PHILOMENA

A TALE FROM THE COR NOVAN SKY ALMANAC

MARK GUINEY

First edition: April 10, 2013
Second edition: May 1, 2016
Createspace Independent Publishing Platform
Radioheart Media, LLC

Createspace ISBN: 978-1484162057
ASIN: B00CAC104Q

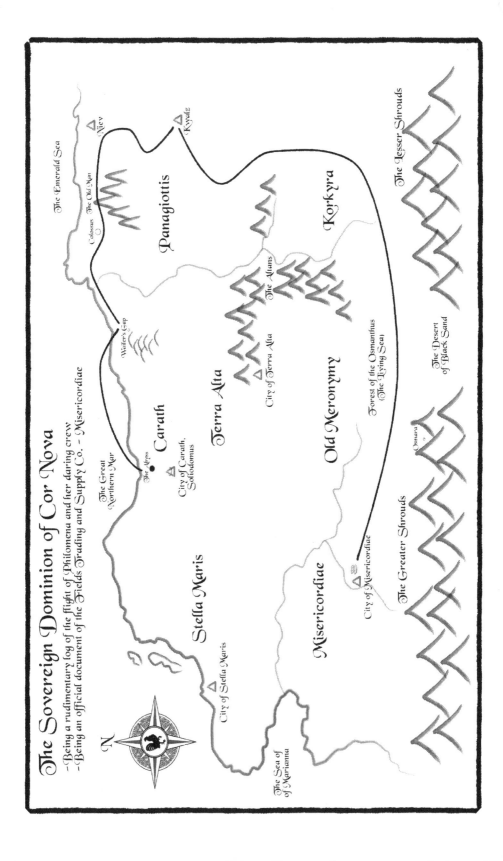

TABLE OF CONTENTS

CHAPTER ONE

The mordonocs roared out of the sky from all directions, talons slashing through the bulkheads, gunwales, rigging, and men of *Grace of the Cedars*. Screams joined the sounds of splintering wood, snapping cable, and tearing canvas that rent the air. The airship pitched and shuddered as the deck exploded into a panicked maelstrom of gunfire, screams, and blood.

"Fight, you dogs!" roared one of the ship's officers, brandishing a rusty cutlass. He dashed toward one of the creatures, sweeping wildly at its snapping jaws. Immediately, the mighty beak seized him by he shoulder and flung him out into the yawning abyss. A fresh wave of terror swept over the deck, and airmen dropped their weapons and ran, stumbling over one another in blind terror.

At the midships gunwale, airmen scattered as a huge mordonoc smashed through the cedar beam, its vicious head whipping back and forth on a long, scaly neck. Dark mats of rotten-smelling feathers sprouted from its wings, and the channels of its beak dripped with saliva that could make a man bleed and bleed till he turned white and cold. Its black eyes, boiling dumb hatred, locked on the airman who stood nearest. This one was not running. His hand rested on the pistol jammed in his leather airman's belt, lanky and loose-limbed in the awkward way only a boy of fifteen years can be.

"That's right, gorgeous," said Cyprian Fields, fixing his storm-grey eyes on the murderous beast. "Come say hello."

With a shriek, the mordonoc whipped itself at him, eager to rip the flesh from his bones, but Cyprian was not in the mood for dismemberment. He drew his pistol and discharged the first barrel

1

directly into the creature's head. One eye exploded in a spray of orange blood, and the mordonoc screamed, lunging with renewed fury.

Cyprian dodged and let loose with a high, piercing whistle. Like a feathered thunderbolt, a proud golden kestrel striped with grey whipped down out of the rigging, flying tight figure-eights around the mordonoc's head. The beast snapped left and right, but was too slow for the old bird. Seizing the opportunity, Cyprian lunged with his deckknife raised high, and drove it to the hilt into the creature's skull. The mordonoc snapped one final time and went limp, sliding backwards off the side of the ship, into the roaring wind.

Cyprian turned back to the deck. Several airmen lay dead or bleeding, and the little courage of the rest was swiftly evaporating. A few of the crew were retreating belowdecks. Cyprian knew they were only delaying the inevitable. At every side, above and below, the creatures swooped and whirled, snapping their beaks in a sinuous vortex of death. The mordonocs would pick the ship clean, one way or the other.

"We're never going to survive!" one airman yelped, hanging on Cyprian's coat.

"Not with that attitude we won't," Cyprian said, grabbing the blubbering deckhand by the collar. "Come on!"

They dashed aft, heading for the war-torn command deck. The wheel was spinning freely in the wind, the helmsman presumably consumed.

"But we can't, Fields…. The shipmaster isn't even…..I have children!"

Cyprian tried to screen out the airman's yammering, his grey eyes piercing the sky as he swept dirty golden hair back on his head with his pistol hand. He did his best to think above the noise and smoke and terror. Cyprian heard a scream and the sound of tearing. Fragments of rigging were raining down on his shoulders. He looked up. The midships envelope was morphing and gushing whorls of white aether. Something with very large talons and a healthy appetite was tearing through. They only had seconds before it was upon them. Cyprian's mind raced. His eyes tracked over the deck. And fell on a cannon. He shoved the stammering airman behind the wheel.

"Come about hard left."

The airman gaped at the wheel as though he'd never seen it before.

"What? You can't.... The shipmaster-"

"Is most likely dead. You've got a family? You want to go home with all your organs? Come about hard left!"

Still blubbering, the airman obeyed. Cyprian seized two more who were cowering behind the gun locker and dragged them to the falconet. Even as the envelope tore to shreds under the strain, they rolled the gun's carriage back into the stairwell of the companionway, so that it crashed onto its breech, barrel pointing skyward, directly into the midships envelope.

"Will this work?" cried one of the airmen in a high-pitched voice.

"There's a simple test for that," Cyprian said, slamming powder and shot into the barrel. "If you're dead twenty seconds from now, it didn't work."

The sound from above was getting closer. A talon sliced through the lower half of the envelope.

"Quickly now!" cried the other airman.

With shaking fingers, Cyprian fed a fuse through the breech and lit it. With a cry, they threw themselves behind *Grace's* rear mast. Cyprian slammed his hands over his ears and hunkered down to avoid the blast, trying not to feel sorry for himself. The morning had started so well.

The last stars were fading above, and the green mountain peaks far below swam through a layer of ghostly mist. Atop the midships envelope, Cyprian could feel every vibration humming up through the rigging of the merchant airship. He seized the line that ran from the top of the mast, snapping it into the brass ropejack studded to his thick airman's belt.

Grace of the Cedars plowed through the dawnstruck sky like a wooden fish through the sea of clouds. Her four great envelopes burgeoned skyward like white cliffs. Brass glimmered, bells chimed and clanged, and aromatic cedar creaked in the wind. In the decks below, twenty-five other souls were at work, but up here, Cyprian was alone. He wrapped his fingers around the tightly braided rope and took a long breath of crisp, cold air.

Over the far rim of the world, the first golden droplet of sun blossomed, and fingers of pink and orange thrust into the sky. Cyprian grinned. Plenty of light to see by.

He took two great bounding steps over the bouncy surface of the midships envelope and leaped, downward and outward, into the roaring dawn. The creak of rope and the clang of brass, the earthy smells of leather and pitch were swept away. The only sound was the rushing of the wind and the thumping of his heart.

Cyprian spread his arms as the wide emptiness of the sky came roaring up, blasting between his fingers and whipping his golden hair into a frenzy. Gold and green and bright, the world turned over and over, and Cyprian caught glimpses of the emerald mountains, the dawnsoaked auburn of the plains, the pale blue ribbon of a river sparkling through the valley below.

Cyprian's heart swelled within him. For this moment, a lowly airman was king, lord of the air, undisputed master of all between the mountainpeaks and the fading stars.

Then, Cyprian felt the rope catch in the rigging, grow tight, and pull. Among the spars and pulleys above, a block-and-tackle slammed home. As the blood rushed into his head, Cyprian gave a colossal whoop and arched his back, catapulting himself backwards to swing under *Grace's* mighty keel.

He twisted his head to see the underside of the ship go rushing by, sharp grey eyes searching for anything that looked like damage or decay. The long planks of cedar shone flawless in the light of dawn, the keel a mighty beam holding up *Grace's* little world.

And then Cyprian flew out from under the ship. He went head over heels again as the rope tightened around the keel and his momentum swung him upwards in a wide arc. Graceful as a leaping fish, Cyprian cleared the gunwale. His soft boots skidded to a stop on the smooth deck, his heart hammering in his chest.

"Hem-hem."

A rotund, red-faced man was strutting up the deck toward Cyprian.

"Dawn inspection completed, Mr. Fields?"

"Yes, shipmaster," said Cyprian, flexing his fingers and setting to the job of coiling up the rope. "Seems like everything's in order."

The shipmaster grunted his approval and pursed his wet lips, which made him look like a large, petulant goose. He fanned himself with his floppy hat, hooking one finger into his overtaxed suspenders. Clouds of white frizzy hair poked out from the sides of his head. Cyprian had served many shipmasters, and *Grace's* was no different from many. He had an excellent mind for calculating profits, and little mind for anything else.

"Well met, young Fields," puffed the shipmaster. When he replaced his hat on his head, the white clouds of hair sagged and flopped. "Well met, to be sure. Never seen anyone work a rope the way you do. I'd say we're doing just as we ought. Just as we ought. Not a bad piece of maneuvering to go outside the shipping routes. Gets us there a bit quicker. Might manage to get a bonus if we come in a few hours ahead of schedule."

"Maybe so, shipmaster," Cyprian replied.

In reality, he didn't think that going outside the shipping routes was a good idea at all. The Imperium Titus was not particularly interested in defending his subjects from bandits. This was not usually a problem, as the sheer number of vessels in the shipping corridors that crossed Cor Nova's skies kept bandits mostly at bay. But, a ship on its own could expect no protection.

"Relieve Grimley at the helm, Fields," said the shipmaster, pursing his lips once more. "Some weather may be coming down from the north. Looks like fog."

The shipmaster trundled away. Cyprian groaned. He had been up since the beginning of the third watch, and now any hopes of a warm bunk and some hot food had evaporated before his eyes.

Cyprian headed aft, toward the raised quarterdeck at the rear of the ship. The Imperium's tariffs meant that no one was making much money on their cargo. Their shipmaster was a wheezy old sod, and the weather had been sour for most of the voyage. The men were old, undisciplined, and inclined to laziness and drunkenness. Cyprian could see the helmsman, an unshaven man with a pipe sticking out of his slack mouth, nodding behind the ship's wheel. Cyprian mounted the creaking steps, and rapped his knuckles three times on the helm.

"My ship," he said to the helmsman.

"Gah! Wazzat! Ah…hem," said the helmsman, jolting into wakefulness. "Ah yes. Your ship."

The helmsman stumbled below. Cyprian ran his fingers over the smooth wood of the wheel, feeling the airship hum with life beneath his fingertips. Above him, the four envelopes, bulging with aether, lifted her to the sky. Her sails, six along each side of the craft, pulled her forward into the dawn. A geometric jungle of cables and stays held the finely tuned rigging in alignment.

Cyprian could feel the giant assembly tugging and pulling at the wheel, the polished brass pitch levers at his right hand shifting in their housings as the wind pulled this way and that. His father used to say that if you held a ship right, you could feel her heart beat.

Cyprian checked the heading of the ship on the brass aetherolabe that whirled in its housing to the left of the helm. The painted sphere rolled on its layer of aether, the numerals painted on its surface bobbing and wobbling as they followed the ship's flight through the sky.

A few deckhands, late for the upcoming watch, stumbled up the companionway that led up from belowdecks, red-eyed and clutching chipped mugs of skip-jack. They were clad in thick breeches and light boots that a man could feel the deck through. Around wiry waists, they wore the traditional airman's belt, wide leather studded with tokens and talismans, souvenirs from a hundred ports throughout the Dominion. Their hands and arms were cluttered with tattoos, the skin scarred and calloused from work in the sky.

"Oy there, Fields," said one buck-toothed man. "Old man keeping you up here again?"

"Looks that way," Cyprian said.

"Well, that's where all the greenies go! One day, you'll be an old hand like the rest of us. Then you get the cake jobs."

Cyprian had no doubt that he could outfly every one of these old skydogs, and was about to say so when a speck broke through the cloud layer beneath them. It came closer, wings pumping as it bobbed and wove through the fibrous layers of whiteness. A long cry, almost like a whistle, rang over the sky.

"Looks like your bird, Fields," said one of the other deckhands.

Cyprian extended an arm as Petros came soaring through the rigging, but the bird swooped past him. Instead, it landed with a graceless thump on the gunwale, shaking a dead vole in its beak and cocking its head at Cyprian in a distrustful way. Cyprian rolled his eyes.

"I don't want your vole, stupid bird."

Golden sea kestrels are often regarded as untrainable. They were powerful and intelligent, but obstinate as feathered mules. Cyprian's father had succeeded in training Petros to a degree, but the kestrel clearly didn't view Cyprian as having the same level of authority. Part of that, Cyprian told himself, was that the bird was starting to feel his age. His once spectacular golden plumage, with its brown stripes and cap, was beginning to fade to gray at the tips.

But today, Cyprian sensed something off about the insufferable bird. His feathers were fluffed and, as soon as he'd choked down the vole, his head swiveled back and forth, scanning the horizon. Cyprian reached out a finger, and Petros only nipped him slightly when he stroked his head.

"Something out of sorts, old boy? You're not the type to be easily scared."

The kestrel nipped his finger again and took wing into the rigging, presumably to glare at any finches that may be passing by. Cyprian shook his head, and reached a hand into his jacket, pulling out a piece of paper. The paper was still smooth, devoid of wrinkles. He had only looked at it once: when he had received it at the kestrel office before they departed.

Mr. Fields,

As I mentioned in my previous letters, the Fields Trading and Supply Company has fallen to my ownership. A recent turn of events has placed me in great need of officers.

In the interest of fiscal success and your own legacy, I ask you to consider returning to Misericordiae so that we may discuss this matter in detail.

Warmest Regards,

Francis Lightlas Proprietor
Fields Trading and Supply Company

Shaking his head, Cyprian crumpled the paper and tossed it over the side of the ship, where the wind snatched it away. It was the same thing he had done with the last three messages, all from Francis Lightlas, all similar in content. He hadn't been back to Misericordiae in four years, and working for his dead father's decrepit trading company didn't make the prospect any more attractive.

Cyprian peered out into the mist again. Despite the brilliance of the day, it was getting thicker. A few more minutes passed. More airmen made their way up onto the deck. Most were bleary-eyed and smelled heartily of brandy. Cyprian looked for the helmsman who would come on duty with them, eager for some hot food and a few hours of sleep. But, as usual, he was late.

"Wings!" cried the lookout from the top of the mast. "Wings at twenty marks!"

Cyprian's heartbeat immediately accelerated. There were a few curses, and the men on deck rushed the gunwales, peering out into the fog.

"Where?" they demanded of the lookout. "Where?"

"Twenty marks! Low!"

Finally, Cyprian saw them, three sinuous forms flapping along the nearest ridgeline. As one, they turned and banked toward the ship.

"What are they?" one of the young deckhands asked, his voice cracking. "Rocs? Oh, please say rocs…"

One of the sun-darkened, experienced airmen shook his hoary head.

"Them's mordonocs if I've ever seen 'em."

Cyprian's grip tightened on the wheel. He had to agree. He could see them more clearly now as they broke through a layer of fog, on a straight course for the ship.

"Another group," cried the lookout, his voice trailing up in fear. "From the west!"

Another chorus of curses went up from the crew. There were three more, skirting a cloud bank on the ship's opposite side. *Grace* was being surrounded, the mordonocs working in perfect concert, like trained dogs. The shipmaster burst out of his cabin, his breakfast apparently disturbed. He was still gripping a sausage in one hand.

"What…" he demanded, his head swiveling back and forth. "What…what…"

"Mordonocs, shipmaster," Cyprian said, pointing. "Twenty marks, coming in from low."

"Collars on 'em?"

"Can't see, sir."

The shipmaster's eyes bulged with fear. He reached forward and clanged the brass bell that hung above the helm.

"Toll to quarters! We run before we fight. Fields, come about."

The portly shipmaster yelled down through the grating into the deck to the shipcore, where the half-drunken machinist stood swaying at his post.

"Dados! Give her full rise! We need more height!"

The pipes groaned and sighed as aether from the brace of casks below rushed up into the burgeoning envelopes. Cyprian felt his feet press into his boots as *Grace of the Cedars* lifted skyward. They would need as much height as they could get.

Playing the wheel and levers like a musician, Cyprian guided the ship into a full turn as she rose. The mountains shrank beneath them, but the mordonocs only grew on both horizons. On the deck, the men struggled to get control of sails and sheets with panic starting to take hold. The shipmaster was getting sweatier with each second, large beads of perspiration glistening on his crimson forehead.

"That's all we're liable to get, Fields, or they'll be upon us! Put her at full tilt with a heading at thirty three marks!"

"Yes, sir!" said Cyprian, slamming all of the vent levers back. The ship rumbled as *Grace* vented four plumes of white aether from her envelopes into the sky. Cyprian felt himself grow light in his boots as the ship descended, her sails converting the energy into forward momentum. With a groan, the ship dipped forward and began to glide.

Grace plunged forward through the sky, her crew working furiously to retract the sails that were holding her back. She bobbed and wobbled in the column of rushing air as she burst through pockets of lift. Cyprian glanced behind them. All six of the mordonocs were bearing down upon them. With each beat of their massive wings, they came closer. Cyprian could almost smell the musty cave-rot odor of them, the last smell an airman smells before the blood begins to flow. There were three large front-runners, and another dozen or so a little ways behind them.

"Collars!" someone yelled, voice cracking with terror.

Sure enough, Cyprian noted, around the neck of each mordonoc glinted a golden collar. Cyprian's blood ran even colder.

Then, the strain of the tilt became too much for the old ship. With a crack, one of the leftward sails ripped right through the center. The deck bucked, sending the crew tumbling across the deck. Cyprian had to throw himself against the wheel to keep the ship from tipping into a deadly spin.

"Shipmaster!" said Cyprian, wrestling the ship back under control. "If we run, they'll chase us down and pick us off. Our only hope is to hit them and disperse them if we can…"

The shipmaster's chins wobbled as he braced himself against the helm. Inexplicably, the sausage was still clenched in one pudgy hand.

"No! Too dangerous… They have collars. They must be Cain's…"

Cyprian pointed to the mountain peaks ahead and below, growing larger every second.

"We're running out of sky, shipmaster!"

Finally, the shipmaster nodded. His hands shaking, he leaned forward and rang the bell three times, shouting over the deck.

"Toll to arms! Prepare the leftward side braking sheets, leftward guns prepare to fire! Stomp in for sunwise turn!"

The deck exploded into furious energy. The crew dropped the sheets and ran to the arms lockers. These opened to reveal rows of rusty muskets and swords. Gun teams manned the six light falconets at the gunwales, as well as the two positioned on the stern. With the heavy clang of iron, each was loaded with a heavy canister of powder and a ball of shot.

Once armed, each airman took up a position along the deck, carefully stepping onto one of the long leather straps studded with nailed brass "frogs" that ran up and down the deck. The brass linkage on the underside of their boots made a satisfying click as they held fast to the frogs, securing them to the deck.

"Prepare for turn!" cried the shipmaster. His jowls were quivering and sweat rolled down his red forehead. "NOW!"

Cyprian slammed forward two pitch levers and rolled the wheel sharply left. The braking sheets on the left side of the ship slammed to attention, bellying as they spilled their wind. With a drunken sway, *Grace of the Cedars* pivoted hard left, the guns of that side turning directly into the oncoming mordonocs. The frogs on the deck pulled against Cyprian's boots, and the gunners struggled to keep their aim true. As the ship whipped sideways, the mordonocs streaked towards the leftward beam. For a moment, they were suspended in time, terrifying collections of eyes, feathers, talons, and teeth. Cyprian had the presence of mind to observe that they were in quite a pickle indeed. The morning had largely deteriorated from that point.

The falconet roared, spewing flames and iron skyward into the midships envelope. When Cyprian peered around the mast, all that he saw were shreds of canvas, burnt pieces of rope, and mats of burnt, rotten feathers. Cyprian allowed himself a small grin.

Then, there was a high call that sounded over the sky. It was a clear, piercing note, almost like a shriek. Slowly, second by second, it climbed until it was nearly too high to hear, and hurt Cyprian's ears.

The mordonocs stopped, some pausing in mid-air. They took one last snap at their prey, and then, reluctantly, they released their grip on the ship and twisted away into the air, back toward a black ship that had broken through a nearby cloudbank. In the fury of the fighting, Cyprian had not noticed it. From its stern, it flew a golden flag edged with black.

The crew, for a moment dazed and relieved, sank into terror once more. Every merchant in the skies of Cor Nova knew that flag. Cain.

"Petros," called Cyprian. The old bird landed next to him with a thump. He seized the bird by its neck and stuffed it unceremoniously down the front of his jacket, poking the squawking mass into quiet.

Within a moment, the ship had drawn alongside *Grace*. Skulls rattled from its bow, strips of foul-smelling leather hung in tatters from its rigging, and its hull was coated with black tar. A flood of bandits trooped aboard, screaming at the airmen to drop their weapons and kneel on the deck.

"By whose authority do you do this?" demanded the portly shipmaster, trembling as they smashed open the hatches and ransacked the holds. "To set your beasts on us and take our rightfully earned proceeds! In the days of the Sovereign…"

The bandit leader was a greasy man with a silver hoop piercing his lip. He wore a long black coat, a permanent sneer, and an odor that suggested he hadn't washed in a quite some time.

"What age are you living in, old man?" he sneered, pressing a pistol barrel into the shipmaster's wobbling cheek. "The Sovereign's been dead fifteen years. You want to know about my authority, you ask Bartimaeus Cain."

At the sound of this name, the shipmaster's eyes bugged out. The bandit leader laughed and spat at his feet.

"Today's your good fortune," he said, as his men finished their search, carrying the meager valuables on board. "I have no mood or time for blood and your ship is a worthless old crate. Today, you fly free."

The bandit shipmaster looked up at the shredded rigging and splintered spars, curls of white aether bleeding into the sky.

"If you can."

The bandit shipmaster's eyes crossed the deck, flicking from face to face. Finally, he found Cyprian. He extended a tar-blackened finger.

"Except you. You come with us."

The shipmaster's jowls wobbled.

"You can't! He's just a boy…"

The bandit leader crossed to the shipmaster, lifted him by the collar and sneered directly into his face.

"You volunteering to take his place, old man?"

The shipmaster's stubby legs kicked dejectedly, his eyes twin saucers of terror.

"I…well…my men need…"

With a bark of laughter, the bandit leader dropped him to the deck, where he lay, quivering.

"Then keep your fat mouth shut."

As the bandits stomped back across their gangplank, one of them seized Cyprian by the collar, yanking him to the bandit ship and throwing him to the deck below the mast. With a grunt, the bandit chief gave the command to rise and they were off, a dozen mordonocs flapping alongside in horrible formation. Cyprian chanced a look behind him, and saw *Grace of the Cedars* disappear into the fog.

CHAPTER TWO

Basil didn't jerk away as the razorback hissed, baring venomous fangs. Its black scales glistened as it twisted against the leather straps that held it fast. The lizard's tail and three unbound legs thumped and scratched against the wood of the desktop, setting rock samples and glass bottles a-rattle.

Basil pushed his iron-rimmed glasses up on his nose, brushing dark hair out of his clear blue eyes. For a boy of fourteen years, he was not particularly tall, and his build was slender, making him even more of an oddity in the hardy mining town of Osmara. The chair creaked as he leaned closer, peering through a series of polished quartz lenses at the razorback's muscular rear leg, which was curiously bent. A hundred images ran through his head, drawn from observation and memorized from the pages of illegal books: networks of bone, muscle, and nerve. A careful tap on the glossy black scales confirmed his suspicions: a break in the smaller of the two forearm bones, near the elbow joint. A few ebony scales were missing, and thick blood oozed through the gap. Basil guessed that the creature had made a narrow escape from a polecat or a timberwolf. Nothing that couldn't be fixed.

Basil looked up, perusing the shelves for the materials he needed. Dust motes winked in the shafts of light that poured through the window of his small loft room, causing innumerable bottles, flasks, and jars to glitter. The shelves, fixed to every available space of log wall, overflowed with potted plants and mosses huddling moistly in bottles. Page upon page of handwritten notes bound with twine and pine slats vied with samples of plant, fur, and fossil for space.

Feathers, beetles, and bones were arranged neatly on pins. Lenses made of hand-polished quartz, forged iron forceps, and flecks of topaz, moonstone, and opal glittered in the sunshine. By the open window, an ancient ebon finch rescued from a swollen mountain stream croaked in its nest-box, eyeing the razorback with clear distrust. Finally, Basil's eyes lit on the tall bank of square drawers above his bed.

The razorback snapped at him as he stood up to retrieve slender pine splints, twine, and bits of soft linen.

"Calm down," Basil said to the creature. It struggled harder, glowering at him with yellow reptilian eyes.

Basil cut a pine splint to fit the lizard's glossy black foreleg. With nimble fingers, he padded it with linen and secured it with loop after loop of handmade cedarbark twine, cord that would fall to pieces after about two weeks. It would be enough to hold the leg until it healed. He was admiring his work when the cabin door scraped open.

"Basil!" a deep rumbling voice called. "Stir yourself, boy! There's work needs doing!"

Basil leaned over the rail of the little loft room.

"What's happening?"

Thon Black was like a weathered pine, growing tall and haggard beside the oaken table and stone fireplace of the cabin. His face and knuckles were rough as broken stone, and his beard tumbled down his long, lean front like a mottled mat of forest lichen. They said that in his youth, Thon Black could break his way through twenty yards of solid limestone in a single day, wielding a hammer in each mighty hand. Of all the men in town, he was the oldest, the wisest, and the best metallurgist in the Korkyran mountains.

"There's a man down at the forge, hurt bad," Basil's father said. "A stranger."

Basil reached for his boots. The people of Osmara were originally skeptical of asking help from one so young, but when they saw limbs repaired and diseases cured, their hesitancy evaporated. Calls came at all hours of the day and night: a broken limb, a fever, a baby on its way. In the past few years, he'd seen a hundred injuries and a thousand ills, but no two were ever the same. Each was a new adventure, an opportunity to learn, to add to his notes. Basil yanked clothes from the pegs on the walls and flipped open his medical box.

It was fashioned from sweet-smelling pine banded with iron, drawers packed with pouches and rattling bottles.

"What happened?" he asked, slinging the box's leather strap over his shoulder. The razorback snapped at him as he swept a few extra vials into the box.

"Probably a vagrant," said Thon Black. "He collapsed at the town gate, coming up the mountain road. They moved him to the forge. He didn't look well. Haste, Basil."

Satisfied, Basil shut the lid of the box and fastened the clasps. He carefully gripped the squirming razorback behind its spade-shaped head.

"What is that?" asked Black as Basil descended the peg ladder set in the wall.

"A razorback," Basil replied. "I found it on the hillsides when I was coming back from the minehead. It has a broken leg, probably from a polecat."

Black pulled the cabin door shut behind them.

"Basil, I have no opposition to you fixing up the people and pretty birds and working animals around here, but you better not let anyone see you healing venomous varmints. Next time someone's baby gets bit, they'll be swearing it was the one you nursed back to health."

Basil had to trot to follow the great, loping footsteps of his father down the path. He stopped for a moment to release the razorback into an old dry creek bed. It scuttled under a rock and hissed loudly back at Basil.

"They don't bite unless they're stepped on," Basil said as he caught up with his father. "Or taunted. They eat to live, the same as anything else."

Thon Black shook his great head as they strode towards the center of Osmara. The small village huddled in a valley formed by the convergence of Osmo Mountain and its foothills. In the sunlit valley, among the cabins and stables of the villagers, the forge longhouse stood as it had for centuries, all cedar beams and great masonry chimneys. Beyond it, the mountainside gave way to a large natural cavern that was open to the free mountain air. The town's name came from an Old Korkyran word that meant "mouth", because it almost seemed as though the great mountain was trying to swallow the little valley. Beneath the mossy eaves of the mountain

15

stood the oxen stables, tool-sheds, and the minehead, where lamplit shafts led down into the mountain's deep, secret bowels.

"That's easier to say," Black said. "When you're not the one swollen up purple with a bite on the leg. You've got a good head for a boy of fourteen years, Basil, but don't let your heart do all it's thinking."

When the forge longhouse doors swung open, a wave of dry heat rolled out. Down at one end, the forges glowed red and hammers pounded to keep the miners' axes and shovels sharp enough to bite into the mountain's stony flesh. The furnaces rumbled steadily, throwing sparks and flame up the chimneys, turning the raw ore into hot rivers of pure iron, copper, and oraculum.

"There," said Black, pointing to the near end.

A few leather-clad miners were standing over a still figure stretched out on a big oaken table. As Basil got closer, he saw the man was deathly pale. His chest rose and fell with alarming speed. His pants were muddy and torn, his boots worn near through. His beard and hair were so tangled and matted it was hard to distinguish their color and his skin was burnt from long hours in the sun.

The young miners took a step back, muttering to each other, as Basil approached the table and felt the stranger's forehead. It was hot and dry. His breathing was shallow, eyelids barely flickering at Basil's touch.

"It's the sunstroke that's got him," said one of the old miners. "Either that or the drylung."

"I don't think so," Basil murmured, opening his box. "Take off his shirt."

The miners did as they were asked, and Basil tapped the stranger's chest, listened for a heartbeat. He lifted the man's jaws, and when he did, he saw that the bloodshot eyes were open, looking at him. The cracked lips were moving, as though speaking.

"Can you hear him?" asked a miner. "What's he saying?"

"Shh! Can't hear with you talking!"

"Shh! Can't hear with you hushing!"

"Quiet," said Thon Black, his voice a hammerstroke quelling the noise.

Basil drew near to the man's mouth, trying to catch the words. But the man's head fell back on the table, eyes rolling upward. One of the miners whistled.

"He's in a bad way, for sure. My old gramps was the same way. Just keeled over like an old tree. Right into his soup."

"What is it, Basil?" asked Black.

Basil looked hard into the man's eyes, picked up his hand to flex the muscles, examined the inside of his mouth. The signs were there, but where was the wound? Basil pushed his glasses up on his nose again.

"I think he's been poisoned."

Carefully, he ran his eyes down the length of the man's body, until his sharp eyes caught a small tear in the man's left pant leg. The threadbare fabric tore with little effort. There, surrounded by the motley purple and brown of rotting flesh, was a small, round puncture. Basil probed gently with his fingers, and felt something hard embedded deep beneath the skin. The stranger moaned, still unconscious.

"Whatever's in there," said a miner. "It'll have to come out."

For once, he was right. Black carefully laid out the instruments from the box as Basil scrubbed his hands with a green solution of winterpine. With a small iron probe and skillful hands, Basil explored the wound and almost immediately located something round and hard. With great care, he pulled out a ball of shot. Turning it over in the light, Basil could see a faint crust of chalky, whitish material beneath the sheen of blood.

"A poisoned ball," said Black. "Who would use a weapon like that?"

Basil chipped away a piece of the solid. He mixed it with a collection of clear serums in his vials as the miners watched in wonder. Finally, one of them shifted in color, clear to yellowish-brown.

"Skrill venom," said Basil. It was a slow but sure killer, exotic and expensive. There was only one group with the coin to use skrill venom with any regularity.

"The Imperium," said Black, his face grim. "This man was running from the Fleet."

Suddenly, a hot feverish hand closed around the front of Basil's shirt, pulling him forward. Beads of sweat rolled down the man's forehead, his eyes bulging, his breath hot on Basil's face. His dry lips struggled to form words.

"Basil Black," he whispered.

The longhouse was silent except for the persistent roar of hot air through the furnaces. The miners stood bug-eyed, stunned.

"Listen to me....," the stranger said, struggling for every word. His eyes bored into Basil, veins bulging. "The Imperium is looking for you. Soon the Fleet will be here, and you must escape. You are a Bookkeeper, a true servant of the Sovereign."

Basil shook his head, feeling pity for the man. He was delirious, the skrill venom taking his mind from him even as it took his life.

"There is no Sovereign anymore," he said softly. "Just lie back."

The man's grip tightened. He pulled Basil even closer. A feverish light burned deep in his eyes.

"There is a Sovereign. There is always a Sovereign. You must escape to Misericordiae. When you get there, there is a ship called *Philomena*. Do you hear me? *Philomena*. Her shipmaster is Lightlas. *Philomena*..."

Basil shook his head.

"I don't understand…"

With a thunderous bang, a young miner burst through the longhouse doors, arms flapping, eyes agog.

"Ships!" he cried. "Coming out of the west!"

"Trader's come early," grunted Black.

"No! Dreadnoughts! A great passel of 'em! One of them flying the sun-and-stars!"

"No..." said the stranger. His grip slackened. "...*Philomena*..."

The longhouse erupted into chaos as, with a chorus of curses, the miners dashed for the door. Basil could only watch the stranger's face helplessly as the venom took hold. As panic permeated the hot air of the forges, the lights of life left the messenger's eyes.

CHAPTER THREE

Fires burned in Misericordiae, chasing Veronica through the haunted night. She whipped around the corner, skirt whispering as she dashed over the cobbles. In one hand, she carried an elegant pearl-handled rapier, her only friend on the abandoned city streets. Lungs heaving for breath, she stopped at the corner and poked her head into the next street.

The boulevard was silent, awash in the mist that stole up from the wharfs on the Ivory River, but Veronica knew there was no peace to be had in Misericordiae tonight. Throughout the city, terrible sounds echoed over rooftop and wall: axes on wood, screaming voices, and the snap of flames. Veronica scarcely had time to catch her breath when, with a clatter and the rumble of boots, a group of soldiers, clad in red wool and black leather, exploded from around the corner.

There were six of them, led by a huge sergeant. Metal masks hid their faces, their eyeholes black, grilled mouths rattling with ragged breath. The sergeant pointed a huge, gauntleted hand at Veronica.

"There!"

Veronica took off, sprinting off the street into a garbage-choked alley. She dodged through the twisting brickwork, toppling barrels and slicing down lines of laundry with her rapier to hinder her pursuers.

But on the soldiers came, unrelenting. They were strong, fast. More than once, they grew so close that Veronica could hear their breath rattling against the iron, feel the drumming of their boots

19

through the cobbles. Veronica could certainly take on one, possibly two, with her rapier. But six trained soldiers? Those were greater odds than Veronica could bet on. Once, a pistol shot filled the alley like a thunderclap, and part of the wall to Veronica's left exploded into shards of brick. The sergeant bellowed something, and there were no more shots. They wanted her alive.

With a rush of space, the alleyway opened up onto the open street again. The boots up the alleyway grew closer, pounding in Veronica's ears. Something white caught her eye. Just to her left, a small house stood on the corner. From the balcony on the second level, a sheet fluttered forlorn and lonely in the breeze. She glanced at the door. It had an old, heavy brass lock.

Veronica's eyes narrowed, an idea blossoming in her mind.

She whipped the pearl-handled rapier through the air, catching a seam in the fabric with the tip and pulling it down. With her other hand, she reached into her hair, done up in a flawless spiraling braid at the back of her head, each ebony lock exactly in its place. From the second spiral, closest to her neck, she drew out two long, thin pieces of metal. With the deftness born of dedicated practice, she inserted one piece into the lock, turned another, and felt the single tumbler click.

And then, the soldiers thundered around the corner. They skidded to a halt, steel glinting in the night as they stared eyelessly at the girl in the open doorway of the house, looking very small and frightened indeed. She clutched a white shawl around her shoulders, and let out an ear-splitting wail of relief when the soldiers appeared.

"Oh, thank goodness!" she said, clutching at the nearest soldier's jacket. "I was here in the kitchen and I heard a commotion in the alley. I just poked my head out to see what was happening, and she came tearing by. She shoved me right back into the house, fairly menaced me with an awful sword, told me to get inside or I'd be done for! She went that way! Up the street, towards the square! Oh, I was frightened so!"

Then, with a keening sob, she collapsed into the arms of the enormous sergeant, a mess of tears. The soldiers looked at one another for a half-second, apparently not stirred by her distress. With a grunt, the sergeant shrugged her off, gave an order, and the whole group went tearing off down the street, leaving the hysterical girl to flop to her knees in the doorway.

As soon as the sound of their pounding boots faded, Veronica allowed herself a small smirk. Fortunately, intelligence was not a quality the Imperium greatly valued in his soldiers.

"Who in the blue hazes are you?"

Veronica wheeled around. There, in the kitchen of the little house, stood a balding man in a long, striped nightshirt, who appeared to be brandishing a rake. A trembling woman and three small children poked their heads around his sloped shoulders.

"Hello," Veronica said, pulling off the sheet and sweeping a lone stray lock of hair back into its rightful place. "You forgot to bring your laundry in. I'll just leave it here on the table."

"Ah," said the balding man, relaxing his grasp on his rake. "I suppose in that case…"

The wisp of a housewife stepped out from behind her husband. The housewife's careworn hands rested on the shoulders of her young son.

"It isn't safe to be out… especially for one so young…"

In times like these, Veronica knew, mothers thirsted for peace more than anyone else. She felt the mousy housewife's concern wash over her, trembling in those brown eyes. It was the love that kissed tiny hands and sent grown men to work and war, a love Veronica had lost.

"I do quite well, thank you," she said, stepping back over the threshold. "Keep your door locked, and turn out your lights. It's not a safe night."

The door closed over the terrified family and, without a word, Veronica was gone. She latched the door behind her and was off again into the dark. The street was mercifully abandoned, mists floating ghost-like over the cobbles.

She kept to the abandoned side streets, staying close to the walls. Every now and then, a Fleet dreadnought or interceptor passed above the rooftops, sending Veronica ducking into doorways and alleys. Further down the hill, Veronica could make out the Ivory River, a ribbon of whiteness through the city. On the other side of the river, the great slope of Keel Hill rose, lamps on its terraces of concourses piercing the fog. The hundreds of ships docked there were still and silent, slumbering beasts weathering the haunted night. At the top of the hill was Topgallant Square, the throbbing heart of Misericordiae's shipping industry. A huge, flickering spindle of

21

orange fire rose over the tops of the buildings, making skeletons of the tower of the Kestrel Office and the Port Authority Rotunda. At the base of those fires, Veronica knew with a surge of anger, were books. Fifteen years before, when she was born, a statue of the First Sovereign Sylvanus had stood in that square. Now there was a monument to the Imperium Titus, and his monuments demanded sacrifice. Forcing herself to stay calm and vigilant, Veronica quickened her pace down the dark streets toward the river.

The River Carillon loomed up ahead, a spired tower of oak and stone among the mills and warehouses that lined the banks of the Ivory River. She crept around the base of the tower, finding the small iron-bound bellkeeper's door located on the far side. She glanced left and right. On road and river alike, no living thing stirred. From the band around her waist, she produced a slim key, and was through the door like a shadow.

The Carillon enclosed her, a great pillar of wood and dust and warm, creaking quiet. She allowed herself to breathe easy for a moment, in and out. Then, she was running again, taking the wooden steps two at a time, a mouse in the thicket of beams and buttresses. Far above, like great looming owls in the dusty recesses, the bells hung silent on their beams.

Up and up Veronica went. Every few steps, she passed one of the narrow windows in the side of the tower. The cityscape was dotted in the squares and in the streets with fires just like the one on Topgallant Square. Throughout the city, soldiers slammed through doors, pulling out suspected dissenters, seizing banned books, piling them up, and setting fire to them. The children screamed. The books crackled and snapped. The Imperium's justice was being done.

Finally, Veronica stopped at the twelfth turn in the stairs. She tapped one knuckle lightly against the wall and spoke into the silence.

"In the last days of the Old World, the shepherd Sylvanus lived with his herds on the Fields of Carath."

A section of wall slid away, revealing the smell of paper, the damp tang of ink, and an old man, cradling his knuckles in weathered hands. With large spectacles and a stooped back, he looked like an apprehensive turtle.

"Veronica!" he said as she drew the hidden door shut. "We thought you hadn't made it."

Behind him, an old oaken printing press stood silent. A stack of papers was paused in its run, but had been so for some time. The ink was dry. The bells had not rung for several hours, and the press ran only in the midst of the ringing, inaudible to anyone near or far.

"Well, I'm delighted to say that I did, Harmon" she said, sitting down heavily on one of the stacks of blank paper. "The ones they had following me were fools. How bad is it?"

"Bad," said Harmon. He pushed open the shutters of a window, looking out over the city. "They've hit everything in our kestrel network. They've found the Hammer Street Press, as well as the ones off Topgallant Square. They also found some copies of the Rule, killed a number of dissenters. We don't know who yet. They're saying that it's Ambry himself in the city. I was worried about you…"

Veronica felt a rush of affection for the old man, and an even greater fear that something would happen to him. It was unfair that friendship could cost so much these days. She rubbed her temples.

"Someone betrayed us. If they've given away Hammer Street and the others, they'll certainly be coming here next."

She looked at Harmon, almost afraid to utter the next words.

"We need to dump the press."

Harmon swallowed loudly, laying a withered hand on the antique press. It was one of the few left in Misericordiae outside of Imperium control, discovered in pieces in an old warehouse. It took Veronica, Harmon, and several others weeks to get all of it into the Carillon and assembled. Veronica knew that if they pulled a lever, the wooden panel wall of the Carillon would swivel out, the platform holding the press would tip upwards, and the press would slide out the side of the Carillon into the depths of the Ivory River. They would be hiding the evidence, but also burying an old friend, their sole weapon against the Imperium.

"Yes…" Harmon said finally. "I suppose we must."

There was a thundering sound on the steps, echoing up through the structure. Shouts. Then, the crack of a pistol. Veronica's heart sped up. They were here already.

"We have to do it now," she said.

Harmon nodded.

"The lever is over by the ink, my girl. I'll loose the hinges. Let's see…"

Veronica had to slide aside two casks of ink to get to the lever, lashed crudely to the floor with a series of thick leather straps.

"Platform is clear, at least I think," whispered Harmon, wheezing as he stood up from the last hinge. The platform was built over the floor, and it contained the press as well as all of the extra paper and contraband printed material. Once the platform went, the river would swallow it all.

Veronica cut the straps and pulled against the lever. It retracted an inch, and stuck. She pulled on it with all her strength. Harmon joined in, his hands thin but strong over her own. It wouldn't budge.

"The mechanism is jammed!" the old man said, squinting into the jungle of pulleys overhead. "Confounded sparrows up there! Pecking at everything…"

Veronica followed the pair of lines extending from the lever, trying to see the blockage. But the mechanism was complicated, and mixed in with the works of the bells. She had puzzled out more difficult problems, but this one would take time. The sounds of boots grew louder, perhaps three floors down. Maybe they would just pass them by. But eventually, some chipper young soldier would notice that there was an area of the Carillon that should not be there, that seemed to have no way in. Then they would come with saws. Or gunpowder.

Harmon pointed up into the pulleys, muttering to himself. The shouts were now close enough that Veronica could almost pick out words.

"Harmon," Veronica whispered. "You need to get in the hatch."

Harmon stopped in mid-rumination, fixing her with sad, bespectacled eyes.

"What? And leave you here?"

"I'll be right behind you. I'll dump the press, then meet you with the others at the safehouse. I travel fast; I'll probably be there before you."

She pulled aside the threadbare old carpet, yanking up a hidden hatch, its ladder reaching down into the dark. Far down below, it dropped into the drainway beneath the Carillon. The old man leaned away from the yawning black opening.

"Please, Harmon," said Veronica. "I will dump the press, and then follow. I've lost enough family as it is."

At her tenderness, the old man's defiance wilted. With Veronica's help, he descended the first two rungs into the darkness. Then, he stopped. There were boots coming up the stairway just outside.

"I never had any children, Veronica," he said in a whisper. "But I hope…. I hope you…"

"I do," said Veronica. Her impatience clashed with a surge of gratitude for Harmon's faith. "Believe me, Harmon. I do. I will see you soon."

The old man nodded, and descended. Veronica lowered the hatch by its iron ring, letting it clack shut. She pulled the rug back over, and the room was silent for a moment, leaving just Veronica, the press, and the sounds of Imperium soldiers racing up the stairs of the Carillon outside.

Then, the stomping of the boots passed by and faded, heading further upward. Veronica forced her breathing to slow. It would be a while before they noticed the hidden section of the Carillon. Careful to make no sound, she glanced back up at the jammed mechanism, searching for the flaw. But something in her mind twitched, a faint discomfort. It was the feeling she felt when a pair of shadowed eyes were on her, when something very dangerous was very close.

There was an almighty crash. Bits of timber and flecks of wood went flying as a large boot smashed through the hidden panel. With a cry of surprise, Veronica fell against the barrels of ink and piles of paper, her rapier twisted from her grip and rolling across the floor.

A single, tall figure stepped over the wreckage, an officer's saber in his right hand. The red wool of his uniform was finely brushed and the leather polished to a shiny, midnight black. Instead of a full soldier's helmet, his masked helm was crested in red and emblazoned with wings. On his shoulders, the epaulets bore an ornately styled rising sun in gold, the rank of a rear admiral.

Veronica felt the pit in her stomach grow deeper. Rear admirals do not go tromping around in the field, brandishing sabers and knocking down doors. They lead from silk-upholstered armchairs in the cartoria of finely outfitted dreadnoughts, with crystal glasses of golden wine dangling from their fingers. Or, at the very least, they go to hunt down the innocent with a crowd of red-backed minions between them and danger.

The admiral's mask was expressionless, but Veronica could feel cold, intelligent eyes on her. She was wishing intensely that her rapier was in her hand. She reached for the hilt.

"Do not move," said the officer.

The voice was flat, devoid of emotion. He might have been asking her the time of day. Veronica brushed a stray lock of hair back into place before she replied.

"I don't follow orders from men who hide their faces."

In a single movement, the rear admiral sheathed his saber, drew his pistol, and cocked back the hammer with a deep, metallic click, clear as the ringing of a bell. Veronica raised her hands in a demure fashion. In this case, she was prepared to make an exception.

Chapter Four

No one spoke a word to Cyprian all day. The bandits bent their tattooed backs to the ropes, sunburnt hands and agile sails casting the ship like a javelin through the sky. Cyprian knew from the position of the sun that they were traveling northwest, but he had no idea where they were. Once, after a few hours, Cyprian decided to stand up to see the surroundings and stretch his legs. The black-clad bandit chief didn't even look at him. He just drew his sword a hand's length from the sheath, so that the shining edge sparkled in the daylight. As soon as Cyprian sat back down, the blade disappeared. With a grimace, Cyprian rested his back against the mast. That was warning enough.

Cyprian heard a few words from the bandits in Sylvan, but most of the time they lapsed into a dirty dialect of Klahk with a mysterious glottal accent. A fat Stella Marian glass merchant had once taught Cyprian two phrases in Klahk when he worked on his freighter: "Good day" and "Swift death awaits those who fondle the master's vases". Cyprian glanced again at the hulking bandits, and decided to use neither.

Hours passed and Cyprian dozed against the mast. He was awoken by a shout from the bandit leader. In response to the command, the ship banked hard to the right, sending Cyprian sprawling across the deck towards the rightward gunwale. With his face pressed against the wood, the land below opened up for the first time. He saw a large, misty valley in an unfamiliar pale white mountain range. Cyprian had memorized his fair share of sky almanacs and atlases, but he couldn't place it.

Then, the bandit ship rounded a turn in the valley. Cyprian's heart plunged directly into his stomach. He realized exactly where he was. The next mountainside was dominated by an immense black hole, a cavern extending back into darkness. Even from this distance, Cyprian could see the enormous stalactites jutting from its roof like serrated teeth, fouled with twisted vines and creeping moss.

Cyprian had heard many lantern-lit airmen's stories about this place in the last few months. They called it Wailer's Gap. It was an occasional haunt of bandits and more adventurous travelers, but too far off the shipping routes to be safe for respectable business. There were rumors that mordonocs had taken up residence in the caves. Cyprian gauged those rumors to be true, but the mordonocs would not be alone. They came at the heel of their master.

The bandit ship took a fast approach to the mountainside. A rushing river poured out from the front of the cave, spilling onto the soft marshy plain before it. Here, the ground was littered with a motley collection of ships. Most were small, skiffs and the like, battered and worn with hard use and poor maintenance. Patched tents rose up on the ground around them, like crops drunkenly sewn. A hundred smoldering cookfires cast thin spires of gray smoke into the dusky sky. A few ragged dogs trotted among them, looking for handouts. The people, too, had a mongrel look. They craned their necks at the bandit ship that passed overhead, then sagged back down, eyes to the sodden earth.

The escorting mordonocs shrieked and flapped over toward the top of the mountain. A mere speck beneath the yawning maw of the mountain, the bandit ship glided under the stalactites. Cyprian blinked, but the darkness was too intense for him to see far back into the cavern. With expert precision and a few grunted phrases in Klahk, the bandit crew lowered the ship into the immense cavern. The dark air pulsed with the sound of rushing water.

"Up, boy," said the bandit leader, grabbing Cyprian by the collar and hoisting him to his feet.

The bandits seized him by the elbows, pushing him down the ship's gangplank into the base of the musty cavern. There were several other ships docked here, all well-armed. More bandits skulked around in the murk, smoking acrid herbs, tossing dice, and muttering in strange tongues.

A stone pathway wound back further into the cavern, and the bandits followed it. They turned left and right in the dark until Cyprian was totally disoriented. Occasionally, something large swooped overhead, leaving behind an odor of cave-rot that made his eye twitch. Then, they came around a jagged rocky column, and Cyprian nearly stopped in his tracks.

An enormous ship gilded in gold took up the whole cavern, tree-like masts nearly to the ceiling. Its rigging appeared to have been disabled or removed, and a large tent in gold and scarlet was set up on the deck. Light brushed at the inside, and a thousand yellow lanterns lit the ship from stem to stern. The sounds of tinkling chimes and raucous music echoed eerily in the chamber, and Cyprian could smell spices and rum.

But no sooner had Cyprian taken in this sight, than it all winked into blackness. The bandits had dropped a foul-smelling hood over Cyprian's head. Again, he was pushed forward. More than once, he tripped and stumbled over unseen rock ledges, but the strong arms of the bandits held him upright.

After a few minutes, he heard voices, muttering back and forth in the strange dialect of Klahk, and there was a sound like an enormous hatch groaning open. Cyprian was suddenly walking on even slats of decking. The temperature changed. It was warmer and less damp, and the air smelled like black pepper and cardamom, then wet pulley grease, then the burnt-rock scent of gunpowder. He heard snatches of whispered conversation, some in Sylvan, some in other languages. Cyprian was led down a long corridor, then up a tight, turning stairwell, then down another corridor and up another stair that felt as though it was inlaid with stone. Finally, Cyprian smelled the cool moist air of the cavern again. Now it was thick with frantic music from pipes and cymbals, shrieking laughter, and the smell of a feast, rank with spices.

Strong hands whipped the hood from Cyprian's head. The gaudy yellow light of the tent was almost blinding, and he almost jumped back in terror at the nightmare that leered over him. Hideous and deformed creatures of all shapes and sizes surrounded him, twisted faces nightmarish in the light. Seeing Cyprian's wide eyes, they leapt forward, raking the air with laughs and jeers. It took a few terrifying moments for Cyprian to realize that they were people, garishly costumed in bright colors and masks. They were festooned in silver and gold, birds and bears and mordonocs and demons. A fire-breather spat a great jet of flame into the ceiling, igniting one of the iron chandeliers that hung above. Serving girls wearing deer masks sauntered among the partygoers, and acrobats and illusionists capered throughout, tumbling and turning and pulling silks from the hot, crowded air.

The partygoers continued to laugh and poke at Cyprian. The music grew more frantic, and a crazed circular dance began. Several strong hands seized Cyprian by the arms, dragging him along in the human maelstrom. He was yanked and shoved in twenty directions. Sweaty fingers ran through his hair and over his clothes.

And then, as sudden as a lightning strike, the music stopped. The crowd parted. Cyprian stood alone in the center of the tent. Before him stood a man.

Rich fabrics rippled over his frame: pantaloons of golden silk banded with a black sash, a loose gold tunic that ran over one shoulder, leaving the other bare. A broad, beautiful hat topped the ensemble. Though his skin was wrinkled and windburnt, the muscles stood out beneath like bundles of twisted cable. Tattoos ran up and down his neck, over his hands and knuckles. Bangles and charms and talismans glittered on innumerable necklaces and bracelets, and his eyebrows and ears were pierced with hoops and metal bars.

Cyprian had heard many stories about the face of the Bandit Lord Bartimaeus Cain, but none prepared him for what he saw. The bandit's eyes were bright and black, his cheekbones and jaw sculpted, the remains of his lips pulled in a confident smile. His right cheek was gone, and in its place was a rippling gold mesh, studded with diamonds, rubies, and oraculum. Around its edges, windburnt flesh grew into the shining links. Through the mesh, Cyprian could see the outlines of yellow teeth. They clicked against the precious studs as he opened his mouth to speak, his voice deep and resonant.

"You have brought a prize, Admetos?"

The bandit shipmaster emerged from the crowd, a somber hunk of black leather among the lights of the party.

"This one killed two, Lord Cain."

Cain nodded, and pierced Cyprian with his night-black eyes, glimmering beneath heavy, dark brows. Cyprian didn't look away.

30

He forced himself to be quiet, to have control, to be calm. It should take more than a nasty facial wound and some unsettling friends to faze the son of Augustus Fields.

"What is your name?"

Cyprian hooked his thumbs into his belt, staring directly back into Cain's black eyes.

"My name is Fields."

"Fields," said Cain, leaning back, almost working the word across his mouth. Cyprian could see his tongue sliding behind the mesh. "How old are you, boy?"

"Twenty."

With a fluid grace, Cain snatched a red-hot knife from a nearby brazier. He held it in his bare hands, but the red-hot metal didn't burn his weathered skin.

"Lie to me again, boy," he said languidly. "And I will cut out your tongue. How old?"

Cyprian had received enough idle threats in his day to know a real one when it bared its fangs. He only hesitated for a moment.

"Fifteen."

"Ah," sighed Cain, sliding the knife back into the fire. Some of the partygoers tittered. "That has the ring of truth. Although you could pass for older if needs be. You have the build of your old man. Ah yes, I knew him. Augustus Fields, the mighty merchant of Misericordiae. The Rooster, they called him. Although, he's not much more than a lesson to all who would try to oppose the Imperium. I'm sure no Fields would be welcome crowing in Misericordiae these days."

Cain dabbled two fingers by his chin, setting the golden mesh wavering.

"Augustus's boy. Let's see. That would make you Cyprian."

Cyprian didn't say anything. Cain's fingers dropped, as though he had become tired of pondering.

"Maybe you're wondering why my men did not leave you to rot or perish along with your incompetent compatriots. I am rather fond of my mordonocs. I myself have a hand in their training; they respond to me. I have commanded my shipmasters to bring to me any prey that manages to slay one of my beasts, and faithful Admetos here says that you have slain two. Is that true?"

Cyprian set his jaw. Cain was stroking his ego, trying to manipulate him.

"Yes," he replied finally.

"Good," said Cain. "I have an eye for talent, particularly talent as prodigious as your own. I would like to make a proposition to you, Cyprian Fields. You can fly for me, as one of my bondsman. You'll have riches, ships, women. Whatever you desire. Crow for me, Young Rooster, and I will make you prosperous."

For a moment, the offer was tempting. In these increasingly lawless times, there was a lot that could be gained from being close to a man like Bartimaeus Cain. But, there was danger as well. Cyprian squared his shoulders.

"I'm no bandit."

"Cyprian, my boy," said Cain, spreading his bare, muscular arms in a patronizing gesture. "Nor am I. I am merely a gentleman of fortune, a man who recognizes opportunity when it knocks. The last Sovereign is dead, and the age of the Imperium has come. There is no place in this new world for men who make their decisions against what is good for themselves."

"I'm no bandit," Cyprian repeated. "My money comes from no one's blood but my own."

Cain's confident smirk didn't waver. The gold of his false cheek flashed in the lamplight.

"You crow just like your father. Allow me to make my point more clear."

Cain uttered a command in an unfamiliar tongue. From the shadows, three hulking masked partygoers emerged. A rabbit, a jackal, and a lizard. From hidden pockets, each drew a hefty club. Cyprian's hand went to his belt, instinctively reaching for a weapon that wasn't there. The partygoers gathered into a frantic ring, delirious with joy at the prospect of bloodshed. Cain settled himself on a silken couch. A trio of serving girls descended upon him, bearing trays of fruit and glasses of wine. The music resumed, a frantic, dizzying reel.

"They enjoy their sport, my men," Cain said, half-formed lips smacking around a succulent purple fruit. "At any time, you may swear your allegiance to me."

But Cyprian had little intention of succumbing or dying. His sharp eyes searched every surface, flicked through every opportunity.

There were no weapons nearby, nothing that could be used. The only thing he had was an old bird in his jacket, who was still, amazingly, asleep. Rabbit, Jackal, and Lizard advanced, clubs smacking against their meaty palms. Someone in the crowd was loudly taking bets on the fight in Sylvan, suggesting ever-diminishing amounts of time that Cyprian might have to live.

Cyprian would have put a few coins on seconds, until he thought to look up. A chandelier hung above, a wrought-iron affair suspended from the tent's wooden framework. It was too high to reach. Rabbit, Jackal, and Lizard were nearly upon him, Lizard at their head with his club held high aloft. Cyprian hesitated only a moment, trying to determine any other plan but the one that had popped into his mind. None arose. So, he ran right at them.

Lizard swung, but his forward momentum was too great, and Cyprian too light on his feet. The young airman whipped past, swiping one booted foot beneath the big man's shin. Lizard came crashing down, nearly taking Rabbit with him. Jackal, quicker than his compatriots, swung around, club at the ready. But, Cyprian was already away and jumping, first on the back of a stumbling partygoer, then to a rolling cart of wines, dodging a wild swipe of Jackal's club. Cyprian launched himself upward into the gold-speckled light, fingers outstretched for the iron rim of the chandelier.

Jackal and Rabbit reached for him, but they were too slow. Cyprian's free hand closed around the warm iron, and he was whirling around the top of the tent, his boots connecting with several unfortunate foreheads. With his free hand, Cyprian wrenched loose one of the ropes holding the chandelier, so that the whole assembly slammed violently sideways.

Flecks of flaming lamp oil rained down in spirals on the partygoers. With screams and frenzied barks of laughter, they retreated, beating out the flames that landed on their sleeves and collars. Even more landed on the fabric of the tent, and the fine silk burst into vibrant flames. Burning drops of oil landed on Cyprian's vest, and Petros, now conveniently awake, burst out, soaring through the tent on agile wings. Below him, Cyprian heard his pursuers regrouping, the ring of swords being drawn, the metallic click of pistols being cocked. There was a blast and a flash in the air below, and a bullet blasted apart one of the iron lanterns.

Then, a single vibration passed through the spiraling chandelier, the unmistakable cracking of breaking wood. The tent, its edges now truly flame, was morphing and twisting. The wooden frame above was starting to give way. Never one to pass up an opportunity, Cyprian decided to help it along. He yanked on the chandelier with all his might. The cracking intensified to an almighty boom.

And suddenly, along with the chandelier, frame, and endless golden silk, Cyprian was falling through the perfumed air. He just had time to throw himself from beneath the chandelier before it smashed into the deck. To his relief, something large and solid broke his fall. To his disappointment, he discovered that it was in fact Rabbit, his mask now askew, and his eyes alight with manic rage.

Cyprian was sure to get a boot into his face when he took off running through a burning hole in the tent's side, up the length of the immense ship. The partygoers were now running amok, stumbling and struggling in a sea of torn silk and flame.

Cyprian glanced behind. Dark shapes bore down upon him. He ran past a forecastle illuminated in red stained glass, until he was standing on the bow of the great ship. There was nowhere else to run. He peered over the edge. The subterranean river rushed below, beating ceaselessly against the rocks, the water black as night. Could he jump it?

Then, there was an almighty blow against his back, and he was tumbling forward. Only reflexes born of life in the rigging allowed one of Cyprian's hands to find the gunwale, leaving him dangling over the dark, rushing abyss. Cyprian looked up. A sinuous figure was outlined against the firelight. Cyprian saw the glint of gold on the face.

"Such a display," said Bartimaeus Cain, his voice smooth, almost amused. "And you have ruined the nicest party. Color me furious, young Rooster, but color me impressed as well. You killed two of my mordonocs, so I will give you a second chance to join me. There is much to be gained. I will make you free to wander and roam and plunder as you desire, the master of the sky you inhabit. A shipmaster at fifteen years old. That would have made daddy proud."

Cyprian's grip was slipping on the gunwale, sweaty fingers sliding against the hard cedar. Augustus Fields had been many things, but above all else, he had been honest.

"I'm no bandit," he said, trying to regain his grip.

"Maybe not," said Cain with a viper's smile. "But there is one thing of which we can be certain, Cyprian Fields. We can be certain that you will do the same as all talented men who come to my side and depart…"

In Cain's hand, something angular and glowing appeared. The knife, red-hot. The gold mesh sparkled in its luminescent glow, dark eyes black as death.

"You will come back."

And he pressed the back of the knife into Cyprian's hand. The pain was like a lance. His fingers spasmed once and then Cyprian was falling through the dark. The roaring of the river rose up into the underground night and swallowed him whole.

CHAPTER FIVE

Basil leaned against the table that bore the dead man, blue eyes trained on the small, sad pile of possessions removed from the messenger's pockets: a few coins, an old pipe, twisted scraps of paper. None of it held any answers for Basil. Who was this man? How had he known Basil's name? His desperate ramblings of Sovereigns, Bookkeepers, and the Imperium filled Basil with a profound sadness.

Basil was no stranger to death. It was just as natural as life, but there was a special pang of sorrow that he felt whenever it happened in pain, confusion, and loneliness.

The furnaces and sluices of the longhouse clanked and rumbled, chewing through their coal like hungry beasts, but no men stood at the anvils or bellows. The only miner left was Thon Black. His big hands hung at his sides, and he was looking at Basil with glistening, solemn eyes.

"I knew this day would come," he said. "I've known it since you came. When you were a little child."

"What?" said Basil, looking away from the dead man for the first time. The tone of his father's voice made Basil suddenly very hot and very cold at the same time. Black was not a man prone to undue emotion.

"Black!" a miner's voice yelled from outside, the voice edging upward in panic.

"Come with me, Basil," said Black, pushing open the door of the forge longhouse.

The miners stood with their backs to the Mountain, peering out over the village. In the waving haze of afternoon sky beyond the mountain, sleek red shapes were plying the air.

"They're coming," said one of the miners. "Just like the stranger said."

Within a few moments, half a battalion of the Imperium's Fleet filled the sky over the tiny village: three dreadnoughts, two sleek interceptors, and a supply frigate. They were trimmed in gold, as beautiful and sleek as stallions. Their agile form and the quick motion of their control surfaces made them seem to Basil like living things. Their decks bristled with long banks of polished guns, empty eyes that stared out at the town.

From the foremost dreadnought's deck, a gangplank extended and a large complement of airmen trooped down into the village in tight formation. The airmen stood at the ready, breaking ranks to reveal a man striding through their midst. The sun-and-stars of the Imperium's Grand Admiral shone on his shoulders, but the rest of his red uniform was rumpled and dirty. He was swarthy with broad shoulders and the brace of pistols at his waist rolled with his long, loping gait. His hair was greasy and lank, his fingernails long and unkempt. His eyes sparked a languid yellow as they swept over the gathered village, like a mean dog on the prowl.

"Basil," said Black, seizing Basil by the arm. "We have to go. Now."

Without a word, Basil obeyed his father. But, they had not gone more than a few steps when the Grand Admiral spoke, his voice booming over the village.

"I come to you in the name of the Imperium Titus, the Undisputed Ruler of the Dominion of Cor Nova."

For a moment, there was nothing but the sound of the wind and the cry of condors circling up the mountain. The people were silent. Fear was thick in the air. The Grand Admiral's lip curled in a contemptuous sneer.

"You don't kneel at the name of your king?" he roared. "I've said his name. Now kneel!"

The miners looked to Thon Black. With a single nod, he knelt to the ground, murmuring for Basil to do the same. The rest of the town followed suit, mothers holding children firmly by the hand.

"Good," grunted the admiral. "The Imperium's kindly face shines on those willing to learn. I am Grand Admiral Lysandros Rast, and I have questions."

Black went to stand up, as if to speak. The Grand Admiral drew a heavy pistol, cocking it and pointing it at his head.

"On your knees, dusty bones. The first man to rise will come to a nasty end indeed. I am looking for someone, rock-herders. I am looking for a boy. In the name of the Imperium Titus, I command every boy between twelve and seventeen on his feet."

Warily, one by one, the boys of the town stood up. Basil did his best to appear brave. He could feel his father's eyes upon him. The Grand Admiral looked them over for a long moment, his yellow eyes settling upon each. He gestured to the officers beside him.

"Load them onto the ship."

The blood drained from Basil's face. Why? The outcry from the miners was immediate, a chorus of surprise and outrage. Some of the women began to cry.

"On your knees!" roared the Grand Admiral, swinging his pistol toward the nearest group. The rest of his airmen drew their weapons, forming two red ranks. "The first man to rise will find his brains suddenly expelled from his head."

The Grand Admiral's swarthy neck twisted as he peered left and right, sniffing for defiance.

"Now," he said. "Take them."

A masked soldier seized Basil by the arm, pushing him toward the dreadnought. The airmen were doing the same with the other boys.

Basil didn't know where the first shot came from, but it echoed over the mountain passes. A Fleet airman screamed, the sound metallic behind his mask, and his glove came away from his shoulder dripping blood. The Grand Admiral's face twisted into a mask of hatred, rage, and triumph.

"Is it blood you want, rock-herders?" he said, drawing a second pistol. "That's just as well. I'm thirsty."

With a roar, he commanded the attack, and the valley erupted into thunder. In a frantic haze of blood and smoke, the miners were on their feet. Some were able to get their hands on guns, others had axes and shovels. In the thick of the fighting, Grand Admiral Lysandros Rast led the charge, the manic light of a lunging animal in his yellow eyes. He dispatched two miners with his pistols, then dove into the fighting with a heavy scimitar.

A pair of hidden dreadnoughts swooped in over the hill, armed to the teeth. Basil could see gun crew at work on the decks. Women and children dashed for the forge longhouse, hoping the walls would save them from the cannons. Suddenly, Basil felt the strong grip of his father.

"Get back!" Black roared to the townspeople as he dragged Basil away. "Back to the mouth!"

Together, they ran through the gunsmoke and the screams of the miners, heading for the cavernous mountainside. The dreadnoughts came about, pointing their guns down into Osmara, where the bolder villagers were making their stand. A bell rang three times from Rast's dreadnought. Immediately, the Fleet airmen in the fighting retreated, so that they stood in the shadow of the immense vessels. Basil saw the torches of the gun crews descend toward the fuses.

"Get to cover!" roared Black, throwing both of them behind a tiny overturned oxcart, hardly any protection at all.

Still caught up in the fighting, most of the miners could not hear. They were totally exposed. The first powder-flash illuminated the rigging. In seconds, Basil knew, the air would be filled with hot, thunderous death. Basil's chest tightened, the horror incomprehensible. These people, whom Basil had known and loved and healed for his entire life, would be destroyed. Suddenly, unexplainably, he felt something stir deep within himself, like a kestrel erupting into wing. A warmth thrummed in his chest, radiating outwards, seeping its way into his lungs, whirling up through him, headed for the free, free sky.

Not knowing why, Basil leapt up. Unbidden, a shout sprang to his lips. It was a sound like the roaring of a hundred mountain storms, the crack of rock, the wind whispering through tiny white mountain flowers. The unearthly words filled the air in front of him, growing and flattening and spinning outward and away in an ever-widening disk of silver. The guns fired. Fire and smoke and thunder filled the world, and dashed itself against the shield that had leapt unbidden from Basil's lips. Basil and his father were thrown backwards with the force of the blast. Then, time seemed to catch up, and all was chaos.

As the words faded away, the shield of air faded away as though it had never been. The fight went on, and Basil felt a strong hand grab him by the collar and lift him to his feet. Basil staggered, exhausted, drained.

"What... was that?" he said.

"I….," said Black, eyes wide. "We have to go. Come!"

"I have to stay!" Basil said. There were people, friends and neighbors, lying all around, blood seeping into the dust beneath them. He seized the clasps of his medical box. "I can help. There are wounded..."

But his father wasn't listening. Thon Black dragged him through the doors of the forge longhouse, seized him by the shoulders, and pulled him in close. Basil saw himself reflected in the old man's hard black eyes, now glistening with tears.

"Listen to me, Basil. Your destiny is outside of this town. It's bigger than you, bigger than me, bigger than all the ore beneath the mountain. I heard what that messenger said. He's told you everything you need to know..."

"To do what?" asked Basil.

"To do what the Bookkeepers have always wanted to do: bring the Sovereign back. You're one of them, Basil."

There was thunder outside, the assault taking on fresh force. The Grand Admiral's orders came in a cackling scream now. Without another word, Basil and his father dashed from the back of the forge, heading for the minehead within the mountain's mouth. As they drew near, a cannon blast struck. The minehead exploded, cables and ropes breaking free and striking like snakes. Black threw himself in front of Basil, but both of them were blown aside by the blast. There was a crash as the mine elevator fell to the bottom of the shaft. Staggering, Black clambered to his feet, and led Basil on.

They took a turn down one of the lamplit shafts that ran back into Osmo Mountain, the sounds of battle immediately swallowed up by the endless rock. They dodged down a side tunnel, switching back and forth through the darkness, until they came to a small passage that Basil had never seen before. Raising a guttering oil lamp high, Black carefully counted the stones, muttering to himself. Finally, he seemed to find what he was looking for. With a muscled hand, he gripped a small granite outcropping, and pulled with all his strength. After a moment, there was a loud crack and chunks of old plaster came free in Black's big hands.

In moments, a piece of the mine wall fell away, revealing a black hole leading off into blackness. The lamplight fell on a single mine-cart, squatting in the dark. Black helped Basil get in, but shook his head when Basil tried to return the favor.

"The cart will take you as far as the creek at the mountain's base. The line ends behind a bluff at the base. From there, go to Old Whetstone, the miller. He will get you safe passage to the Road. Then, it's on to Misericordiae. Don't come back here. There will be nothing to come back to."

Then, Basil saw the glistening wetness on the front of Black's vest. He remembered the blast from the minehead, how he had staggered after the blow. It was bleeding as only a mortal wound bleeds. Basil reached out his hand, trying to stop the flow of blood, but Black caught it and held him still. Basil's head was swimming, tears turning his vision to a blurry soup.

"No," he said. "I have to stay! I have to help..."

Black clasped one rough, worn hand to the side of Basil's face. He looked deeply into Basil's eyes.

"Here in this village, you have healed. You have helped. Now, others are in need of you. You have a gift, Basil. Find the Bookkeepers...for Osmara, for the whole Dominion..."

"But...!"

"Remember what the messenger said. Go to Misericordiae and find the ship *Philomena*. Boy, never forget that I have loved you. We all have. Have courage, Basil."

With tears glistening in the crevices of his eyes, Thon Black gave the cart a push, and Basil was suddenly rushing into the dark, calling out for his father. Into a diminishing square of light, everything that Basil had ever loved and ever known disappeared.

CHAPTER SIX

The upper levels of the Carillon creaked under the rumble of booted feet. But, in the secret room off the twelfth turn in the stairs, all was quiet. The bells hung above in silent witness as the masked admiral trained his pistol on Veronica's chest. The eyeholes of his mask were twin pools of darkness. Unflinching, Veronica stared right into them.

"A pistol is a coward's weapon," she said.

The admiral appeared unmoved.

"Sit down on the floor," he said, flicking the barrel of the pistol downward.

"It is not becoming of a lady to sit on the floor."

"Then it is good that I am not speaking to a lady. Rather to a foolish young girl who has placed herself in mortal peril. Sit."

With a prim nod, Veronica folded herself onto the floor, settling her hands neatly in her lap. The admiral's armored head swiveled on his shoulders, taking in the hidden room. His gloved hand fell on one of the stacks of freshly printed documents, each thin volume pressed between strips of cheap pine.

He lifted one, then glanced again at Veronica. After a moment, he reached up and lifted the crested helmet from his head. By Veronica's judgment, he had once been a handsome man. He had a broad face with a strong chin, the skin now lined with worry, his beard a faded gray. His eyes were hard, but a sadness seemed to weight his body. This was a man who saw things, who noticed, who remembered. A man who would send his soldiers on while he stayed behind, following a hunch, finding a secret room. Veronica felt the wheels of her mind begin to turn, then seize. She knew this man. Every dissident in Cor Nova knew this man.

His eyes roamed across the page in front of him. After a moment, he shook his head, and dropped the book fragment at Veronica's knees.

"The Rule of Sylvanus. Not the type of material a young girl should be reading. Or spreading."

Veronica primly rearranged the folds of her skirt.

"You're well-read enough to recognize it. Clearly we printers are doing our jobs."

"It is not admirable to distribute trash into the hands of the uneducated rabble."

Veronica patted delicately at her braid.

"I've never seen soldiers so singularly preoccupied with burning massive amounts of *trash*. It must be garbage of a startlingly provocative variety. I have to say, I've heard many stories about the great Admiral Khyber Ambry, the Imperium's Hunting Dog, and a great many of them involve you tracking down people who print and distribute this book, among others. Surely, our Imperium has greater tasks for a man of your talents than merely collecting trash. If there is no danger of the Sovereigns returning, then why is the Imperium so afraid of the book that guided their rule? Unless of course, he has reason to believe that a Sovereign *will* return. I have found, Admiral, that it is men who wrongfully clutch the power of others that fear losing it the most."

The Admiral took a step closer to her, gazing down at her impassively. With a squeak of leather, he squatted so that their eyes were level. Then, he dealt her a slap that sent her sprawling, her vision dancing with stars, her cheek burning.

"When you address me next, you will do it with some respect. In a few moments, my men will be returning empty-handed from the floors above. So, we have a little while to talk."

Veronica glared at him with fire in her eyes. She glanced at the pearl handle of the rapier. She had fallen toward it, but it was still too far away. The Admiral rested on his haunches, his voice quiet, almost a whisper.

"One night, two years ago, I was called from my patrols in upper Terra Alta. Apparently, there was a high-level dissenter against the Imperium at work in Terra Alta City, a scholar. He was connected with a dissident organization called the Bookkeepers. That night, we raided his house. It was a large, stylish mansion, the grounds lined with willow trees and flowering lavender."

Veronica suddenly felt as though she had been plunged into ice. She could see the house in her minds' eye, its spires reaching up into the moonlight. She could hear the boughs of the lavender trees whispering against one another, the crackle of wood in the fireplace, the smell of coriander in the kitchen. Her mother was a sliver of ivory in the moonlit window, leaning over her most recent canvas with a brush of golden ochre in her hand.

"When the moon rose, we broke through the door, found the scholar in the anteroom, with sword and pistol at the ready. Somehow, he knew we were coming. He fought like a tiger, an able swordsman for a scholar. He took down two of my men before he was subdued. Even then, it took us considerable time to acquire the necessary information from him. Then, we carried him to his library. We put him inside, on a big mahogany table that he had."

Veronica could feel her resolve wavering, a surging wave of hot, angry tears. She pushed it down. She couldn't lose control. It was what Ambry wanted.

"He was delirious, losing blood. He wasn't making any sense, just saying a single name over and over. There was nothing more that he could tell us. We tied him to the table, and set fire to the books."

Veronica lunged at Ambry, unable to stop the firestorm of hatred that boiled out of her, but the Admiral was fast. With a blow that drove the wind from her lungs, he seized her by the throat, lifting her feet from the floor.

"And what name do you think he said?" Ambry demanded, as Veronica fought for breath in his grip. "What name came from the scholar's lips over and over? Veronica. Veronica."

And then Veronica was lying on the floor in a tumbled heap. Rear Admiral Khyber Ambry stood over her, his somber gray face looming among the bells. He pointed a gloved finger at her.

"Hector Stromm's destiny was a function of his choice. He chose to spread dissent against the Imperium, and he paid the price. You, though small and frail and female, have a choice to make as well.

And you must make it now. The age of the Sovereign is over. The age of the Imperium has come. Whether you choose peace or war is up to you."

Veronica stumbled to her feet, still reeling from lack of oxygen. Her left foot landed on something that rattled. She looked down. A pearl handle glinted beside her toe. With a practiced kick of her foot, the blade sprung up to her hand. Like lightning, the admiral swept up his pistol, but Veronica was faster. She swiped downward savagely, and with a clang, the pistol skittered across the floor. Ambry leapt back and drew his saber.

"I choose the Sovereign's peace," Veronica said, raising her blade to meet Ambry's. "And if that's the Imperium's war, then so be it."

The admiral looked at her for a long moment. All it would take, Veronica knew, was one loud call out into the Carillon, and his men would come running. But instead, Ambry pressed the attack. Veronica rapier whizzed through the air as she blocked Ambry's heavy blow and countered with her own. Ambry sidestepped and knocked the attack away.

"You're well-trained," he said.

"By the best," Veronica replied. "A scholar."

The duel continued in a dizzying ballet of thrusts, parries, and lunges. Ambry's style was methodical, his strength immense. As quick and precise as Veronica's footwork was, he would overpower her with sheer endurance given enough time. She had to end this fight. Quickly. Turning another vicious blow, Veronica chanced a glance upward. There, in one of the hidden press platform ropes hidden among the bellworks, there was a kink, a loop of rope jammed in the pulley. The fault in the platform mechanism. Veronica's mind began racing.

Sweat now beading on his brow, Ambry came down with an almighty stroke, smashing into Veronica's rapier with a jolt that shot through her whole arm in lances of hot pain. With difficulty, she parried and lunged, but Ambry was quick to exploit her weakness. In two brief swipes, the saber whipped at her, the first blow grazing her arm, the second smashing into her right shoulder. The rapier fell from her hands, and she sank to her feet, momentarily blinded with searing pain, hot blood seeping across her chest and down her back.

"Perhaps you've learned a lesson, foolish girl," Ambry said, chest heaving. "This is the fate of all who oppose the Imperium."

Veronica steeled herself, pushing away the pain that throbbed through her sword arm. There was something hard under the free hand she put down to steady herself, something cold and metallic. Ambry's pistol, still cocked.

Ambry froze as Veronica trained the pistol on his chest.

"Drop the saber," she said.

Flushed as he was, Ambry's expression didn't change, his grey eyes impassive.

"You're not going to shoot me."

Ignoring the screaming pain in her shoulder, Veronica rose to her feet.

"You are wrong about that. You're an instrument of a tyrant. You're the man who tortured and murdered my father. Nothing would give me more pleasure than to shoot you where you stand."

With a grim glare, Ambry thrust his saber, point-first, into the floorboards.

"Step back," she said.

Ambry complied, boots thudding onto the platform that bore the printing press.

"On the night when you killed my father," she said. "There was a woman in the house."

"Yes," Ambry said.

Veronica struggled to keep her voice from wavering from pain and fear. Did she have the courage to ask the next question?

"Did you kill her?"

"That is a Fleet matter."

Ambry's stolid, grim defiance made Veronica's blood boil.

"Listen to me. You have exactly two options at this moment. You can either tell me where my mother is, in which case I will allow you to live. Or, you can refuse, and I will shoot you dead. Choose quickly. There isn't much time. If I didn't know that some similarly uniformed murderous cockroach would step up to take your place, I would have shot you already."

Ambry didn't seem afraid, but something flickered in those dark grey eyes. A thought or emotion that Veronica could not identify.

"Your mother," he said, his voice flat, as though reading from a report. "Amelia Stromm. Apprehended from the Stromm residence in Terra Alta while attempting to foil the arrest of Hector Stromm. She was interrogated and relocated to the Imperium's labor force."

Veronica felt a sudden thrill. She wasn't dead.

"The Imperium's labor force," Veronica said. "Where?"

"If you don't know that," Ambry replied. "You are not your father's daughter."

Veronica nodded. She knew what that meant. In the highs and lows of Misericordiae, she'd heard the same story in a hundred forms. There was a pit in the Fields of Carath, a wound in the earth, and that is where the prisoners went. They didn't come out. It was all the information Veronica needed.

"Congratulations, Admiral," Veronica said, backing toward the door, pistol still trained on Ambry. "You've saved your miserable life."

"You are making a mistake," Ambry said. "Why oppose the Imperium in his might? The path to peace is not to divide the Dominion, but to unite it under his rule. I bring order. You sew chaos. Why oppose the inevitable?"

Veronica smirked.

"It's as you said earlier. Because I, though small and frail and female, have a choice to make as well. And I'm making it right now."

Veronica aimed the pistol upward, and fired. The ball obliterated the kinked pulley, releasing the rope, and the platform's release lever slammed the rest of the way forward. With a wrenching clank, a whole section of the floor swung free on huge counterweights, carrying the press and Admiral Ambry with it. The wall levered outward on greased pulleys, the press groaning as it broke free from pins on the floor. In the blink of an eye, the press, platform, and admiral went sailing outward into the night amid a rain of paper, ink, barrels, and crates. Ambry's fingers reached out for Veronica even as he plunged with the press into the milky whiteness of the Ivory River.

Veronica allowed herself no time to gloat. Shouts of alarm and surprise sounded from above, and boots hammered down through the Carillon. She picked up her rapier, and took off down the staircase, every step cruelly jarring her shoulder.

In moments, there were shouts and yells behind her. A hail of shot struck the wood all around her. Finally, she barreled out into the haunted black night, streaking through the streets and toward the myriad of bridges that led over the River toward Keel Hill. She chanced a glance back. There were even more soldiers.

A gunshot sounded. A lance of pain suddenly tore through Veronica's back. She stumbled on, fighting the pain with every step. As though it was her last hope, she gripped the pearl handle of the rapier, her only friend.

Chapter Seven

Once, the Road of Sylvanus was alive with traffic, the wagon trains of prosperous merchants forming moving cities as they transported their wares through the seven provinces of the Sovereign Dominion of Cor Nova. But now, in the age of the airship, the Road was largely abandoned, its once-majestic flagstones cracked and uneven, its markers weathered to lumps of mossy stone. Now, it was a way for the poor and forgotten, or for those who wished to pass unnoticed.

Cyprian Fields, nursing a thunderously bad mood several days in the making, considered himself all three. For the twentieth time in an hour, Cyprian decided he hated walking, and would do as little as possible in the future. His thin airman's boots were nearly worn through. His blisters had developed blisters. In the sky, a man dashes, leaps, climbs, and crawls, but he doesn't plod along in one direction for hours unending like a peasant. A few times, he'd been lucky enough to catch a ride on the back of a rare farmer or trapper's cart. But mostly, he walked. The back of his hand, the outline of the knife's blade etched white into his flesh, still burned like fire.

Noon had only just passed, and the day was hot. Occasionally, Petros dove off into the underbrush, swooping among the trees. Other times, he sat on Cyprian's shoulder, pecking idly at the mosquitoes that plagued the young airman. Cyprian was still

deciding whether he was going to forgive the old crow for finding
something else to do while Cyprian was outrunning Bartimaeus Cain
and his lackeys. It had been more than a week since he'd washed out
of the river from Wailer's Gap somewhere farther down the valley,
bruised and aching in a hundred places, and it had taken him a
whole day of walking to get to the nearest one-goat Korkyran village.
Once there, he had no money to pay for food, so he had to dig
potatoes for several hours, then sleep in a small barn before
beginning his trek towards civilization. In his nights and days on the
Road, he had dodged a few overly inquisitive forest creatures, two
highwaymen, and a crazy old fortune-teller lady who followed him
for a quarter league, loudly predicting a pair of unfortunate meetings
in his future. Once, he saw a large troop of Imperium soldiers
marching from the direction of Misericordiae, but he kept his head
down and they gave him no trouble. His spirits finally lifted when he
saw a tell-tale rise in the old Road as it cut through the trees ahead.
Merchant's Respite.

It was the spot where merchants, footsore and tired of fighting
and struggling their way along the Road, saw for the first time the
city they had come for: Misericordiae, the Ivory City, the Merchant's
Kingdom. Hazy over the vast plains, the city rose up at the far end of
the valley, resting across the swell of three great hills. On Keel Hill,
the furthest and highest rise, long concourses of ships arrived and
departed, speckling the sky with the flags and masts of a hundred
vessels. Misericordiae was an old city, its history a mad whirlwind of
rogues, heroes, and shipmasters. It was the place where Cyprian had
grown up, and now, against his better wishes, he was going back.
There, he would find a ship and his way back to the open sky.

Night was falling by the time Cyprian skulked his way past the
Imperium soldiers at the city gates, pulling the ragged collar of his
coat up high and tucking his head down. Once, the sky-blue
uniformed officers of the Lord Grand Chancellor of Misericordiae
had stood there, but the Imperium had removed the heads of all the
provinces, replacing them with his Fleet admirals.

Even before Cyprian passed the gate, he could smell it: the scent
of the city. There was the bitter tang of vented aether and pulley
grease, the sweetness of oranges and sliced green melon drifting over
the rooftops from Topgallant Square, the musk of dank alleys and
raucous taverns, the warm exotic aroma of spices and soft leather

and wine. It rolled over Cyprian like a wave, almost the same as when he'd left. But, there was something new in the air as well. He had felt it in a hundred cities and towns, great and small, all over Cor Nova: the sharp scent of fear. The glance over the shoulder, the hurrying of children along, the unwillingness to meet the eyes of strangers. On every corner, the soldiers of the Imperium stood, faceless, clad in red, gloved hands resting on polished pistol butts.

Cyprian did his best to blend in with the crowds, and pressed forward up Keel Hill. Topgallant Square, crammed with people, was dominated by the Port Authority Rotunda with its cupola of glass panes and the twin spires of the Kestrel Office, streaming with the passage of dark wings. Cyprian had to grab Petros by the talons, as his neck strained toward the mass of kestrels.

"Easy, old bird."

Above their heads and further down the hill, the high oaken concourses stretched east and west, the wooden bellies of ships large and small huddled around them. In the midst of this teeming world above Misericordiae, merchants, artisans, and airmen hurried past one another like ants at work, tabulating yields and calculating profits, all attempting to thrive in the cutthroat jungle of decks, ropes, and aether. Loadmasters argued with shipmasters who argued with merchants who argued with port authorities over deals, agreements, prices, and taxes. Winches bore crates, bales, and boxes aloft between ship and concourse. For a moment, Cyprian stopped in the square, looking up at the great multitude of ships above. He could find work on one of them.

But, something twinged within Cyprian's heart. The little streets that wandered off from Topgallant Square splintered into even smaller capillaries, each crammed with tiny shops and businesses. Against his better judgment, Cyprian set off down one of them. He passed rope-vendors and textilers displaying wares on spools, grimy moneyhouses with sweaty proprietors, sleazy airmen's bars with jangling concertinas, leatherworkers selling belts and boots. Finally, Cyprian stopped in front of a tiny building that was once painted blue. Now peeling and dilapidated, it squatted between a blacksmith's forge and another shipping office. Above the grimy windowpanes, a chipped wooden sign emblazoned with a faded golden rooster swung in the spice-laden breeze. It read: "Fields Trading and Supply Company".

Cyprian tried the tarnished brass latch. It didn't budge. Cyprian looked through the pane, but the glass was scratched and hazy. He braced himself against the door, preparing to drive a shoulder into it.

"This is how Augustus's son returns? By breaking down an old man's door?"

Cyprian wheeled around. A man stood in the street behind him, watching Cyprian with curiously bright blue eyes. His once-tall frame was now slightly stooped and he leaned heavily on a bronze-headed cane. His hair was a peppery gray streaked with white, and his neatly combed beard fell halfway down a fashionable green waistcoat. As neat and carefully dressed as he was, his weathered, stony features gave him the look of a man who had fought through many a hard sky. He extended a hand, about to introduce himself, but the name swelled up from Cyprian's memory to his lips.

"Francis Lightlas."

Lightlas bowed slightly. He had been one of his father's loadmasters, Cyprian remembered, in charge of keeping track of cargo and aether. A stern man, he remembered, but never unkind.

"How did you know where to send your letters? I've been in the air for a long time."

"Let's see," said the old man, leaning on his cane as he counted with his fingers. "Three years ago, you piloted a schooner through the Berellus Straits during a blizzard. The Lammastide following that incident, you were discovered aiding in the break-in of an Imperium outpost, successfully retrieving a captured comrade. Then, you were captured by the Bowman-McCoys and imprisoned in the ruby mines of Kerrag-al-Gaat, from which you escaped by instigating a modest slave revolt. And now there's some wild talk that you managed to get yourself wrapped up with Bartimaeus Cain…"

Cyprian shoved his hands in his pockets.

"I take your point. Perhaps I haven't kept the lowest of profiles."

"And smashing down an old man's door is not a good way to escape notice," said Lightlas, producing a tarnished key from his waistcoat pocket. "Step aside."

Daylight pierced the murk of the shipping company office like a lance. When Cyprian was a child, this room had bustled with the activity of four clerks and a steward, and there was always some shipmaster stomping in through the door, boasting of profits and holding a fistful of victorious documents. Those days were long over.

The place smelled like mildewed paper and dry leather. Several old desks, a broken aetherolabe, and a few chairs formed islands in the middle of the scuffed hardwood floor, holding up reams of ancient paperwork: faded shipping receipts, crumpled permits, and moth-eaten manifests. A yellowing map hung above the fireplace at the rear, its surface pocked with tiny colored pins marking the positions and routes of ships long lost.

Lightlas lowered himself into a creaking chair.

"Do you know what has happened here since your departure from Misericordiae?"

Cyprian poked the old aetherolabe.

"Not much, by the look of it."

"Well-observed. For the most part, the shipmasters who chose to join your father's rebellion were slaughtered or scattered to the four winds. This left the trading company with precious few ships and no business. By the law of the province of Misericordiae, the ownership of the company fell to his most senior officer. That man turned out to be the first in a depressing parade of drunken and slovenly scoundrels who squandered what was left. I bought the remains a year ago for a mere pittance."

Cyprian nodded, but didn't feel too much pity. This company had stopped being his inheritance on the night his father died.

"And now, you have an actual contract."

"The first," Lightlas said. "The only. And I would like to have you on board to see it done."

Cyprian shook his head.

"I'm done with this place. I wish you the best of luck, Mr. Lightlas, but I'm shipping out on the next freighter that will have me."

Lightlas nodded slowly, lips pursed, cane tapping thoughtfully on the floor.

"I see. What then brings you to the old headquarters?"

Cyprian shrugged.

"Morbid curiosity, I reckon."

Lightlas seemed to ignore this explanation, instead handing Cyprian a neat stack of rough paper, emblazoned with a crowing rooster at the top. Cyprian took the offered parchment, tilting the page so that the light fell on the flowing, meticulous script. It requested the shipment of a large quantity of reinforced wooden crates from a warehouse in Misericordiae to Carath. It specified a date and, Cyprian was surprised to note, an exceptionally large sum of money.

"It can't be real," Cyprian said, jabbing at the figure. "That amount? For a courier service?"

Lightlas arched an eyebrow.

"I presume the client finds these crates especially valuable. A large sum of money was enclosed. Exactly one quarter of the offered amount. It is in the safe. The rest can be retrieved from a bank in Carath. I sent a kestrel. The sum of money in Carath exists."

"You have no ship."

Lightlas shook his head.

"I have done some digging through the records at the Port Authority. As it happens, you are mistaken. Fields Trading and Supply Company maintains exactly one vessel."

"Which one?"

"*Philomena.*"

The word dropped on Cyprian like a rock. He looked up at the old man.

"What?"

Francis Lightlas massaged his old knuckles, wincing at an apparent rheumatic stiffness.

"She is cradled under the Old Concourse. Lot 363, I believe. The Fleet impounded her following the rebellion, but the statute of limitations on her seizure has expired. I believe the Imperium has forgotten about her…"

Cyprian stood up, suddenly very eager to be out of the office.

"I should go."

"Where to?"

"The concourses. I'm going to find a vessel and ship out to someplace far from here."

"And what do you imagine you are going to find in that place far from here, Cyprian?" Lightlas asked, his blue eyes piercing. "You've been traveling for four years, without direction, without guidance. Take it from someone who has done his fair share of running away from the past. It's no way to live a life. It's not something your father would ever have done."

Cyprian scowled. The old man was trying to manipulate him. He was on his way to the door when Lightlas seized him by the hand.

"On a more practical level," he said. "I don't believe you will find many options on the concourses. It seems to me like the rumors are true."

Lightlas pointed to the back of Cyprian's hand, where the scar of Cain's blade stood out white.

"No shipmaster that I know of will be interested in taking on a deckhand who has been marked by Bartimaeus Cain. True, you may be able to hide it. But if they discover it, they'll be afraid of Cain coming after you with unfinished business. That won't end well."

"I'll take my chances."

With a sigh, Lightlas stood up.

"No, you won't. Because you're an intelligent young man. Your father was kind to me. I've been reaching out to you because I know that you're an airman capable beyond your years, and trustworthy officers are hard to come by in times like these. I need a deckmaster. A second-in-command. Someone who can manage the affairs of a ship in flight when I am otherwise engaged. Do you want to be a wandering deckhand for the rest of your life? I'm offering you the chance to be a ship's officer."

Lightlas reached into a dusty desk drawer and removed a heavy package in brown paper. He opened this to reveal a pair of polished oculi, one silver, one brass. They were engraved with the image of a three-enveloped freighter topped by a crowing rooster. Lightlas took the silver shipmaster's oculus and stuck it in his jacket pocket. The brass deckmaster's oculus reflected the light dully in Lightlas's hand, the telescoping body and lenses polished to a shine.

"Reclaimed from the Fleet at significant expense," said Lightlas. "It's yours. If you want it."

Cyprian looked for a long, difficult moment at the oculus, then back at the white outline of the knife on the back of his hand. Finally, against his better judgment, he accepted the oculus. It was warm in his hand.

Lightlas grunted his approval, then dropped a heavy, rust-covered key into Cyprian's palm.

"Now, you take this. I'm too old to be mucking around down by the Old Concourse."

"What does this open?"

"The lock," Lightlas said, his blue eyes twinkling. "To Lot 363."

CHAPTER EIGHT

The skeleton of the Old Concourse stood at the very base of Keel
Hill. It was the first concourse built in Misericordiae, under the
direction of the Sovereign Maximillian, the wonder of its age. But as
the decades passed, the structure became weather-beaten and
rickety. After a celebrated incident in which a small circus troupe fell
through the most eastward section, it was repurposed as a storage
area for unused vessels. The ancient beams of the Old Concourse
separated Keel Hill, Topgallant Square, and Market Circle from the
narrow, crowded streets of the southern regions of the city. In the
daytime, truant children played among the abandoned ships. On
rainy nights, the eyeless hulks were witness to shady deals between
men who hid behind the collars of long coats. The abandoned ships
were cradled, nestled behind locked shutters under the concourse.
Within their enclosures, they stood boarded up and bare-masted,
old-timers awaiting a second birth into the sky.

The light of day was fading as Cyprian walked beneath the
concourse's gray eaves. Ahead of him, a long line of shutters stood
like silent sentries. Petros wheeled in and out of the beams, snapping
at drowsy, unsuspecting pigeons. Cyprian massaged the burnt back
of his left hand. He tried to concentrate on the cobbles of the street,
on the stars in the sky, but he could only think of what lay ahead, of
the past that lurked behind one of these locked doors.

Lot 363 came up even more quickly than he thought, a pair of huge shutters identical to the others. The wood was cracked and split in places, the heavy iron lock caked with rust. When Cyprian inserted the key, a shower of red metal flakes fell on his boots. He had to wrench with all of his strength to get the old mechanism to turn. Then the door came open, rusted hinges groaning. The meager light of dusk fell on an enormous hulk shrouded in canvas, the cloth streaked with bird leavings and mildew.

For a moment, Cyprian felt the impulse to turn around and leave, to find a ship on one of the concourses with a crew that didn't speak Sylvan, to leave the brass oculus behind and fly out with the dawn to somewhere strange and wonderful. He had spent four years running. A few more wouldn't hurt. But, Lightlas's words had the sting of truth. It wasn't something his father would have done. Cyprian clenched his teeth, willing his heart to stop its rapid beating.

Yanking his knife out of his belt, Cyprian stepped up to the ship's canvas-clad side and slashed at the nearest rope. The dry fibers parted with a snap. Cyprian slashed again and again, cutting ropes and slicing the panels of canvas that stretched down amidships. Petros perched on one of the open shutters and watched Cyprian with a golden eye.

"I don't suppose you'd mind putting that beak to work and helping me for once?"

The kestrel clicked his beak.

"Of course not."

It may have been minutes or hours by the time all of the ropes hung vine-like around the ship. Cyprian stood, chest heaving, shirt clinging to the sweat on his back, beneath the right side of the bow. He reached up, seized one loose rope, and pulled. With a dusty rippling, the enormous patchwork mess of canvases on the ship tore up the side, splitting along seams and sliding over the gunwales. The canvas fell away, revealing a sight that Cyprian had not seen for over four years.

And suddenly, Cyprian was twelve years old again, clambering his way up the weather tower as fast as he could go. His limbs ached and his lungs burned by the time he was high enough to see all of Keel Hill. Far above on the platform, he could hear the booted footfalls of the weathermaster, logging the temperature, air pressure, and windspeed and sending them out on kestrels to the Port

Authority Rotunda. The great birds flapped out every few minutes, but none paid any attention to Cyprian. The city was quiet. All of Misericordiae, dark and sleeping, stretched out in front of him.

Far out in the port, several great lights hung, coloring the clouds grey and gold. Dreadnoughts, heavy with loaded guns and masked airmen. They had hovered there night and day for the last two weeks, stopping all trade. Save the Fleet ships, no one came and no one left. Precious goods languished in hundreds of holds. There was no fresh food at the market. Misericordiae, the Merchant's Kingdom, was starting to fester and roil from the stillness.

For a long time, everything was still. Cyprian was relieved. Maybe it wasn't going to happen. Then, somewhere in the port, a bell rang.

Then again.

And again.

On the third ring, the blackness of the night gave way. Lanterns sprung to flickering life along the gunwales of a dozen ships, then thirty, then fifty, then a hundred. The merchant ships, mostly freighters and clippers, rose from the concourses, ghostly stars climbing through the fog. With another clang and a roar from the decks, the merchant ships tilted toward the dreadnoughts that blocked the port. Even in the cloaked darkness of the night, Cyprian could hear heavy guns rolled into place across the decks, musket balls pushed down the length of rusty barrels, steel drawn.

For a moment, the Imperium's mighty ships were silent and still, watching the merchants charge. Then, the firing began. The cannon blasts were dull thunder, the flash from the barrels orange lightning. Cyprian guided his little tin oculus back and forth across the sky, searching everywhere for his father.

Then, he saw him. Augustus Fields' red shipmaster's coat billowed out behind him, his great white teeth bared beneath a dark mustache as he roared orders to his helmsman from the bow. He stood, a mighty statue, with pistol in one hand and sword in the other. His merchant freighter, *Philomena,* rolled like a graceful cloud under him, responding to every direction of the helmsman. Even with her three envelopes burgeoning with gas, she slipped through the air like a knife. Augustus Fields had rigged her himself. It was the first ship Cyprian had ever flown, the ship his father truly loved.

Sometimes, Cyprian lost *Philomena* in the smoke and fire, and was sure that he wouldn't see her again, that she would rain to earth in ashes and splinters. But, she plunged in and out of the fray, his father leading her crew from the bow. Finally, *Philomena* emerged for the last time. Augustus Fields still stood to the bow, holding a wounded man up by the collar and roaring for the attack. Then, he jerked strangely. Cyprian never heard the gunshot. It was lost amid the roar of battle. Even from such a distance, Cyprian saw his father's gaze turn from sharp and close to distant and far away. His father slumped to the deck, and *Philomena* disappeared again into the fog of battle.

Cyprian fell to the deck of the weather tower, the oculus rolling from his fingers into the night. The Merchant Rebellion ended before dawn, but Cyprian never knew. The bells of the Carillon on the Ivory River pealed the victory of the Imperium over the rebels, but Cyprian didn't hear them. He cried his father's name until the sun came up.

The high call of Petros brought Cyprian back to his senses. He blinked, furious with himself, forcing the shadows of the past back into his memory, where they belonged. The kestrel swooped over *Philomena,* resting himself contentedly on a gunwale. It was once a home to the old bird. And to Cyprian. Not so anymore.

The ship was a wreck. A splintered side hatch, a mast cracked from top to bottom, a burned section of gunwale, the tattered remains of her canvas and envelopes reminded him that Augustus Fields was dead. Gone. Scattered to the winds that were his livelihood.

Cyprian sagged to the ground, letting his head hang between his knees, gazing into the dusty cobbles. The sadness that dragged him down did nothing to cool the anger that burned in his gut. Again, he saw the fiery death lights of the Merchant Rebellion, heard the cry of dying men. Cyprian didn't know what made him open his eyes and look up. The effort was almost too much, but when he dragged his head back upward, someone looked back.

Carved from the end of the enormous cedar beam that made up *Philomena's* keel was a beautiful figurehead, a breathtaking work of Misericordiae cedar. It depicted a young woman, crowned with the stars, robed in graceful windswept layers, with a globe beneath her feet. She looked forward, into the darkness of the alley, down on

Cyprian, with an expression of calm and certainty. If he turned his head, Cyprian could just see a tiny smile playing at the corners of her lips. It was almost like she was laughing at him.

Then, something moved in the long alleyway behind Cyprian, a human shape in the shadows. Cyprian jumped to his feet, drawing his pistol in a fluid motion.

"Unless you want a window in your liver, it would be best if you announced yourself."

The figure took a hesitant step forward. The first thing Cyprian saw was a pair of glinting eyes, round and impossibly large. It took Cyprian a moment to realize the figure was wearing iron spectacles. He was young, only about Cyprian's age. There was a seriousness about his pale face, overhung with dark brown hair, and his arms hung at his sides, reserved. He carried a bedraggled rucksack and a wooden box with a handle. He wore dark brown pants, a threadbare black vest, and a coat, all covered with the dust of miles. There were a fair number of bums and vagrants floating around the Misericordiae shipyards, trying their best to stay out of the eye of the Imperium soldiers, but none of them looked anything like this one.

"I didn't mean to startle you," said the boy.

Cyprian holstered his pistol.

"You're lucky I'm the relaxed type."

"Is this your ship?"

"No," Cyprian said.

The boy's eyes suddenly caught Basil's, blinked with realization. Cyprian sensed that he was being scanned, inspected like an insect beneath a looking glass.

"Is this…" he asked. "*Philomena?*"

"Yes," said Cyprian. "That's what they used to call her. Move along now. The streets aren't safe at night."

But the boy didn't seem to hear him. He took another step closer.

"Do you know a Lightlas? Shipmaster Lightlas?"

Cyprian's eyes narrowed. There was something about this boy, something about the way that he looked at him, as though he was his last hope.

"Who are you?" Cyprian asked.

The boy shouldered his rucksack as he replied.

"My name is Basil Black."

CHAPTER NINE

Ambry's boots beat a precise march over the Way of Kings, an
elevated bridge of white marble that extended from the outer walls of
Soliodomus in towards the Sanctuary.

Ambry let his gaze fall on the first alcove on the right, the alcove
that used to hold a statue of Sylvanus, the first Soverign and founder
of Cor Nova. But instead of the tall, bearded Sovereign Father, a
mortal man in a red Imperium Fleet uniform stood at rigid attention.
In each of the alcoves down the way, there used to be statues of the
Sovereigns. Hundreds of them, immortalized in marble. Now, their
places were filled by Imperium airmen, silent as stone, muskets and
masks agleam. In the pale light of the afternoon sun, they might have
been statues themselves. As Ambry passed, he could feel the unseen
eyes behind those masks watching his every measured footstep.

With a soldier's precision, Ambry removed the admiral's helm
from his head and tucked it under an arm. He was resplendent in
brushed red wool, shining black leather, and gold piping. The rising
sun insignia of a rear admiral glimmered in gold on his shoulders.
His heavy saber beat a rhythm against his leg as he strode. It was a
brand new uniform. His old one had been ruined in the process of
disentangling himself from a dissident printing press sinking in the
Ivory River. It hadn't been one of his better evenings.

Finally, the Way of Kings opened onto the Round Plaza, where an enormous map of Cor Nova lay emblazoned in every type of stone between the Shrouds and the Great Northern Mar, seven provinces in all the colors of the earth. Misericordiae was in green corundum, dotted with emeralds. Terra Alta in sandstone and peridot. Korkyra in ribbons of brown schist and green quartz. Panagiottis a great expanse of gray granite. Stella Maris in seastones and glittering mica. Old Meronymy shone in yellow feldspar striped with pyrite. Finally, Carath shone in white quartz. At its center stood Soliodomus, the great hall where the Lord Sovereign of the Sovereign Dominion of Cor Nova was protector and governor of all. Not so anymore.

At the end of the Plaza, like a great white leviathan leaping against the darkening purples of the sky stood the Sanctum of Soliodomus. The Nicholas Gate rose at its mouth, a masterwork of polished bronze that had guarded the entrance to the ancient seat of the Sovereigns for over eight hundred years. Dwarfed by the immense portal, a Fleet officer stood just left of center, beneath the scene of Sylvanus protecting his people from the storm of the Old World.

His yellow, rheumy eyes took Ambry in from beneath arched eyebrows and his dirty fingernails tapped on a pair of heavy pistols shoved into his scuffed leather belt. His red uniform showed none of the careful attention of Ambry's. The brass was tarnished and dark stains spotted the cuffs. In lieu of the traditional saber of the Fleet officer, he wore a shining curved scimitar. A golden emblem of the sun and stars shone on his epaulets. Only one man in all of the Imperium's Fleet could wear that rank.

Ambry drew his saber in salute, placing it across his palms and bowing. Grand Admiral Lysandros Rast snorted. His smile exposed jagged rows of yellowing teeth. His face, pocked and scarred, twisted with the effort.

"You're early," he growled, waving the sword aside.

Amber reseated his weapon and stood at respectful attention.

"A useful habit, I have found, Grand Admiral," he said.

Rast grunted.

"It got you this far. To be honest, I only half-expected to see you here. Some wagered you'd be running for the hills by now."

The Grand Admiral gave his twisting smile again. A summons from the Imperium was not always an honor. Sometimes, it was a death sentence.

"I come when my Imperium calls," Ambry said.

"Even if he calls you to swing in the breeze over the Moon Gate by sunset? Be careful with how much honor you want to have, Ambry. It may be just enough to hang yourself."

Rast stepped across Ambry to stand over by the colonnades surrounding the Round Plaza. As he passed, Ambry caught a whiff of his rancid scent.

The sun was setting over Carath, the first province of Cor Nova, seeming to catch the white bulwarks of the city walls ablaze. In the distance, something shimmered in the haze above the plains. There were great trellises and scaffolds extending over a yawning black rim, and enormous piles of rubble and rock grew beside it, mountains bled onto the earth. There were many names for that place. The Black Mouth of Carath, the Bloodpit. The Abyss.

"Every day, the Abyss goes deeper," said the Grand Admiral. "Every day, the Imperium gets closer."

"Closer to what?"

"Whatever lies below. That's where disloyal men go, Ambry. Take a good long look at it. It may be the last time you ever see it from aboveground."

Ambry repeated one of the many maxims from his Fleet training days.

"Honest men fear nothing."

"A soldier to the core. We'll see how well it serves you. The Imperium is nearly finished entertaining his guest, I'm sure. Open the gate!"

A guard snapped to attention and struck a bell with a large mallet. With the turning of ancient cogs, the Nicholas Gate groaned open, the burnished bronze giving way to murky darkness.

Ambry marched into the Sanctum, just behind Grand Admiral Rast. Vast stone columns looked like giants in the shadows, stretching up into the darkness above. A few unshuttered windows cast faint beams of yellow light here and there. Figures moved in the dimness, conferring with one another in low voices. From somewhere ahead of them came the high, urgent breathing of someone enduring pain.

At the dais that rose above the floor at the end of the Sanctum, a tall figure strode, encircled in the yellow twilight that fell from the high windows. Ambry almost didn't recognize the Imperium Titus. He wore a red Fleet uniform with polished leather boots. He was rail-thin and his hair was a startling white in the gloom. It was his voice, high and commanding, that broke the silence.

"You will tell me about the boy."

He appeared to be speaking to a pile of crumpled rags on the floor, which did not respond.

The Imperium's blue eyes hardened, and he rested his hand on the pommel of the fine black Fleet saber that hung at his belt. The hairs on the back of Ambry's neck stood straight up, and he had to suppress the instinctive urge to reach for his own weapon. Even Rast seemed tense. The Imperium's lips parted and words emerged, a language otherworldly and ethereal. High Sylvan. Or at least a form of it. The sound raked over Ambry like a set of claws. Like living, spidery things, the words almost seemed to shudder and jump through the air, black and spindly with too many legs, leaping up columns and dancing through the polluted light of the windows, converging on the crumpled figure on the floor. Like a ghostly scarecrow, the frail shape was lifted up in the air, suspended so that his wizened head lolled like a rag doll's. He was wearing only a nightshirt, his bare toes just visible beneath its hem. He groaned faintly.

"Now," said Titus. "Tell me about the boy. Tell me...Bookkeeper."

The old man straightened, his eyes sunken and tired. Streams of tears ran down his weathered, bloody cheeks. His voice was a wheeze.

"No."

Titus's eyes became harsher, more blue.

"Well then, Galen, if you are not helpful, no doubt I can find someone who will be more forthcoming. Cor Nova lives in the past no longer. My brother is dead and so are his kind. The age of the Sovereign is ended, and the rule of the Imperium has begun. Thrive in my keeping, or die, if that's your wish."

With the last syllable, the Imperium spoke a new syllable of High Sylvan, as harsh and fast as the crack of the whip, the snap of a bone.

With a tremendous jerk, the figure whipped around and came crashing to the floor, his limbs at odd angles. Ambry could clearly see the whites of his eyes as he trembled once, then lay still, a crumpled leaf on the floor of the Sanctum.

The silence that fell was absolute. Ambry had seen death many times. He had inflicted it. One less traitor to deal with. When Ambry tore his eyes away, he saw the Imperium was looking at him with his icy blue gaze. The court was gently applauding the spectacle. A few soldiers emerged from the dark recesses, removing the body of the old man. Somewhere, a group of players began to make soft music. Servants lit a few lamps, chasing away the forbidding twilight. The faceless figures in the porticoes began to talk quietly amongst themselves once more.

"My Lord Imperium," grunted Grand Admiral Rast, saluting at the first step of the dais. "Rear Admiral Ambry, as you requested."

The Imperium descended the dais, arms extended in greeting. His smile was genuine, his bearing warm. In those blue eyes, Ambry saw again the friend who had once stood beside him in Fleet Training, offered his hand when the two were navigating their exercises so many years ago.

"Ambry," said the Imperium, his grip firm and warm. He made a casual gesture to the pale shape now being carried away by the soldiers.

"It's a pity that your return is marred by such a spectacle. Unfortunately, as you well know, every ship has its rats, and they must be purged. He was a former court doctor under my brother. A dissident that needed my attention."

The Imperium snapped his fingers, and a servant immediately appeared.

"We'll walk on the East Balcony. Bring my admirals some refreshment."

With the open sky above his head, Ambry could almost relax. The day was draining away over the western horizon and lights began to appear in the city of Carath. Servants lit great torches on the East Balcony. The Fleet Concourse was just off the farthest walls of Soliodomus. Ambry could count his ships in the midst of the red dreadnoughts, interceptors, and ships-of-the-line.

"Old friend," said Titus, his smile warm again. "Your Imperium has much to thank you for."

Ambry accepted a cup of chilled Terra Altan wine, rose-red and sweet.

"It's my pleasure to serve."

"Of course," said Titus, raising his own glass to Ambry. "As it is every dutiful officer. But not many can boast your accomplishments. You've kept the peace everywhere you've been sent. Tracked down bandits. Eliminated dissenters. Put down the Misericordiae Merchant's Rebellion. Even driven Cain from his last hole. You bring great pride to the Fleet and to your Imperium."

"Thank you, my lord."

"For this reason, I have a new duty for you. Grand Admiral Rast, please summarize the report for our benefit."

Rast nodded.

"Two weeks ago," he said in a low growl. "The Fleet was tracking down a rumor. Thanks to an informant, we were able to retrace the steps of a dissident group called the Bookkeepers, who want to return the rule of Cor Nova to the Sovereigns. Most were eliminated in a purge years ago, but several went into hiding. It appeared that their plans concentrated on a boy, who we traced to a mining village in the mountains of Korkyra. I led the mission to locate and arrest him."

The Imperium turned to look out over Carath, his fingers drumming on the marble. The Grand Admiral went on.

"However, the miners were resistant to the Fleet. When we attempted to collect the youth, a fight broke out. Not surprisingly, the miners were mostly annihilated. I at first hoped the boy was among them, but then…"

Rast paused, faltering for a moment.

"In the midst of the fighting, a boy spoke High Sylvan-"

"What?" Ambry said, his mind suddenly awhirl. What did this mean? The Imperium nodded, as though commiserating with Ambry's surprise.

"Please allow the Grand Admiral to continue."

"It created some kind defensive wave," Rast said. "Like a shield wall, protecting most of the village from our first volley. He escaped through a rathole leading out of the mountain, although we killed the man who was protecting him most of the way."

Titus nodded. He turned around, his startling blue eyes fixed on the Grand Admiral. His hand closed around the hilt of his saber.

The hair on the back of Ambry's neck stood up again. Something was not right.

"Is that all, Grand Admiral?"

Rast nodded, looking uncertain.

"Then you have expended your use to me. You've lost Basil Black once. Now it is the turn of someone else to serve. Thank you."

The Imperium moved like lightning, a single word of High Sylvan on his lips. Rast barely had time to reach for his weapon before he was run through with the Imperium's shining blade. Ambry was stunned. It was unnatural how quickly it had happened. Rast slid to the marble, the lights fading from his eyes, his uniform even more crumpled and now dark with blood.

Suddenly, Titus was mere inches from Ambry's face. It was like standing against a cold pane of glass. From the base of those icy blue eyes something strange and terrifying welled up, a blackness that called to Ambry out of the deep.

"The Sovereigns died with my brother," Titus said. "You are part of a new engine. You serve me before all else. Under my command, you have tortured men, imprisoned wives and children, commanded your ships to rain fire on village and fortress alike."

Ambry looked into the frightening abyss of Titus's eyes and saw his own deeds, smoke and fire, blood and steel. He saw farmers fighting against the onslaught of his ships, dissidents crouching over their printing presses. He heard screams, smelled blood, tasted the salt of tears.

"What you have done has turned you over to me," Titus said. "On the day your determination flags, your loyalty falters, I will find you, old friend. And you will beg for the Abyss."

Titus bent down to the prone form of Grand Admiral Lysandros, and wrenched the sun and stars insignia from his shoulder.

"Now go," said the Imperium, delicately placing the golden insignia in Ambry's hand. "Grand Admiral Ambry. And bring me Basil Black."

Ambry bowed, the taste of blood in his mouth. He had bit his tongue. He swallowed, blood and all.

"Yes, my Imperium."

CHAPTER TEN

"A vagrant boy, you were saying?" asked Lightlas, leaning on his cane and squinting up at *Philomena's* figurehead. "Hanging around the ship?"

Cyprian nodded, taking an enormous bite out of a crisp vermillion nutapple. The early morning light made the dusty freighter look a little more hopeful, but not much. He jammed the nutapple in his mouth, and pulled himself into the murky framework around the ship's hull.

"Said his name was Basil Black," he said around the piece of fruit. "Some kind of messenger sent him to find the ship. And you. I told him to beat it."

"Odd," said Lightlas, following stiffly after Cyprian.

Cyprian worked his knife into the jamb of the large hatch in the hull. He heaved once, and with a snap of dry-rotted rope, the cedar door slammed to the ground in a cloud of dust.

Cyprian took a final bite and pitched the nutapple core aside. Then, he stepped up into the cavernous main hold. Fingers of light stretched into the darkness from the grating on the main deck, illuminating a few bits of paper and torn canvas lying on the floor. A few old ropes spanned the hold, like the leavings of a drunken spider. The hold-deck corridor ran forward, leading to the crew's quarters

68

and water storage. Cyprian helped Lightlas up the step. The old man thumped his cane on the decking and wrinkled his nose.

"Smells like cats," he said. "All right. Might as well see the rest of her. This way."

A series of hatches led off to the right and left, carved symbols showing their uses: sail storage, pantry, powder locker. Finally, they reached a spiraling stairwell that led upwards. Cyprian put his hand on the worn cedar. The first step creaked, just like he remembered. From the time he was very young, this was one of his favorite things about the ship, how he could dash up and down in circles and the three decks would spin past. The airmen would dive to the side and tell him to be careful, or rumple his hair and laugh.

Lightlas thumped his way up through the darkness to the middeck landing. He yanked aside a thin piece of wood nailed over the porthole, flooding the middeck corridor with light. Ahead, there was a thick hatch that stuck firm when Lightlas tried to open it.

"The ship-core, if I remember rightly," he said. "I expect you'll have to put your shoulder into it, young man."

Cyprian grunted in agreement, slamming his weight against the door. It splintered in half, and Cyprian jumped a foot in air as several dark somethings streaked past his legs, yowling. It took a moment for his heart to stop hammering.

"Reckon we found those cats," said Lightlas, whacking the last one in its flight with his cane.

Cyprian peered into the shipcore. Once, it had been a marvel in carved cedar and polished brass. Large pulleys turned effortlessly on their spindles, bearing the cables that ran from the helm to the sails and ailerons. Banded casks of aether were stacked two high, polished brass outlets sealed with oakum and oil. Saws, shears, and hammers hung in orderly rows on the wall. Now, it was a desultory wreck. Even the sunlight that came through the grate to the main deck seemed to fall in an apologetic way. The pulley-wheels were broken and the cables hung bowed and shredded. Brass pipes were bent like reeds, rusting tools scattered across the floor. And over it all, the overwhelming smell of cats hung.

Together, Cyprian and Lightlas explored the galley with its upturned benches and small oven hanging open, the barren officer's quarters, and the tiny medical cabin. When Cyprian opened this last door, he was nearly crushed beneath an avalanche of old buckets, rotting cordage, and a hefty bin of what appeared to be petrified oranges. Finally, they climbed the stairwell again, this time beneath the command deck that rose up at the ship's stern. The stairwell dumped them directly into the cartorium, where an immense oaken map-table dominated most of the space. A jumble of navigational equipment, charcoal pencils, chalk, and maps made a tangle across its surface, and two large cabinets in the corner hung open, spilling rolled maps onto the floor. At the rear of the cartorium was a door leading to the shipmaster's cabin and more officer quarters.

Cyprian opened the two large doors that opened outward onto the main deck, and climbed up onto the command deck, surveying the grounded ship with her bare masts. The helm stood empty. The aetherolabe and other instruments were long gone, probably taken by a scavenger. Only the sturdy ship's wheel remained, fastened by a set of stout iron pins. Lightlas grunted as he climbed up after Cyprian.

"She is in rougher shape than I hoped. However, the Imperium could have had her burned, so we're lucky to have her at all."

Cyprian shook his head. He had been afraid that she would be too familiar, too much a reminder of his past life, for Cyprian to live on her. But, it was almost as though it was a ship he had known in a dream, like a pale ghost of the one from his childhood. He had memories of standing on this very spot, his father holding his hands on the wheel, the wind singing its free song as she swooped through the sky. Now, she was an empty wreck underneath a rotting concourse in a dank corner of Misericordiae. The old *Philomena* was gone. Maybe that was for the better.

"Well, Shipmaster Lightlas," said Cyprian, running a finger along the ship's wheel. "Unless you feel like rigging a ship by yourself, we're going to need a crew."

Lightlas snorted.

"I assure you, Cyprian, my rigging days are over. I put out the word at all of the taverns a few hours ago. The word will be spreading."

Sure enough, the very next morning, airmen turned up, ambling up the road beneath the Old Concourse alone or in pairs, eyes cast appraisingly over the old ship. They were tall and short, dark and light, tattooed and pierced, cleanshaven or sporting beards braided to their knees. There were Terra Altans, Misericordians, Stella Marians and many others. A dozen languages colored the air.

Even as the first potential crewmembers climbed the rickety gangplank, Cyprian could see them murmuring skeptically to one another. He found it hard to blame them. The ship was an old beaten tub. Her shipmaster was an old man, and a friend of Augustus Fields to boot. They came alone and in pairs, but they left in groups, shaking their heads and headed for the taverns.

At least, most did. A smattering of airmen stayed, forming a ragged line over the deck. And they were not the cream of Misericordiae's crop. With the Imperium in power, times were lean, and able men were looking for jobs that could sustain them. The desperate group that was left was none too impressive. They were very young and very old, arms in slings or missing entirely, some bearing the shifty look of men on the wrong side of the law.

"All of those not able to find work on other ships," Cyprian muttered to Lightlas as he shoved aside the junk on the cartorium's maptable.

"Perhaps there will be some rubies in the clay," said Lightlas, straightening his waistcoat.

One by one, they called the men into the map-room. Immediately, Lightlas turned away a pair of boys no older than twelve, a one-legged man who seemed only capable of communicating by swearing, an airman with immensely bushy black hair who concluded his interview by jumping on the map-table, gobbling like a turkey. Finally, a pair of airmen emerged into the cartorium, both looking scrubbed and rather shifty.

"Clip McElhaney, if you please, shipmaster," said the shorter one. He had a wide gap-toothed grin, a patched cap that rested aslant on his shiny, bald head, and a pair of airman's breeches that were entirely too large for him. They were belted up high around his wiry waist.

"And my associate, The Right Honorable Nolan Paschal."

His comrade was tall, dark, and muscular, with a shining golden earring through one ear. His boots were polished a solid, midnight black. He stood with his tattooed arms crossed, giving a single nod at his introduction.

"We are a duo of airfaring gentlemen well-versed in the aetheronautical arts. Nobody swings a rope like my friend Paschal.

On the day I was born, I slipped right out of my grandmother's arms and landed in a bucket hanging from the clothesline, which I then proceeded to propel across the street by fashioning a rudimentary sail out of my swaddling blanket. I'm a natural. Between us, we boast over thirty years of experience on a variety of vessels. In fact, Paschal and I once-"

Lightlas, as enraptured as he was by this discourse, held up his hands. McElhaney's mouth snapped shut like a trap.

"If you are such tremendous airmen, why look for work here? Why don't you ship on board one of the big freighters or with a large trade union? The money is better."

"Well, you see," McElhaney said, flopping his cap back and forward between his hands. "We had a bit of a misunderstanding with our previous shipmaster. We were under the impression that it was all right to play a bit of a joke during the course of the voyage. At least, nothing that got in the way of the job, you know. It was a food freighter, and it must be said, our shipmaster was a bit of a prig."

Lightlas raised an eyebrow.

"Go on."

"Well, we were carrying this load of peaches. And the shipmaster was always prattling on about how important it was that we had these peaches. So much so, that it became a joke amongst the men. Well, one day the shipmaster says he's only going to pay us half for the voyage, we... Well, we..."

Nolan Paschal's face remained passive as he finished the story for his friend.

"We loaded one of the falconets with some powder and all of the peaches and blew the whole lot through the shipmaster's cabin window. It was not my idea."

Cyprian roared with laughter and slapped the table. Lightlas shook his head ruefully as McElhaney finished the story, a grin exposing his gapped teeth.

"The shipmaster found out it was us, and raised a lot of trouble with the magistrate. Turns out the peaches were going to Carath, to serve the court of the Imperium, so we had to skedaddle. And now we're keeping a low profile."

Lightlas hired them, with the understanding that all peach-related antics were to be kept to a minimum.

Following McElhaney and Paschal, there was a mountainous farmboy from the Misericordiae plains. He had muscles like bulging sacks of oranges running down his arms and his great black eyebrows protruded from his forehead like hairy caterpillars.

"Name?" Lightlas asked.

His reply was a bass rumble.

"Castor Benttree."

"You have no experience working on ships?"

"No."

"Have you ever flown on a ship before?"

"No."

"Then what do you work with?"

"Hogs."

"Aha. And why are you leaving that?"

The huge man shrugged.

"Tired of hogs."

"And what," asked Lightlas. "Makes you think you would be a good fit for *Philomena*?"

The huge farmboy looked at Lightlas and Cyprian for a moment, his brow furrowed. Then, in one effortless motion, he placed a massive hand on the underside of the oaken map-table, lifted it up, and swept it onto his shoulder. He narrowly avoided smashing a corner through the stained-glass transom above the door.

Cyprian and Lightlas shared a look.

"Always good to have a strong man," said Lightlas, adding his name to the roster.

Next to make the roster was a small, spry man named Hugo Masterson, whose face was mostly obscured by an enormous, pristinely groomed mustache. Every few minutes, he took a swig from a beaten brass flask. His references stated that he was a helmsman, and capable of "landing a three-legged cow if needs be." Some time after him, Lightlas hired a bandy-legged, tobacco-spitting machinist with a red bandana named Bartholomew Oakum. With the air of a visiting duke, he swaggered around the ship and said he could "fix 'er right up, yessireebob".

Then, there was a redheaded, acne-speckled youth who was dragged before Cyprian and Lightlas by a lady in a lacy purple dress.

"Come on, Burt," she said. "Now, no more whining. Beg your pardon, shipmaster. This is my boy, Burt Spacklebrook. He's plenty strong, just has a liking of sitting around my house and doing nothing but eating. He just needs a taste of the world to toughen him up. He's a bit of weenie, truth be told."

Lightlas blinked.

"Ma'am, I don't know that I can accept…"

"And you don't have to pay him!" the lady countered, waving her handbag as the boy sulked beside her. "In fact, I'll pay you."

"Good to have him on board," said Lightlas, adding the name on the roster. "Every ship needs a cook."

At the end of the day, fourteen men filled *Philomena's* roster. Fewer than they needed, and less skilled. But, to their credit, all of them showed up the next day, blinking in the early morning sunlight, for the first day of work. And work was in no short supply.

Everything made of canvas or rope had dry-rotted to a crumbling, useless mess. In addition to cleaning, scrubbing, and scraping every conceivable surface in the freighter, *Philomena* needed a full overhaul of her envelopes, rigging, and ailerons. The ship's old aetherolabe, along with most of her other hardware, were long missing, so one of the new crew members had been charged with scavenging hardware from the boneyards. Under Oakum's direction, Paschal, McElhaney, and Masterson spent several days crawling through the tiniest spaces in the ship, running new cables and ropes through the ship core so that she could be controlled from the helm. A few nasty surprises were also uncovered, including a number of melon-sized wasp nests, a few volatile casks of mysterious fluid that no one could identify, and a second colony of feline stowaways wedged firmly in the steerage.

It was on this last occasion, while pursuing a yowling tomcat up the forward yardarm, that Cyprian caught sight of someone watching the ship from further up the alley, a person in a black vest and round spectacles. But, when he looked again, the figure had disappeared.

Finally, the turn of the next week brought a clear day. The sky beckoned.

"Is she ready, Mr. Oakum?" Lightlas asked.

The bow-legged machinist wiped his greasy brow with his bandana and spat a hock of tobacco spit over the gunwale.

"Ready as she'll ever be."

"Then let's give her wings. To quarters!" Lightlas said, ringing the brass bell that hung off the helm. "All hands to the beam and prepare to counterbalance if anything shifts below! Mr. Masterson, get on the helm!"

Philomena's new crew shuffled into position, taking up slack and snapping the sails to the wind. A few scurried up the ratlines that led into the rigging. Up above their heads, three requisitioned envelopes, threadbare canvas stitched with surgical precision, hung limp. Smooth lumps of sea sponge rose like muscles beneath the canvas.

Lightlas called out over the deck.

"Mr. Oakum, give her the aether! All hands hold steady and prepare for lift!"

With a grunt from Oakum and a rattling hiss, the aether from the ironbound casks in the shipcore flooded the copper pipes, pouring into the envelopes. As the seams began to pull against one another, the crew hurriedly spooled out netting and line, balancing the three burgeoning envelopes together and working out kinks. Paschal and McElhaney moved through the men, keeping a lookout for anyone liable to be cinched down by a tightening rope.

One by one, the lines grew tight. Cyprian held his breath, but everything held true as the weight of the old freighter was transferred from her keel to her great cedar masts. There was a chorus of creaks and groans as the earth begrudgingly released her from its jealous grip. For the first time in four years, *Philomena's* keel stood a full yard off the beaten ground. That night, *Philomena* found her dock among the other ships on Misericordiae's concourses and Lightlas allowed the men a celebratory night on the town.

But despite their work, *Philomena* wasn't bound for the sky yet. Refitting and calibration would take some time, and a good amount of the ship was still filthy, reeking of cats and worse. Already, the crew was starting to show signs of tension. The crew was respectful in the presence of Francis Lightlas, but Cyprian often caught them murmuring and casting him furtive glances when his back was turned. Clearly, they felt some resentment at following a deckmaster so young. Amongst themselves, too, there were struggles. Bartholomew Oakum's voice was reedy, full of arrogance and disdain much of the time, a quality which grated on all of the airmen. Masterson was prone to half-drunk silences and Spacklebrook complained endlessly. Even McElhaney and Paschal, the only truly competent airmen on the ship, were starting to realize it, and they had developed an annoyingly cocksure attitude.

A few days after *Philomena's* initial flight, Cyprian was showing Benttree and some of the others a braiding technique when a chorus of shouting erupted further forward.

"I tell you, Oakum," said McElhaney, letting his planer crash to the deck and driving a finger into the machinist's narrow chest. "You get in my face one more time, and I'll feed you that stupid bandana."

"I'd like to see you try that!" retorted Oakum, shoving McElhaney against the mast. The rest of the crew turned to look, just in time to see Paschal clock Oakum across the back with a piece of old decking.

Then, Masterson came barreling out of the rigging on a rope, swinging into Paschal with a weird yodeling cry. Several more airmen set to, fists swinging.

Cyprian came storming up the deck, firing a pistol into a nearby water cask. With a thunderous crack, splinters and flecks of water peppered the combatants. They looked up surprise.

"THAT'S ENOUGH!" roared Cyprian. He tossed the smoking pistol to the deck and pulled off his jacket. The men were silent, still, speckled with water. Tense muscles went slack, all eyes on the boy deckmaster.

"I know," said Cyprian, sweeping a finger at every man on deck. "What you think, what you say. You say that I'm too young to be an officer of this ship. You say that I'm unworthy because of my father. My father was a fighter, a thinker, a flyer. He was the Rooster. Well, I'm the young Rooster, and I learned from the best."

He strode through the group of men, staring into the eyes of each.

"You think you can outfight me? Outthink me? Outfly me? Then try. Right now, and we'll decide who's the master here. Get your sword or your gun or your fists. Get on the wheel."

The men were still. There was the sound of shuffling feet, soft coughing.

"No one?" Cyprian said. "Then I see we have nothing else to discuss. So every last mother's son of you can get back to work."

Cyprian picked up his pistol, cleared the pan and shoved it back into his belt. Then, he turned and strode aft. Petros only just had time to swoop in before he slammed the door of the cartorium behind him so hard that the panes rattled. He landed on the maptable, now laden with an enormous map of the land between Misericordiae and Carath, mountains and rivers stenciled in ink, with trade routes flowing in blue chalk. A few nutapple crates served as chairs around the map-table. Francis Lightlas occupied one, papers in careful stacks in front of him.

"I was watching through the plate-glass," said Lightlas, gesturing toward the bow. "Masterfully done. The men will benefit from a bit more…guidance. Mr. Black, this is my deckmaster, Mr. Fields."

Cyprian had not even noticed that there was someone else in the cartorium. There, seated on a crate, was Basil Black. He regarded Cyprian with those blue eyes, awash with uncertainty. Cyprian felt a sudden rush of irritation and mistrust. They had enough trouble to worry about without adding this mysterious boy to the mix. Basil Black pointed to the bird on the table.

"A golden sea kestrel," he said. "It's beautiful. They're very rare."

"So," said Lightlas. "You were telling me you're a miner's son from…"

"Osmara," said Basil.

"Right," Cyprian said, leaning over the map and tapping the location. "A nowhere mountain town over two hundred leagues away. And a mysterious messenger comes to your doorstep and tells you that you should come to this ship."

Basil nodded.

"Yes."

"And here you are," Lightlas said. "Did he say anything else?"

"Nothing important. At least, nothing that I understood. He was dying. He'd been poisoned by a shot laden with skrill venom."

Lightlas frowned.

"Which almost certainly means he was shot by the Imperium's men. And you're acting on his word?"

"The Fleet destroyed my town," Basil said. "I have nothing else to act on."

Cyprian preferred not to look at the pain in the boy's eyes, so close beneath the surface. He pushed the pity down. Basil Black wasn't the only one with troubles.

"You can't come on board this ship," Cyprian said.

"But…why not?"

Lightlas raised an eyebrow.

"I was under the impression that I was the shipmaster. I must ask along with Mr. Black. Why not?"

"Because someone is obviously looking for him," said Cyprian. "And you said the man was poisoned with skrill venom. If the Imperium didn't want him to reach you, they didn't want you to come here. And we have enough problems with the Imperium as it is. Besides, do they train men to be airmen in your little mining town? I didn't think so. There are no mines on a merchant ship. You would be a burden."

"I'm a physician," Basil said, lifting his box. "I know how to cure ailments and mend wounds."

Cyprian looked askance at the boy.

"A boy physician?"

"A boy deckmaster?" replied Basil Black.

Cyprian raised his eyebrows. The kid had pluck. He could relate to that. He tapped his finger on the blue lines between Misericordiae and Carath.

"There's a major trade route between Misericordiae and Carath. Even if you're a great healer, we're within a half-day's flight of a physician at every point along the way. We don't need one on board."

Basil's silence was broken by a racket from somewhere up the midships corridor, the sound of clanging and rushing feet came up the stairwell.

"Water!" someone roared from aft.

"A bucket! For heaven's sakes, somebody lay hands to a bucket!"

There was a thundering of boots in the corridor beneath the maproom, a long string of foreign curse words trailing down after them. Cyprian dashed down the stairwell and into the midships corridor, where nearly collided with Clip McElhaney coming back from the galley.

"No need to worry, deckmaster," he said. A dripping bucket dangled from his fingers. "A little blaze in the galley. Seems young Spacklebrook managed to set his apron alight. It was all the frills that done it. He's a bit soggy, but all is well."

As if on cue, a blackened and dripping Spacklebrook stumbled into the corridor, trailing a thin line of smoke from his singed hair.

Francis Lightlas stumped down behind Cyprian, with young Basil in tow. He smacked his cane on the decking and grunted.

"A youth that careless has no business being in charge of the oven. Besides, his biscuits are better suited for masonry than eating. And in my day, I've eaten leather boots more appetizing than that pork he served up yesterday. Pity there's no time to find another one."

Lightlas's eyes narrowed. He turned to look at Basil Black.

"Mr. Black. I'm going to ask you a question. And I trust you won't take offense."

"Of course not."

"Do you cook?"

Basil seemed taken aback for a moment.

"Yes," he said. "Simple things. Nothing fancy."

"Look around you," Lightlas gestured to the rough timbers of *Philomena*. "Does anything look fancy to you? If you want to fly on this ship, you're a cook."

Cyprian willed Basil Black to turn down the offer. What if the Imperium came looking for him? He could endanger all of them.

But, after a moment, Basil nodded.

"I'll do my best."

Basil Black was true to his word. *Philomena*'s next morning on the concourse broke with the smell of wheat biscuits, a thick oat porridge with dried plums, and a tall mug of tea that had a pleasant spice in it that Cyprian couldn't identify. The crew was impressed, and Basil seemed at home in the galley, which was now very orderly and clean.

The next day, the cargo arrived, an island of unmarked reinforced crates amid the bustling thoroughfare of the concourse.

Finally, *Philomena* was a new ship. Her age was still apparent, but her deck planks were solid, her envelopes burgeoned with aether, her brass shone in the sunlight. When Cyprian spun the wheel at the helm, he felt the motion of a slick jungle of pulleys through the ship, counterbalancing and pulling the ailerons into position to turn left and right. The pitch levers moved back and forth on greased cantilevers.

One or two cats still skulked in the bilge, and the airmen were still occasionally finding new caches of disused junk. There were temperamental kinks in the ship's mechanisms, and the oddities of her crew were all too often apparent. But she was whole, and she could fly.

"Cast off the lines and prepare to break daylight!" Lightlas called over the deck, as soon as the last crate was winched into the main hatch.

Lightlas took his place at the command console, looking more vital than ever in a long shipmaster's coat. Masterson stood statue-like at the helm beside him.

"Ship the gangplank and lines away, Mr. Paschal," said Lightlas. "Mr. Masterson, bring her about twenty marks sunwise!"

One by one, the concourse tethers fell slack. There was a whoosh of aether and the envelopes swelled. *Philomena's* hull floated evenly with the concourse, then began to rise, first slowly, and then quickly above the masts of her sister ships. Cyprian felt his feet grow heavy in his boots as the concourse grew smaller and smaller beneath them. With the sharp rush of wind and the creak of cedar and rope, *Philomena* rose from the colors, smells, and clamor of the shipyards into the fierce, clear sunlight of mid-morning. Then, Masterson turned the wheel to the right, allowing *Philomena* to make a complete smooth rotation as she ascended, so that the lady on the bow looked east out of Misericordiae.

For Cyprian, the experience was exhilarating and terrifying at the same time. The last time this ship had flown over Misericordiae, his father had been at the helm. Lightlas gave the order, and the ship tilted forward into the sky beyond.

BOOM.

Cyprian leaned over the rail of the command deck just in time to see a plume of white smoke jet into the vivid blue of afternoon sky. The falconet rolled back on its carriage from the recoil.

"That's another keeper, shipmaster!" said Oakum, smacking the breech of the gun. "On to the next, boys!"

Philomena's old falconets were long gone, stolen or sold by the Imperium. Oakum had bought a complement of used light guns from a scrapper, stripped from an ancient Fleet dreadnought. Most had not been fired in years, so it was necessary to test and sight each one. The process began as soon as the ship was free of Misericordiae's city limits.

"Load!" cried Oakum, as the gun crew converged on the next cannon, midway up the leftward gunwale.

Benttree, Paschal, McElhaney, and Masterson levered a charge of powder and a large ball of shot into the cannon's barrel. Benttree brandished the tamping pole with ease as McElhaney fed a fuse into the cannon's breech. With a groan of rope and wheels, the cannon rumbled forward, pointing to the open sky.

"Prime!"

A burst of flame from the starter.

"Fire!"

The harsh, ringing scream of rending metal rocked the entire ship. The breech of the gun was a lump of hot twisted metal on the deck, and the barrel had long cracks spidering up its length. In the haze of smoke that clouded the scene, Cyprian could see several figures, staggering or prone. Some were moving, some were not.

"To quarters!" Cyprian roared, slamming the bell once and leaping over the command deck rail. He charged into the rapidly dissipating smoke.

Flames licked up the side of the wooden carriage, eating through the ropes that held it fast to the gunwale. The deck planks were shredded and embedded with shot. With a snap, the ropes gave way. It rumbled toward two airmen sprawled on the deck. The first was Masterson. He lay just outside the falconet's path, blood darkening one of his pant legs. The other was Benttree, who was directly in danger. Yelling for help, Cyprian seized Benttree around his ankles. With no more than a second to spare, Cyprian and McElhaney yanked the massive man backwards. The wooden wheels of the cannon knocked the cap from his head as they rumbled past. Then, the falconet tipped backward into the hatch of the main hold, smashing through the grating and into the hold below

Cyprian tried to take stock of the damage. Masterson was screaming. Benttree wasn't breathing, the big man's chest still as stone. The crew stumbled through the smoke, trying to help, dazed and disoriented. Lightlas emerged from the cartorium, stumping over as fast as he could. Time seemed to slow. Suddenly, another figure emerged in the smoke, clad in a black vest, iron spectacles, and a cook's apron. He held a wooden box in one hand. Basil Black.

Cyprian was about to warn him away, when he knelt beside Benttree, placing skilled, pale hands under the massive man's jaw and on his chest. He was silent for a moment.

After a second, he took a long needle joined to an iron tube out of the depths of the box. Basil tore open the man's shirt, fingers probing for a spot on Benttree's chest, then, apparently finding it, he jabbed the instrument through the airman's skin. Cyprian and the crew lurched forward in alarm at this apparent attack, but a huge, agonized gasp from Benttree stopped them in their tracks. He coughed and wheezed, then collapsed on the deck again. His breath was shallow, but regular.

Stunned at Basil's treatment of Benttree, the airmen backed off when he knelt beside Masterson. The smoke was almost completely dissipated now, exposing the mangled mess of Masterson's leg. Masterson's normally impassive face was a twisted mask of agony.

"Leg's going to have to come off," grunted Nolan Paschal. He appeared to be right. Cyprian's stomach turned at the sight. Wounds like this seldom ended with living men, let alone whole ones. If the wound didn't kill them, the infection that followed almost always did. But Basil wasn't listening.

He turned to the open trunk, silently pulling open drawers and drawing out vials and a neat sleeve containing another set of shining metal implements. He took up one small vial that was filled with a clear liquid.

With a speed that surprised Cyprian, Basil seized Masterson's jaw and placed a careful dab of the liquid on his lips. Within seconds, Masterson began to struggle less feebly, his sight unfocused, his cries dwindling away.

"Heavens have mercy," murmured Oakum. "Did you ever see such a thing…"

The crew stood in silent wonder as their ship's cook, in sure, swift movements, set and bound the broken leg, fixing a splint and applying a green pine-smelling paste to the skin. Then, he set to binding up the other men who had received light burns or cuts from shrapnel.

"Thank you," Lightlas said, when all was finished.

Basil Black nodded.

"Of course."

Cyprian remembered unpleasantly his comments about not needing a physician on board. Rather than meet Basil Black's eyes, he decided to assess the damage left by the falling cannon. He peered down into the hold. It was hard to see from the brightness of the deck, but he could see the falconet lying askew below, wheels still spinning lazily. Its barrel had punched through the planks that lined the bottom of the hold. On its way down, the cannon had partially crushed one crate and clipped the sides of several others. Cyprian slid down a stayline to inspect the damage. Paschal and McElhaney thumped down beside him in the dimness.

Then, in the silence of the hold, Cyprian heard a sound. He went to the damaged crate closest to him.

The inside was filled with spools of linen, but they didn't fill the box completely. Instead, there was a gap at the top where air flowed through freely. Cyprian stuck his head inside. There was a lump in the midst of the linens, a figure sprawled in the darkness. Even in the dimness of the hold, the linens around the lump were a deep and rusty red.

"Blue hazes," said Paschal, eyes wide.

"Get Basil Black," Cyprian said, yanking aside loose planks. "And tell him to bring his box."

CHAPTER ELEVEN

Veronica awoke to the feeling of something cool and moist against her forehead. She imagined that she was lying under a waterfall, the mists washing over her. Standing on the highest rock beneath the falls, she waved to her mother, seated on the bank waving back, to be sure that she was looking. Then, she ran and jumped, crashing into water that was icy cold and crystal blue.

Veronica opened her eyes, but it wasn't her mother that she saw. Instead, it saw a boy about her age seated on a stool. His iron-rimmed glasses glinted as he tilted his head in a concerned way. An apron stained by work was tied around his waist, and the bottom of his black vest was flecked with flour and salt. He was holding a piece of moist, clean linen.

"Hello," he said.

Veronica blinked, and tried to sit up. She nearly hit her head against a heavy cedar bulkhead. Sunlight streamed through a single porthole. It was cracked to admit a cold rush of wind and the fierce blue of an afternoon sky. She tried to lick her lips. Her mouth was overpoweringly dry.

"Where am I?" she croaked.

"You are on the merchant freighter *Philomena*. Headed for Carath."

"What happened…? I…"

"You were found stowed away in one of the crates. That's where you'd be still, if the crew hadn't nearly dropped a cannon on your head. I'm Basil."

"Ship's doctor?"

"Ship's cook," he said, wringing out the cloth into a basin. "Although I'm equally comfortable patching up people and peeling potatoes."

"My head hurts," she said.

Basil nodded.

"Probably an aftereffect of the skrill venom. The ball passed clean through your side, more of a graze than anything. Little enough of the poison got into your system that the antidote had effect, but the wound itself will take some time to heal."

Veronica's hand went to her side, where she felt the corners of a clean linen bandage beneath her cotton shift. Her dress was neatly folded on a shelf above her bunk. The cabin was small, rough, and smelled vaguely like pitch. It had none of the regimented polish of a Fleet ship.

"You said this is a merchant freighter," she said.

"That's right," Basil replied. "No Imperium here. If you've been poisoned with skrill venom, I suppose that's who you were running from."

Although she had no reason to suspect this boy, Veronica said nothing. Too much trust had cost her before. Suddenly, the cabin's hatch scraped open. A light airman's boot entered, followed by a long gangly leg, then the tall frame of a boy about her age. He wore an airman's jacket, and sturdy canvas breeches. A battered brass oculus, a knife, and a pistol were jammed into his belt. His sandy hair hung down around the back of his neck, and he regarded Veronica with bright, suspicious eyes.

"She seems to be alive, Mr. Black," he said. "That's a point for you."

"Thank you, deckmaster," said the young ship's cook. He turned to Veronica. "The deckmaster of *Philomena*. Cyprian Fields."

"Is she in any danger?" Cyprian asked.

"The poison has run its course," said Basil, folding the cloth neatly. "All should be well."

"In that case, you can go back to the galley," said the young officer. "I'd like to speak to our…guest."

Veronica was sad to see the young ship's cook go. She didn't like the look of this Cyprian Fields. He had a confident strut, but there was an apprehension about him, which he seemed very keen on hiding.

"I suppose you have questions for me," said Veronica after the young doctor left.

"She speaks the truth," said Cyprian, folding his arms and leaning against the bulkhead. "Who are you?"

"My name is Veronica Sewell," she said, the lie coming easily. "I'm a traveller, trying to get back to my aunt's family in Stella Maris. I had a run-in with the Imperium guards, and there was a dispute over the paperwork. I panicked, tried to run. One of them managed to clip me with a ball of shot. By the time I reached the warehouse district, I was exhausted and looking for a place to hide. The crate was on a warehouse loading dock. The top of one of them was loose. I crawled inside. And then I awoke in this bunk."

The end of her story was no lie. She had been nearly delirious from the poison by the time she got as far as the warehouses. She knew that if she didn't find shelter soon, her life would be over. The open shipping crate had been her salvation.

"What sort of paperwork issue?" Cyprian asked, his mouth a grim line.

"One of my passports was missing the Imperium seal."

"May I see it?"

Veronica recognized the skepticism in the boy's storm-grey eyes. He had been lied to before. Many times.

"The soldiers still had it in hand when I fled."

"You're telling me that the Fleet has solid identification of you? And now you're on our ship. When we arrive in Carath, she may very well be searched. The customs officer will ask for a full report of all persons and goods. If your name appears on that list, what will happen?"

Cyprian Fields unfolded his arms. He seemed to grow taller.

"Do you know the typical punishment for stowaways on a merchant vessel?" he asked. "Stowaways take the long step."

Veronica imagined standing on the edge of a gangplank that extended out into the nothingness, nothing but mists and winds. And far below, the unforgiving earth. She imagined stepping into that nothingness, falling until her world ended. She suppressed a shudder.

"I'm not a stowaway."

"Possibly not. But you are a fugitive from the Imperium's justice. Which is worse."

"So, you're threatening to throw me off your ship? To my death?"

"It's within the sphere of possibility."

Veronica crossed her arms. She looked into the young officer's eyes. They were hard, but not the eyes of a killer.

"I want to speak to the shipmaster," she said finally.

The young shipmaster's grimaced with annoyance.

"The shipmaster is not up yet. But I'll be sure to make him aware of the situation."

And he left. Veronica tried to puzzle him out, to think about the young ship's doctor and this ship she found herself on. But her head and her side were throbbing. Inevitably, when sleep came to take her away, she didn't resist.

Veronica awoke with the dawn the next morning. She immediately decided that her best hope would be to find the shipmaster. Hopefully, he would be more helpful than his second-in-command. Still groggy with fatigue and with her side aching, she threw back the rough covers and unfolded her dress. She found her personal effects in a cabinet beneath the bunk: scuffed leather shoes, a few charcoal pencils, some paper. The pearl-handled rapier was missing.

Veronica pushed open the unlocked cabin door. The short corridor, studded with doors leading to other cabins, wrapped around *Philomena's* stern. It was deserted. Veronica found the small spiraling stairwell that led up to the main deck.

Veronica had been on airships before, many times. But each time, it was with her parents, always on a comfortable cruiser outfitted with polished ebony gunwales and lustrous brass fittings. The command deck was furnished with red leather couches, fine glasses, music, and the lounge was staffed by airmen in pressed white uniforms. When Veronica emerged onto the main deck, she saw that there was not a leather couch to be found on *Philomena*. She was a working man's vessel. This was a ship for hauling grains and bricks, casks of oil and sheep. Every surface, rope, and plank was scuffed and worn with hard use. But here and there, little touches of care shone through. A set of artful stained-glass windows were set above the doors of the cartorium that opened to the main deck. The scrolling woodwork was polished, and what little brass plating there was shone in the dawn light. Several airmen, burnished with sun, were scrubbing the deck and taking in sail. They were a ragged group, the kind to scoff at pressed white uniforms.

"Oi there!" said a bald, gap-toothed airman with a floppy cap, smacking his fellows on the shoulders to get their attention. "Look, boys! It's our stowaway!"

"Blessed poor luck to have a woman on board," murmured a tall glowering one with an earring and tattoos, looking askance at Veronica as though she was a cobra about to strike. "A working ship's no place for the females."

"Have you got a name, child?" asked the first man, who introduced himself as McElhaney.

"Veronica," she said. "Veronica Sewell."

"Veeeronica!" laughed McElhaney. "I used to have an aunt named Veronica."

"Used to?" asked one of the men.

McElhaney shrugged.

"Turns out she wasn't my aunt. She'd attend the odd family gathering and she always pretended to be on the other side of the family. Used to chase the children around with her false teeth, the old bat."

"You any good on a ship?" asked another airman. "Know any ropes? Any sails?"

She knew this type. They were airmen, men that lived from day to day, who took life as it was and made the best of it. While the young deckmaster seemed none too kindly, it would be useful to get them on her side.

"I don't know any ropes or knots," she said. "But I can do things with sails."

"Well, I hate to tell you, girl," said the tattooed man, who McElhaney introduced as Paschal. "But to make sails obey, you must have ropes to hold them."

"Have you got a trimming?" Veronica asked.

The men looked at one another for a moment. Finally, someone reached into a pocket and pulled out a rumpled triangle of sailcloth, trimmed from a larger piece. Veronica took the piece of canvas and spread it flat across the gunwale of the ship, where the wind tugged its edges. She pulled a charcoal pencil from the sleeve of her dress. Veronica took one look at Paschal's face, then set to work. The pencil dipped and swooped over the rough surface. Veronica stopped only to sharpen the pencil with a tiny jackknife from her pocket.

"Crazy girl," murmured a pimply youth named Spacklebrook. "Just scribbling on an old piece of canvas like a…"

"Hush," replied Paschal, who was leaning over the Veronica's shoulder.

The airmen huddled in closer. Veronica made a few final strokes, shading carefully in places. Then, she handed the trimming over. A dozen chapped, blistered hands reached out for the canvas. There, preserved in charcoal, was Nolan Paschal: the earring, a tattooed arm, the hard look of a man who had spent his life looking into the horizon. Veronica couldn't keep from smiling as their mouths dropped open like a school of fish.

"Sweet drunken stars," said Clip McElhaney. "It's magic!"

"It's me," said Paschal in a faint voice, reaching out to touch the canvas. "It's me. It looks…"

"Ugly," snickered Spacklebrook. Paschal punched him in the arm.

The airmen looked at Veronica, still gaping.

"Can you do us another one?"

Veronica smiled. It was good to have friends.

In the end, they insisted on showing her the whole ship, with Nolan Paschal as head guide. Although Veronica declined to travel to the top of *Philomena's* rigging, they went through just about everything else. They named all the ropes, sails, and ailerons. She met the temperamental machinist Bartholomew Oakum amid the turning wheels, pulleys, and cables of the ship-core. She saw Basil Black, the ship's cook, in the galley, which was small, but neat as a pin. He smiled and offered her a freshly cooked ship's biscuit, which was stuffed with almonds and raisins. She was also taken through the crew quarters forward, a long cabin beneath the main deck strung with hammocks and chests, overrun with unwashed articles of clothing, which the men kicked out of the way ahead of her, red-faced. A mustached man nodded silently from one of the bunks, where he was laid up with his leg in a cast. Cyprian Fields, mercifully, was nowhere to be seen.

She was finally rescued from the tour by exactly the man she'd been hoping to find. With a wave of his hand, Shipmaster Francis Lightlas ordered the men back to work and offered her a seat next to the helm on the command deck. To her relief, he seemed quite sympathetic to her.

"My deckmaster has shared your conversation yesterday with me," Lightlas said, stroking his grey beard. "Of course, he's right. It would not be advantageous to anyone for you to remain aboard as we get nearer to Carath. There is a lively trading post that we will pass by late tomorrow. We'll drop you off there, and you should be able to find transportation anywhere that you wish. In the meantime, you're welcome to join the ship's officers in the cartorium this evening. Our ship's cook will be preparing dinner."

Grateful, Veronica accepted immediately. The rest of the day passed quickly as she moved among the crew, hearing their stories, learning ropes and sails and songs until the bell for dinner rang.

Philomena's cartorium, true to form, was nowhere near as grandiose as the ones from Veronica's childhood. Instead of crystal chandeliers, oil paintings, and picture windows, the cartorium was furnished in yellowed maps, pewter candlesticks with squat tallow candles, and the smell of ink and old paper. In place of silent waiters in white vests bearing platters of fruit and delicate cheeses, Burt Spacklebrook slouched around the table plunking down serving bowls of hot roasted pork and steaming wheat rolls.

The assembled group was very small, consisting of Lightlas, Oakum, McElhaney (who, Veronica learned, had been promoted to acting loadmaster) and the young deckmaster. McElhaney was the life of the party, countering the bawdy jokes of Bartholomew Oakum with his own more tasteful brand of wit. Even the old shipmaster chuckled now and then, but young Cyprian Fields was largely quiet.

He seemed unwilling to meet Veronica's eye. He clearly didn't trust her, and he seemed uneasy about her familiarity with the crew.

"Ms. Sewell, where did you learn to draw?" asked Francis Lightlas, when Spacklebrook stomped out with the last of the food. There was the loud crash of a dropped tureen in the stairwell, but Veronica politely took no notice to the muffled curse that followed.

"When I was a little girl in Stella Maris," she said. "It was one of my favorite past times when I wasn't working for my parents. I used to make portraits for people sometimes, using the backsides of posters on the streets."

There was a loud knock at the door, which quickly opened to reveal Nolan Paschal. A faint sheen of sweat covered his normally stoic face.

"Begging your pardon, Shipmaster," he said. "There's a ship off the eastern horizon. Long profile. Hard to tell in the moonlight, but she looks like a three-envelope ship."

"A dreadnought?" said McElhaney, his jolly face instantly serious.

"Could be," said Paschal.

"Or a bandit," said Cyprian, rising from the table.

"Douse the lights on deck," commanded Lightlas.

Paschal nodded.

"Already done, sir. We're running dark."

Spacklebrook slouched back into the cartorium.

"Should I cover the rolls?" he asked as the officers hurried out onto the deck. Veronica was quick on their heels. "So they don't go stale."

"Spacklebrook, we have greater issues to deal with at this moment," McElhaney said as he leapt up after the others. He stopped for a moment. "But, yes. Cover the rolls."

The night air was cold. In the distance, Veronica could make out breaks in the cloud where the silver light of the moon shone through, illuminating the rough fabric of the rolling forests of eastern Misericordiae. The running lamps on *Philomena's* bow and stern had been extinguished, plunging the deck into darkness.

The airmen of the third watch huddled on the leftward gunwale, peering into the night. Veronica rubbed her eyes, willing them to adjust more quickly to the darkness. Finally, she could pick out a dark shape, moving along the near ridgeline, a dark mass against the cloud cover.

"Any indication that they've seen us?" Lightlas asked Paschal in a low voice. "Did they change course? Change speed?"

"Not that we've seen, shipmaster. They're just running along the ridge. We didn't see them until just now, on account of the cloud cover."

Lightlas nodded, then turned to Masterson, who was seated at the helm in a specially rigged chair.

"Come about fifteen marks sunwise and take us low, Mr. Masterson. We have to reduce our silhouette."

Masterson acknowledged the order with a low grunt, and turned the wheel. With a low groan of wood and the spooling of cordage, *Philomena* began a quick bank and turn. The crew was eerily silent as the ship came about to the west, whipping through the night towards the dark carpet of forest.

"Keep an eye on the cloud cover. We need to avoid the moonlight," said Lightlas. He pulled out his silver oculus, fixing it on the ship.

Veronica squinted as well. She thought she could pick out the low scoop of the hull, the broad swell of envelopes, the leap of the command deck above the main, but it may all have been a trick of the light. Whether it was a merchant ship, a Fleet vessel, or something more sinister, Veronica couldn't say.

The bandit gangs that patrolled the trade routes of Cor Nova were not to be meddled with. Whether it was the riotous Bowman-McCoys of Korkyra, who forced their victims to cut the envelopes of their ships loose after plundering them, or the Mazurkas of Stella Maris, who were known for the bizarre rituals associated with their pillaging, or Bartimaeus Cain himself, the bandits were a scourge of the skies, a source of nightmare for merchant and villager alike.

Suddenly, there was a loud crack over the empty sky, an orange flash of cannon fire.

"Morningstar!" gasped Clip McElhaney. "We're too close!"

Veronica was about to ask Francis Lightlas what this meant, when suddenly, the sky erupted into light, as though a small sun had dawned off the leftward beam of the phantom ship. It was a projectile, slicing a blinding arc into the sky. For a single moment, Veronica could see every particle of dust and wisp of cloud in the air, and the deck of *Philomena* was flooded with blinding light. In the wide sphere of brilliance, she could see the outline of the other ship plainly. She picked out a red hull, three towering envelopes, rigging in regimented lines, two decks of fourteen guns each, gazing out like silent eyes. The deck crawled with men in red and black. The morningstar faded, plunging the night into even darker blackness. But the flare had done its work.

"A dreadnought," said Lightlas, slamming his fist against the gunwale. "If we had run with our lights on, they might have let us go. Since we were running dark, they'll be coming aboard to search us. Masterson, come about twenty marks!"

"I have to hide," said Veronica. "If I'm found on board…"

The old shipmaster's brow furrowed, thumping the cane once against the deck, as if in decision.

"Get the winch ready," he said to McElhaney. "We have only a few minutes before they're on us."

"What are you talking about?" Veronica said. She had to hide. What did the winch have to do with anything? But Lightlas didn't seem ready to negotiate.

"You're going off ship. We will try to outmaneuver the dreadnought, or submit to a search if it looks favorable. Don't wander from this spot. We will return for you."

The crew looked stricken as Veronica stepped aboard the platform that now hovered a foot off the deck, borne by the mechanism of the winch. There was a creak of wood. Veronica looked beside her to see the youthful face of Basil Black, his face pale and fearful beneath the veneer of calm. He climbed beside her on the winch platform.

"My presence here may not be appreciated either," he said to the shipmaster. "Besides, you'll have to come back for me. None of you can cook for beans."

The crew murmured their assent. Lightlas nodded.

"Your safety will be seen to," he said. "Deckmaster Fields will go with you."

The young deckmaster looked up from priming his pistol, his face suddenly white.

"What?!" Cyprian said. "But the ship-"

"Mr. Fields, you will not contradict my orders. Quickly now. Time is short."

Begrudgingly, Cyprian Fields stepped aboard.

"Lower away! And quickly," said Lightlas.

With a bump and a rattle, the winch arm rotated over the side of the ship, and crew began to feed the cable through a clamp, allowing the winch to lower the platform into the night. Rapidly, the sounds and smells of the deck faded away. They were replaced by only the creak of rope, the scent of pine, and the croak of peepers. The treetops rose up around them. Branches brushed against the underside of the platform as it descended through the canopy and down to the pitch darkness beneath.

With a bump, the platform connected with the forest floor. Without a word, Basil and Veronica stepped off with Cyprian directly behind, all immediately sinking knee-deep in a swampy mire. The empty platform began to rise back into the night. Suddenly, there was a blast of cannon, illuminating the dreadnought in a spasm of light. The ball missed *Philomena*. Her dark hull was flying away, venting aether and pulling as hard as she could into the valley ahead.

And as quickly as that, they were alone.

CHAPTER TWELVE

When the ships above had departed, the sounds of the forest night closed around them: the faint hum of insects, the whisper of wind-blown trees, the low hooting of owls. Under normal circumstances, Basil would have been quite at home here, listening to all of the marvelous creatures of the forest produce their symphony in the dark. But, as it was, Basil was profoundly uncomfortable. On the first part, they were entirely abandoned in an unknown section of Old Meronymy forest. Second, to say that Cyprian Fields seemed tense would be well beyond an understatement.

As soon as the lights of the ships disappeared through the treetops, the young deckmaster stomped off into the dark, glaring upward and muttering angrily to himself.

"Where are you going?" Veronica asked. "Shipmaster Lightlas said we were to stay here."

There was a tremendous rustling and the creak of branches as Cyprian swung himself up into the boughs of a large pine. Cautiously, Basil and Veronica followed to the base of the tree, peering up at the climbing form of the young officer. Veronica squinted to see through the branches.

"I don't think you're liable to see anything. They were headed over th-"

There was a series of thumps in the branches, and Cyprian landed lightly on the ground in front of them in a rain of stray needles and pinecones. He was glaring at Veronica.

"I don't know if you had noticed, but I am not particularly interested in your advice. Perhaps if I need to know anything about being a dirty stowaway then I will consult you."

The look that came across Veronica's face was so severe, Basil thought it best to seek refuge behind the trunk of the tree.

"Look, you arrogant prig, I didn't ask to come aboard your ship."

"Correct! You didn't. And look where that's landed us! The Fleet may very well gun *Philomena* out of the sky! And if she does by some miracle come back for us, it's anyone's guess what or who is roaming woods like these in the middle of the night!"

On the last point, Basil disagreed. It was well known what roamed the woods. At least, it was to people who read the right books. He glanced into the dark forest around them. He was suddenly aware of how far their raised voices must be carrying among the trees.

"Fields," said Basil, extending a hand toward Cyprian, bespectacled eyes scanning the darkness. But, Cyprian wasn't paying attention. He and Veronica were now quite distracted.

"How can you blame me for this?" Veronica demanded, the blood rising to her cheeks. "I was fleeing for my life and I went the only place I thought I could. Wouldn't you have done the same?"

Cyprian turned away in disgust.

"Do you mean to tell me that cock-and-bull story is anywhere near the truth? Who takes refuge in a shipping crate? An open shipping crate? And what kind of merchant leaves their crates open for fleeing dissident girls to climb into?"

"Fields," Basil said, a little more pointedly. "I don't think you should yell."

"You stay out of this!" Cyprian bellowed. "Who knows what truth there is to *your* story! For all I know….you…"

Then Cyprian's voice faded. His face grew ashen. He had heard it too. Silence. Silence so deep it was almost loud. Their heads swiveled around, and the darkness pressed close.

Then, Basil saw something, a shape in the trees just behind them. It slipped smoke-like through the vines and creepers, a darker blackness, ethereal and mountainous at the same time. Then, the moon broke out from behind the clouds, and the forest was flooded with ghostly silver light. The dark shape rose up, black eyes glistening, midnight black fur slashed with red, ivory spikes rattling from its mane, its back, its massive shanks.

With a sound that rent the night, the witchbear roared. Like an avalanche, it smashed to the ground on massive forelegs, eyes black with menace, and charged. For a moment, they were paralyzed, stunned.

"Run!" cried Cyprian, grabbing both Veronica and Basil and charging into the night.

Branches and leaves slapped at Basil's face as they dashed through the underbrush. Trees leapt ghostlike out of the gloom ahead. The ground pitched downward, and they found themselves slipping on the thick layer of wet leaves that coated the forest floor. All the while, the wave of blackness came behind them, claws raking chunks from the soft earth. At the base of the hill, they crashed through a stream, sliding on the wet rocks and thick mud of the opposite bank.

There was a lightning flash, the smell of gunpowder, and a thunderous roar. Basil didn't bother to look back. Cyprian's pistol would do no good against the beast. The witchbears were rumored to be creatures beyond nature, the souls of sorcerers trapped forever in an animal cloak. Airmen wrecked in the woods were known to have fired whole casks of small shot at a witchbear, only for it to keep coming, a bloody nightmare, teeth grinning all the more.

As the trees whipped past, Basil was suddenly aware of more loping shapes in the darkness beside them, more ivory spines and black-mottled-red. The slobbery breath of hungry cruelty filled Basil's ears, flooding his heart with panic.

Basil's strength was flagging when they burst through a copse of trees and stumbled into a clearing. With a roar that sprayed hot saliva onto Basil's vest, the witchbear gained the tree line and came crashing towards them, blazing red mane and ivory claws reflecting beads of moonlight. From the opposite treeline, more witchbears emerged, slaver dripping from their jaws. Basil had often wondered how death would come, how it would feel. Now, he would observe it for the first and only time.

Then, something sprang from one of the trees at the edge of the clearing, arching high into the air over bear and man, glinting silver in the moonlight. At first, Basil thought he was seeing another morningstar. But, it landed gracefully on two legs, and two arms emerged, along with a head flowing with silver hair on a graceful neck. She was clad head to toe in smooth buckskin, and a beaded bag hung at her side. There was something wild about this strange figure, and Basil wondered whether they were in less danger, or more.

Then, she opened her mouth, and a familiar, luminous sound filled the forest. It was the same sound that had left Basil's own lips during his escape from Osmara, the living words that had protected the village. The words began to rise, lift, dance. And they took Basil with them. He forgot about *Philomena*, about the forest, about Cyprian and Veronica, about the witchbears that gathered around. He was suspended in a moment, caught up in wonder, as though the words were a rapturous melody. As the strange language rolled over the forest clearing, it sounded like the snap of lightning, the roar of trees ablaze, and the bright spark of iron on flint. It was a language that no human had invented, the words that had written the world.

Then, with a glowing, crumbling crack, the words blossomed into fire.

"High Sylvan," Veronica whispered, wide-eyed. "The Tongue of the Sovereign."

Basil opened his eyes. The strange woman stood in the center of the forest clearing, a pale globe of flame suspended between her pale, delicate hands. Whether she was young or old, Basil could not tell, but her face was fearsomely beautiful, illuminated by the golden, leaping light of flame that now enveloped the whole clearing. With roars and groans, the witchbears receded into the blackness, backing down from the light, leaving Basil and his companions shining with sweat, hearts hammering.

The woman sat down in the center of the clearing, cradling the fire between her fingertips. She set it carefully on the ground, whispering and feeding it with sticks until it blazed lustily. Then, the forest woman spoke, her eyes not leaving the fire.

"I don't take kindly to those who come trespassing in the forest, bringing their shouts and their weapons."

Basil expected Cyprian to say something, but the young officer seemed dumbfounded. They both looked at Veronica, who cleared her throat.

"We don't mean to trespass. We've lost our ship-"

The forest woman dropped a cascade of pinecones and crumpled brown leaves into the blaze, nodding slowly.

"You've lost your ship, so you feel lost? Better to be lost, Anne says. No use to the wooden monstrosities. Waste of good trees. Plants are meant to grow in the ground and men chop them and nail them and twist them and put them in the air. And it's the same men who wonder why the wide world is in the state it is."

Confronted with this clearly crazed forest hermit, Cyprian looked about ready to take his chances with the witchbears. Basil would have felt the same, if the woman had not spoken in High Sylvan, as Veronica called it.

"Names!" the woman cried suddenly, leaping to her feet. They all jumped. "I must have names."

She beckoned them to the firelight and leaned in close, inspecting each of them in turn with luminous silver eyes.

"Your names," she said. "Names mean something. Names are a beginning. That is where everything starts. The beginning."

She leveled a finger at Cyprian.

"You," she said.

Cyprian only faltered for a moment.

"Cyprian Fields," he said finally. "Cyprian Augustus Fields."

"Ah," said Anne. "What's in between has weight. A son who carries his father's name. A heavy burden."

Her eyes fell on Veronica next.

"Veronica Sewell," she said.

"Lie not!" cried Anne, loud enough to make them jump again. "Anne Stormalong knows the truth. She knows."

"Veronica Stromm," said Veronica, eyes downcast. Basil felt Cyprian stiffen beside him. She had lied about her name. At least some of Cyprian's suspicions were founded.

"Another name that weighs heavy," said Anne. "You are one who is searching, looking. That is easy. It is the finding that is hard."

When her silver eyes landed on Basil, he did his best to hold her gaze. Those luminous eyes looked all the way into him, probing, searching. Deep in those silvery eyes he saw a past fraught with pain, with the wonder of youth, and at the very depths, power. Power that Basil somehow recognized.

"And you."

"Basil Black."

The silver eyes widened, then narrowed.

Then, Anne Stormalong was off in a flurry of movement. Leaping and sliding through the underbrush, she snatched dry brush, pinecones, and sticks from the underbrush, dropping them onto the fire. A strange wind blew up, whirling skittering leaves into the blaze.

The weak orb of golden light around the fire grew, pulsing further into the darkness that seemed to exude from the brooding trees. Far beyond the light of the fire, Basil could make out fell, slinking shapes in the darkness, rattling their spines. By the time Anne Stormalong was settled again by the fire, it rolled up toward the heavens, sending sparks to spin among the stars.

"The dreadnoughts will see us," Cyprian said, his eyes scanning the ridgelines.

"I have sent friends to deal with your pursuers," said the forest woman woman. "Sit."

They sat. Cyprian more knelt, careful and wary. His eyes didn't leave the outer rim of the darkness, his hand lingering near his pistol.

"The witchbears will come no further as long as the fire burns bright, and the fire will burn bright as long as I feed it," said Anne Stormalong. "There is work to be done, talk to be had."

She pointed at them all again.

"Three with fathers lost. One a shipmaster, one a Bookkeeper. But you, Basil Black, who is it that you have lost? Anne would wonder, but Anne knows."

Basil immediately thought of Thon Black, preserved in Basil's memory like stone. Strong hands, piercing eyes, words of reason. A dead man.

"A miner," he said finally. "A metallurgist."

"No."

Anne Stormalong's expression was stern, but not unkind.

"He was a father to you, indeed. Anne knows. But he did not give you life. Your fathers were of a different lineage."

Then, into the silence, Anne Stormalong spoke High Sylvan again, the words washing over Basil like the waves of a long-forgotten ocean. The wind pulsed with each rise and fall of the syllables, and the flames of the fire swayed and bowed, twisting themselves into strange and luminous shapes.

Then, the shadowy figures in the flames began to acquire heads and shoulders, arms and legs of golden light. They rose and fell, one after the other. Each wore a crown about their head and a round amulet around their neck. Every left hand bore a tall staff, and every right a heavy book. There was a great, somber man in long robes, a young girl as slender and quiet and delicate as a lily, a portly jolly man in a garden, a moody soldier with a large dog by his side. There were hundreds of others; they flew past, rising and falling in quick succession.

And at their backs, shadows in the flames, was the Sovereign Dominion of Cor Nova through the ages. There were cities and mountains and rivers, festivals and feasts and laughter. But amid the laughter, there was weeping. Plagues swept through the provinces, wars burnt the land black, floods and famines and ruin did their terrible work. Through the stormy sea of time, the Sovereigns were a rock against the waves.

And finally, the fiery shade of Lorus stood in the flames. The last Sovereign. He was tall, resolute, and handsome, resplendent in amulet, crown, and staff. Then, the flames rose up around him, a towering figure of orange horror. It crashed down, engulfing the Sovereign. From the ashes, rose a tall, hard-bitten man, his skin sallow, his hair white, his eyes empty. He wore neither amulet nor crown, carried neither staff nor book. The Imperium Titus stood alone in a Fleet uniform, a black saber by his side, drinking in the light of the flame. Basil thought he saw something shifting, moving witchbear-like, in the flames behind them.

The eyes of Titus's phantom were trained on something in the flames before him, a small lump that was growing and coalescing amid the embers, rising up out of the ashes. The figure wore a black vest, iron-rimmed glasses, and carried a square wooden box. Titus leered over Basil's phantom with an expression of contempt and hatred hotter than the fire itself. Out of the fire around them, more flames licked up, forming a round amulet, a crown, and a staff.

Then, the shapes disappeared. The song of High Sylvan had stopped. The forest was silent but for the blowing of the wind and the crackle of the fire.

"No," Basil said. His head was awhirl. All he knew of the world was mining and medicine and books. What did this mean?

"I'm Basil. I'm from Osmara. I'm a miner's son. I can't…"

Veronica seemed similarly stunned, and Cyprian wore an expression of extreme discomfort.

"Lorus had no heir," Veronica said. "He had no children. His queen gave birth to a stillborn child a few weeks after Titus rose. He can't…"

For the first time, Anne Stormalong's eyes seemed truly gentle.

"Unless a lie was constructed, designed to keep the truth from those with no right to it. The court doctor declared the child stillborn. But the child, though small, was very much alive. He was smuggled out of Soliodomus, taken to a place where Titus would never think to look for him. A tiny mountain town in Korkyra, called Osmara."

"The Bookkeepers," said Veronica.

"My father," said Basil, his mind still rebelling against all of this. "Said I was a Bookkeeper."

"Basil Black," said Anne Stormalong. "You are not a Bookkeeper. You are the one for whom the book is kept."

She reached into the beaded satchel that hung about her waist, and pulled out a large rectangular object. It was heavy, bound in supple red leather burnished by the years. And it was scarred. At one time, it had been sliced clean through, a single cut clearly visible between top and bottom. Polished brass braces had been mounted to the cover, holding the book firmly together. It was warm and heavy in Basil's hands. Somewhere behind him, Veronica gasped.

"Is that…?"

"The Rule of Sylvanus," said Anne Stormalong. "The book that the Imperium Titus hates the most. The very one stolen from Soliodomus on the night when Basil, son of Lorus, escaped his uncle's clutches. And thanks to the Imperium's purges, one of the last complete volumes in the world."

"This can't be true," said Basil, running his fingers over the book. "I don't… I never…"

Suddenly, Anne Stormalong was on her feet, all the more strange and terrifying. The fire leaped high, roaring skyward, sending sparks and heat into the darkness.

"Is it your choice to make?" she demanded, a pillar of luminous silver in the night. "Many bend their backs beneath the weight of the Imperium! Have you heard their cries? Have you? Anne has. Anne knows. Anne carries them with her. Doom rises. And Cor Nova will face it as she always has: with her leader."

The fire receded. Anne took her seat. It was a long moment before Veronica finally spoke.

"Doom?" she asked. "What doom?"

"The Abyss," said Stormalong. "Grows deeper with each passing day, and blood seeps into its base. If Titus is not stopped, night will fall, and this time, the sun will not rise."

"But, the Sovereign…" said Veronica. "The Sovereign has High Sylvan! You have it! How is that so? Are you a Sovereign?"

Anne Stormalong shook her head.

"No, my time has come and gone. High Sylvan must be stirred, must be summoned to you, Basil Black. To do it, you must recover what has been lost, what the Bookkeepers sacrificed so much to hide. Three relics of Sylvanus. Time grows short. The fire is dying."

The three objects, outlined in fire, flew through Basil's mind again: crown, amulet, staff.

"But how?" he said, still numb. "How will we recover them?"

"Look to the Rule," said Stormalong. "The Rule will guide you, as it has guided your forefathers before you."

The coals were dwindling, and the heavy breath of huge things in the darkness drew closer. Suddenly, a dark shape swept over the ridge, turning and coming to stop over them. The creak of cedar and the high, reedy voice of Bartholomew Oakum cut through the air. They had lit the bow and stern lights.

"*Philomena,*" said Cyprian.

"A name," said Stormalong. "A name that means something, a name that is a beginning."

Then, the fire went out and Anne Stormalong was gone. The night rushed back in around them, and the snarling in the underbrush grew alarmingly close.

There was the loud crack of musket fire, and plumes of dirt erupted from the forest floor as shot penetrated the deep loam. More than one witchbear roared in fury, harried by the gunfire. A trio of ropes spiraled down snake-like from the gunwales.

"Time to go!" Cyprian cried.

He whipped ropes into Basil and Veronica's hands. At once, *Philomena's* envelopes burgeoned with aether, lifting them skyward. As the snarling witchbears grew small beneath them, Basil clung to the rope with one hand. The Rule of Sylvanus was clutched under his other arm, heavy and still warm from the fire. Veronica was shouting something to him, but Basil couldn't hear her. In his mind, he saw only the face of Thon Black, tears running down his cheeks. He had not thought it possible to lose his father twice.

CHAPTER THIRTEEN

Ambry looked up the valley, watching gray clouds roll in from the west. The wind made waves in the treetops, rousing blue cranes from the bows and rocking the Fleet warships moored in the trees. Like an enormous red cliff rising from the forest, Ambry's battleship, *Mercy of Titus*, with her five massive envelopes and three decks of guns, dwarfed the two dreadnoughts that swayed to her right and left. From each ship, a collection of ladders and winches spooled down to the forest floor.

Allowing himself a deep breath of the cool afternoon air, Ambry scanned the clearing again. The grass was smooth and dotted with flowers, a near-perfect island in the sea of trees. His search parties had found three sets of running footprints leading to the spot from further up the valley. Even now, the airmen were spreading further out into the wilderness in a precise line, looking for any sign of the fugitives.

One of the sergeants leading the search parties made a low whistle and put his hand in one of the enormous bear prints that pocked the ground.

"Witchbears," he said. "No chance of anyone escaping from this. Not with all of their insides where they belong."

In the center of the clearing, a circle of ashes covered the ground. Ambry drew his saber, using the blade to turn over the chunks of charred wood. It was fresh, but not hot. Less than a day old. Ambry's brow furrowed. Once witchbears seized on prey, they didn't relent. Ever. If some madness drove these three to stop and build a fire, the creatures would have destroyed them. Messily. When the three ran into the clearing, had the fire been waiting for them? What happened then? If they had met someone else, there was no sign of them. Ambry had no answers, but he was certain of one thing.

"They escaped," he said, reseating his saber. "A bloodlusting witchbear is not a cleanly animal. If the three had been killed here, we'd know. Sergeant, call the search parties back to the ships. They won't find anything. Bring me Shipmaster Correll."

With a salute, the sergeant went stomping into the underbrush, yelling orders. Ambry watched the red uniforms of the Fleet airmen retreat back through the valley, headed for their vessels. They had almost reached the ships by the time Shipmaster Correll emerged through the treeline, red-faced and puffing mightily. In his youth, he'd been known as "Correll the Rock", a fierce fighter who rushed into battle with a granite club in one mighty fist. It seemed to Ambry that the rushing stream of time had worn him to a pebble, round and mostly useless.

Shipmaster Correll bowed, face running with sweat.

"You called for me, Grand Admiral Ambry?"

"I wanted to clarify a few of the details about last night," Ambry said. "So, your lookout saw the merchant freighter while on your search pattern?"

"Yes, Grand Admiral. We were running dark two ridges over, keeping an eye for ill doings of any sort. They were running with lights on, but as soon as they made notice of us, they doused them, hoping we hadn't seen. We continued on our usual course, waiting to see what happened. We saw the winch descend. My signalman made note of the location, so that we could come back and check after the ship had been detained. We supposed they were dropping contraband."

Ambry nodded. The jowly old shipmaster was right about that, at least. But they weren't smuggling books or spices. This contraband lived and breathed.

"Well," Correll went on. "I ordered a morningstar fired, clearly saw them. Fortunately, my signalman thought to take note of their colors. When they appeared to flee, we fired a warning shot. They fled, and we gave chase."

"The colors" Ambry asked. "You have this information?"

"Yes, Grand Admiral. I had it sent to the signalman on your flagship as soon as you arrived."

The old man had done at least one thing right. With any luck, the signalman was already checking the registry to identify the mysterious freighter.

"But you failed to apprehend them. Because of..."

"Sparrows, sir," said the shipmaster, flapping his arms languidly. "A whole flock of them. They blotted out the sky, weighing down our rigging, taking wing at the crew. More than a few of my men were badly....err...pecked. I've never seen birds behave that way in all my life. It was as though they'd been set upon us. And the state of my deck... the mess is horrendous."

Ambry breathed out slowly through clenched teeth.

"A flight of sparrows harried you, allowing the freighter to escape."

"That's right, Grand Admiral. By the time we were able to drive them off, we had fully lost sight of the freighter."

Ambry was silent for a moment. Fleet airmen were trained to fight through storm, fire, and lightning to accomplish their orders. And this pompous old curmudgeon had turned yellow at the sight of a flock of songbirds. Apparently sensing Ambry's annoyance, Shipmaster Correll flushed pink. Finally, Ambry took a step towards the shipmaster. The older man seemed to shrink beneath Ambry's gaze.

"If that is all...shall...shall I return to my post?" asked Shipmaster Correll.

"You will not be returning to your post," Ambry replied. "Give me your insignia."

"But...why?"

"For three reasons. Because the Imperium has no need of men who cannot complete their mission, because a man more suited to your duties would not ask me that question, and because your Grand Admiral has commanded it of you."

Correll cringed as Ambry whipped the golden insignia from his shoulders. The shipmaster's eyes were wide, as though he was suffering a nightmare.

"But...I have served the Imperium for his whole reign..."

"You will serve him still: as a deck sweeper. You will enjoy the rank of able airman under Shipmaster Boylan."

Correll's jowls wobbled with disbelief.

"I will not suffer this indignity..."

Ambry's patience ran out. His saber sung from its scabbard, shining in the air before the quivering shipmaster. He called for a sergeant who was standing nearby.

"Indignity presents a problem for you? Then I should make you more acquainted with it. Sergeant, give this man fifty cracks of the whip, relieve him of his clothing, and lash him to the mast. He can remain until he is prepared to take on his duties."

A pair of hefty airmen seized the protesting shipmaster and escorted him to one of the dreadnoughts. Even as they disappeared into the trees, a tall thin airman whose shoulders bore the golden kestrel wings of a signalman emerged from them. He waited at a respectful distance until Ambry gestured for him to come forward. Bowing in salute, he handed Ambry a sheet of paper.

"I managed to cross-reference the flags seen on the ship, Grand Admiral. It's fortunate that we updated the registry before departing, as it was one of the newest entries. It's a merchant freighter named *Philomena*. It has a valid registration. Shipmaster is Francis Lightlas, Fields Trading and Supply Company, Misericordiae."

Ambry nodded. He had known of a *Philomena* in Misericordiae once, owned by a boisterous shipmaster named Augustus Fields, a man as loud and brash as he was principled. He raised a rebellion in Misericordiae, stirring his fellow merchants to oppose the Imperium's trade embargo. Fortunately, there were men in Misericordiae city who would sell their allegiance for the right amount of gold. The Imperium managed to find them.

Ambry had been a shipmaster on that night, standing on the command deck of his own dreadnought, every man poised for battle. When the thunder of cannons lit up the sky, it was the merchant freighter *Philomena* who led the charge, with Augustus Fields calling the attack from the bow.

"I did not know that this ship survived the Merchant Rebellion."

"According to the registry, she was seized, Grand Admiral," said the signalman. "But being of no use to the Fleet at the time, she was cradled and her documents archived. I believe the Imperium's lease on her lapsed, allowing the ship to fall back into the hands of whoever owned the shipping company."

"The shipmaster," Ambry said. "Lightlas."

It was a coincidence too great to be ignored. A ship bold enough to attempt to out-run an Imperium vessel, a dreadnought much less, surely had something to hide, and this ship had a history.

"Send a kestrel to the Port Authority Rotunda in Misericordiae. I will have all their information on *Philomena*, most importantly her roster and registered plan of flight. Then, blacklist her. Make sure that every vessel in the Fleet and port in Cor Nova is keeping a lookout. The Imperium offers a reward."

As the signalman returned to the ship, Ambry squatted down beside the charred remains of the fire. He scooped up a handful of charcoal. There, curled among the black, was a single silver hair, as delicate as glass and shining like a star in the sunlight.

"More questions," Ambry murmured to himself as he crushed the burnt wood in his hand, tarnishing silver with black.

CHAPTER FOURTEEN

Cyprian stood beside the stained-glass windows of the map-room doors. The sun rising in the east splashed crimson and purple across his face. Veronica, Basil, and Shipmaster Lightlas were sitting around the table. Petros slept wheezily on top of the map cabinet, nestled among some shredded aetheronautical charts.

At the moment, they were silent, pulled in by the gravity of the Rule of Sylvanus, lying open on the map table amid charcoal pencils, brass marking tacks, and the great map of Cor Nova. The book's pages swam with text, embellished at the headings and borders with breathtaking scrolling and images. There was history, poetry, song, and exhortation. There were drawings, calculations, tactics of war, and winged beasts. The slice of a blade that must have been perilously sharp clipped each page into two halves, so that Basil had to carefully turn each page's top and bottom together. Francis Lightlas touched the pages with a weathered hand, like one greeting an old friend after many years.

"My family had one when I was a boy," he said in a quiet voice. "Almost every family did. My father would read a little bit of it every night. Sometimes from the actual Rule, but more often from the Songs of Analisa, some from the stories of Proteus and Obelius. It was always different, not just a book, but a collection of books, with the first chapter being the actual Rule of Sylvanus, written by the first Sovereign himself. The following sections were added by his successors, all the way up to Corinna. Lorus never got to write his, although it's said he very nearly did it many times. They say he was a man who always expected more time."

The old loadmaster's eyes shone brighter than usual. He picked up the heavy tome, flipping through page after page.

"You are all too young to remember, but this was the first book Titus had sent to the fires. Most gave it up willingly, some cried but handed it over, some refused. It came to blood then. Those nights, fires lit up the cities like day. The wisdom of eight hundred years of Sovereigns burns bright."

He turned the pages as though to flip through them from the beginning, but stopped on the inside of the front cover with a surprised grunt. Cyprian saw clearly that there was handwriting there, neatly penned in orderly lines.

"This does not belong..." said Lightlas. Basil and Veronica leaned closer to see. Cyprian, begrudging his own curiosity, leaned over their shoulders. The writing was written in a firm, round hand, in neat lines that went all the way down the page.

Three from one, one from three.
A world turned back, the light to see.
Three for one, a dreadful choice
To make the Sovereign find his voice.

The Sovereign's heart, in living sea,
'Neath bleeding elm and twisted tree.
Only one and one alone
Lonely is the shadow throne.

The Sovereign's arm, the strength that reigns,
In the frozen north remains
Beneath the Old Man's Tooth. She sleeps,
Colleena of the valley deep.

The Sovereign's eye, that sees from height,
Turns on brows of wooden sight.
Third and sixth and third once more.
At Ivory's first, behind the door.

Three from one, one from three,
A world turned back, the light to see.
Let Cor Novan hills rejoice
When the Sovereign finds his voice.

"Curious metrics," Veronica said. "It's almost like a Terra Altan sonnet…"

Cyprian snorted. Somehow, the great weight of the last few hours came thundering down on him all at once.

"That," he said. "Is a very astute observation for the daughter of a Stella Marian fisherman. That sounds like something an educated girl would say, someone who grew up in a big house, went to an expensive school, and was fed with a silver spoon."

The temperature in the cartorium seemed to drop; every eye shifted to Cyprian. Basil leaned in toward the book, as though absorbed, and Veronica stood up.

"What do you want from me?" she asked.

"Well," Cyprian said. "If we're going to talk about what I want, I'd start with being told the truth. You already lied about your name. What else is there to know?"

"Fine," Veronica said, folding her arms, dark eyes flashing. "My name is Veronica Stromm. I grew up in Stella Maris. My father was Hector Stromm, a scholar at the university. He aided the Bookkeepers, and the Imperium killed him three years ago. My mother was imprisoned. I escaped, and I've been traveling ever since. I spent the last four months illegally printing this book in Misericordiae. That is the truth, if you need it so badly."

"So," Cyprian said. "You lied and got yourself aboard *Philomena*. No Imperium airmen forced you into that shipping crate. You saw where it was going and snuck aboard. You intentionally endangered us all with your presence, then lied about it."

Veronica shook her head.

"That was never my intention. I had no idea where that crate was going. I was wounded, delirious, unaware of where I was."

Cyprian shook his head.

"Considering the colossal mess we're in," he said. "I don't think your intention matters for one lean lentil at the moment."

Veronica was a full head shorter than Cyprian, but her brown eyes didn't waver. For a moment, Cyprian was sure that she was going to punch him.

"Mr. Fields," Shipmaster Lightlas said, his voice low and commanding. "That will be all."

With a resentful grunt, Cyprian turned back to the window.

"Well as it is, here we are," the shipmaster said, tapping his finger on the handwritten lettering in the book. "We have all taken risks, foolish ones perhaps. The question is now what to do with the situation in which we now find ourselves. Choices must be made."

Turning her back to Cyprian, Veronica pulled the Rule of Sylvanus toward herself, clever brown eyes still sparking with anger as she searched the lines.

"This must point to the three relics. We have to figure out what the Bookkeepers were trying to tell us."

"We?" said Cyprian, unable to contain his fury. "Us?"

Veronica's mouth opened, then closed. Basil looked at the ceiling, as though wishing he could disappear. Lightlas was looking at Cyprian with annoyance, but Cyprian didn't care.

"Am I right in thinking," he said. "That you are prepared to face the wrath of the Imperium, risk everything, just because some cracked old forest lady told you a fairy tale? The Sovereigns are dead. All of them. There has never been any evidence that one survived Titus's takeover. The only person with Sovereign blood who is fit to sit the Just Throne is Titus himself, and he doesn't seem to be interested in giving it up anytime soon."

"But Anne…" Veronica started.

"Is a crazy lady who lives in the woods and talks to bears. You're going to just trust her on this? Basil!"

Cyprian turned to the ship's cook, who slid down a little further on his crate, bespectacled eyes wide.

"Are you a king?" demanded Cyprian. "Are you the Sovereign of Cor Nova?"

The cartorium went silent, all eyes on Basil. He looked down at his hands, folded in his lap.

"I…don't know."

Cyprian slapped the table, setting pens and rules a-rattle.

"A vote of confidence if I ever heard one! Let's all become revolutionaries! We'll take up spoons and ladles against the Imperium!"

"Clearly," Veronica said, nearly shouting. "The Fleet thinks he's a person of interest!"

"Ha! How interesting! Let's assume for a moment, that Basil is the Sovereign of Cor Nova, the lost son of Lorus. He has no resources, no allies, no ships. He could march right into Soliodomus and stake his claim to all of Cor Nova, and what is Titus going to do? Hand it over to him? No! He's going to kill him so quickly it'll make his head spin. Right off his skinny shoulders."

Veronica shook her head, fists resolutely clenched at her sides.

"If he's the Sovereign, he has a right to the Just Throne."

"Yeah, and I have a right to be named the Duke of the Starfairies. My point is that even if Basil's claim is legitimate, it doesn't matter. Nothing is going to change. It won't. It can't. The Imperium has hundreds of ships, maybe thousands. Any kind of rebellion will be put down. Quickly. Basil would be much better off as a living ship's cook than a dead challenger to the reign of the Imperium."

Cyprian could feel his heart pounding, flush with victory. But the look of defeat that was clouding Veronica's eyes immediately dampened his spirits. He found himself regretting the words, then resenting himself for regretting them.

"So," Basil said, finally meeting Cyprian's eye. "What are you going to do?"

"What are we going to do?" Cyprian said. "We're going to land this ship and drop you both like a hot cinder at the very first settlement that emerges from the horizon. Then, we're going to take our cargo to Carath and get paid."

Lightlas stood up, his voice firm.

"Fortunately, that decision is not yours to make. I think you've said quite enough, Mr. Fields. Get out."

"But-"

"Boy! That's enough."

Cyprian's eyes fixed for a moment on the Rule of Sylvanus. It lay as a silent witness, forcing itself upon Cyprian, and his anger was suddenly rekindled. He clobbered the doors aside, setting the stained-glass panes a-rattle, and went out onto the deck.

Cyprian fumed his way all the way to the stern rail. On the far southern horizon, grey clouds were massing. Cyprian seethed right with them.

After a while, there was the muffled thump of a cane against the deck, and the shipmaster appeared at the rail beside him. Francis Lightlas was silent, gazing out with Cyprian into the fitful morning sky, the wind tugging at his grey beard and setting his weathered eyes blinking. For a moment, Cyprian felt the urge to rage at him, but the desire was ebbing with every passing moment, as though throwing the tiny rock of his rage into Lightlas's great pool of calm would leave hardly a ripple.

"It's insanity," Cyprian said finally. "All of it."

The old man nodded.

"Reality too often is."

"You can't possibly believe them."

"It doesn't really matter if I do or not. If you stopped for a moment to think rationally about the situation, you would realize that a chain of events has been sent into motion that we can't stop. You're forgetting about the morningstar last night."

Immediately, the flare burst in Cyprian's mind, and he remembered how it had illuminated the ships like day, how he had been able to see every detail of the pursuing Fleet dreadnought. The Fleet men had seen them as well, and probably had been able to identify *Philomena*. As soon as the Imperium Fleet could communicate their information, she would be blacklisted at every major port in Cor Nova, marked for arrest as soon as her bow came in sight. The roster would be published and made available in every city, perhaps with rewards for information. Or bodies. Cyprian imagined flying into Carath, with a full delegation of Fleet soldiers awaiting them on the concourse.

Cyprian was silent. With the anger gone, he felt strangely empty, despondent, like the rain-sodden, charred wasteland that is left after a forest fire. He remembered the hurt in Veronica's eyes, and felt a pang of guilt.

"Cyprian," said Lightlas, rubbing the top of his cane with one gnarled hand. "As soon as we are within a port of call, or spotted by a Fleet ship, we will be taken, interrogated, executed, or sent to the Abyss. A similar fate will await the crew. They can't escape any of this either. Similarly, I don't see the wisdom in blaming Basil Black or Veronica Stromm. They both perhaps acted rashly, but they expected this journey to be every bit as uneventful as you did. Keeping that in mind, I believe there are two options."

Cyprian nodded, rubbing his temples.

"Which are?"

"First, we can attempt to escape. Whether that means abandoning the ship, growing beards, and taking up ranch work somewhere in Korkyra, or trying to make the passage over the Shrouds out of Cor Nova, I wouldn't know."

"I've never liked cows," said Cyprian. "And I wouldn't attempt that passage in a Stella Marian cruiser, much less this old tub. The second option?"

"The second option you will not see unless you take some time to think very carefully. That book in there is very real. There is no faking or copying that. From the markings on the inside, I would guess that particular copy belonged to Lorus himself, marked by the Bookkeepers to be found by his son."

Cyprian turned on the older man. He almost couldn't believe his ears.

"Really? You really do believe it. You believe that the ship's cook is the Sovereign of Cor Nova. It's absurd…"

But there was no joke in Lightlas's old eyes.

"Cyprian, there is a very real chance that Basil Black is the son of Lorus. And if you believe that to be true, the second option is the only option. Think about what has happened in the dominion over the last fifteen years. If there was a chance to roll it back, a chance to do something about it, wouldn't you take it? Even if the chance were small?"

"Those are odds that no businessman would take."

Francis Lightlas shook his head, looking back out into the gathering dawn.

"Those were the odds your father took."

Suddenly, the Imperium was clear in Cyprian's mind, leering over everything. Piles of burning books, masses of citizens skulking under the eyeless gaze of masked Fleet soldiers up and down the street. The disappearances, the whispering, the fear. He remembered his father, how he had died, fighting the Imperium to his last breath. Fighting although he knew he was taking himself away from the people who loved him most.

"If we pull this off," Lightlas said. "There'll be glory. And with glory, comes gold. Imagine knocking on Bartimaeus Cain's door with a dozen heavily armed cruisers at your back."

Cyprian rested his head against the stern rail.

"You're manipulating me."

The old man smirked.

"Is it working?"

When Cyprian pushed open the doors of the cartorium, Basil and Veronica were leaning over the Rule of Sylvanus again. Basil was hunched, worry etched across his face. Veronica leaned over the book, aggressive, like a fighter. Cyprian drew up a crate, sitting down heavily at the table.

"I don't trust either of you."

Veronica nodded.

"The feeling is mutual."

"For the record, I am not convinced that our ship's cook is anything more than a ship's cook. But the shipmaster doesn't see any other way for us to go forward. We can't dock in any port of call. We can either run, turn ourselves in, or pursue this bizarre course of action."

Veronica nodded.

"And where is the shipmaster now?"

"Telling the men that we are having a change in plan. We'll see how well they take it."

Cyprian slid closer to the open Rule of Sylvanus.

"So, if we're going to make this bid, what do we have to do? Our friend Anne wasn't too forthcoming on the details."

"Oh, I think she was," Veronica said, still clearly mistrustful but thankful for cooperation. "Basil and I have been talking."

She produced a charcoal pencil from her sleeve and set to work on a piece of spare parchment. Within a few moments, she roughly reproduced the final scene in the fire. It included the figures of Titus and Basil, and around them, three more shapes: an amulet, a staff, a crown.

"*Three for one, and one for three,*" said Veronica. "Three relics that every Sovereign has worn since Sylvanus made them. The Riverstone Amulet is worn over the chest: a heart. The Elm Staff is a symbol of power, of action: an arm. The Astral Crown resides on the head, a symbol of wisdom: an eye. The Bookkeepers hid them, scattered them so that no one could find them without a map. And the poem within the Rule is the map."

"You seem to have a good handle on this," said Cyprian.

"My father was a scholar," said Veronica. "He studied history, specifically the early Sovereign era. He never stopped talking about it. I guess that's how they found him…"

Basil traced his hand over the rough parchment, fingers passing between the amulet, staff, and crown.

"So, what do they do, the relics? Why bother hiding them? Or finding them?"

"Like Anne said, they help to unlock the power of the Sovereigns. High Sylvan," said Veronica. "It says *'to make the Sovereign find his voice'.*"

"Right," Cyprian said. "High Sylvan. A language that can control nature."

He would have normally scoffed at the idea of High Sylvan as a fantastical daydream of those who missed the days of Sovereign rule, but Anne Stormalong had eradicated any chance of that.

Veronica read from the Rule's cover again.

"The Sovereign's heart, in living sea,
'Neath bleeding elm and twisted tree
Only one and one alone
Lonely is the shadow throne"

"It doesn't mean anything to me," said Basil, his brow furrowed. "I don't know of any elm species by that name…"

"The Living Sea. That's only a few days west of us," said Cyprian. Basil and Veronica looked at him, eyebrows raised.

"The Living Sea," he said again, pushing the Rule aside to expose the relevant section of the map beneath, a dark circle enclosed with trees. "The Osmanthus. It's a forest about three hundred leagues from here. Dangerous place, filled with wild men and trees as old as the earth. They say the bottom of it is so dark, the creatures there are blind."

Basil nodded, his eyes full of doubt and fear. He looked very un-king-like to Cyprian.

"It's a start," he said.

CHAPTER FIFTEEN

"Reach for it, Spacklebrook!"

"Aye there, boy, stretch out those long chicken arms!"

"And remember to keep your mouth shut, or you'll wind up with a bug in your- Oh, look there, what did I tell you?"

Basil pushed open one of the galley's small portholes in time to see a sputtering Burt Spacklebrook go sailing past the hull, upside down, apparently gagging on a large, winged insect. A thick rope ran from his ankles to the winch above. A number of windburnt faces poked over the gunwale, looking on with interest. Even Cyprian's old kestrel was perched on the winch boom. As best as Basil could tell, Spacklebrook was integral to a scheme for catching some of the succulent purple fruits that were clinging to the lush treetops in thick bunches.

"Now come on, Spacklebrook! Reach like a man!" McElhaney's called from above. "Make that old mother proud!"

"We should've signed her on," said Bartholomew Oakum. "We'd probably have better luck dangling her over the side!"

In spite of the gale of laughter from the deck, Burt Spacklebrook sputtered even louder as a bunch of leaves whacked him in the face.

"You fellows come down here and try if it's so blessed easy!"

Basil couldn't help but grin as he latched the porthole. He returned to the business of lunch, stirring more rosemary into a pot of white beans.

"Has he caught anything yet?" Veronica asked, not looking up from the Rule of Sylvanus.

She sat on one of the benches in the empty galley, a small pile of dates on the table in front of her. She chewed them thoughtfully as she turned the pages. He and Veronica had spent the last few days poring through every line of the poem, but there was little progress.

"No," said Basil. He glanced out the porthole again. "Looks like it's not going- ooh."

"Hit a branch?"

"Another bird. This one is a little more pecky."

Rather than dwell on Spacklebrook's misfortunes, Basil shifted his gaze to the forest that skimmed along beneath *Philomena's* keel. The Osmanthus was a wonder, a Living Sea if there ever was one. The leaves of the treetops were not rugged or pine-needled like those in Misericordiae, but flat and broad, endless green occasionally streaked with yellow. The boughs undulated like waves in the constant rush of the warm wind. Occasionally, the airmen caught sight of marmots catapulting themselves across the canopy, snatching dragonflies and greedy handfuls of fruit before vanishing back into the dim understory. Once, an enormous roc burst out of the treetops ahead of them, the blast from its colossal tawny wings blowing the ship yards off course. With every spare minute between meals, Basil was on deck with his vials, capturing any specimens of butterfly or leaf that happened to blow on board. He even had Veronica draw a few sketches of the creatures they saw, which she did with much applause from the crew.

Lightlas had ordered the ship down low over the forest, so that the topmost layer of vegetation nearly brushed the underside of *Philomena's* hull. Lookouts on both sides of the ship were ordered to look out for an elm and a yew tree, growing near one another. But, the last two days had yielded nothing, save a memorable moment when a marmot had darted over the side and led the crew a merry chase through the main hold.

"Basil, did you read this opening story?" Veronica asked, flipping through to the beginning of the Rule.

Basil nodded. He had read it many times.

"Read it again."

Veronica nodded, swallowing another date before beginning.

"In the last days of the Old World, the shepherd Sylvanus lived with his herds on the Fields of Carath. He drank from the streams, slept beneath the trees and the stars, guiding his sheep in birth and death. Even as a young man, he was known to be wise, and people walked many roads to ask his counsel. In those days, men worked wonderful deeds, because they were young, and had not yet forgotten the words that knit the world together.

"For many years, all was well. Then one day, black ash fell from the sky and the first wild-eyed refugees appeared, stumbling sick and injured to the Fields of Carath through the mountain passes, their dead left behind. Sylvanus knew that the Old World was crumbling. The greed and fear of that age was spilling over. In the north, king rose up against king, lord against lord, brother against brother. With the words, they wrought evils that could not be opposed or understood, living storms that plowed down crops and destroyed cities, invisible assassins, and most horribly, phantom armies made of tortured creatures long dead. The evil had not yet breached the Fields of Carath, but its pollution crept in anyway, a prophet of doom. As the grass withered and the streams turned black, Sylvanus's sheep sickened and died. Sylvanus, with all his wisdom, could not save a single one.

"And so, Sylvanus buried the last of his sheep and went off by himself. He knew that the weapons of the Old World were crafted from the words that formed the world, twisted by man's pride and greed. And so, it was only the words that could turn the evil back upon itself. Sylvanus determined that he would learn these words.

"In the morning, he walked beneath the trees, and listened to their murmuring. He learned to recognize their low, sweet hum of their voices. When he asked, the trees gave him a straight staff of elm wood. With the sun high, Sylvanus bent down to the last clear stream of the Fields, a tiny trickle of clear water. He heard it whispering, and whispered back. At his lips, the waters parted. And in the stream's tiny bed lay a smooth, green stone. That night, Sylvanus lay beneath the stars, and they glimmered with their silver light. Their speech was high and clear, the hardest of all to learn. But Sylvanus was patient and wise. And when he called, the stars sent a part of themselves streaking over the heavens, a piece of molten silver that smote the earth a mighty blow. Sylvanus fashioned from this into a bright, round ring.

"When Sylvanus awoke, the meager sunlight was red. Ash rained from the sky like hoarfrost, and the grass was brittle and dry beneath his feet. The far mountain ranges crackled with fire. And over the peaks of the mountains, dark shapes came. Sylvanus held the staff of elm in his hand, the river's stone on a leather strap around his neck, the star's ring on his head. And, gazing into that red dawn, he spoke the words that had formed the world, words that mortal men had twisted. With their power, he turned the corruption of the Old World back on itself, locking it away beneath the Fields of Carath.

"It was upon that morning that the Sovereign Dominion of Cor Nova was born and the Rule of Sylvanus was written."

Basil shook his head as Veronica sighed and closed the book with a thump. As tantalizing as the story was, it still held no answers. Clearly, the three relics were mentioned: the Elm Staff, Riverstone Amulet, and Astral Crown. Beyond that, it left Basil feeling only more confused.

There was another shout of encouragement from the deck, and a boo of disappointment as Burt Spacklebrook swung past a choice purple fruit once more.

"Do you think Lightlas or Cyprian has caught wind of all this?" Veronica asked, letting her gaze drift up towards the porthole.

"I suppose not," said Basil, carefully slicing wedges of salted pork. "I can't imagine that dangling one of the crew over the treetops would be something Cyprian would particularly like."

Veronica shook her head.

"Not unless he came up with it himself."

They heard a loud shout from above, and some apologetic scrambling.

"Ah, there it is," said Basil.

But the ruckus didn't subside. There were a few loud creaks, then urgent voices, then panicked shouting.

"Something's wrong," Basil said. He pulled the handle that loosened the stopper in the clay jar beside the stove. It glugged, releasing water into the oven compartment, filling the galley with steam. Stopping only long enough to seize his medical box, Basil dashed after Veronica into the corridor and up the stairwell.

The deck was in a state of utter chaos. All of the men were gathered around the winch, yelling as the great assembly of wood and rope groaned under some great weight, its line stretched into the canopy.

"Something's got Spacklebrook!" McElhaney yelled to Basil as he charged past, coils of rope slung over his shoulder.

Basil could see Cyprian at the front of the press of men hauling back on the line, still berating the men even as they struggled against the unseen force dragging Spacklebrook down.

"What blessed foolishness…?" Francis Lightlas roared, emerging from the cartorium.

Suddenly, there was a buzz and whistle in the treetops beside them. A hail of small black objects whizzed out of the trees to *Philomena's* right and left, trailing thin cord. They arched over the envelopes, draping the thin ropes over her. Then, they began to tighten.

"Sweet drunken stars…" said Paschal as the rigging groaned above.

In an instant, Cyprian's deckknife was flashing in his hand, his storm-grey eyes alight with danger.

"Keep pulling Spacklebrook up!" Lightlas cried, waving a deckknife. "The rest of you, cut the lines!"

With a scramble of knifes and hooks, half the men charged to the gunwales, hacking and slicing at the cords that netted the ship. The fiber, though thin, was tough. By the time Basil had sawed one away, his arm was aching. Veronica, on the other hand, was a whirlwind. Her rapier, which Lightlas had returned from a weapon's locker, sliced through three lines at a blow.

A second wave of the cords arched over *Philomena*, and then a third. Their grip on the ship tightened with each passing second. Even with all the airmen slicing away and Veronica's rapier singing, it wasn't enough. Basil could hear the sound of branches scraping against *Philomena's* hull.

"They're trying to pull us under!" Lightlas called. "Oakum, give her all the rise we have!"

Oakum shouted his assent from the shipcore, yanking open the valves that released aether into the envelopes. The canvas burgeoned until the overflow valves gasped and vented aether into the sky. The ship sank even faster. Yet another wave of the lines bound *Philomena* even tighter.

"It's useless!" said Veronica, driving her rapier through another set of lines.

Lightlas rang the bell at the helm.

"Toll to quarters!" he roared. "To the guns! Whatever's down there is about to realize it's made a mistake!"

Racing to load muskets and pistols, the airmen ducked as the first boughs of the trees cleared the gunwale, branches springing inward toward the deck, flinging leaves and blossoms everywhere, pulling through the rigging and scraping on the underside of the envelopes. With a crunch, the foliage closed over the ship. The ropes went slack, hanging limp over *Philomena's* gunwales. All was still.

The air beneath the canopy was hot, perfumed, and still, and the light shone down through the treetops in mote-stricken shafts of gold, illuminating twisting trunks, succulent mosses and, and flowering vines. The faint hum of insects and the distant call of birds echoed through the treetops. The dappled light left shadows, twisting among the seemingly endless boughs.

Suddenly, the buzzing of the lines filled the air again, and Basil was whipped off his feet, now bound together by intricately braided, green fiber. His head struck the deck, knocking his spectacles askew. In the blurry chaos that followed, Basil heard a cacophony of voices rising from the deck around him.

"Curses to the blazes! Masterson, my knife. Grab my knife!"

"Did anybody see where they came from? Did anybody....erf..."

"The guns!"

The rims of Basil's glasses were poking into his mouth, and he worked his lips, pushing them back up towards his face. Finally, with a lucky toss of his head, he was able to get them back onto his nose. Through the crystal lenses, the world came back into focus.

Green lines criss-crossed the deck like a spiderweb, and the crew wriggled beneath them like flies. Cyprian, cursing loudly, was pinned beneath Oakum and several others. Paschal, and McElhaney were tightly lashed to gunwales, others splayed across the deck and against masts. Shipmaster Lightlas was prone on the deck, apparently knocked unconscious against the helm. A dozen strong lines bit into Benttree's muscle-bound arms and chest as he practically rocked the ship with his struggling.

Veronica, though trapped against the steps leading down from the command deck, was perfectly still, looking out into the forest around them. Creatures were stirring in the boughs of the lush canopy, shadows of moss and lichen, lean shapes with bright eyes. They wove through the trees as nimble as fish in a stream, supple and swift. In skillful hands, they held tight the lines that lashed *Philomena's* crew to the deck, running them out and taking them in as they moved around the ship. Casting lines up into the treetops, they swung into the void.

Midnight-silent and feather-light, they lighted on the rigging and skipped to the deck on bare feet, bodies bent in a lean crouch. It took a moment for Basil to determine that they were, in fact, human. They wore tunics woven from bark, lichen, hanging vine.

Basil could just barely see Cyprian, who was trying mightily to extract himself from beneath Bartholomew Oakum.

"You'll get off my deck!" Cyprian said to the interlopers between clenched teeth. "If you know what's best for-"

One of the forest men lashed out with a line that wrapped itself tight around Cyprian's neck, leaving the young officer sputtering and red.

With a few muttered words between them in a lilting tongue, the strange men set about collecting the crew, forcing them into a group near the midship line. One of them loosened Basil's bonds, only to throw him in between Cyprian and McElhaney, rebound at hands and feet. Another forest man appeared over the side of the ship, bearing on his shoulder a bundle that Basil recognized as a remarkably purple-faced Burt Spacklebrook. A few of the captors stood guard, glaring down at the crew with eyes that were delicate brown flecked with amber. In the breaks of their mossy armor, Basil could see tattooed red whorls on their forearms and legs, somehow giving their light, freckled skin the texture of leaves and dappled light.

The rest of the forest men stood up around the edge of the gunwale, whirling their lines in a green blur above their heads. Then, in a near-mechanical sequence, they released them into the shadowy light of the forest, so that they wrapped tight around nearby trees. Then, alternating back and forth, they pulled on the lines and *Philomena* began to slide through the canopy.

Despite their circumstances, Basil couldn't help but wonder at the Osmanthus, the Living Sea. If it was majestic in its vastness above, a whole new world erupted below. Trumpeting flowers with blossoms bigger than Basil's head stretched up and down the canopy in vines, and birds with voices like trilling flutes called through the undergrowth. There were pearl-skinned lizards, swarms of emerald beetles that swirled and sped off into the undergrowth as the ship advanced, long-necked cranes that fed from pools collecting in the treetops. There were whole kingdoms of species that Basil had never seen or even read about.

Hours passed. Basil tried to track the sun across the sky, but it was getting more and more difficult as *Philomena* sank deeper into the green and the boughs grew thicker above. But as the daylight expired, the trees began to thin out. The tangled growth of boughs gave way to truly massive trunks, rising like mossy columns through the murky twilight.

Finally, they stopped. One of the forest men stood on the bow, giving a high ululating shout that rose and held, a single note ringing in the vaults of the forest. After a moment, an answering shout came from up ahead, echoing through the trees. And, as though a key had been turned, the Living Sea blossomed with light.

In the midst of the soaring trunks of the Osmanthus giants, a thousand lanterns and braziers caught fire, forming starry pinpoints in the murk. The light soared up to the canopy, revealing an immense, multi-tiered scaffold that embraced the moss-covered trunks high above the dark forest floor. Winding walkways and rope bridges connected towers and soaring halls made of bark, wood, and woven fiber. Some of the trees were carved through their hollow centers, supporting multiple exquisite levels. Above and below, laughing children swung on vines between bridges, walkways, and porticoes. Birds wild and domestic called softly in the night and the air smelled like nectar, aromatic woodsmoke, and herbs that Basil could not identify.

Torches in immense baskets suspended from branches above illuminated hundreds of faces. The people had light, freckled skin, with curly copper hair that was tied back with braided bands. They came pouring out of doors, down rope lines, springing from tree and branch.

Philomena's captors brought the ship up short, and without a word to one another, each man roughly seized a captive, gripping them tightly around the chest.

Basil felt his heartrate build as he was ground against the mossy breastplate of a forest man, locked in the iron embrace of his muscular arms. Along with several of his compatriots, the ranger stepped up on the edge of the gunwale, cast his line out into the treetops, and leaped into the misty abyss toward the waiting city. The thick, perfumed air of the forest streamed past Basil, and he was vaguely aware of the moaning of Burt Spacklebrook somewhere below him and to the left.

In seconds, there was a clatter, and a hard deck was beneath Basil's feet. They had landed on a well-lit platform at the edge of the city. All around him, the rest of the rangers and *Philomena's* crew were landing amid the lanterns and eagerly peering crowd, all chattering in the same strange tongue. They looked on with interest as Spacklebrook vomited loudly, and when Hugh Benttree, flown by four rangers in formation, was deposited hog-tied in their midst. A rough stretcher was brought for Lightlas, who was still unconscious.

Finally, once all were assembled, they were marched through the city, and Basil couldn't keep his eyes from roaming. From the endless platforms, twisting walkways, and monstrous tree trunks, Basil heard piping music and smelled the scent of meat cooking over braziers. Everywhere, they were watched with extreme interest.

After several minutes, they came to a tree that was bigger than all of the others. At its center, a great natural doorway, inscribed with runes at its edges, yawned inward. In a line, they were led through. The walls of the great elm (as Basil identified it) were carved with scenes of victorious battle against fearsome creatures lurking in the forest deep. Finally, they emerged into a large room, roughly circular, lined on each side with more ornate carvings that stretched up to a ceiling dotted with fireflies, flashing azure and gold in the dimness. The crowds were gathered around the center of the hall where there was a great stone basin on a mighty carved plinth. Curls of steam rose from the green water, filling the air with exotic perfumes and the smell of burning charcoal.

Like a pale leviathan rising from the sea, a man stood up from the basin, steaming water running over the whorled tattoos on the white freckled skin of his arms. He was of middle age, with a large head and aggressive red eyebrows. He crossed his tattooed arms above his prodigious belly, surveying the crew of *Philomena* as the rangers marched them before him. He licked his pouty lips, and smiled broadly, as though awaiting an introduction. The crew looked to their unconscious shipmaster, and then at each other. Cyprian stepped forward.

"Sir," he said, making a small bow to the man in the basin. "I believe there's been some kind of mistake. We're merchants, under the protection of the Imperium."

"Ha!" said the man, slapping his chest and sending water droplets scattering.

The people laughed as well, nudging each other and gesturing at Cyprian.

"Who is this manling that he speaks for you?" the man in the basin asked. "He is your chief, this beardless boy? Tell me, manling, do you see the Imperium here? You think Titus is hiding in my bath, yes? I am the only one who rules here. I have many names, but in your tongue, I am Samuel, Lok of the O'Larre. You will tell Lok Samuel your business. Why do you come to the Living Sea? Perhaps I can help, indeed."

Basil thought it unlikely that this chief wanted to help. There was a glint to his eye, a fleck of iron in his smile.

"We are simple merchants..." said Cyprian. "Lost..."

"Ha!" roared Lok Samuel. "And you deal in what? Treetops? Flowers? Marmots, yes? You have been flying over the Living Sea for two days. You seek something different, yes? Something hidden, yes?"

A tiny servant lady shuffled beside the stone basin, holding a large wooden platter crawling with a pile of blue speckled beetles. The Lok reached out and scooped up a handful, popping them into his mouth and crunching loudly. He looked down on their silence with a victorious, lip-smacking grin.

"I have guessed correctly," he said. "But there is little to be found in the Living Sea, save what is alive, and few men come looking for that. There is only one place where an outsider may come seeking treasure. The Bleeding Elm, yes."

Basil immediately caught Veronica's look. *Bleeding elm and twisted tree.*

"Yes," said Veronica immediately, forgetting herself in the moment. "What do you know about it?"

"Your servant girl speaks for you now?" the Lok said, whipping his fingers through the green water to clean them of beetle pieces. "The places outside are getting stranger, indeed."

Veronica's fists clenched.

"I am NOT a…"

"CLEARLY," Cyprian continued, taking another step forward and bowing again. "You are a most discerning and wise king. As you guess, we would be interested in learning more about this Bleeding Elm. I'm a businessman. We could reach a deal."

"Ha!" The Lok smacked his great white hand against the surface of the water, spraying water into Cyprian's face. "We will reach a deal, indeed. But you are in *my* city, interrupting *my* bath. So, I shall make the deal, and you shall agree to it, yes?"

Basil had to give Cyprian credit. It is hard to look resolute while dripping, but the young deckmaster did his level best. The Lok selected a spindly insect from another tray, plucking off its legs and eating each with a loud crunch.

"The Bleeding Elm," he said around a writhing leg. "Is a tree, yes, once one of the Twelve Giants, a brother of the one in which we stand. Before the corruption took it, it stood over the tomb where all of our dead slept. Many generations, many years. When I was a younger man, a Bookkeeper came to see my father, then the Lok. He was tall and thin, and spoke like a man learned in your ways. He paid my father to place a treasure deep in the crypts of the Bleeding Elm, a treasure that a worthy one would come to find, yes?"

"Are we the first?" Veronica asked.

Lok Samuel paused, considering her a moment. Then, he flicked a chitinous bit of insect away.

"Maybe so, maybe not. That is not for Lok Samuel to say."

Basil shifted uncomfortably, and mustered up the courage to speak.

"Lok Samuel," he said. "What about this tree is corrupted?"

Lok Samuel looked at Basil, seeing him for the first time. His intelligent eyes narrowed. Then, like a tremendous boulder falling to earth, Lok Samuel splashed back into the basin, sending waves of green fragrant water cascading over the edge of the basin, soaking Cyprian's boots.

"So many questions, yes!" bellowed the Lok to the whole chamber. "Here in the trees, we have little use for silver or gold, but my artisans could use it to drape my women with sunlight and moonlight. I will show you the Bleeding Elm. Should you return with the treasure, you will give me my share, and I will let you on your way with your old ship. Should the Elm take you, I will keep your crew and your ship. It would be a lesser addition to my collection, yes."

"And what is the amount of your share?" Cyprian asked. "If there is a deal, there must be terms."

"Three pieces of every four," the Lok replied, gesturing with thick, pruny fingers. "That is the Lok's share. You will keep one piece out of four. And your lives. That is a generous arrangement, indeed."

"And what if we refuse?" Cyprian asked.

Lok Samuel looked at Cyprian for a moment, as though he didn't understand. Then, he roared laughing, the water rippling as his belly wobbled with delight.

"I don't believe that you understand. I am the Lok. This is my deal. These men will stay here. Send the manling and his friend with the glass eyes if he wants to know more about the Bleeding Elm. Also, the servant girl. Maybe she will do their fighting for them."

The last they heard of Lok Samuel as they were marched from the throne room was a great bellowing laugh.

The basket was made of a woven mesh of heavy fiber. It swayed as Basil stepped aboard. Begrudgingly, the O'Larre had given Cyprian and Veronica their weapons, and Basil his wooden box.

"Only three blessed balls of shot!" said Cyprian, checking the pistol. "What am I supposed to do with this?"

Deaf to Cyprian's protests, a pair of O'Larre rangers in full garb stepped aboard, launched their lines down into the darkness, and drew them downward with strong muscles. The lights of the city faded as they descended. All around, Basil could hear the slithering in the trees, the faint rush of wings, the steady hum of insects. Finally, the basket struck the forest floor. The rangers drew out a pair of grey rocks that they struck together, lighting a trio of heavy torches from the cascade of sparks. Without a word, they passed these out and pushed the three off the platform. The basket rose until it was only a ghostly outline rising back toward the faintly glimmering city above.

Basil tried to get his bearings in the dark, misty world in which they had been thrust. Here and there, mushrooms shone a pale green, and algae a faint blue up the side of the monstrous, moss-covered elms. The light of their torches could barely penetrate the layers of mist that hovered around them. The air was thick with the smell of moist soil and decay.

"Well," Cyprian said, his boots squelching. "This is fabulous. And my feet are wet. Lok Samuel and his bath."

"I've met lots of men like him," Veronica said, with an edge to her voice that Basil was relieved Cyprian did not pick up on. "Still, I suppose we're going where we'd like to be. To the Bleeding Elm."

"That's one way of looking at it," said Cyprian, lifting his torch higher and peering into the mist. "Personally, I'd rather go with some trained, competent airmen at my back."

"You could do worse than Basil and I," said Veronica.

Cyprian shrugged, not looking convinced.

"This looks like a path. Come on. I'm sure whatever is going to eat us down here would prefer a moving target."

Cyprian started off on the pale stripe of ground that meandered off into the darkness.

It was well packed, once beaten by the passage of many feet. As they went along, Basil could only think of funeral processions, of the O'Larre bearing their dead with slow, lilting song through this dark, misty underworld.

After a few minutes, Basil heard the rushing of a river beneath them, as though they were walking on a cliff. Then, the sound faded into the steady hum of the forest night. Basil had the sense that things were prowling through the darkness, taking wing above, burrowing far beneath. More than once, Basil thought he caught a glimpse of clusters of orange eyes in the farthest reaches of their torchlight. He tried desperately not to think of witch-bears.

Finally, they came to what seemed to be an immense wooden wall, caked with lichen and moss. Basil raised his torch higher.

"A wall?" Cyprian asked.

"No," Basil replied, running a hand along the rough surface. "A root."

As one, they looked up. A rare lance of moonlight shot through the canopy above, illuminating an enormous elm that ended about fifty yards up in a jagged crown of splinters. From the crevasses in the horny bark, crystallized rivers of sickly orange sap flowed out, washing over the roots and covering the forest floor with a hard, orange stickiness. Basil had the feeling that he always had when seeing a body, still and silent, a shrunken shadow of itself. Veronica and Cyprian looked pale in the light of the torch. Cyprian had reflexively drawn his pistol.

"Are you going to shoot the tree?" Veronica asked, a small smile tugging at her lips.

"I haven't ruled it out," Cyprian replied, reseating the pistol, somewhat red in the face. "I'd say this looks a lot like a Bleeding Elm to me, wouldn't you?"

Basil nodded.

"An elm, certainly. Once very large, then very sick, now very dead. What could have killed a tree like this… I don't know."

Basil swallowed. These elms were mighty creatures, carved from the very bones of the earth and as old as Cor Nova, some said. To kill one was no small matter. And, if they were right, the Riverstone Amulet of Sylvanus lay somewhere within. Or beneath.

"Didn't the Lok say something about going in?" Cyprian said, scouting up and down the root. "There must be an entrance. Unfortunately."

It took a long time to find it. Basil felt like an ant as they navigated around the labyrinthine roots of the tree. More than once, they nearly stumbled into immense crevices in the ground left by shrunken roots. After half an hour of searching, Veronica spotted it. In the crux of the two largest roots, there was a rough circle of blackness. When Cyprian swung the torch into the gap, Basil could see an opening. A set of carved steps led off into the darkness, heading under the dead tree.

"Oh joy," murmured Cyprian.

"No more dangerous than flying on a ship thousands of yards in the air," Veronica said.

"As a general principle," Cyprian said. "I prefer to keep the earth at a distance."

The passageway was wide enough for two to walk abreast, but they went single file. Cyprian led the way with pistol and torch, with Basil in the middle and Veronica bringing up the rear, rapier in hand. Basil made rapid note of the surroundings as he passed. The rock beneath their feet was a grey limestone streaked with quartz. The heartwood above was black and rotted, dripping with moisture. Basil would have thought that being underground would remind him of home, but the tunnels under the tree were nothing like the mineshafts of Osmara. Everything here smelled of death and decay, and something sharp and unpleasant that Basil couldn't exactly identify.

The tumbled rocks and brittle roots of the underground were mixed with the bleeding orange sap that seeped down in frozen rivers from above. Endless fissures disappeared off into the darkness. Some were niches carved into the walls at regular intervals. They bore long, bundled shapes, and Basil could see traces of decayed vine and the brittle whiteness of still bones. Following the only path, snaking downward into the earth, they passed through crypt after crypt. This was a Bleeding Elm indeed. Now for a twisted tree.

"Blue hazes, look at this one," said Cyprian, lifting his torch over one of the niches. "I had a shipmaster once who had teeth like this. By which I mean none."

"Oh come on, Cyprian," said Veronica, pushing ahead. "Show resp- what is that?"

Basil looked around her shoulder. A long trail of something silver lay across the narrow passage. It was as wide as a man, glistening in the light of the torch, and emerged from one of the side passageways into a large fissure on the other side.

Cyprian bent down, smelled the substance and grimaced, then offered his slime-covered fingers to Basil.

"This kind of thing is your department. What do you reckon?"

Veronica reached out and touched the slime as well, her dark eyes straining to see in the torchlight. Basil rubbed it between his fingers. It had a thick, slimy consistency and the smell was musky and overpoweringly rotten. It made Basil's eyes water.

He flipped open his box and pulled out a vial. He scooped up a portion of the slime and funneled it into the vial before corking it.

"I don't know," he said. "I'll take some back to the ship."

"Fine," Cyprian said. "As long as it doesn't show up in dinner."

They kept on going. The passageway widened and narrowed as they went, sometimes leading off towards more niches and bigger chambers. Finally, they reached the largest chamber they had yet entered. It was surrounded on all sides with smaller doors carved into earth, rock, and root. Basil was nearly knocked over when Veronica stumbled into him, her face alarmingly pale.

"I…I think I need to stop," she said, leaning against the wall, breathing quickly. "You all didn't hear…voices, did you? Nothing like…"

"No. You're going crazy," Cyprian said. But he looked pale as well, the sweat glimmered on his forehead. His focus seemed distant. "We can't give up the ship…"

Basil felt himself, too, slipping. He reached into his pocket, felt the hard glass of the vial between his fingers. Even as the passageway began to swim left and right in his vision, a flash of realization lit up his mind. He had been stupid. So stupid! He should have known!

Then, the focus of this thought wavered, and the tunnel seemed to close in. There was Thon Black again, falling away into the darkness as Basil rushed down a dark tunnel. Sovereigns long dead danced in the fire of his mind. Desperately, breathing hard, he dropped his box to the floor and flipped the lid, fumbling through a series of packets. The words on them were blurred, obscured by darkness and fire. He would never reach the right one in time.

Basil fell to the ground and retched. He barely had strength to keep himself from collapsing against the rock. The tunnel grew small and distant, and the only thing he could hear was the crackle of flames, the rush of roaring darkness, and a low, far-off sound, echoing through the rock.

Slithering.

CHAPTER SIXTEEN

Titus sat on the Just Throne, a red pillar of indifference, looking down on Ambry.

"Have him brought here," the Imperium said to his guards. The chair was the only artifact of the Sovereigns that Titus had seen fit to keep. It was like him in a way: lifeless, marble, unflinching. A soft muttering ran through the court of the Imperium. Faces, some quietly jeering, others silent and stony, watched Ambry like grotesque statues. Their gazes were slimy fingers on his neck.

"My Lord Imperium, I had the man soundly punished..."

Titus silenced Ambry with a wave of his hand. After a few moments, the old shipmaster, Correll, was brought, his sniveling echoing in the Great Hall. He was red-faced and wore a rumpled uniform with no insignia. His jowls wobbled as he trembled in the Imperium's presence.

"My Lord Imperium... You will not believe what this indecent excuse for a man did to me. I was lashed to the mast... left to the elements...I have served you faithfully for many years."

Ambry tried to make eye contact with Correll, willing the old fool to stop sniveling, for his own stupid sake. Titus rose from the Just Throne.

"That is true, Shipmaster...Correll, was it? But it seems to me that you have allowed a known fugitive to escape. Is that so?"

For the first time, Shipmaster Correll saw the danger. His eyes grew wide.

"Yes, my Lord Imperium..."

"That is all I need know. Such failure has a price, I am afraid. But, as you say, you've served me faithfully. Throw him."

"What?" Shipmaster Correll asked, his face blanching.

With mechanical ease, the guards lifted the protesting Correll, dragged him to the nearest window, and tossed him, a simpering lump of supplication, over the brink. Then, a sound rushed through the Sanctum. Titus had risen from the Just Throne, his hand locked on the hilt of his black saber. The High Sylvan that sprang from his lips was high and cold, like icy wind over a mountaintop. It raced around the enormous columns, roared in the vaults of the Sanctum. It blasted outward, rushing over the brink into the depths, where the disgraced shipmaster was falling to his doom.

And suddenly, Correll was lifted back up to the level of the window, the wind tearing at his face as the rushing blast turned him over and over like a leaf in a storm. He was red-faced and puffing, his eyes wide with terror. He reached for the window once with pudgy fingers, but was thrown back by the gust.

"Don't look so displeased, Shipmaster," said Titus in normal speech, over the roar. "I have given you your due. As you say, you've served me for many years. I have given you an airman's death. In the air."

The Imperium spoke another word of High Sylvan. The phantom wind vanished, and Shipmaster Correll plummeted once more. This time, nothing caught him.

The Imperium mounted the dais back to the Just Throne. He reclined, knitting his fingers together and regarding Ambry. With a wave of his hand, he dismissed his court.

"Old friend, you think I am a monster," he said after the last shuffling feet had disappeared.

Ambry swallowed before he spoke, governing his mind, quelling his fear.

"I think you have done what is necessary."

Titus raised a finger toward Ambry, as though reprimanding a small boy.

"Clearly you don't. Otherwise, you'd have done it yourself and thrown the useless old waste over a gunwale as soon as I called you back to Carath. Now, to the question that must be running through your mind. I have given Correll his just desserts for failing me in apprehending Basil Black. But, you too have failed me. Shouldn't I do you the same courtesy?"

Ambry bowed.

"I live to serve your will, my Lord Imperium. As an officer of your Fleet, I stand ready to give my life in your service. However you may require it."

Titus stood up. A sudden, icy light was glinting in the Imperium's eye as he descended the dais, step by step. He drew the black saber, leveling the point at Ambry's chest.

"Oh, I don't think that's true. Is it, Ambry? We both know that this little charade of the gallant admiral only goes so far. Or have you forgotten?"

The black blade whipped through the air, but instead of tearing his life from him, the point of the blade gently rested against his cheek. High Sylvan rushed over Ambry, crackling through his brain like lightning, and sounds and images and smells erupted into being. The Sanctum flickered around him. Titus's gaze disappeared, but he could still feel it, watching over his shoulder.

Suddenly, Ambry was in another time, another place. He knew that his body was still in the Sanctum, but Titus had forced his mind to recede back to someplace forgotten, to memory. The night was cold; the dusky purple of the sky was turning to black, and the wind howled over distant, lonely mountaintops. Ambry's breath crystallized in the air in front of him, the wisps turning to silver in the light of his lantern. He glanced left and right. A string of lanterns juddered across the moor, a long line that disappeared on either end into the dark. They lit a pale strip of the grey rock and twisted shrubs of the Boneless Moors.

The young airmen bearing them were not clad in the red of the Imperium, but in the black and gold of the Sovereign livery, faces bared to the biting wind. These were not untried boys, but men, square of jaw and hard of eye. They had sworn upon the Rule, before the Riverstone Amulet, by the Elm Staff, under the Astral Crown. Their minds devoted only to duty, they advanced through the darkness, with sword and pistol at the ready.

Ambry stepped high over a rock, holding his lantern high. His limbs were supple, his eyes sharp. Closely cropped black hair framed his youthful face. To his right, a handsome youth with brown hair and bright eyes was marching with steel bared, his easily smiling mouth hard with concentration. His lieutenant's rank glimmered against the field of black on his shoulders. Titus, the brother of the Sovereign. The two walked side by side, brothers in arms.

Young, weren't we?

The Imperium's voice rattled through from outside, and then was gone.

The airmen stalked on, each man with his eyes fixed forward, watching. As the night deepened, the mists fell. The lights of the men were swallowed one by one, and suddenly, Ambry couldn't see anyone to his left and right, just darkness and his own meager lantern lighting up the fog. With every step, he thought he saw faces and figures emerge from the mists, only to have them fall away to nothing. Ambry listened, heart hammering, watching for the thing that dwelt in the mists.

"Titus," he whispered as loud as he dared.

"I'm here," said the Titus of the past, emerging anew from the mist.

"I can't see the others," Ambry said. "What do we do? Double back?"

Then, out of the mist, came a scream, guttural and piercing. Then another, closer. On the right, on the left. It echoed off the fog, muffled and yet terribly close. Ambry felt Titus's shoulder against his own, their blades drawn to meet whatever lurked in the dark.

"Stay in the light," Titus murmured. "Whatever you do, Ambry, don't go out of the light."

There was another scream, very close. Then came a silence that pressed down on them with a clammy cold.

Suddenly, it was upon them, something huge and black and cold, streaming out of the air, trailing the scream of its last victim. It was part liquid, part solid, and Ambry couldn't tell where the creature ended and the fog began.

Ambry's blade was up in a flash, slashing downward at the creature. It whipped away and circled them, screaming. Ambry caught the sight of a powerful, muscled leg, then a set of talons, a rattling scaled arm, propelling the thing forward. Its steps were juddering and strange, almost like a limp. It had the desperation of an animal that is more dangerous for its wound. Enormous shoulders formed the top of the creature, great reaching arms, beating wings, no head. It leaped, and it seemed to Ambry that a part of it devolved into mist as it came, reformulating and solidifying when it hit the ground.

Titus fired both of his pistols, their orange radiance stabbing the dark in two quick thrusts. The creature may have flinched, but it didn't stop. Ambry leaped at it with saber in hand, throwing his body to the left. The creature, stopped, regrouped, then came at them again. It lunged at Titus, bearing down upon him as he bore his saber upwards. But, the Sovereign's brother didn't move. He stood his ground, blue eyes fearless. Ambry opened his mouth, trying to warn his friend before the creature sliced through him.

Then, Titus did something Ambry had never seen him do before. They said that only the ruling Sovereign could use the full power of High Sylvan, but others of Sovereign blood could speak it at times of great need. And Ambry supposed it must be true, because Titus spoke High Sylvan into the rushing night. Bands of the mist solidified, tightened, swooping in from the air around them like silvery cords and snapping themselves around the creature. It screamed and struggled, headless shoulders surging against the bonds. But, still the beast came. Its clawed fingers, wrapped in silver filaments, reached out for Titus, to tear and rip and destroy. Titus swung his blade. The saber's ringing strike rattled every bone in Ambry's body, thundering across the Boneless Moors.

When Ambry opened his eyes, the mists were disintegrating, giving way to clear moonlight. Titus was on his knees, cradling his right arm, which was bent at a strange angle. Blood poured from a gash in his forehead, but he seemed oblivious. Instead, he was looking at the sword that was buried half its length into a boulder. The blade smoked, the leather of the hilt charred to nothing, the steel now a harsh and unforgiving black.

"Well," said Titus, with a grin, once Ambry had managed to get him to his feet. "Altogether, I'd say that went better than expected."

The moor faded into the darkness. High Sylvan sounded in Ambry's ears again, and suddenly he was nearly blinded by light. Another time, he knew, another place.

It was two weeks later. The Sanctum of Soliodomus was bathed in a cascade of colored light. The great windows of the galleries poured forth their scenes of victory, defeat, and struggle in golden yellows and emerald greens. The ceiling high above sparkled with constellations in azure and sapphire.

"And it was destroyed?" Lorus asked.

He was a relatively young Sovereign, with all the power of Cor Nova at his fingertips, resplendent in a green tunic embroidered with gold. His beard and his hair were a darker brown than his brother, but his eyes were the same clear blue. The Riverstone Amulet shone against his chest, the Astral Crown on his head, the Elm Staff in his hand.

"Utterly," said Titus, his fingers drumming against the hilt of his saber, now newly rebound in handsome black leather and silver.

"And you weren't able to gain any information from it?"

"Only what we saw, what we felt," Titus said, drumming more quickly. "Ambry and I both gave reports."

The Sovereign shook his head.

"I've read them. It's not enough. If this creature really was a Sidiom, we need to know something about it. Where it came from. Why it was apparently wounded."

"Well, I apologize," said Titus, an edge to his voice. "Next time, I'll stop it to ask questions."

Lorus shook his head.

"This is not a joke, Titus. Any time a piece of the Old World resurfaces, it brings with it turmoil unimaginable, the chaos and ruin of that age. We have to know where it comes from to know how to stop it in the future, should the need arise. That is the task that Sylvanus charged us with above all."

Fool, hissed the icy voice in Ambry's ear.

"Quite an observation for you to make from your throne," said Titus. "You weren't out risking your life to stop it."

Lorus stood up, eyes flashing.

"For the love of our mother, I'll allow you to reconsider that statement."

Titus gave a resentful bow and retreated from the Great Hall. With respect, Ambry did the same and followed. When they reached the Round Plaza outside, Titus stood against the balustrade and looked out over the white city of Carath, one hand on the hilt of his black saber, fingers resting against the guard. Titus had cleaned the blade and repaired the hilt himself. Ambry hadn't seen him without it since the Boneless Moors.

"Did you see me, Ambry?" Titus asked finally. "Did you see how I destroyed it? If that creature had come at anyone else, anyone but me, what would have happened? More death. It would still be ravaging the villages out there, maybe heading for a major city. Azimuth or Kwalz. Even Misericordiae."

Ambry's brow furrowed. It was unlike Titus to talk this way. He would celebrate his accomplishments when prompted by others, but it wasn't in him to muse on his own greatness. There was a hardness to him now, a bitter edge.

"It was an amazing thing to see," Ambry replied finally.

Titus nodded.

"Yes. It was. My brother would have tried to talk it to death, to communicate with it. Senseless. Anyone who was there knows the folly of that. You would think a Sovereign would be more considerate of reality."

"I'm an officer of the Fleet, Titus," Ambry said. "Far be it from me to know the Sovereign's mind."

Titus shook his head and gave a resentful snort.

"The Sovereign. My great brother, the benevolent Lorus. The wise Lorus. He may be older, but he's not wiser. I think one day, Cor Nova will find that her great king was not all she made him up to be."

Ambry didn't know how likely that was. The word around Soliodomus was that Lorus's child would be born within the month. And that boy or girl would inherit the Just Throne before Titus. Ambry looked up and down the plaza. No one was close enough to hear them. Such talk was likely to draw stares.

"The Sovereign is not the only man with influence in Cor Nova."

"Of course not," said Titus. He grasped Ambry by the shoulder. The old familiar light of his eye was back. The black mood had passed like a storm, leaving behind only Ambry's friend. "Thank you, Ambry. Well, we've returned the conquering heroes. It's time we celebrated like some. I think some drink is in order."

Again, Ambry felt the stab of High Sylvan in his mind, and the vision changed.

The daylight had faded, replaced by a torch in Ambry's face. The blaze of the torch passed by his bunk, racing down the length of the elegant officer's quarters in the Southern Courtyards.

"Fire! Fire in the Sanctum!"

There was no time for a uniform. Ambry seized his boots and his sword, polished to a sheen over the idle days awaiting his next assignment. A month had passed since their return to Soliodomus.

A small army of young officers was already pouring into the hallway, dashing out into the gardens of the Southern Courtyards. The Sanctum of Soliodomus loomed above them to the north, a soaring white giant against the night. The fire that escaped from the windows glimmered an unnatural blue at its edges. With a chorus of shouts, the officers tore off, some to rouse more men, others calling for ships with water to stem the blaze, still others heading directly for the Sanctum. Ambry was in this last group, but he had spent his youth crawling over all of Soliodomus with Titus. He knew every nook and every cranny. He took off through the alleyways.

He reached the Great Hall before anyone else. Ambry slashed through the burning timbers of the nearest side gate. As the burning timbers fell away, the sounds of war broke through. High Sylvan washed over Ambry, and a fresh gout of fire roared upward, this time a wall of searing purple. Layers of dense smoke choked the Sanctum, and Ambry stumbled over fallen pieces of masonry and fragments of colored glass. Another word of High Sylvan rolled through the hall, rumbling the pillars, shaking the floors, and driving Ambry to his knees.

Then, there was a break in the chaos, and Ambry saw a tall form in the midst of the smoke. The fire glinted off dark brown hair, and the figure raised the Elm Staff above his head. He roared a defiant unearthly syllable that sounded like the waves of the sea crashing against a rock, and from the thin air around him, a mist collected in a rotating ring, spinning and flattening and coalescing as the green water increased in density and form until a rotating wall of water surrounded the Sovereign Lorus.

A second voice rang in the high rafters, lost in smoke, and this one sounded like the eruption of a volcano. A colossal tower of flame erupted into the ceilings, illuminating the pillars in glowering orange.

For a moment, there was silence. The fire fell. The water rose. The two collided. Ambry barely had time to throw himself behind a pillar before, with a vicious roar, flame and water enveloped one another, sending a blast of steam, smoke, and rubble through the Great Hall. And then, he heard voices, speaking in common Sylvan.

"Titus!" cried Lorus, crouching on the ground, bleeding from his head, his robes in tatters. "Come out!"

Ambry peered around the pillar, drawing his pistol from his holster. Lorus struggled to his feet, the ceiling of the Great Hall arching up over him. A dark figure emerged from the midst of the steam and smoke. The smoke seemed to cling more closely to him. He wore his Fleet uniform, not black but a deep red, resplendent in his insignia, almost insolent in his control and calm. His saber was in his hand, glinting unnaturally in the light of the fires.

"Here I am," he said, a smile tugging at the corners of his lips.

"Stop this. Whatever is troubling you, we can end it. There's no need…"

"Oh yes, there is need," Titus said, his eyes unnaturally bright. "And now, I'm more powerful than you."

A word of High Sylvan, ringing with something dark, and a wind charged through the Great Hall, from the direction of the dais. In its center, it bore an object that fluttered through the breeze. The Rule of Sylvanus landed in Titus's hand with a thump. He smiled at his brother again. Lorus paled.

"What are you doing?"

"What I was born to do."

Titus tossed the book upward, setting it spinning into the air, and the saber sang through the air. The book hit the ground in two pieces, bleeding pages from its bindings.

Ambry couldn't believe what he saw. For centuries untold, a copy of that book had lain by the Just Throne, growing and expanding as each Sovereign added to it. And here it lay, a sad pile of lacerated paper twitching in the storm of unearthly battle. The Sovereign seemed to fade, to wilt. There was no rage in Lorus's eyes, only sadness. He slumped to the ground, picking up a half of the destroyed book.

"What are you going to do?"

"Everything," said Titus. He slammed his boot into Lorus's chest, smashing him to the marble. The Astral Crown and Elm Staff crashed to the floor with a ringing clatter, and Titus dangled the

Riverstone Amulet from the end of his saber. "You won't need these now. Goodbye, Lorus."

Ambry tightened his grip on his pistol, preparing to spring to action. What he would do, he didn't know. But, he had to do something. He dashed out into the Sanctum.

He had not come two steps when Lorus lifted his head from the floor, and caught sight of Ambry. The Sovereign, his hair singed and blackened, his noble face stricken with fear, reached out. His hand quivering, his blue eyes begging. The most powerful man in Cor Nova fixed his eyes on Ambry, his last hope. Then, a word of High Sylvan, harsh and abrupt as a mountain crag, rang out and Ambry was slammed onto his back. It wasn't Lorus's face he saw when he opened his eyes. It was Titus who looked back at him.

His friend's smile was a ghastly mask. The eyes bore down into his very soul, and Ambry felt fear, deep and animal, grasping with icy claws at his heart. His eyes not leaving Ambry, he raised his sword over Lorus. Ambry felt as though his legs were stone. Every fiber of his being screamed at him to help the Sovereign, to throw himself under the blade, to die in defense of his king. But the fear took vicious hold, fear at dying at the mercy of this bizarre creature, fear at confronting Titus, his friend since childhood. And Ambry dropped his pistol and ran.

He ran as though a legion were after him.

He ran past smoke and flame and ruin.

He ran. But he couldn't outrun the words of Lorus that rang out from behind him.

"We're brothers. We're brothers!"

And then, Lorus didn't speak anymore.

There was a harsh crack of High Sylvan and suddenly, Ambry was back in his own boots, in the dark and sullen Sanctum.

He was standing before the Imperium, tall and severe in his red Fleet uniform, older and leaner. But, he wore the same manic smile, and he removed the blade of the black saber from Ambry's cheek. Ambry felt drops of blood run down his chin.

"Fail me again," the Imperium said. "And I will make sure that you die as you lived. Not Ambry the Admiral, but Ambry the Coward. Every man in Cor Nova will despise your very name. Now, go. And if you desire to not be crushed as I have crushed others, bring me Basil Black."

CHAPTER SEVENTEEN

"Well, Cyprian, my lad," said Augustus Fields, grinding his pipe between his teeth and slapping Cyprian on the shoulder with his great big hands. "It's a fine day to fly. A fine day if there ever was one."

Cyprian started. He was standing at his father's side, Augustus Fields at the helm of *Philomena*, flying her straight into an oncoming wind.

"Dad?" Cyprian said, and then the question came tumbling out, the one that kept him up at night. "Why did you leave?"

Augustus Fields laughed his big laugh, teeth like white tombstones behind his thick mustache. He reached into the pockets of his long red shipmaster's coat, drawing out a tobacco pouch to refill his pipe.

"Well, it's like I say, Cyprian, there's always gold to be had in Terra Alta."

Cyprian shook his head.

"No, I mean, why did you leave? Leave me? To go fight in the Merchant's Rebellion? Why did you choose the fight over me? Why couldn't I have at least come with you?"

The big shipmaster just laughed again, the great booming laugh that earned him his nickname. The Rooster.

"Oh, some things are hard to know, boy."

He relit the pipe, throwing the match up into the air so that the wind caught it and sucked it away over the stern.

"Like I say," he said. "It's a fine day to fly."

He laughed his laugh again, and with a sudden movement of his massive arm, he shoved Cyprian over the gunwale into the open sky. Cyprian cried out in fear and surprise, and the blue burnt to a dark angry purple as Cyprian plummeted.

The ground tilted up to meet him, an endless grassy plain. When he hit, Cyprian had expected it to be more violent, more painful. It really just felt he skidded for a moment, receiving a mouthful of grass. As he tried to spit out the incredibly bitter plant, and the whole world grew faint and watery. He nearly gagged when something shoved more of the grass into his mouth. When Cyprian opened his eyes, he saw a mouse bounding up to him, flicking its head sideways. In its paws was another handful of grass, which it shoved towards Cyprian's face.

"Cyprian!" it said, whiskers twitching. "Get up!"

The grassy plain flickered, giving way to dripping rock and musty air. Cyprian was in a dark cave, and suddenly everything came rushing back. Basil Black was leaning over him, and shoving a green leaf into his mouth, one hand on his jaw, forcing him to chew. Cyprian sputtered and choked, sending flecks of green onto Basil's vest.

"I'll- hrrk- rip your tail off and feed it to you, you-!"

"Please don't," said Basil, helping Cyprian to sit up. "Get your pistol."

With a groan, Cyprian managed to get himself onto a knee, trying to keep the world from spinning. The leaf was bitter between his teeth, but every time he chewed, he felt his head becoming clearer, his senses returning. His nostrils were filled with a heavy, damp scent, the smell of something rancid and rotten, growing more powerful with every second.

"What is that blessed reek?" he asked.

Basil pointed down the way they had come. Something was flowing wave-like out of the darkness.

It was tall as a man, rolling over the ground, the flesh of its glistening pale belly expanding and contracting at a rapid rate as it came. Luminescent green stripes ran down its back, flaring and flashing in the dark. Its mouth flexed, exposing row upon row of jagged teeth. Rapidly flexing appendages sprouted from its sides, each bristling with spines of dirty purple and green. It tensed its whole body, and leaped from the floor of the cavern to the wall, then launched itself to the ceiling before crashing back down to the floor, tendrils awhirl.

"What is that?" Cyprian said as he pulled himself to his feet, searching for his pistol.

"Venegast," Basil said, slamming his box shut.

"A what-the-bloody-heavens?!"

In front of it, half its height, was a single figure with rapier and torch. Veronica. She wasn't steady on her feet. The slime must have caught her as well. Cyprian cocked back the hammer of his pistol, and felt a small thrill. Time to be a hero.

Cyprian dashed down toward the end of the cavern, every other footstep betraying him, where the enormous misshapen lump of the venegast was sliding down its length. Basil was close behind, his box whacking occasionally against the wall of the tunnel.

"Aim for the head and stay clear of the spines! Poor eyesight but their smell is excellent, so quick movements. Don't stay in one place for long."

"How do you know that?"

"Books. I read books."

Even with chewing the herb, Cyprian struggled to keep a straight line. The world was swimming around him, the rocks shifting beneath his feet. The lights of the cavern morphed to different colors, and he suddenly felt sick to his stomach. He chewed the leaf hard, but he was half bent over by the time he reached Veronica. She was slowly backing away from the advancing creature, rapier point like a star in the lamplight.

"Stay back!" Cyprian called to her, gesturing with his arms.

She glanced at him, rapier point a-quiver. He was struck by how perfectly coiled her black hair remained, how she managed to look like she had just stepped out of one of her drawings. Could all girls do that? Maybe he just hadn't noticed before.

The creature was only a few yards away, and didn't show any signs of stopping. Cyprian caught a glimpse of a dozen unblinking eyes that stared out above the gaping mouth.

"You stay back!" Veronica said. "You're half out of your senses!"

"Oh yes?" Cyprian said.

With a smoothness born of practice, he drew his pistol from his belt, fixed his eye on the advancing creature, and fired. In the cavern well behind the venegast, a shelf of rock exploded to dust. Cyprian stood aghast. He missed. He never missed.

"Oh, that's blessed brilliant," said Veronica. "Basil-"

But, she didn't have time to finish the statement. The venegast let out a ghastly shriek, and lunged at Veronica with one of its appendages. It moved faster than Cyprian would have thought possible. Veronica swung, managing to deflect the spines that rattled along the wall, but the thing kept after her. She fell backwards, swinging upwards again and detaching one of the reaching arms.

Cyprian felt his senses sharpen, and gave himself over to instinct and reflex. He lunged forward, grabbing Veronica's sword hand. He wrenched the blade from her fingers and hurled it with all his strength.

The blade arced end over end toward the thing, flashing in the lamplight. It struck the venegast directly in the fleshy white warmth of its mouth, and dark blood bubbled and pooled, mixing with slime as it streamed down the creature's front. It emitted a strange guttural shriek and its appendages flailed, slapping against the rock, leaving long trails of silver slime. Finally, it slid to the floor, and its lights faded to a dull gray.

Cyprian went to help Veronica to her feet, but she shoved him away.

"What the blue hazes was that?"

Cyprian backed up. He had expected gratitude, not fury.

"Basil called it a vedeplast... I call it the most blessed horrible garden slug I've ever-"

"Not the creature. That stunt with my rapier! I had it under control!" she said, her dark eyes flashing. She went up to the venegast and yanked the blade from its mouth with fury, sending flecks of blood everywhere. "I had it right where I wanted it."

"Yeah," Cyprian retorted. "If you wanted it to be sucking the marrow from your bones."

Basil was leaning over the faded venegast, inspecting the creature with a careful eye.

"I've never seen a subterranean species like this," he said rather loudly, as though trying to divert the conversation.

"You think that just because I'm a girl, I can't be trusted to handle myself. I'll remind you that I got along just fine by myself for years before I ever met you."

"Now look here, miss prissy-"

"It can change the pigment in its skin, allows it to blend in with its surroundings. It probably lays these slime traps for victims, then retreats until the victim is unconscious."

"-pardon me if I wasn't thinking about your feelings when I saved your blessed life."

"Perhaps if I had been in need of saving, you arrogant prat!"

"MOST LIKELY SOME TYPE OF MOLLUSK."

"Just because you have a sword doesn't mean that you know how to use it."

The venomous glare that pierced Cyprian made him wish he was toe-to-toe with the slug again. Veronica seized the sword from Basil, handle first. The blade cut the air in one swift movements. Cyprian looked down, and his thick, leather airman's belt was on the ground in two pieces. Cyprian's cry was outraged.

"I've had that belt for seven years!"

"I've been holding a sword for longer than that."

"I apologize for interrupting," Basil said. "But there are almost certainly more of these creatures, and we'd never see them."

Cyprian glared at Veronica. She glared right back.

"We will settle this once we're not in moral peril," he said finally.

"Suits me fine," she said, sheathing her rapier.

"We may not see them, but we'll smell them," said Cyprian, wrinkling his nose at the putrid remains of the venegast. He collected the remains of his belt and threw it over his shoulder. "Let's find what we're supposed to find and get out of here."

They proceeded in icy silence. More chambers followed, one after the other, each crammed with nooks and bodies and the smell of death. They saw no more of the pale slime, or the fearsome beasts that dispensed it. Finally, they came to what appeared to be the end of the long corridor. The rock here looked rougher, unfinished. Only one nook went off the left. The other rock faces were bare.

Within the solitary mausoleum, shelves that would have held bodies were empty, with the exception of a single tomb that stood against the wall, a large oaken marker erected to cover the rock. The marker was sealed with wax around the outside. Veronica ran her fingers around the seal, then swiped her hand across the front of the sarcophagus. The dust cleared, revealing a bent, spindly tree carved into the wood.

"*Twisted tree*," said Veronica. "Bleeding elm and twisted tree."

Cyprian jammed his deck knife into the wax seal around the outside of the sarcophagus. It chipped away in a large, yellow chunk, revealing a crack in the stone beneath.

"I guess we'll just have to pray we don't meet Lok Samuel's old dead grandmother in here, won't we?"

Basil gave a half-hearted laugh, but Veronica shook her head and went to work on the wax. Within a few moments, the wooden door of the tomb was loose in its housing. With a nod from Basil, Veronica slid her rapier into the gap and pulled. With a scrape and a groan, the door clattered to the floor of the crypt. Darkness yawned beyond. All three of them peered into the gloom.

"Well, you know the proverb," said Cyprian. "He who kills venomous slugs doesn't have to go first."

"That's not a real proverb," grunted Veronica.

"I suppose it is now," said Basil, lifting his lamp ahead of him, stooping slightly, and going into the dark.

Cyprian was close behind. They entered a small passage, only big enough to pass through with head bent. The air was chilly and damp. Before the tunnel's ending, a niche was carved in the rock on the lefthand side. Set in the niches were silver lamps, each loaded with a braided wick and solid fat. They were fashioned with fine quartz panes, Terra Alta craftsmanship if Cyprian had ever seen it. A freighter full of these would earn a respectable pile of coin in Misericordiae.

Then, the passage opened into a cavern. It was big enough that the meager light of Basil's torch didn't reach outward to find the far walls. Instead, he stood in a sphere of golden light amid the gloom, peering into the darkness. A faint, low rumble could be heard through the rock.

Veronica emerged behind Cyprian, bearing a lantern she had plucked from the niche. She lit it with her torch, and the wick burst into lusty flame. The white fat in the base of the lantern quickly melted, yielding more fuel for the fire. She lifted the silver lantern high, and light poured out into the darkness.

All three gasped, and Cyprian's hand went to his pistol. The cavern was filled with people.

"Blessed heavens," Veronica said. "Statues."

Cyprian nodded, allowing himself to relax. The cavern was of the natural variety, its walls and floors and ceilings veined with pink and orange crystal, worn by the passage of time, the drip and flow of the earth's life blood. The statues stood upon ledges, stone feet in wells of swirling water, set in the many layers of the floor. There were at least a hundred, each as tall as a man.

Each wore a simple crown, a round amulet, a staff in one hand. The left hand of each was extended, fingers curled upward, as though beckoning.

"They're Sovereigns," Basil said. "All of them."

Cyprian looked at the inclined stone fingers, his mind whirling.

"They look as though they're supposed to hold something."

Cyprian retrieved his own lantern, lighting it with his torch and carrying it further into the chamber. He set the lantern on the hand of the nearest Sovereign statue. There was a crack and a boom that rocked the whole chamber. And suddenly Cyprian was enveloped in blackness and piercing cold, and a rushing, roaring monster tugged at his boots. Wet wind filled his ears. He felt something yanking at his collar, and he was heaved back onto the wet stone. Somehow the lantern was still in his hand, although the wick was dark and two of the panes were now broken out.

Gasping and blinking, he looked up to see Veronica, her face blanched white. Basil was behind her. He too seemed to have lunged, but he was either too far away or too slow to reach Cyprian. Before them in the floor, a gaping blackness remained where the statue had been. It had disappeared, along with the floor around it, down into the subterranean river below. Cyprian's hand was still entangled with Veronica's, and he hurriedly extricated himself. He helped her to her feet, and this time, she didn't resist him.

"Well," Cyprian said with a gulp. "I reckon we're even."

"I reckon so," she said, avoiding his gaze as she helped Basil up.

They all took a moment to breathe. Finally, Basil spoke, pushing his glasses up on his nose.

"So, the lanterns have to be put in the hands of the Sovereigns. In the right hands. The question is, which is right and which is wrong? We have to look for differences. Judging by the number of lanterns, we're looking for seven that are different from all the others."

Veronica and Basil began to scramble over every inch of the statue chamber. Cyprian did the same, but was soon tempted to give up in frustration. They were the same as far as he could tell. All were tall, with long beards, simple crowns, tall staffs, and amulets around their necks. At the feet of each, a book rested. They were carved of the same stone, identical in every way.

"It's the amulets," said Veronica, finally. She pointed to the round emblems around the necks of the statues. "They're different. Some of the details… look."

Cyprian and Basil gathered around. Cyprian saw no difference. Basil began to flip pages through the Rule of Sylvanus, which he pulled from a special slot in his medical box. He found an image of the Amulet, transcribed in close detail. Near its center was a large, ornately faceted stone, but all around the inner border there were constellations, animals, and plants, the sun and the moon. The clouds of the sky and the waves of the sea ran around the outside, weaving in and out of one another. Basil carefully examined the amulet on the statue Veronica pointed to.

"We have to find the true amulets. The ones that match the picture. There should be seven. This one looks to be correct. We have to be sure."

Carefully, Basil lifted his lantern to place it on the stone hand of the statue.

"Wait," Cyprian said. "Give me that."

He took the lantern from the bemused ship's cook, set its handle on the end of Veronica's rapier, and carefully extended the lamp out, guiding it onto the stone hand. The crack of rock didn't sound. The stone held firm, and the Sovereign statue held a lantern to light up the eternal night.

"Well," Basil said. "That's one."

It took over an hour to find the first four statues. Cyprian didn't find any of them, but they used his method to place the lanterns on each. The next two were harder and took another hour by themselves. Basil had shut the Rule of Sylvanus in exasperation for a fifth time when the smell of death and decay crept into the chamber.

"They're close," said Basil. "Or already here."

"Keep looking," Cyprian said, drawing his deckknife and watching the walls for morphing shapes. "Quickly."

The smell grew stronger over the ten minutes it took for Basil and Veronica to track down the final statue.

"Found it!" Basil said. He set the lantern on the last stone hand.

Suddenly, it was though a combination had been unlocked, as though a precise balance had been struck. The seven lanterns blazed like stars in the night, casting their beams through the quartz panels into the darkness, so that their rays glittered among the salt pillars that ran through the walls. They illuminated purple, green and pink, casting their radiance in pale shards of color.

The beams converged on a spot high up on one of the bluffs, rippling and spilling over the natural jutting of the rock. In the spaces between the strips of light, was the shadow darkness that formed the clear shape of a chair.

"*Only one and one alone,*" said Basil, the light sparkling on his spectacles. "*Lonely is the shadow throne.*"

But that was not all the light revealed. Dozens of shapes glistening with slime emerged from fissures in the rock. Appendages slapped against rock and shrieks filled the air.

"The light," said Basil. "It's attracting them."

Cyprian felt the hair on the back of his neck stand up.

"We need to go. Now."

"Not without the Amulet," Veronica said.

"It's just a necklace!"

"Don't talk nonsense. We need to get up there. Alive. Think!"

But the creatures were nearly upon them. Within seconds, they were backed against one salt-veined wall of the chamber, with half a dozen venegasts blocking their exit. More were appearing out of holes and seams in the rock, their skin rippling and mottling the colors of the stone. The smell was overpowering.

Cyprian checked his belt for the fifth time. Plenty of powder, but only two balls of shot. He had no weapon but his deckknife, and that was only good for one at a time at most. Veronica had her rapier, and Basil had nothing. At least, so he thought.

As Cyprian watched, a hunk of pink rock hit one of the venegasts directly in the center of its fleshy body. The creature shrieked and flailed, its flesh white and foaming where the rock had struck.

"What was that?!" Cyprian said.

"Salt from the walls," Basil replied, winging another hunk. "It irritates their skin. More from books."

Cyprian's mind began to race, turning over and over on itself, until an idea appeared.

"Basil, your books might just save us. Give me some salt. Quick!"

Hurriedly, Basil passed Cyprian a handful of small pieces. Cyprian rammed them down the barrel, crushing them to smithereens with his ramrod. Then, he picked the closest creature, aimed, and fired. A brilliant cone of fire and vaporized salt erupted outward. The chamber erupted into furious shrieking as the creature writhed and twisted, its flesh blanching a sickening white and the glowing stripes of its back flashing green.

Taking up the idea, Veronica smashed at the vein of salt with her rapier. She picked put up the fragments in her hand, crushed them as best she could, then flung them headlong into the oncoming venegasts, keeping the more aggressive ones at bay with the point of her rapier. Basil had somehow mixed the salt with something green from his box and the water that lay in pools beneath their feet. Wherever the droplets hit the venegasts, their skin foamed and smoked. The chamber was suddenly filled with shrieks and spastic flashes of venegasts, but they kept coming.

"Good!" Veronica said. "We need to go up the rock face! Towards the shadow throne!"

Cyprian saw no point in arguing. The things had already cut off their escape. If they were going to fight through, they may as well go all the way.

Foot by foot, inch by inch, they pushed forward. Burned venegasts lurched left and right, but new ones slithered over their fallen brothers in a seemingly endless stream. Flecks of toxic slime broke through here and there, and Cyprian wiped them off his sleeves as fast as he could, hoping their effect wouldn't take his mind. The barrel of his pistol was red-hot and glowing by the time they gained the top of the cavern, where the ghostly luminous throne shone against the rock.

Cyprian and Veronica covered Basil as he probed at the wall. There, in the heart of the shadow, where the chest of an occupant would have been, there was a ring of slightly paler rock.

"Here!" Basil cried above the din.

"Just get it!" Cyprian yelled back, slashing at the mass of lunging tendrils.

Basil reached into his pocket, pulling out a long, metal instrument with a thin blade at one end. Gently, he worked it into the gap, and worked free a smooth stone disc that fell out into his hand. Behind the disk, there was a cavity in the wall. Basil reached in, and pulled out a round object covered with a piece of thick, soft cloth.

"Come on!" Cyprian said, trying to find a way back down to the entrance tunnel.

"There are too many!" Veronica said. "There's no way through!"

The waves of venegasts pressed up toward them, flashing colors and brushing up against the pair of Sovereign statues. Cyprian picked up a hunk of rock, hefted it, and flung it. It met its mark, and struck the stone Sovereign's beckoning hand directly on the tips of his fingers. With a crack and roar, the statue jerked downward, taking a great piece of the floor, and a host of venegasts, with it. The rest huddled away from the rushing water.

"There!" Cyprian cried and ran for the gap, grabbing Basil by the arm and beckoning Veronica.

They skirted the roaring hole, leaping over rocks and dodging swinging spiny appendages. Cyprian saw the entrance of the cavern, where they had picked up the lanterns, looming ahead of them. He ran even faster.

They were making steady progress when a scream, a human scream, went up in the chamber. Behind them, Veronica had been surrounded. Her rapier struck and cut like lightning, but there were too many. A spiny appendage lashed out, striking her savagely in the stomach, another came out from behind, seeping poison into the back of her neck. They came closer; Veronica's lunges grew weaker.

"Basil!" Cyprian yelled. Behind him, the young ship's cook had lobbed a vial of green concoction directly into the maw of an enormous venegast. Its pale white vomit, streaked with dark blood, was smeared all over his waistcoat. Cyprian could see the lump of the Amulet outlined in his pocket.

"There's an opening! Up the passageway! Take the Amulet and go! Don't wait for us."

Basil opened his mouth, closed it, then ran.

Once he was safely past, Cyprian fired off another shot, blasting two venegasts approaching from the left, then he took off at a dash back toward Veronica. A venegast lurched into his way. With a flying leap, he slammed his bootheel directly into its skull, launching himself up and over the advancing creatures, slicing his deckknife through the appendage of a creature that was crawling along the ceiling.

For a moment, he hovered over the sickening creatures. Veronica's scream was fading. And, like an airship descending into the piercing mountains, he fell.

CHAPTER EIGHTEEN

Veronica slipped in and out of her dreams. The tall posts of her bed back in Terra Alta loomed high above her, stretching to the starry ceiling. Long ago, her mother had painted the constellations in silver on a dark blue field. Every night, she would point to them and tell Veronica stories. Stories about Ila the Sunmaid and Od the Snowkeeper, about the Three Hunters and the Silver Tree, about The Cobbler and the StarKing. Then, the stories about all the Sovereigns past, of Sylvanus and the Sidia, Proteus and his laughing gardens, gentle Analisa, proud and sad Sebastian, the twins Linus and Leos.

Now, shapes arched over her in a posture of concern. She felt the bed rustle underneath her, as though it were moving, but the constellations remained still. The shapes coalesced into a single one, slender and gentle. In the light of the stars, she saw her mother's face. Her mother, Amelia Stromm, with long brown hair so much like her own, her chin an easy slope of ivory. A silver pendant hung around her slender neck. Veronica tried to raise a hand to touch her, to grasp her arm. She could save her mother. Her father was gone, but she could save her mother.

"Do you remember the way to the basket?" her mother said, her face full of concern. "Back to the city?"

What basket? What city? Veronica tried to form the words, but her mouth wouldn't cooperate.

Then, another shape appeared from the darkness, large and squarely built. Even in his evening smoking jacket, Hector Stromm cut an impressive figure with his strong jaw and thick beard. One large hand wrapped around Veronica's mother's waist. He too looked down at his daughter.

"I think so," he said in his bass rumble of a voice. "As long as we retrace our steps on the path. There was another large elm further on…"

There was a thump and, all of a sudden, she was on the ground, thick muck and crawling things pressed against her cheek. Then, she was wrenched to her feet. She struggled to open her eyes; it was as though her eyelids were made of lead.

When she came to again, she was running down a dark corridor. The Imperium's soldiers, their masks glinting in the darkness, were pressing after her, boots hammering against the ground. Her mother and father were practically carrying her on either side. She could hear their heavy breathing in her ears.

"Basil!" her mother said. "She's getting paler! You have to give her some more of that leaf stuff."

"You focus on the venegasts," her father said in more measured tones. "I'll take care of Veronica."

Then, Veronica tripped. Her mother and father went spinning off into the darkness. Veronica cried out, frantically searching left and right. The soldiers bore down on them, masks flashing in the darkness. There was fire, the crackling and crumbling of books ablaze. And then, silence for a long time.

She thought she heard the lilting voice of a foreign tongue, the groan of wood and rope, the clamor of a crowd. Then, she felt something cold at her lips, a liquid with a bitter tang that was almost metallic. She felt like she was going to retch, but someone forced more of the concoction past her lips. Then, everything went black.

Veronica's head was pounding. She opened her eyes. She was lying on something smooth and warm. Above her, the ceiling glittered with blue and gold fireflies. The throneroom of Lok Samuel. A bitter aftertaste remained in her mouth, but the intense feeling of disorientation was gone. All around her, the men of *Philomena* were standing, bound and silent. Benttree had an O'Larre ranger on each side. Burt Spacklebrook was pale as a sheet. Veronica was relieved to see that Lightlas was now conscious, although slightly bruised and looking somewhat testy. Clip McElhaney noticed that she was awake. He extended a finger and raised an eyebrow.

"Hey there, girlie," he murmured. "You were in a bad way there for a moment."

A ranger tapped a knotted cord against his back in warning, and McElhaney fell silent. The O'Larre were quiet, attentive. Veronica had to peer through the legs of *Philomena's* crew to see anything.

The steaming stone basin had been drained, and an impressive throne carved from tree roots placed in its depths. It gave the impression of a blossoming flower, with the Lok at its center. His chest was bare, and the blue light seemed to make his tattoos luminesce. Serving girls bearing incense, steaming dishes, and carafes orbited him, but his eyes flashed discontent. Basil and Cyprian stood before the Lok, rangers at each side. Both were muddy, bedraggled, and pale. Cyprian seemed to be bleeding from his leg, and Basil looked respectably battered, his coat still covered in slug vomit.

Lok Samuel crossed his mighty white arms.

"So," he said. "You have returned from the Bleeding Elm, yes. If you have found silver and gold, you have hidden it well."

"There was no treasure," said Cyprian, hocking a blood-and-dirt flecked gob of spit. "Only your dead. And poisonous creatures."

The Lok shrugged.

"For many centuries, the Bleeding Elm is where the O'Larre have sent our lost ones to rest. The scourge that now creeps in those sacred halls keeps us out. My warriors have failed to take it. Many times, yes. An elm of the Living Sea is a hard thing to kill. Humans are a good deal more frail, as your woman almost found out."

Lok Samuel picked up an object from a platter in the hands of a serving girl. The Riverstone Amulet glimmered in the light. Its reflection cast faint speckles across the carved scenes on the throne room walls.

"A pretty trinket, yes. The bauble of Sylvanus."

"The only thing of value in the crypt," said Cyprian. "Unless you value bones and statues."

"Ha!" said Lok Samuel. He threw the amulet back onto the platter with a clang. "And so it is mine. As is your ship and your servitude."

"We had a deal!"

The guards around him immediately leapt between Cyprian and the Lok, who didn't seem disturbed in the least.

"And our deal is finished. I will claim three of the four parts of all the treasure you obtain from the crypt. This Amulet and your ship I will take as my share, your lives you will take as yours, yes. But, my physicians have saved your woman, and you have defiled our most sacred ground, yes. For these things you owe, and as payment, I accept your servitude."

The warriors moved in, lines at the ready to bind and take them away. Veronica tried to get up, but she was too weak, her head impossibly heavy.

"You're making a mistake," said Cyprian as the rangers surrounded him.

"Preachings are not becoming of a slave, manling," said the Lok.

But Cyprian didn't stop talking. He slung words like bullets, his only weapon.

"Are you afraid, Lok Samuel? Afraid of what is coming? Because you should be. Titus crushes all who don't submit to his rule. Don't give me that fool look. You may be the lord of the Living Sea. There may be no enemy you can't defeat in the trees. But do you honestly believe that Titus's Fleet will come that close? Let me tell you something, Lok Samuel: Forests burn."

There was a flood of angry murmurs from the crowd, but the Lok spread his hands for silence, his once jolly face now truly livid.

"Such words are not to be uttered in the Living Sea!"

But Cyprian didn't stop, he swung his finger around, indicating the whole city.

"When the Imperium Fleet comes here, they won't come through the treetops for you to pick off and tangle up. They'll come during the dry season, with barrels of red pitch. They'll light them with torches, roll them off a hundred ships. They'll fall on your forest like rain. And when they're finished, the liveliest thing in the

Osmanthus will be the Bleeding Elm. If there's anything left for your rangers to defend, they'll have to do it from a pile of ash."

The Lok was glaring at Cyprian in silent rage, but Veronica saw real fear behind his eyes. Cyprian pressed his advantage.

"That is what will happen to you, sooner or later, regardless of what you decide today. But I say why have one great enemy when you could have one great friend? A Sovereign is a powerful ally."

The anger in Lok Samuel's gaze didn't waver, but Veronica could see the cold shrewdness of a longstanding chieftain beginning to take over. He had clearly had suspicions about Basil from the start, and Cyprian had confirmed them. But, Lok Samuel played the fool.

"The Sovereigns are dead, indeed."

"Well that's clearly not true, indeed," Cyprian said, seizing Basil by the shoulder. "You have nothing to lose and everything to gain. Your fathers were allies to the Sovereign. There's no reason you can't be as well."

The Lok stepped over the rim of the bowl, handling his girth with muscular ease. He walked to Basil, looking him directly in the eye.

"And if you are the son of Lorus," he said. "What is it that you will do for me, boy who wishes to be Sovereign?"

Basil was silent for a moment, and the two regarded one another. Small and large. Black and white. Basil reached into his bag, and pulled out an angular hunk of pink crystal.

"Do you know what this is?" Basil asked.

Lok Samuel's eyes narrowed a bit, but he accepted the offered rock. After a cursory glance, he licked it.

"Salt," he said.

"Yes," Basil replied. "That is rose salt. There are veins of that running as wide as a man's hand in the rock underneath the Bleeding Elm."

The Lok's hand closed around the salt.

"But this is mine," he said. "You give me nothing."

"In your hand, you're holding the silver and gold you wanted. Rose salt is a preservative, an exfoliant, a seasoning with a hundred uses. And even now, it's a valuable commodity in any port city. You're also holding the key to the Bleeding Elm. Venegasts are naturally weak against salt; you hold the weapon that you could use

161

to drive them from the burial grounds of your ancestors. Certainly, it lay beneath your own ground, but I've told you how to use it. I give you knowledge, friendship, the key to a better life for your people. As Cyprian says, we're valuable friends. Who knows what else lies beneath?"

The Lok stared hard at Basil, rubbing the hunk of salt against his lip, the throne room silent as a tomb. It was Francis Lightlas who broke the silence.

"I believe," he said. "There's a fine cask of Terra Altan wine in the galley of my ship. We can drink to friendship."

The Lok nodded grimly. Then, his face erupted into his great toothy smile.

"Ha!"

With one muscular arm, he tossed the Amulet to Basil. It glinted, turning over and over in the blue light before landing in Basil's hands. Then, with great loping footsteps, Lok Samuel crossed the throne room, and enveloped Basil in a strong embrace, pressing him into his sweaty, tattooed chest.

"The son of Lorus returns to bring back the old ways, and the O'Larre will cheer him onward! A feast!"

The people clapped and smiled, and Veronica couldn't help but join them when she saw Basil do his best to not be smothered in the embrace, his face emerging with glasses askew from the tattooed arms.

The feast was a tremendous affair, beginning with the O'Larre slinging their ropes into the vines and branches above the city like a coven of weaving spiders. Then, there came woven squares, cleverly linked together by braids of fiber. Within moments, a great, shifting platform hung suspended in the canopy. The O'Larre hung lanterns and lit fires in stone basins. The forest night came alive with the smells of exotic foods and the lilt of whirling music.

Veronica couldn't sketch fast enough to keep up with the spectacle going on around her. As one, the O'Larre flipped and twirled and spun in their dancing, faster and faster around the fires. *Philomena's* crew did their best to keep up, with giggling copper-haired girls trailing them by the hands. McElhaney, Benttree, and some others roared with laughter at each surge in the reeling pipes and drumbeat. Francis Lightlas looked on with a cup of nectar in one hand, a small smile just showing behind his beard.

Veronica surveyed her latest sketch: lanky Burt Spacklebrook turning violently red as an O'Larre girl fluttered her copper eyelashes at him.

"It a good likeness," said Cyprian Fields, emerging into the lamplight.

The young deckmaster sat down beside her, his deckknife and oculus clunking on the platform. Petros fluttered down to settle on the tip of his boot. Veronica couldn't help but smile. They were similar in that way, Cyprian and Petros. In the sky, they moved with finesse and skill. On land, they were downright ungainly.

"Thank you," Veronica said. "Somehow, it's good to capture moments like that."

The beat of the music picked up as a few of the men joined in with their own instruments. The twang of Oakum's mandolin and McElhaney's concertina took up with the drums. Veronica cast a sideways glance at the young shipmaster. The lights of the feast were dancing across his golden hair, flashing in his grey eyes. He absentmindedly tossed some kind of fried rodent out of a bowl to Petros, who choked it down with gusto. She could tell that he was worried, thinking. Even when he was still, his mind was elsewhere, hundreds of yards in the air, soaring somewhere at a breakneck pace.

"Thank you," Veronica said.

"You already said that."

"No. I meant for everything in the Bleeding Elm. You saved us."

Cyprian grinned, pushing his hair back on his head.

"Twice."

"Now, don't go spoiling it. But really, you were very brave, even if you were a bit of a pig. I owe you."

Cyprian grinned. Now, he seemed more relaxed, almost relieved.

"Well, you weren't exactly quailing either. We did it together, the three of us."

"I suppose so," Veronica agreed.

A squat serving lady with a large bowl of shiny, red centipedes came around. Veronica politely refused, as did Cyprian. Petros pecked at one, then flew away. On the other side of the feast, Paschal and McElhaney were watching in fascinated horror as an O'Larre ranger crunched his way through an entire basket of baked spiders. Masterson munched a lizard on a stick, his face impassive, mustache bobbing up and down.

Basil was over by the biggest fire, doing his best to laugh when Lok Samuel slapped him heartily on the back.

"You really believe in him?" Cyprian asked, nodding his head toward the boy. "Really?"

Veronica looked at Basil again, now being forcibly dragged into the dance by a skippy O'Larre girl, apologizing profusely with every misstep.

"Yes. I do," she said. "I take it from that question that you're still on the fence."

"I don't know. It's a lot to take in. I suppose I expected the Sovereign to look different. Taller, definitely."

"He saves lives," said Veronica, tilting her sketchbook to capture a trio of rangers watching the celebration from the canopy. "And there's nothing fake about that Amulet. If Stormalong didn't have me convinced, that does."

"So, that means we're going to do this for real. We're going after the staff and the crown."

Veronica nodded.

"There's no turning back now. There wasn't any to begin with."

"And what about you? You're a stowaway, not on any records. You could slip away and never be seen again. What keeps you close to him?"

"It's...the right thing to do."

Cyprian snorted.

"What?" Veronica demanded, putting her sketchbook down. Cyprian's pale grey eyes searched her face, mocking her. She could feel her gratitude waning. They had been doing so well. Now he was going to ruin it.

"No one does that," Cyprian said. "Everyone has an angle, Veronica. Something they want. Something they need. One thing that you learn in business, nothing is free."

"You're a cynic."

"I'm a realist," said Cyprian. "I believe in gold and wind and the bottom line. Those are the things that get me along. I'm here because there is no choice for me. I have to see this through, or die. So, I ask again. What about you? Looking for something?"

Veronica sighed, turning back to her sketchbook.

"Someone?"

"You know what?" she said, gripping her pencil a good bit tighter than was necessary. "You should mind your own business."

"Never stopped you," he said with a cunning smile.

"I imagine you think yourself very charming."

"Oh, I don't imagine. I know. So, go on. Why are you here?"

Veronica put her sketchbook down, but kept the pencil in her hand. She turned it over and over in her fingers, and watched the dancers for a moment.

"When Titus first came to power," she said finally. "There was a group of people that tried to subvert him. They saw that he'd abandoned the Rule, subverted the power of the Sovereign for his own personal gain. So, they banded together in an attempt to stop him, or at least slow him down."

"You're talking about the Bookkeepers."

Veronica nodded.

"My parents were part of them. My father was a history scholar at the University of Terra Alta, specializing in the Old World, the time before the Sovereigns. He was a good man, a kind man. He taught me all kinds of things. How to fight, talk, pick locks. My mother loved him dearly. Together they raised me, educated me. They gave me the best life they could."

Cyprian was looking off into the fire, listening intently.

"My father came to suspect that someone had double-crossed them. When I was ten, my parents sent me to one of the few boarding schools left, in Azimuth. They enrolled me under a false name, thinking it would keep me safe if anything should happen to them. For years, I listened for any scrap of news from my parents, always afraid. One day, there was a rumor that a scholar in Terra Alta was murdered in his house by soldiers, that Admiral Ambry had done it himself."

Veronica took a long breath.

"I ran away. Lied my way onto a ship for Terra Alta."

She remembered how the house had looked from the street on that hazy afternoon. A burnt shell, black spars penetrating the sky like broken bones. There was no door on the hinges, only the remnants of stone foundation, the places where the floors had not burnt through, where she could still see remnants of wallpaper, fragments of parchment. It was a wasteland, a desolation where she had once known warmth. Ash was ankle-deep on the marble floor of the landing. Her foot had tapped something buried below. She reached down and pulled out a pearl-handled rapier, the blade still biting into the mask of an Imperium soldier.

Veronica brushed her hair back over her ear, focusing more intently on her drawing. She knew she didn't need to tell Cyprian the rest of the story. He could read it on her face. The tears came, as they always did, but Veronica wiped them away. They didn't change anything, they didn't help.

"My father died protecting what was left of my family. I'll find my mother, even if I have to die doing it. I think she's in the Abyss."

"The Abyss…" Cyprian said, his voice growing small.

"I know," Veronica said. She looked out over the party. An O'Larre ranger was throwing big satchets of herbs onto the large fire at the center of the platforms, sending blue and purple flames high into the canopy. Basil Black, now hoisted onto Hugh Benttree's shoulders, was a mere fleck against the roaring blaze.

"The only way the Abyss opens is if Titus falls. And the only hope we have of that is your ship's cook."

CHAPTER NINETEEN

Basil crawled over yet another boulder, the coarse gray granite rough beneath his fingers. There was no soft moss here, no blooming lilies, no leafy trees. Instead, the endless craggy mountains were pocked with tough, pale lichen, scrubby bushes, and lean hemlocks lashed by the wind. They didn't talk as they climbed, Cyprian at the front, with Veronica and McElhaney behind. Finally, they reached the rocky peak. Waves of white dust came off the top of the mountain in ghostly sheets, calcite sand swept up from the white plains below. Basil had to shade his eyes from the onslaught as he peered out over the valley.

"There she is," McElhaney said, as they poked their heads over the ridge toward the northeast. There, a red precipice at the edge of the white plains, was a city. The stone was the dark gray of the mountains veined with crimson, the city skyline a series of tall, swirling spires of red and purple, rosebuds in the sea of white and gray. Immense plumes of steam, emerging from a thousand ancient stone vents, pierced the blueness of the sky. Basil had read that steam was the lifeblood of Kwalz, rushing in hot ceramic channels beneath the streets, bubbling through the baths and meetinghouses, a guardian against the frost that swept down from the mountains.

McElhaney sighed and scratched at the shiny dome of his head.

"Good times I spent in those bathhouses at one time. I'd give a good piece of coin for a nice bath. You would not believe the layer of crud on the back of my neck-"

"Look," Veronica interrupted, pointing. "Dreadnoughts."

Basil followed Veronica's finger. Ships were coming and going from the concourses: lean, icicle-bedecked freighters from the north and big-bellied caravels from Stella Maris. And indeed, the lean forms of dreadnoughts, sleek as predatory animals, cut wide circuits around the city's borders.

"They're patrolling," said Cyprian, pulling a piece of thick parchment from his belt. He traced his finger around the map of Kwalz and the lands surrounding. "There's no way we'll get through without being seen."

"Are they looking for us?" asked Basil.

"Most likely," said Cyprian. The young deckmaster slid down behind the rock, thrusting his oculus back into his belt. "One thing's for sure. If we're caught sneaking into that city, we're chopped kidney. There'll be even more redbacks at the port. And we need that information. And the food. Do we have enough to keep us to a relay station or another port?"

"Unfortunately not," said Basil. The barrels in the hold were running low. His tally showed that the food had dwindled to only a few meals. And they'd been eating potatoes and red beans for a week.

"Fine," said Cyprian. "Then we're going to Kwalz."

"How?" Veronica asked. The young deckmaster's jacket flared out behind him as he bounded back down the hillside to where *Philomena* was moored, a great, ugly swan nestled among the cairns of mossy rocks.

"Fortunately," said Cyprian. "The shipmaster and I have a plan."

Basil shook his head as he stumbled down over another boulder. Cyprian's strategies were bold, always fueled by a reckless confidence. Whatever the harebrained scheme was, the crew would most likely do it whistling. It was a quality that Basil found himself envying. He couldn't imagine ever swaying a group of people like that. Maybe the Bookkeepers had the wrong man. Basil could imagine Cyprian on the Just Throne, the heir of the Sovereigns. In all honesty, that would be a relief.

By the time they got back to the deck, the crew was gathered around the midships mast, where Francis Lightlas stood on the command deck, the wind tugging at his long coat.

"What's the verdict, Mr. Fields?"

"I think it'll work, shipmaster."

Lightlas nodded. He rang the bell over the helm. When the crew was finally assembled, he extended his finger to the east.

"Over the crest of that hill is the proud city of Kwalz, the Ruby of the East! We need food, and we need information, and this is the only place we're likely to get either. The problem is that the Imperium has it surrounded. It's possible that they are looking for *Philomena* in particular, so if we're going to get what we need and put this place to our stern, we will need to have a plan and stick by it."

The men nodded, grunting their assent to one another. Lightlas pulled the shipmaster's coat off his shoulders.

"That's why, from this point forward, there is no *Philomena*. There is no Fields Trading and Supply Company. There is no Shipmaster Francis Lightlas. Instead, this ship is *Fortune's Muse*, and she's a freighter of the Big Windy Trade Union out of Terra Alta, mastered by..."

Lightlas pushed the red coat into the hands of Clip McElhaney, who raised an eyebrow, then put the coat on. Lightlas also passed him his oculus and a roll of papers.

"Shipmaster Willas Hennings. We'll run out the colors of a Terra Alta freighter, rig the envelopes in a Terra Altan style, replace the name-plates, and give the hull some stripes. If you can't speak with a Terra Altan accent, don't speak at all. If anyone breathes a single word of *Philomena* or Misericordiae, we're lost. "

"And you, shipmaster?" asked Hugh Benttree in his deep rumbling voice.

Lightlas yanked a bandanna down over his left eye and rolled up the sleeves of his linen shirt.

"I'm One-Eyed Tomm," he said. "Deckhand."

The crew grinned at one another. McElhaney was already demanding to be referred to as "Old Rotgut", and practiced an imperious strut up and down the deck. Spirits were high, but Basil knew they were taking a tremendous risk. Capture by the Imperium could mean death or the Abyss for all of them. But Lightlas and

Cyprian were turning it into a game, a daring trick. It was the sort of melodramatic showboating that airmen loved.

"Quite a plan," Veronica murmured. "I'll be interested to see if we survive."

The next hour was filled with furious activity, and even Basil and Veronica were caught up in the maelstrom of rigging, painting, and rehauling that turned *Philomena* into a different ship altogether. Petros was relegated, squawking, to the shipmaster's cabin, as it was possible that such a distinct bird could draw the Fleet's attention. The one detail that was difficult to hide was *Philomena's* figurehead, with the smile of the fair lady looking ever forward. The best Oakum could do was rig a tangle of blocks and tackle to the bow, obscuring most of her.

When dusk began to fall, the fictitious Shipmaster Willas "Rotgut" Hennings clanged the bell and ordered a course for the port of Kwalz. Cracking the frenzied sort of jokes that nervous men make, the crew obeyed.

Moments after they cleared the ridge, an Imperium dreadnought was already making its way toward them. Basil was clad in an incredibly grubby deckhand's coat that someone had found in a storage locker. Veronica, working at one of the sails next to him, was wearing a pair of breeches and concealed all of her black hair underneath a large floppy hat. A liberal amount of dirt and rope grease helped to conceal her features. Cyprian had borrowed one of Oakum's red bandanas to conceal his distinctive golden hair. With a loud order from McElhaney, the crew fell in together, standing in a neat row on the deck, ready for inspection.

"All stop," said McElhaney, digging his hands into the deep pockets of his leather coat. With a large pipe jammed between his teeth and a pompously feathered hat on his bald head, the acting loadmaster effected the cocky poise of a shipmaster well.

With the snap of her braking sheets, *Philomena* slowed to a standstill in midair. The Imperium dreadnought came sailing out of the murky twilight towards them, the running lanterns suspended off its bow and stern giving it a strange, skeletal look. With unsettling precision, the dreadnought came to rest in the air directly beside *Philomena*. The deck was alive with red-uniformed men, who fell rapidly into regimented lines. With a whistle, a gangplank was thrown down, and twenty Imperium airmen came thundering across. A few systematically began to search the crew, patting pockets and scrutinizing faces. The rest went down into the holds, through the corridors, inspected the rigging. Basil could hear the roll and thump of airmen's chests being overturned.

"Documents," said the ranking Fleet officer who stomped aboard, extending an armored hand.

"Naturally," said McElhaney. As if without a care in the world, he handed over the forged papers, puffing idly on his pipe.

"Port of origin?"

"Terra Alta."

"Destination?"

"Niev, by way of Kwalz."

The officer stared McElhaney down with his eyeless metal face, and it seemed to Basil that he was looking into the fake shipmaster's soul, searching for the lie that dwelled there. Were there eyes behind those black holes, a living man of flesh and blood? Or just the Imperium's thoughtless machine? Finally, when his men returned to the deck and trooped back over to their own ship, the officer spoke.

"Concourse B. Dock 17."

"Boundless thanks," said McElhaney, bowing graciously as the officer followed his men back over the gangplank. All around him, Basil could almost feel the sigh of relief that passed through the crew. Once the dreadnought was clear, McElhaney snickered.

"Once again, Rotgut Hennings wins the day."

Misericordiae's concourses flowed like wooden rivers above the maze of streets and alleys, but the concourses of Kwalz were stone, set in three rigid lines that ran along the city's eastern rim. Gusting winds kicked up the flames of the immense torches that lit the concourse as Masterson navigated *Philomena* to her dock. A storm was blowing in from the east. With the ship secured, Francis Lightlas gave final instructions to Cyprian and the other officers in the cartorium. Basil listened just beyond the hatch.

"Mr. McElhaney, you'll be going to the depot we talked about. They'll be open even after hours. They specialize in cases like ours. Get as much of whatever they have. In our position, we can't be picky. Mr. Fields, you will go to see the Silverspoon as we discussed. Mr. Oakum, set about as usual, checking the lines and so forth. We want to give the impression that we are a merchant ship looking to meet a deadline, which we are. We're stopping and leaving in a hurry. Am I understood?"

With a chorus of grunts and the scrape of crates, the officers went about their work. Basil ducked down the staircase, jogged through the mid-deck corridor, and popped up through the deck hatch at the bow. On the main deck, *Philomena's* crew was busy getting the ship ready for a swift departure. The lanky form of Cyprian, still disguised, swept along the leftward gunwale, before mounting the gangplank and disappearing down onto he concourse. Basil glanced again at the airmen on the main deck. If he tried to follow Cyprian down the gangplank, he would certainly be seen. He would have to find another way to the concourse.

Basil dashed down into the galley, which was mercifully empty. He wrenched open the large porthole by the stove and stuck his head out. He was nearly level with the concourse. Using the stovetop as a brace, he hefted himself up and wiggled his shoulders through the porthole. A few seconds of graceless struggling sent him tumbling the rest of the way onto the concourse. Above him was the leftward gunwale. No one on *Philomena* would be able to see him unless they peered directly down.

Basil scrambled to his feet, setting off in the direction Cyprian had taken. But, as he ducked through the straggling crowd on the concourse, he saw no sign of Cyprian. As he stepped around a pile of crates, he was suddenly seized by the collar and dragged into the shadow.

"What the blue hazes are you doing?"

"Cyprian! You startled me."

"Good," Cyprian said in a low whisper. "You're going to be a lot more startled if some redback arrests you and sends you to the Abyss. Get back on the ship. Now."

Basil stood his ground.

"I know you're going to see a Silverspoon. I have questions as well. Questions I need the answers to."

"Now's not the time."

Basil shook his head.

"Do you believe that I'm the Sovereign of Cor Nova?" he asked finally.

Basil searched the young officer's face. Cyprian said nothing, but the confident jut of his chin, the knowing light of his eye, flickered for just a moment. Beneath the façade of confidence, of calm control, there was uncertainty.

"I'm not sure either," Basil said. "There are things I need to understand. And I'm not going back to the ship."

Cyprian opened his mouth. Then closed it again.

"What will Lightlas say?"

"You'll tell him that I threatened to cause a scene if you did not do what I asked. Which is true."

Cyprian shook his head at Basil, grinning ruefully.

"You might actually be learning something after all," he said. His face suddenly fell, as though realizing something terrible. "Veronica's going to be furious."

"We can deal with that later," Basil said. "Just stay a rapier-length away in the meantime."

The city smelled of soot, the sharp tang of frosty nights, and the sweet spiciness of Kwalzian cuisine. Basil was grateful for their disguises, but no one in the city seemed the least bit interested in them. The merchants, mongers, and housewives moved with heads down, passing like ghosts through the red stone city. The creeping fear was present here, even stronger than in Misericordiae. Only the Imperium soldiers swaggered down the streets with impunity, staring through the mists with masks and weapons at the ready.

Wordless, Basil and Cyprian passed through the main square into the narrow streets beyond. At the far end of one such windy avenue, an old boardinghouse slouched, flanked by two boarded-up shops. A few mercantile offices also crowded for space amid a graying shipping supply depot. The smallest, seediest storefront of them all was a small, tumble-down affair that at one time had plate-glass in the front. This was now replaced with some old boards with slivers of yellow light peeking through. Back in its depths, Basil could hear a wheezing concertina and rowdy voices.

When they were nearly at the door, Cyprian seized Basil by the collar of his jacket, yanking him back. He barely missed being plowed into by a man with more toes than teeth, who came stumbling out the door accompanied by a blast of some bawdy airman's ballad. Recovering his balance through a long, roundabout step, he stumbled into a standing position and rendered a bleary, slack-jawed salute.

"Well, good evenin', nob'dy-n-particl'r. May the Imperiumsh windsh blesh yer cotton bloomersh...."

The man proceeded to cackle uproariously, turn, and make it about three steps before collapsing, with a tremendous snore, into an abandoned empty barrel beneath a wooden noticeboard on the wall. Of the hundreds of disintegrating flyers and leaflets that still clung to the surface, Basil's eye was drawn to one in particular. He squinted to see through the steam. Cyprian grunted.

"Blue hazes, Basil. Stop staring. Did they not have any drunks in that village...?"

Cyprian's voice trailed off, following Basil's eye. There, pinned with care among the top layer of notices, was a flyer emblazoned with a reproduction of *Philomena*. She was drawn down to the last cable and sail, and all of her crew were identified by name in a list down the side. The red seal of the Imperium shone dully from the corner of the parchment. Cyprian groaned, swiped the notice off the board, and jammed into his pocket. He grabbed Basil by the elbow and marched him toward the tavern door.

"More reason to be done with this as quickly as possible. Now, when we go in here, remember that you're nobody. Don't talk to anyone. Don't look at anyone. Don't even be around."

After checking for more oncoming traffic, they pushed through the loosely hanging doors. Immediately, the smells of spoiling sausage, bad beer, and pipe smoke washed over Basil. The posts of the walls were tilted at strange angles. The ramshackle tables and chairs appeared to have been repaired again and again, victims of brawls too numerous to count.

"Isn't it great?" Cyprian murmured. "The Crooked Mast. Best airman's tavern in the province."

Basil did his best not to choke on a noxious purple cloud of pipe smoke.

"I'd hate to see the worst."

Carefully, they picked their way to the bar through the singing, swaying, roughhousing crowd of airmen and townspeople. Shouting over the out-of-tune concertina, Cyprian ordered a pair of drinks. The one-toothed barman smacked two dirty glasses containing what appeared to be dishwater garnished with slime on the bar. Murmuring his thanks and hoping that whatever goop was on the outside of the glass wouldn't burn through his hand, Basil accepted the beverage and followed in Cyprian's wake through the crowd. They made their way around a sailor reciting a decidedly off-color limerick and a game of Noq that was quickly devolving into a fistfight, to the line of booths along the wall, each lit with a dirty oil lantern.

In these secluded nooks, sky-weary merchants talked in hushed voices, a pair of women attired entirely in fur cast ivory dice over and over on the tabletop, and a man with orange spectacles glanced in their direction, fingering a crystal glass that appeared to contain a live lizard. Cyprian steered clear of all of these.

"Remember," he said to Basil, just loud enough to be heard over the carousing. "Ask no questions that you don't want to have answered."

Finally, Cyprian approached the most secluded booth in the tavern, jammed in the farthest corner with a large, stuffed mordonoc head above it. Cyprian slid into one seat, beckoning Basil to sit next to him. A pile of rags lay on the opposite bench, making no sound save a deep, rhythmic thrumming that made the table vibrate every few moments.

Cyprian raised his glass a few inches, then cracked it down loudly on the table. With a snort and an oath, the pile of rags jerked into a sitting position. Basil jumped in surprise, nearly spilling his drink all over himself.

The man swayed like a tree in the wind for a moment. His face was slack, the skin a pale grey with pink veins and silver stubble. He blinked blearily at them, smacking cracked lips, before digging a large pipe from one of the pockets of his voluminous leather coat. His vest seemed to have once been purple, embroidered with what might have been stars. A tarnished silver spoon was stuck into one of the unused buttonholes. Cyprian cleared his throat.

"How much does a- ?"

The Silverspoon raised a ringed finger, silencing Cyprian. Then, he tapped tobacco from a packet into his pipe, packing it down carefully. He winced as he did so, and Basil noticed a soiled bandage on his right hand. The brown cloth was spotted with red and the faint stench of decay pricked at Basil's nostrils.

The rumorman lit a match from the guttering lantern overhead, gingerly lifted it to the bowl of his pipe, and leaned back as the pungent, sweet smell enveloped the booth. He flicked his finger again, inviting Cyprian to speak.

"As I was saying," said the young officer. "How much does a rumor cost these days?"

"Well, sir," the Silverspoon's tongue ran across yellow teeth. "Varies according to what a man has. Men with much give more for what they want."

The fumes from Basil's drink were making him lightheaded. He pushed it away from himself. The Silverspoon grabbed the glass, drained it in a single gulp, and slapped the glass down on the table. Cyprian did not blink.

"You didn't answer my question," he said. "Prices first, then business."

"And I suppose that *is* the way gentlemen do things," the Silverspoon said, licking his teeth again. "All right, stranger. S'true that rumormen are getting a little difficult to come by. The wearing of the silver spoon is becoming slightly… perilous. It's not just lotteries and fishwives these days. Information is always a dangerous business when times get dark."

Cyprian leaned forward.

"Well, in this case, you stand to benefit. I'm interested in darkness."

The pipe smoke seemed to twirl aside as the Silverspoon inclined his head.

"I see, and into what areas of obscurity do you desire to venture?"

"I need to know about the Old Man's Tooth. It would be something in Panagiottis, not too far north of Niev."

"Ah," said the Silverspoon. "Well, if I knew something about that, it would be worth ten regals."

Cyprian snorted.

"Five."

"Ten."

"Seven."

"Ten," said the Silverspoon. "Don't haggle with me, boy. That is what the information is worth, and that is the price."

Grimacing, Cyprian slid the money across the table. The rumorman licked his teeth again, about to speak, but was interrupted by a man who came crashing onto the table, apparently thrown by his comrades from the other side of the bar. Unconscious, the man rolled into Basil's seat and lay face down, snoring loudly, on the table. The rumorman pointed at the slumped form.

"It's extra if he's going to listen."

"He's not with us," said Cyprian as Basil nudged the man. He was alive. Thankfully, his carousing comrades came and retrieved him, feet first. "Now, my rumor."

The Silverspoon leaned back in the seat, his eyes closed. He breathed in and out. In the faint light of the single candle, Basil could swear that he saw the pipe smoke gather close around him, swaying like dancers in the dark.

"The people of Niev have a name for the mountain that overshadows their city," said the Silverspoon. "The old maps call it Kamallak, but the people of Niev call it the Old Man. There's a place toward the peak of the mountain where the wind blows ungodly quick towards the face. In the old shipping routes, when ships tried to make it to Niev and were caught in the thick of a storm, they couldn't see the Three Giants. More often than not, they wound up around Kamallak, and got blown into the mountainside. The place is marked with a spire of rock. They call that Old Man's Tooth, and it has ghosts a-plenty."

Basil nodded. It sounded like a good place to hide something.

"What about the name Colleena?" asked Cyprian.

The rumorman dug a dirty finger into one ear.

"Never heard that name. If you're looking for a girlfriend at the Old Man's Tooth, let me tell you that she's most likely frozen solid."

"No, Colleena isn't a person," said Basil slowly. He imagined a wasteland at the top of the mountain, where vessels went to die. He turned to Cyprian, realization dawning. "She's a ship."

Cyprian nodded.

"That's what we came for."

He got up to leave.

"Wait," Basil said, turning again to the Silverspoon, now in the act of extinguishing his pipe. "Tell me what you know about Lorus."

Basil slid some coins across the table. The rumorman looked at the money, shining dully on the stained wood, for a moment. He blinked blearily at Basil.

"Stranger, most people in Cor Nova understand the considerable risk involved in the asking of such questions."

"I'm one of them."

Basil held the rumorman's gaze. He could sense something otherworldly flickering behind those watery eyes, like starlight through a cloudy sky. The rumorman's eyes widened, and he leaned forward, peering closely at Basil. The pipe smoke around them seemed to grow thicker, the silver spoon a sliver of moonlight in the haze.

"I reckon that you are," the rumorman said finally. "But, in the eyes of a Silverspoon, all people are the same. All people have secrets. All people have fears. So do you. And that amount of coin isn't enough to offset my unease. Especially now. Go."

"That's all the money I have."

The rumorman leaned back in his seat, making a dismissive gesture toward the door.

"I would wish you luck, but it wouldn't do you any good."

"I have more than money," Basil said. "Let me see your hand."

"Why?"

Basil caught another glimpse of the poisoned hand as the Silverspoon cradled it. The scars of stitches poorly done, the bandage improperly wound, the pus pale and yellow.

"It's a poisoned cut," said Basil. "And three others have tried to fix it and failed. The third one used a mercury tincture. And made it worse."

The Silverspoon's eyes grew wide. He nodded.

"A dissatisfied customer didn't like what he heard. Came at me with a poisoned knife two months ago. No doctor nor medicine man nor shaman has been able to fix my hand. One of them did some funny stuff with needles. Now I can't feel much."

The rumorman let his hand fall on the table, not taking his bleary eyes off Basil for a moment. Basil carefully unwrapped the dirty bandage. The laceration ran through the rumorman's palm and curled down towards his wrist. The skin was mottled and clammy, the veins nearly black. Basil reached for the roll of tools stashed in his pocket. He'd left his box on the ship, but he never forgot to throw a few things in his pockets. He pulled a vial out of his vest. The rumorman inhaled sharply as the Basil poured the liqueur of hollyoak onto the wound.

"I… I can't feel my hand!"

"It's temporary," muttered Basil, bending over his work. With a few lightning quick movements of a flat, sharp instrument, he cut out graceful slivers of dead flesh. Then, he dove a second instrument into a vial of green paste and slathered it delicately onto the open wound. He pulled a needle and a piece of thin, clean thread from his vest pocket, drawing the flesh together with neat stitches. Only a few minutes after beginning, he wrapped a fresh bandage expertly around the hand. The rumorman flexed his hand slowly as Basil put his implements away.

"My kind hear many things," said the Silverspoon, gazing at the precise stitching. "Rumors from every corner of this land. In recent days, there have been many about you. And it is beginning to seem to me that they are true."

"And now he's paid you," said Cyprian. "You owe the answers to his questions."

"Very well," replied the rumorman. He lifted his pipe to his lips, but the light had gone out. He didn't seem to notice. For a moment, the tavern faded around them. The rumorman's voice and expression changed; he was more distant, almost whispering in the low voice of secrets. The light seemed to waver and shift, sliding around the booth.

"Lorus," the Silverspoon said. "Was a good Sovereign. As had his faithful forebears, he lived by the Rule of Sylvanus, vowing to exercise his power for the good of the Dominion. He had a love of nature, of books and learning. He was always more suited to them than his brother, Titus, who was a military man at heart. But, Lorus had his faults. He was proud and a bit arrogant, as men of power often are. He'd always wanted a son, they said. And, he was excited to learn from his queen that one would be coming to him. Lorus had great dreams for the future of Cor Nova."

The rumorman's voice dropped, growing darker still.

"But, all wasn't well everywhere. In the wastes, something terrible and dark had awoken from slumber. It preyed over the people, fed on their dreams, raked their children with claws in the night. It was a living shadow with a hundred forms. It breathed nightmare into their days, despair into their nights.

"The people petitioned the Sovereign Lorus, who heard. He dispatched a battalion of the Sovereign Fleet to deal with the creature and return it to Soliodomus for examination. The chase was long and hard, costing many lives and several ships. The night it was captured, an additional ten men were killed. It was Titus who captured it. He used High Sylvan to keep the creature at bay, then managed to destroy it with his sword, a Fleet officer's saber. He returned to Soliodomus, with all the pomp and glamor of a returning hero.

"But, Titus was never the same after that. He became dark and brooding. He was often found in strange and deserted places, deep in thought. And he was never seen without the sword. It was at his side, day and night. Some said that he was afraid that the thing was coming back for him, and that he couldn't bear to not have his weapon handy. On one night, Titus made a move to claim the throne for himself. He fought his brother, Lorus, in the very Sanctum of Soliodomus. At the end of all of it, Lorus was dead, and Titus had everyone believing that he'd almost died to try and save him. But the lie did not hold. Dark suspicions welled up."

"Which were?" asked Basil, leaning forward.

"The Sidia," said the Silverspoon. "Are the shadow soldiers, weapons made of man's greed and a perversion of the language we now call High Sylvan, birthed during the destruction of the Old World, and finally defeated by none other than Sylvanus himself eight hundred years ago. They are merciless creatures, passing from form to formless in the space of a thought, capable of horror unending, and near indestructible. Such creatures cannot be killed, but they could be imprisoned, perhaps in such an unassuming object as a sword."

"Titus's saber," said Basil. "The Sidia is trapped in the saber. And it gives him the power to speak High Sylvan without the three relics."

"So goes the rumor," the Silverspoon replied.

Basil nodded, heart hammering. It was almost too much to take at once.

"And what does Titus want to do now?" he asked.

"The Abyss," said the Silverspoon. "Titus wants the Abyss, and what lies at its base."

"Which is?"

"When Sylvanus faced down the Sidia at the end of the Old World, he was unable to destroy them. He could only imprison them, hold them at bay with the use of three objects recorded in the Rule of Sylvanus: the Elm Staff, the Riverstone Amulet, and the Astral Crown. Using them, Sylvanus locked the Sidia away, in a place the book calls the Sarcophagus. Its whereabouts have been unknown, even to my brothers and I, until now. Now, Titus is digging day and night, into the Fields of Carath. If one Sidia gives him power, he wonders, what will he be able to do with a thousand?"

Suddenly, the Silverspoon's rheumy eyes flew open.

"Time is up. They're here."

Cyprian cursed and grabbed Basil by the arm, dragging him out of the booth. The rollicking in the tavern had not diminished, and Cyprian had to push and shove even harder to get to the door. Basil chanced one glance back through the throng. He saw the Silverspoon raise his bandaged hand, as if in farewell, before the tavern doors swung closed over him.

There were thundering footsteps in the street, people fleeing the square, headed for shelter. The sky was growing dark and green above them; lightning flashed from the east. The wind whipped plumes of steam into writhing columns. The storm was close.

"Quick, Basil!" said Cyprian. "Back to the concourse!"

But when they entered the square, Basil immediately saw that getting back to *Philomena* would not be an option. Looming huge against the green sky, five dreadnoughts had docked at the concourse, along with an enormous battleship flying the standard of the Grand Admiral. Heedless of the approaching storm, troops of soldiers moved across the top of the concourse, down the ramps into the city. Some bore containers overflowing with books, papers, and scrolls. They dumped these into a large pile in the center of the square, massing around them in formation. Crowds of citizens stood stunned, cut off from their homes. They could only watch as still more soldiers drove the butts of their muskets through doors, ransacking houses and bringing out more books.

"There's no way up the concourse," Cyprian muttered. "Too many coming down."

But Basil wasn't listening. A man was standing at the head of the enormous pile of books, which grew ever taller behind him. His hair was a dark, silvery gray, his red uniform immaculate, his admiral's helm under his arm. The sun and stars of the Grand Admiral rested on his broad shoulders. With a signal from one of his aides, the enormous battleship fired one of its cannons, and the mass of airmen and citizens fell silent. His voice carried into the square, bounced from every building.

"People of Kwalz," he said. "You would do well to listen to what I have come to say. I am Grand Admiral Khyber Ambry, a devoted servant of our Imperium Titus. I have come because certain stories have found me. Perhaps they have found you, too. Perhaps you've heard stories about the boy Basil Black, about a return of the Sovereign. You may rest assured that these stories are nothing more than seditious hearsay."

Ambry accepted a pitch-covered torch from an aide. Its golden light whipped back and forth in the winds of the approaching storm. Then, he threw it in a high arc into the fitful green sky. It landed amid the discarded pages and papers behind him. Fueled by the keening wind, the blaze whipped skyward, bathing the square in orange light. Ambry was a pillar of orange and red in its glow.

"The Imperium is a kind and generous ruler, giving much to his loyal subjects. But, if the offense is great, so too is the punishment that he justly gives."

The ranks of the Imperium airmen parted, and several came forth, carrying tied bundles. Basil gasped. They were people, bound hand and foot with rope and chain. Men and women, large and small. Some were still, others defiant and struggling, each face awash with the orange light of the blaze. Ambry raised his arm to the night sky.

"If any man so much as breathes the name of Basil Black, unless he is doing so to turn him over to the justice of the Imperium, he shall perish for this crime."

Ambry's arm fell. With the thrust of strong arms, the captives were thrown headlong into the fire.

Basil couldn't hear. He couldn't think. The blood was pounding in his ears, driving out everything but a new lone voice roaring up from somewhere deep within him. Basil felt nothing but overwhelming pain and grief and rage. For the first time in his life, Basil wanted to hurt, to kill, to maim. He wanted to reach out and destroy the Imperium's soldiers, rip off every mask and stomp it into the dirt, to go after every man of them with pistol and sword. If only he had the power of Sylvanus, the power that had imprisoned the Sidia, he would make them pay. They would pay for every soul lost, for every page turned to ash. The Amulet was a weight against his chest, a cold, useless weight. He rushed forward, frantic to do something, anything. Strong hands grabbed him by the arm.

"Basil!" he heard Cyprian's voice say in his ear. "Don't be a fool. There's nothing you can do for them."

Basil yanked against the young shipmaster's grip, but Cyprian was stronger. He pulled Basil through the crowd, towards the concourses. The ramps were now empty, all eyes focused on the terrible scene in the square.

Barely had they started when a shout rose up from the red ranks. Someone had seen them making for the gangplank. There was a shift in the crowd, citizens thrown aside, red-uniformed shoulders muscling through. A gunshot. Then more. Cyprian broke into a sprint, fairly dragging Basil up the ramp and over the concourse. A mass of soldiers was converging on them, masks glinting in the receding firelight. Up ahead, Basil could see the silhouette of *Philomena* against the stormy sky. Several figures were out on the concourse, returning fire at the oncoming soldiers.

"Full rise!" Basil heard Lightlas roar as they closed the distance. "Every man on deck!"

Cyprian dragged Basil along as he leaped the gap. Basil was vaguely aware of Veronica, McElhaney, and Paschal alongside them, all shouting at once. Another hail of gunfire fell from the gunwale, trying to slow down the pursuing Fleet soldiers. There was the rush of aether, the creak of rope, and the concourse, now awash in red soldiers, was falling away.

Two of the dreadnoughts rose in pursuit. The enormous storm was bearing down over them, a great green wall sweeping towards the city. The men were shouting to each other, disorganized, confused. But all Basil could see was the great orange fire, growing ever brighter in the square below. The dark, bound shapes within the coals had been swallowed.

"Twelve marks sunwise!" Lightlas cried. "And full tilt!"

Another wave of gunshots. Clip McElhaney jerked spasmodically, falling to the deck clutching his neck.

"Basil!" Paschal roared as he leapt to his friend, dragging McElhaney toward the relative safety of the command deck.

"We're headed straight into the storm!" said Cyprian, cracking off another shot at the pursuers.

"Better to fight the sky than to fight the Imperium," said Lightlas. "To your posts, and hold fast!"

The crew stormed around Basil as he worked furiously, trying to stem the bleeding from McElhaney's neck. Wherever he pressed, blood welled up between his fingers. Suddenly, Veronica was at his side, handing him whatever he asked for.

Basil tried to keep focused on his work even as *Philomena* tilted directly into the roiling, green wall of the storm. The ship groaned as her hull was swung sideways, and hammering rain smashed onto the deck. The lightning crashed, the thunder rolled, and *Philomena* shuddered as she passed into the darkest part of the storm. Basil slammed a desperate fist against McElhaney's still chest, hearing nothing but the scream of wind and Lightlas's orders barely audible over the chaos.

CHAPTER TWENTY

Cyprian was lying on something hard. And it was cold. Why was it so cold in his cabin? He let one eye slide open. He wasn't in his cabin at all. He was on *Philomena's* deck, his back against the helm. All at once, the previous night came rushing back.

Philomena's lines and cables had hummed and buzzed in the colossal winds. The rain hammered on the envelopes and sent cascades of water pouring down onto the deck. The deck bucked and rolled beneath them, threatening to throw unsuspecting men out into the wailing abyss. Lightning ripped the sky into pieces.

Men had to yell to be heard as they struggled to control the swinging sails and ailerons that threatened to rip free from their mountings. Cyprian seized the wheel from Masterson, holding the ship's bow steady into the storm. The rain and wind were so thick that he could barely keep an eye on the aetherolabe. They were flying blind, desperately fast. Directly ahead, the bow of a Fleet dreadnought stabbed through the murk like a knife, lights ablaze and gundecks bristling. Only a quick course correction from Cyprian prevented a ghastly collision, and the dreadnought careened off into the storm. It was then that a cry went up; they had lost McElhaney.

But now, everything was quiet. The wind blew sharp and cold. It was snowing. Every snowflake seemed to shine from a hundred glittering facets, like jewels suspended in the sky. Cyprian dragged himself to his feet. Masterson sat in his chair at the helm, eagle-eyed with long icicles dangling from his mustache. *Philomena's* figurehead was clad in a gown of glittering white. Below them, jagged mountains stretched off to the horizon, abandoned snowy valleys between them.

"You know, Masterson," he said finally, checking to see that his ears weren't frostbitten. "You could have woken me up."

"Didn't seem advisable, deckmaster," said the helmsman. "You were quite peaceful."

Cyprian grumbled at this, trying to get his feet beneath him on the icy slipperiness of the deck. A slender hand appeared at his shoulder, offering him a lift up. Veronica stood there, still clad in a rough airman's jacket, pants, and boots. Snowflakes glittered in her hair, white on black. He was surprised when she pushed a warm mug into his hands.

"You could have told me where you were going," she said.

Cyprian was taken aback. It wasn't a challenge, or a reproach. Her tone was sad, almost regretful. The mug was warm between his fingers, and, in their own way, so were Veronica's brown eyes.

"Well," he said. "I didn't have much choice. How is Paschal?"

"He's coping," Veronica replied. "He told me all about the two of them. How they grew up together in the Misericordiae streets. He and McElhaney were practically brothers. The other men are helping, Benttree especially. He is more sensitive than he looks, that man."

For a moment, Cyprian was envious of her. He would have had no idea what to do in that situation, what to say. In a very real sense, she knew more about the crew than he did. He sipped the hot drink. And made a face.

"This is awful. Usually Basil's skipjack is better than this…"

Veronica's face grew even more somber. She drew her coat even closer around her.

"That's because Burt Spacklebrook made it. Basil isn't in the galley. He's…in a bad way…"

"What?" Cyprian asked, his heart sinking. All kinds of things can happen to men in a storm. The wind and pitch of the deck can drag men over the deck, cargo and equipment can roll over them on the deck, uncontained ropes can break limbs and crush flesh. What hope was there for any of them if Basil had been hurt? They were being pursued by an enemy that could only be defeated one way, and without Basil, that way was forever closed. But Veronica shook her head.

"Well, he's not injured or anything. He's just... come and see."

The main hold was like an icy cavern inside *Philomena*. The great crates that they had picked up in Misericordiae were still there, stacked high up to the wooden rafters. The icy white light of the outside shone through the grating in the main deck above.

Francis Lightlas sat at the base of one of these stacks, his fingers knotted over his cane. His eyes opened as Cyprian and Veronica approached. Basil's medical box, its contents scattered across the floor, lay at his feet.

"Shipmaster," Cyprian said. "Where's Basil?"

"He's out of sorts," said Francis Lightlas, pointing to the top of a stack of crates. "Well out of my reach."

"Basil?" Cyprian called. There was no reply from the dim recesses of the hold.

There was only silence. Lightlas, Veronica, and Cyprian all looked at each other.

"You're sure he's up there?"

Lightlas nodded.

"He's there."

Cyprian seized the bands around the crate and clambered his way to the top, peering over the edge. There was Basil, slumped against the crate like a crumpled leaf, his black vest a sad, tangled mess. He was wet, presumably from fighting the storm, and there were rope-burns and what looked to be dried blood on his hands. His glasses lay abandoned beside him.

Cyprian cleared his throat. His type of talk was loud and brash, the haggling that happens between ship's officers, the shout that makes airmen jump to the rails. Words that give comfort were not his specialty. He glanced back to see if Veronica was following him up the crate. But it didn't look like she had. He was on his own. He cleared his throat.

"I just had some of the worst skipjack I've ever tasted. If you don't get back in the galley, we'll all be either starved or poisoned before we make it to Niev."

Basil didn't even look up. Cyprian was about to turn and head back down when he finally replied, in a low, small voice.

"Is everything a joke to you?"

"I…" said Cyprian, caught off guard. "I find that it's easier that way."

Basil nodded, a vacant gesture.

"Where is the closest city?"

"At this point, the closest city is Niev. It's two days away, I reckon. North of us."

"I want to disembark there. I'll continue on."

"What? Leave *Philomena?*"

"Yes," said Basil.

Cyprian shook his head.

"You can't do that, Basil. It would be suicide."

"Shut your mouth," said Basil, and suddenly he was looking directly at Cyprian, his clear blue eyes flashing. "Since when do you care about me? Since when does it matter for a moment to you what happens in the grand scheme of things? Just so long as you come out of it with pockets full of gold! Don't you pull that wounded face at me! If the Bookkeepers wanted me on board this ship, they were fools!"

"Look, Basil," said Cyprian, now genuinely stumbling for words. "I'm not a bandit."

"Oh yes?" Basil said. He reached into his belt, pulled out a deckknife, and stabbed it into the wood of the crate. "How does that feel? That's all you care about. Your ship and your cargo and your money. You don't care about me. You don't care about Cor Nova."

"Now, Basil…"

But Basil was on his feet. Cyprian was momentarily afraid that he was about to make a lunge for him.

"And why does it matter anyway? You saw what happened in Kwalz. And in Misericordiae, and in every other city in Cor Nova. The Fleet owns the sky. The Imperium owns the Fleet. If I'm the son of Lorus, so what? In my studies, do you know what I have found? I've observed that the strong survive. And sometimes the strong are completely capable of having offspring that are weak."

Basil slammed the deckknife into the top of the crate.

"Titus has a Fleet. And because of that sword, he can speak High Sylvan. And what do I have? One merchant freighter with a ragtag crew. No weapons to speak of. And this old book and a few fragments of the Sovereign are supposed to give me what I need to overcome the Imperium?"

"Basil…"

"Shut up! Tell me how this is going to work. Tell me how this is going to help! Better yet…"

Basil jabbed a finger back towards Kwalz. Tears shone brilliant at the corners of his eyes.

"…Tell McElhaney how this is going to help. Tell THEM how this is going to help. I stood in that square and did nothing to help those people. They burned alive, Cyprian. And there was nothing I could do for them. Nothing! Why is anyone else in Cor Nova any different?"

"Basil, there's a plan," said Cyprian. "The Bookkeepers…"

"Hang the Bookkeepers!" said Basil. "Clearly their plans are not to be trusted if they're all dead. We need a new plan. Our only hope is to raise a fleet. One that can counter the Imperium."

Cyprian breathed once, in and out, slowly.

"Basil Black, are you saying that you want to start a war?"

Basil's spectacles flashed.

"There's already a war, Cyprian. And we're losing. If you don't recognize either of those things, then you're blind."

Basil pushed his way around Cyprian, climbed down the crates, and stomped his way out of the hold, slamming the hatch behind him. A beat of silence passed, then Cyprian climbed down as well. Veronica and Lightlas watched him. Their eyes held no solutions either.

"I don't know what I can give him," said Cyprian.

"The same thing we can give Paschal," said Veronica. "Time."

Two days passed, and dusk was falling as *Philomena* travelled over the last frozen hilltops before the coast. The crew worked day and night with mallets, breaking loose the ice that caked on the rigging and deck. The sky was permanently gray, the air laden with frozen crystals.

When Cyprian entered the cartorium, he was accompanied by a blast of frigid air. After slamming the cartorium door shut, Cyprian stamped the ice from his boots. The biscuits and salted pork on the table were long cold, but Cyprian ate some anyway. Against all odds, the men had gotten most of the food loaded before their hasty departure from Kwalz.

"I have flown through Panagiottis many times," said Francis Lightlas from behind the map table. He had several ledgers open in front of him, a scarf around his neck. He was tallying figures. "But I never remember it being this cold. Old age, I suppose. Have all the men switched their bunks?"

Cyprian nodded. They had moved all the men lodging in the forward berths of the ship into the galley, where the small wood-burning stove, closely guarded by a pair of airmen on watch, kept warmth circulating. Any cabins directly exposed to the sides of the ship were perilously cold. An airman left to sleep in such a cabin could very well never wake up. It was all just as well, Cyprian thought. The loss of McElhaney had been hard on all of them, . His raucous singing voice, loud laugh, and cheerful wit were much missed. It would be good for the men to be together.

"At least our ship's cook is back," said Cyprian.

"That he is," said Francis Lightlas. "Albeit reluctantly."

Cyprian nodded. Basil was indeed back in the galley, but more silent and withdrawn than usual. He refused to meet Cyprian's gaze most of the time, and there was little that anyone could do to sway his attitude.

"I don't know what to do with him. He thinks that I am just after the money, the prestige."

"Are you?"

Cyprian jammed another biscuit into his mouth.

"What am I supposed to be after? I'm an airman. Not some kind of altruistic do-gooder."

Lightlas cocked a weathered eyebrow at Cyprian.

"Hmm."

"Don't you start on me now."

"I'm not starting on you now," Lightlas said, closing his ledger, folding his hands neatly on top. "I'm asking you if he is wrong. We're taking a risk, and our lives are at stake. If you are in this, you had best not be for the money."

Cyprian was about to remind Lightlas that the old shipmaster had been the one to dangle the promise of gold and glory in front of Cyprian's nose at the start of this adventure. Then, he thought again about Anne Stormalong and her fire, about the way that the rumorman had looked at Basil. Shaking his head, Cyprian took another monstrous bite.

"Time will tell."

"What is that?" asked Veronica, peering off the horizon to the north, where what looked like miniature mountains poked up. They were like green glass, frozen in perfect geometrical shapes with sloping emerald ridges, capped by white crests.

"The Emerald Sea," said Cyprian, pulling out his oculus. "They say in the days of the Old World, it froze solid in a single night, stilled by the dying command of an army of mages. They're still under there somewhere, they say, encased in the ice."

There were other stories, of course. Stories about the ancient beasts and ships that lay frozen beneath the waves, and why the mages stilled the sea in the first place. No one knew how far down the ice went, whether the waters still flowed in the black, icy depths. The people of northern Panagiottis crossed it in sledges with blades for runners, flying over the frozen green peaks with canvas sails full of frozen wind.

"Three Giants, Mr. Fields!" called the observer in the lookout. "Four marks off the leftward bow."

Cyprian turned his oculus north. There, twinkling on the banks of the Emerald Sea, were three pinpricks of light. As they approached, the tiny dots grew to enormous luminous pillars, a trio of fiery fingers reaching skyward.

"The Three Giants," Cyprian said when Veronica asked. "Burning plumes of natural gas accidentally ignited over four hundred years ago. They serve as beacons for Niev, guiding ice sledges and airships back to the city. Without it, they'd freeze to death before finding their way."

Beyond the Three Giants, the tiny suggestion of a town come into view, huddled on the coast of the Emerald Sea. Niev sat at the base of an enormous, jagged shape that rose against the grey sky. Kamallak. The Old Man. The mountains' peak was obscured by dense, gray clouds. Somewhere on that mountain, the Elm Staff was hidden. Cyprian exhaled. It was just a pile of rocks. No airman should be intimidated by rocks.

"Spacklebrook," said Cyprian, ringing the bell on the helm. "Go and let the shipmaster know we've arrived. Masterson! Bring her about seven marks moonwise and make for the mountain. If the wind starts to pull us, make sure I know it right quick."

Veronica looked up at the mountain. She pulled out her sketchbook, loosed one hand from her glove, and began to draw. Tiny as it was on the horizon, the jagged peak sliced the sky like a knife.

"Sometimes," said Veronica. "I wish that the Bookkeepers had chosen happier places."

Despite himself, Cyprian laughed.

"What would be the fun in that?"

Under Masterson's control, *Philomena* skirted the edge of Niev, drawing ever closer to the treacherous slopes of the mountain. As night fell, Cyprian tried to rest in his cabin, but the cold and the knowledge of the great gray mountain kept him from rest.

Towards dawn, he lifted a squawking Petros from where he perched on Cyprian's wardrobe and emerged out onto the deck, tossing the kestrel into the frigid morning wind. Petros flapped and wheeled, ducking under *Philomena* and emerging at the opposite gunwale, fixing Cyprian was an accusatory golden eye.

"Don't try to guilt me, bird. If you spend another day sleeping in my cabin and eating pork, you'll get too fat to fly. Go find yourself a nice mouse or something."

Cyprian spent the rest of the morning helping the crew to remove some of the ice that built up on the gunwales and rigging. *Philomena* cut through fluffy hills of blindingly white cloud that scattered the morning sunlight into thousands of rainbows. Somewhere below them and to the north, the little town of Niev sat at the mountain's base. Oakum was on the wheel, having relieved Masterson some hours before. His bandana was frozen to his forehead.

"Aye there, deckmaster," he said with a desultory nod. "Come out to catch some of this blistering sun, have you?"

"No sign of the strong current the Silverspoon described?"

"Not so much as a tug," replied Oakum. "Hey now, what's that?"

Cyprian caught only a glimpse as a vessel came out of a cloud beside them. It was trimmed in thick furs on the rigging, and spots of silver trim sparkled here and there in the sun. But, Cyprian was sure that they wanted no company of any kind on this mountain.

"Move, Oakum!" he said, and shouldered the protesting machinist to the side. With a whip of the wheel, he turned *Philomena* moonwise, burying her in the nearest bank of cloud. It was white and the icy mist clung to everything, but at least here they would be invisible from whatever ship was out there. There were legends about fearsome bandits that roamed these parts, fleeing bloody wars with other clans. It was not a good place to meet strangers.

"Do you reckon they saw us?" Oakum said, rubbing his shoulder where Cyprian had pushed him.

"I don't know," Cyprian replied. Then, the wheel juddered beneath his hands, once.

"What..."

And then, he felt the wheel tugging left. At first he could resist, and the wheel turned as both he and Oakum hauled back on it, but the tug was coming harder and harder, pulling on the wheel until it sprung out of their hands, spinning left so that the ship tipped into the wind.

Then, they were out of the cloud, and the mountain loomed dead ahead.

"Take in every sail!" Cyprian roared as he threw himself at the wheel. "The wind is pulling us in! Rouse the shipmaster!"

The airmen on watch set to with a will, and Oakum had the presence of mind to ring the bell, summoning the other watches to the deck. Within moments, every piece of sail was lashed to spar and mast, giving the merciless wind less to grip. Cyprian fought against the pull of the current, but the wheel kicked back savagely, the pitch levers grinding in their housings. The current pulled them inexorably toward the cloud-shrouded mountain.

Then, Cyprian saw a flat patch of clear land on the side of the mountain, free of boulders and crags. He acted quickly, pushing all of the pitch levers forward.

"Dump the aether!" he shouted down to Oakum in the shipcore. "Open her wide!"

In three jets of white, *Philomena's* vents poured aether out into the frigid sky. Her envelopes shrank above, and Cyprian felt himself grow light in his boots as the freighter descended rapidly. He shouted direction to Oakum, who feathered the amount of aether released. Too much, and the current would dash them against the mountainside. Too little, and they would fall like a rock. With a bit of luck, they could guide her into the mountainside. *Philomena* descended fast. The crew braced themselves and held their breath, waiting for the telltale crack of a splitting keel. Snow hissed and rocks thumped against the side of the hull, flying away in twin plumes as the ship settled against the mountainside. Finally, *Philomena* was perched alist on the side of the Old Man. And all was silent, save the keening of the wind.

Cyprian wiped the sweat from his brow, trying to still the shaking in his hands. At that moment, shipmaster Lightlas appeared from within the cartorium.

"Nicely landed, Mr. Fields," he said, looking up the mountainside. "I'd say it's time for a little walk."

Chapter Twenty-One

Veronica was wearing layer upon layer of leather and wool, but the cold cut through like a knife. They had been trudging through the snow for well over an hour, and it felt like they had barely gone ten yards. Veronica looked behind her. *Philomena* was an island of brown in an ocean of white. A series of cables held her fast to the mountainside as the winds buffeted her envelopes left and right. The hunched figure of Francis Lightlas could be seen on the command deck, watching the away party through his oculus. Not that there was much to watch. It was slow going.

Hugh Benttree forged the way, a human plow creating a trench in the thigh-deep snow for others to follow. Cyprian was directly behind Benttree, giving the big man direction every now and then as to the best course to take. Behind him were Spacklebrook, Oakum, and Paschal. Paschal, usually reserved, had grown even more so since the death of his friend. He looked gaunt and pale behind his bushy black beard, but he moved with steady determination, willing himself to work. Veronica and Basil brought up the rear, with Basil stumping along behind her in silence. Normally, she would expect him to be examining the snow and the rocks with interest, committing their characteristics to memory, careful to grab samples where he could. But, he too kept his head down doggedly, the snow collecting on his dark brown hair.

"Bloody snow," mumbled Spacklebrook, digging himself out from where another pile had collapsed in on him. "Doesn't have the decency to be rain. Has to stop and make a show of itself."

"Disgraceful," muttered Oakum, balling up a full fist of the snow and pelted the back of Spacklebrook's.

As they climbed higher, large rock outcroppings sheltered them from the wind, allowing them to move and breathe easier, although the cold became more biting with each step. Finally, when *Philomena* was a mere fleck of cedar in the white expanse below, they broached the top of a long ridge marked by a fang of rock jutting up towards the sky. Above them, the peak of Kamallak continued to rise. At their feet, as though a giant hand had gouged into the side of the mountain, lay a natural basin. Listening to the weird keening of the wind, Veronica found herself remembering the dark entrance hall of her home back in Terra Alta. This place had the same lonely desolation. The airmen cursed, reaching for good luck talismans and spitting over their shoulders. Even Cyprian seemed stunned at the sight. He pulled the hat off his head so that his golden hair blew in the wind.

"So many ships."

The basin was a grey sea of wrecked vessels. The derelicts lay on their sides and on their keels, most smashed and splintered into pieces, snapped spars jutting like broken bones. Shreds of tattered sailcloth and ruined banners hung from the beams, flapping forlornly in the wind. Veronica half-expected to see the ghosts of a thousand airship crews moving out among the twists of icy wind. There were caravels, schooners, trawlers, dreadnoughts, and clippers. Skiffs, freighters, and bandit caravaneers. All silent. All empty. Victims of the vengeful Old Man.

"So many men," said Basil, his sharp eyes hard behind the frosted crystal of his spectacles. They were the first words Veronica had heard him speak since leaving *Philomena*.

Cyprian yanked his hat back down over his ears, eager to be done quickly.

"*At the Old Man's Tooth, she sleeps. Colleena of the valley deep.* We're looking for a ship named Colleena. Somewhere in this…mess."

"What's the plan?" Veronica asked.

Cyprian scanned the basin with his grey eyes, looking for any telltale signs.

"We can't search the entire thing. It would take weeks. Months. And we have hours. Maybe not even that much, if that dodgy ship comes back. There must be another clue. Something else- Oi!"

Veronica, seized by an idea, had snatched the oculus from Cyprian's belt. She swiveled the glass back and forth over the sea of wrecks. Cyprian went to take the oculus back, but she swatted his hand away.

"What are you looking for anyway?"

"Valleys," she said. "Hush."

Then, as she swiveled to the east, she saw it. A dip in the floor of the basin. The ships around it were tilted inward and descending, as though being sucked down a frozen whirlpool in the Emerald Sea. Abandoned masts and spars jutted up out of it. There were ships at the bottom.

"Colleena of the valley deep," said Veronica. "She'll be there. In the valley."

Cyprian took the oculus from her.

"Hold fast there, wisdom incarnate," he said, pointing off to the west. "Look at that over there, just beyond that big freighter. That looks like a valley, too. Maybe even bigger than the one in the east."

The flush of victory quickly fell away from Veronica.

"There isn't enough time to search them both," she said. "We'll have to split up and search them independently."

Cyprian fell silent. Veronica could tell that he didn't like the idea of separating. It made a possible ambush all the easier. Anyone could be hiding in the labyrinth of derelicts. He looked out into the sky around them. There were still no ships in sight.

"All right," said Cyprian finally. "We'll divide into two crews. I'll take Spacklebrook and Oakum and search the west. Paschal, you can take Benttree, Veronica, and Basil to the east. We'll meet back here in two hours. If you run into trouble, fire off two rounds."

The airmen nodded and the two groups went their separate ways. Veronica and Paschal trudged behind Benttree, who once more cut his way through the snow. Basil trudged behind them, sullen and silent. Finally, they reached the nearest edge of the crashed ships. The wind moaned sadly through open hatches and scorched bulkheads. Where they blocked the wind, drifts of snow and thick icicles built up. Here and there, a vague path was available between the hulks, but sometimes a large wreck cut it off, dead-ending or blocking the way with debris. It was clear that Benttree's strong-arming technique would not work as well on wood as it did on snow. They would have to be more creative with navigation.

"Time to lean on mother steel, big man," said Paschal, clapping Benttree on the shoulder.

"Looks that way," grunted Benttree.

He pulled a large axe from his belt, running a massive thumb along the blade to test the edge. The axehead bit hungrily into the brittle wood, and, with a steady stream of splinters in their wake, they pressed forward into the boneyard. Paschal kept a steady eye on his compass and used the peak of the Old Man as a landmark, giving Benttree direction every now and again. More than once, they had to double back to find a more favorable route. After an hour, Benttree was starting to get tired, his enormous shoulders cramping with soreness from swinging the mighty axe.

"A bit more," said Paschal. Every so often, Veronica noticed that he would glance at whatever patch of white sky could be found, wary for the shape of an approaching ship, for the sound of a cannon fired on the exposed hull of *Philomena*. But none came.

Veronica was starting to wonder if they had missed the valley completely, when they almost fell into it. Benttree swung his mighty axe, bulling through a thick cedar plank that was blocking their way, and the force of his blow nearly dragged him out into open space. The valley was more like a chasm, a deep gash in the basin floor lined with quartz-speckled rock.

"Well, blow me down," said Paschal, snapping his compass shut. "If it ain't just like you said."

Veronica was the first to scramble over the side of the valley, watching her footing carefully as she stepped from rock to rock.

"We need to spread out," she said. "*Colleena* could be any one of these."

One by one, they followed her, Basil last, until all were wandering separate paths among the ships, searching. Veronica's eyes roved the broken hulls. Some had brass nameplates. Others had names in Klahk or Miri or foreign runes scratched into the wood. Still others had no discernible name at all. There was *Blonde Bette, Flower of Terra Alta, Skipper Rae*. But no *Colleena*.

She finally came upon a tiny skiff. While weatherbeaten and old, she did not have the look of being crashed or even damaged. Rather, she was perched quite prettily among the abandoned and disused hulks. She bore the remains of the handsome black livery of the Sovereign Fleet. Some gold piping was still visible along her flanks. Her envelopes had even been neatly removed, leaving her bare masts to jut up into the sky. One of her hold doors was open, the cables binding it cut and blowing in the breeze. Her heart began to beat faster.

"Veronica!" came Basil's voice from the skiff's deck.

Veronica followed through the door. The inside of the skiff smelled like cedar and old parchment, and it was as neat as a pin. One hatch led forward to the berths, another back towards the stern. The hatch leading up onto the deck was open, the ladder rungs dusted with snow.

"Basil!" she called to the darkness.

"Up here!" came his voice from above.

Veronica breathed a sigh of relief as she seized the lowermost rung of the ladder and climbed upward. When her head cleared the deck, Basil offered a hand to assist her up.

"Look," he said, pointing to a brass plate affixed to the rear of the stern mast. "*Colleena,* it says. A Sovereign skiff, in the service of Lorus. This ship must have survived the transition between the Sovereign and the Imperium. It's still black."

"The staff," Veronica said. "Is it here?"

Basil pointed to the forward mast. There, at its base, was a chest that was as long as Basil was tall. It was weather-beaten and covered with a faint sheen of ice, but of the finest construction.

"Oak with brass bindings and hinges," Basil said. "If I wanted to keep something safe in a place like this, that's where I would keep it."

"Is there a lock?"

Basil indicated a thick slot on the chest's front, just the right shape to accept a disk. He pulled Amulet out of his pocket and Veronica immediately understood. What better key could there be?

"You should open it."

"Yes," said Basil. "I suppose I should."

Basil stepped forward to the chest. Veronica stood a yard or two behind him. Carefully, he inserted the Amulet into the slot, then gave it a quarter turn. With a metallic thunk, the mechanism slid home and the latch released. Basil withdrew the Amulet and pushed the lid open.

For a split second, Veronica saw inside. There was a bed of thick, black velvet. In its center, lay a long, thin dip, as though something had once rested there, safe in the confines of the chest.

Then, there was a sound like a banjo string breaking, a muffled thump and crash. Veronica felt something whip past her feet, striking her around the ankles and flipping her onto her back. A hiss of aether sounded, and a small envelope burst into life above Veronica. She bolted up just in time to see the net that had sprung from a hidden compartment beneath the deck wrap around Basil, entangling his limbs and dragging him upward into the icy sky.

She heard Paschal shout something, followed by two pistol shots, but Veronica knew they wouldn't get to him in time. Basil was gone.

CHAPTER TWENTY-TWO

The Fleet outpost in Kwalz was a damp, musty affair, the walls and floors constantly oozing with brownish muck. Ambry didn't notice the smell of decay and rot; he'd spent a lot of time in prisons. He slammed the gate of the smallest cell behind him, then turned to face its occupant.

The Silverspoon lay against the back of the cell, his long legs splayed out in front of him, his coat lying open so that he looked like a dying moth. The stars on his purple vest glimmered oddly, and the silver spoon in his coat loop hung askew. He opened his eyes when Ambry entered, but did not move. Ambry's shadow was a line of black across the rumorman's face.

"I want to know everything," said the admiral.

The Silverspoon's eyes were even blearier than before, his face lined and sagging.

"You know the limits of my kind."

"Money for information," said Ambry. The legacy of the Silverspoons was old, their lore and laws secretive, with each man bound to them for life. That was to be expected of rats who hoarded seditious lies. It was good that Titus had set about eradicating them. With a grim look of distaste, Ambry reached into his pocket and removed a short stack of gold coins. He dropped them, one by one, to the rumorman's feet. "My gold is good. Tell me what I want to know."

The rumorman made no move for the money.

"A wearer of the silver spoon must be at liberty to refuse. You are coercing me."

"You have a choice," said Ambry, suddenly feeling extremely tired himself. "Information or the Abyss. Now make it."

The Silverspoon was silent.

"Tell me about *Philomena*."

"A common merchant vessel," said the Silverspoon. "It used to belong to Augustus Fields, the founder of a modest trading company in Misericordiae. Now it belongs to one of his former employees, an old man named Lightlas. There is nothing more to know about it."

"Tell me about the two boys you gave information to. What did they want from you?"

"I cannot do this. As you know."

"It is odd to me that men who peddle lies and rumor are so set on defending their wares."

The rumorman glared at Ambry.

"It is odd to me that a man who abandons his Sovereign becomes the Grand Admiral."

Before the Silverspoon had a chance to take his next breath, Ambry had him by the throat, smashing him savagely against the wall of the cell.

"And how came you by that particular lie?"

"Many ways," the Silverspoon choked out, a trembling scrap of bedraggled cloth in the Grand Admiral's hands. Ambry took solace in the knowledge that, with one hand, he could choke the life from this sad creature. But something glimmered far back in the rumorman's eyes, something that saw past Ambry, past the filthy cell, onto the far slimy wall, where Ambry knew a crumbling message board was posted.

Almost compelled, Ambry turned his head to look. Among a few muck-stained, rotting notices, hung a sheet displaying a Misericordiae merchant freighter.

"Truth has many ways of escaping," the rumorman gasped, struggling for his last breath. "And that is why Basil Black will slip through your fingers."

Chapter Twenty-Three

"So, then I tell the guy, Spacklebrook... I say to him 'Friend, if the sky was any bluer, I'd slap your mother!'"

Oakum chuckled, slapping himself on the thigh and dealing Spacklebrook a punch in the arm that sent the gangly redhead sprawling through an old hatch.

"Oakum, do us all a favor," said Cyprian, yanking Spacklebrook to his feet. "And shut up."

"Your loss, rooster boy," said Oakum with another snicker and a sigh. "A man needs humor. Keeps him young."

Cyprian shook his head, casting another apprehensive glance to the sky.

"Stop chattering and look."

"I've been looking," said Oakum. "I don't see no *Colleena*. I've seen *Green Aelanthe*. *Duchess Grace*. *Cordelia Marie*. Used to know a girl named Cordelia in Azimuth. She was one of those fancy dance-queens with the big hair."

Suddenly, two harsh cracks shattered the windy emptiness of the valley. Cyprian's blood ran cold.

"Did you hear that?"

"Hear what?" Spacklebrook mumbled, still brushing himself off.

"Yes," said Oakum, suddenly sober. "Two pistol shots."

"Back to the ship," said Cyprian, and took off running. He hurdled over snowdrifts and broken spars, ducked under loops of rotten rope, never breaking step. Cyprian kept an eye on the sky as it flashed in and out of view. It was empty of ships, but directly eastward, he spotted something moving. He paused for a second, watching the object rise. It looked like a small envelope, with something in the bottom, a burden in a net, swinging back and forth.

"Rat-trap," wheezed Oakum, as he ran up next to Cyprian. "Bandits."

Cyprian ran faster. He was imagining Veronica, swallowed up into the freezing nothingness above. Or Basil. Or one of the crew. Not that any of them were not in mortal danger at this point. If the trap was sprung, the bandits would soon be coming to collect their prize.

By the time they reached the edge of the basin, they were out of breath. Spacklebrook's face was as red as his hair; he looked ready to throw up. They paused for a moment at the edge of the basin. The envelope was out of sight, disappeared into the clouds above the mountain. On the eastern edge of the boneyard, a trio of figures emerged, one very large, one bearded, one smaller and dark-haired outrunning them all. Cyprian's heart soared when he saw Veronica, but plunged when he thought about the ship's cook.

"Basil!" Paschal called as he neared the top of the hill. "They got him before we could do anything! Rat-trap!"

At Cyprian's order, they half-ran, half-fell down the mountainside, stumbling down the wide track of their earlier passage. Finally, they reached *Philomena's* gangplank.

"To quarters!" Cyprian yelled over the wind, seizing one of the mooring lines in the ground, yanking it from the ice and pulling himself up the side of the ship hand over hand. "To quarters, you rogues!"

"Report, Mr. Fields!" said Francis Lightlas, stumping over as the deck exploded into furious activity.

"Bandit rat-trap at the staff's hiding place, shipmaster. They got Basil. Someone was here before us."

"A rat-trap," the old man said, suddenly pale. "With an envelope?"

Cyprian nodded.

"They're probably still going up as we speak, if they haven't been intercepted by now. If we go quickly, we might be able to collect them before whoever is up there does."

Lightlas nodded.

"Prime the guns!" he ordered.

The gun crews brought up powder and shot as the deck crews cast off the final lines leading into the snow. With a wheeze of aether, *Philomena* took to the sky. Cyprian handled the ship carefully, preparing to navigate her around the corridor of rushing air that flowed into the Old Man's Tooth. Within moments, they would be racing toward Basil. But suddenly, the air seemed colder. The lookout called out, his voice high and panicky. Shapes were appearing out of the frozen mist around them. Lean, long shapes coated with ice, bristling with guns. Four of them. A hunting party. Cyprian recognized the shapes now, the vicious cuts of the hulls, the hulls dotted with skins and silver beads, the rigging a symphony of intricately braided leatherwork.

"Marauders," he said.

He had grown up hearing tales about them. No one could fly like Marauders, no one could kill and thrive in the air like them. No one.

"What do we do?" Spacklebrook wailed. "What do we do?"

Cyprian's mind raced, rolling through every option as fast as he could. They were outmanned, outgunned, and outmaneuvered. The Marauders already had the high ground. Then, like a morningstar rising in his mind, he had an idea.

"Shipmaster Lightlas, do you trust me?" Cyprian demanded of the shipmaster.

The lean old man regarded him for a moment. Then nodded.

"The deckmaster has command!" he yelled over the deck.

Cyprian nodded.

"Vent the envelopes and fire the guns!" he said.

"There's no shot…" protested Oakum.

"Fire anyway! Don't aim. Just fire!"

Paschal's jaw was slack.

"Now?"

"When did you imagine? Blessed yes, now!"

There were three guns loaded with powder, but no shot. They fired, blasting orange radiance into the whiteness. The Marauder ships stopped, as though confused. The noise of the cannon report rolled away, and Cyprian listened carefully, hoping, wishing.

He allowed himself a small smile when he felt a deeper rumbling, almost too low to be heard, through the keel of the ship still grounded on the mountainside. And, above them, there was a subtle shifting in the white snow cover, slowly building to a roar. In moments, a wave of white was rolling down the mountain toward *Philomena*, growing with every moment.

"It's a…a… an anvil blanch!" stammered Burt Spacklebrook.

"Give her all sail!" Cyprian roared over the rising thunder. "No aether until I give the word, do you hear me? Now brace!"

Like a mighty fist, the wall of snow that whipped down from the Old Man's Tooth smacked *Philomena*, spinning the hull around like a toy. The men scattered left and right across the deck, seizing masts and gunwales as the ship lurched.

"Aether now!" cried Cyprian, holding fast to the wheel. He spun it left, and watched the sails respond. With a creak, they caught the wind, pushing *Philomena's* keel into line with the flow of snow. Now would come the hard part. He pulled two pitch levers back and placed his hand on a third. The snow began to shift and rumble beneath them, and they were moving.

With a roar and rush of tumbling snow, *Philomena* passed beneath the stunned Marauder ships, down the mountainside. As *Philomena* picked up speed, they turned to follow, and Cyprian saw the pilot lights of guns at the ready. The Marauders were apparently not amused by this trick. The avalanche grew more violent with every passing moment. Chunks of rock and spikes of ice rose and fell in the oncoming rush, bearing *Philomena* along with it. The terrified crew did their best to keep the sails filled, but they were out of their element. They were used to air beneath the hull, not a mountain's worth of frozen water. The hull dipped downward, plunging the figurehead into the rushing snow. Waves of powder washed over the deck, covering everything in white. There was a triplet of almighty cracks behind them, and three shots hissed in the snow close by. The Marauders were gaining.

"More sail!" cried Cyprian.

"What is the plan, Cyprian?" asked Veronica, suddenly at his side.

"I'm working it out as I go…"

"What?!"

"You should be thankful!" Cyprian said, hauling the wheel left. "We've survived this long!"

Francis Lightlas nodded grimly, holding onto the helm.

"He has a solid point, young lady. Blue hazes, boy, watch those trees!"

Philomena was now whipping down the mountainside, smashing through sparse trees. Thankfully, the snow was deep enough to bury any rock outcroppings up to his point, but they were getting bigger as they descended the mountainside, and the trees were growing larger with every passing moment. A large enough tree or rock striking the hull near center would be enough to whip *Philomena* sideways, sending her tumbling down the mountainside or ripping out her keel altogether.

Cyprian did his best to ignore the next round of shot that fell around them. One clipped *Philomena's* stern, sending splinters of wood into the air. The ice particles in the air ahead of them were stabbing at Cyprian as he tried to see forward, tugging the wheel left and right to avoid the oncoming debris. The ship's barely responded with the force of boiling snow pulling on her keel.

"All hands brace! Forward windbrakes at the ready!"

Cyprian held the ship steady for a few more seconds.

"Brace! Brace!" he roared, slamming the third pitch lever backward. The forward windbrakes snapped to the wind and their spars groaned. *Philomena's* bow jerked skyward, leaping upward into the grey sky. The rumble beneath the hull diminished and stopped as the ship lost contact with the snow. The crew held tight as the ship shot upward, rapidly gaining height.

"We need lift! More aeth-" Cyprian called to the crew.

But he was cut off by an almighty wail and a crash as a Marauder shot slammed into the leftward side of the deck, exploding a section of the leftward gunwale and the hull. The blow smashed the hull downward on the left side, and the forward windbrakes flailed in the breeze. The wheel bucked Cyprian off, whacking him in the lip with a spindle. *Philomena* pitched perilously downward, and slammed her keel into the earth with a blow that rattled the old ship from bow to stern. She slid to a sickening stop at an angle on the mountainside. No one was seriously hurt, but the fire from the cannon shot was still crackling.

"Put it out!" Lightlas called to the stunned crew as they picked themselves up from the deck. "More aether! We can still…"

His voice trailed off. On four sides, the Marauder vessels surrounded them, guns alight. There was no more snow to carry them away this time. They were cut off.

Chapter Twenty-Four

Basil awoke into a world of dull, throbbing pain. His head pounded. Something tough and braided bit savagely into his wrists. Hard wood ground against his knees, and he was bitterly cold. Trying to ignore the soreness in his shoulders, Basil pushed himself upright. He winced against the blinding light that sliced through what looked like the hull of a ship. It was as though all of the upper decks had been removed, leaving only a large, empty base. A set of circular windows in the far end of the hull, where the stern would have been, allowed beams of silver light to penetrate the space, sliding among the tapestries.

Basil couldn't stop his mouth from dropping open in amazement. The tapestries were huge pieces of braided cloth, each formed of thousands of threads in limitless colors, their ends terminating in tassels intricately braided and ornamented with glistening silver beads. Across each tapestry, scenes of battle and treaty, peace and war, feast and famine sprawled out in vivid color. The figures in the images had pale skin, almond eyes, and they were clad in brown ornamented with silver. Strange runes, weird faces, and animals that Basil did not recognize filled the borders.

The air was still. The sound of the rushing air outside was very soft. Basil could swear that the tapestries were undulating slowly, as though brushed by invisible fingers. Basil could almost swear he heard whispers in a harsh tongue uttered in the air around him, always too faint to hear the words exactly. Then, down the length of the ship, there was a sound like a door opening, and enormous footfalls that shook the very floorboards. The figure was enormous, a black silhouette cut by the silver blades of light.

As he came closer, Basil could see the man more clearly. He was as tall as Benttree, with legs like tree trunks. His skin was almost ivory, his eyes sharp and a pale almond color. His beard and mane of brown hair was braided into a single wild tangle. An enormous silver gauntlet emblazoned with runes encased his wrist. Across his mighty back hung an enormous battleaxe. He stopped, staring at Basil as though he had discovered a particularly unsavory insect that he would very much like to crush.

"Do you admire our history?"

His voice was rough and thickly accented, like two ancient boulders rubbing together. For a moment, Basil was speechless. The huge man continued to stare, and Basil stumbled for words.

"The tapestries... are beautiful."

Beneath the great tangled beard, the man's lip curled into a disgusted sneer.

"Yes," he said. "They are. This Lorehall contains the story of my people, a story that I have no doubt you do not know."

Moving more quickly than Basil would have thought possible, the enormous man seized Basil's face, his rough skin rasping against Basil's chin. In the pale brown of the huge man's eyes, a frightening fire burned.

"This is a face that I know. A face that many Marauders have cause to know. It is the face of the Liar. The Sovereign, as they called him, who stood by as my people froze and starved in the farthest reaches of his dominion."

Basil could barely move his jaw against the great Marauder's grip.

"I have never known my father..."

"And yet you share blood. You are of the same flesh. I am Redleg Melloch. My son is Caspar Melloch. He dwells within me always. A man begets his son, and his son is a part of him. Likewise, your father is a part of you."

"I don't know what my father did with Marauders."

"Nothing!" Melloch hissed, directly into Basil's face. "That is what your father did. When I pleaded that my people had been trod underfoot for two centuries, when I demanded that his justice extend to Marauders, who built his dominion on their backs!"

"I am sorry," Basil said. "If my father didn't treat you well. I want to set things right. I'm sure Lorus-"

Melloch jumped to his feet, throwing Basil back against the wall with a roar of rage.

"You do not utter the Liar's name in this place!" he roared. He extended a mighty hand to the nearest tapestry. "It is because of him that Marauders hide in this frozen wasteland like rats, because of him that we died by the hundreds in the Bourdigan Pass, because of him that our riches and our land were taken from us, because of him that our children are dying. You will not speak his name!"

Basil lay helpless on the ground, his hands still bound. The Marauder's fury was boundless. What could he say to quench it?

"I'm sorry," he said finally.

Melloch snorted.

"I do not value your apology. Will you bring back my strong sons and my nephews? My aunts and my mother? They dwell among us only in the tapestries now. The Murderer has condemned them to be so. Blood has been spilled. And blood must be repaid."

If Lorus was the Liar, Basil could guess who the Murderer might be. Perhaps if Melloch understood that he was opposed to Titus, he would listen. But Melloch didn't seem to have any such plans. He slammed a single great booted foot down on the decking. The Lorehall echoed with the sound of the blow. Somewhere far away, the sound of gears and ropes groaning permeated the walls, and the far stern of the great hull opened up, folding outwards like an enormous gate. The blast of icy air struck Basil like a fist. He was instantly shivering. It was a cold unlike anything he had ever experienced, chilling him to his very core. Melloch, however, breathed in the cold air with relish.

"I knew that one day," he said. "The Liar's followers would come to retrieve his staff. And when they came, I would be here to deliver them to justice."

Redleg Melloch reached behind a tapestry, and pulled out a straight staff of gray elm with a gold cap that twinkled in the paltry light.

"This is what you have journeyed into the wastes for? The stick of the Liar?"

Melloch lifted the staff, and with a crack that resounded through the Lorehall, snapped it in half over his knee. With a flick of his mighty arm, the two broken halves went flying over his head, towards the mighty open door. They bounced, then slid, then fell out of sight into the abyss, and Basil saw all of his hopes go with them. Redleg Malloch snorted derisively at Basil's despair. Drawing out a shiny, curved knife, he sliced the clothes from Basil's limbs, until only the thin pair of breeches under his sturdy airman's pants remained. Basil shivered harder as the cold bit even deeper.

"Sovereign blood runs just as red as any Cor Novan's," said Melloch. "If you die tonight, Basil, it will be the fault of the land that you rule, not mine. The tapestries will freeze to solid sheets, but our ancestors do not feel the cold. You will, though. When I come to retrieve you in the morning, I will throw you from the portal, and when your body strikes the rocks, it will crumble into a thousand pieces."

Redleg Melloch returned to the door, the breath from his mouth misting into crystals as he spoke.

"Good night, Basil, son of Lorus. May your dreams be of death."

In the first hour, Basil shivered so much that he could not move. He tried to remember from his books how to treat hypothermia. But none of the information had included the eventuality of being forcibly tied down in a Marauder vessel, and the information became harder and harder to recall as he grew colder.

In the second hour, his mind began to wander. The tapestries were frozen. Colors muted by ice, they barely moved in the frigid wind that came from the portal. He began to think about Osmara, about the tiny white flowers of the mountain, of peace and tranquility at his desk in the cabin. He thought about Thon Black, with his great beard and his wisdom. If only he were here now. His hammers would break these chains, and they would leave together, forgetting all the horror of the days that had passed. And then, with little explanation, his mind turned to *Philomena*, to Veronica and to

Cyprian, to all the crew. It was true that in Osmara he had lost all the friends or family he had ever known. It had never occurred to him that someday it might be others who would lose him. Would they feel the pain that he felt? Miss him the way that he missed his father? Maybe, he thought. But maybe not.

In the third hour, he decided that if he had ever believed he was the Sovereign, he didn't anymore. Here he was, chained and nearly naked, with the cold starlit night sucking his life away. The shivering had stopped. He could feel his heartbeat slowing down. He imagined the tall, stern figure of Sylvanus, a ghostly vision with the amulet, staff, and crown, the Rule balanced in one strong hand. The glowing Sovereigns in Stormalong's fire danced in front of him, passing one behind the other in wild succession, taunting him as they went. Then, Sylvanus was there, with a fiery hand extended toward Basil's chest. He drew nearer and nearer, the faint sensation of heat growing warmer and warmer, pulsing like a living thing.

And, suddenly, there was real fire, a lantern in front of his face, and warm hands on his body, rubbing his chest in circles. A warm, spiced liquid was poured down his throat. He didn't have the strength to cough as it burned its way down to his stomach. Basil forced his eyes open.

The figure that was ministering to him was not Sylvanus. Instead, it was a hooded woman, clad head-to-toe in brown fur. A silver necklace hung around her neck. Her breath made plumes of mist in the frozen air. Although her wide hood covered the majority of her features, Basil could tell by the line of her pale cheek that she was relatively young. Basil opened his mouth to say something, but she held up her hand. The way that she did it reminded Basil a lot of Veronica. It was the motion of a woman not to be trifled with.

"You are Basil," she said, still tending to him.

Basil couldn't tell if this was a question or a statement. Either way, he couldn't adequately respond. The shivering had returned, and his lips were vibrating too much to communicate. He settled for nodding his head.

"Is it true that you are the Liar's son? The Murderer's nephew?"
Basil nodded again.

"And you are a healer?"
This time, Basil was able to take some command of his lips.
"Y-y-yes."

This seemed to satisfy the woman. From a thick haversack on her back, she pulled out a thick overcoat, a pair of high-topped moccasins, and a wide belt.

"Put on these clothes," she said. "Quickly."

Basil found his fingers too cold to bend, so the woman assisted him in putting on the hooded overcoat. It felt oily and had a strong animal smell, but it instantly shielded him from the cold. Under the weight of the coat, he struggled to put on the moccasins. With a look of agitation, the woman gestured for him to sit down and briskly put the moccasins on. The strange woman gave him a once-over, then pushed a weathered stick into his hands.

"Follow me," she said. "Do not look at or say anything to anyone. Do not stop."

She turned and began walking briskly up the hall, the frozen tapestries swaying with her passage. His joints still stiff, Basil had to lean on the stick to keep his balance. The heavy coat pressed down upon him, and the thick waves of fabric undulated, throwing its weight left and right as he walked.

They went through a large carved doorway into a corridor, which dead-ended and turned up a stairwell, winding its way up several decks. The color and grain of the wood changed, and they were walking down another corridor. Basil couldn't be certain, but it seemed to him that this one ran at a different angle than the one they had just left. The corridor itself was strangely constructed, with some doorways purposefully blocked. Silver talismans and strange sigils were embedded above haphazard doorframes and in the middle of random stairs. Around them, the sounds of life began to come through the walls: voices, low mournful music, and the boom of things being rolled and dragged and hammered in far-off places.

The way twisted and turned, occasionally opening into a small room or stairwell. Other passageways opened up in unnatural ways, clearly cut into what had once been a bulkhead or wall. Once, they crossed over a landing that sported a round window. As they passed, Basil reached out and touched the frosty glass. It was extremely cold. Beyond the pane, the clouds below looked so hard and unforgiving that they may as well have been the ground.

Spread out above the clouds was an immense ramshackle circle of bulkheads, decks, and gunwales, an amalgamation of dozens of ships, connected and stacked into a giant, floating ring. The window through which Basil was looking was positioned on the inside of this ring, and allowed a view of the immense circle above and below. A vast network of cables, pipes, and ladders extended upwards into the gray sky above, connecting the ring to a enormous collection of envelopes that bore the structure aloft. Here and there, the lean outlines of Marauder ships stalked the frozen sky. Somewhere on the far side, Basil could see several docking with the structure where the ring's "deck" would be.

"Haste," hissed the woman. "I will explain later."

Basil tugged his eyes away from the sight. Finally, they arrived at a round door. Beyond the door was the brisk sound of human activity. She gestured subtly for Basil to stand on her right, then pushed the door open and walked through. Entire decks had been removed, allowing the hull to open up hugely on the inside. Stall upon stall was set against the high-planked walls, fitting neatly between the gunwales. The warm clamor of business being conducted filled the space, which smelled of stale bread and animal hide.

The marketplace was crowded with people, mostly clad in thick fur like Basil's mysterious guide. The Marauders didn't look much like the terrifying race that Basil had been raised to believe in. They were mostly tall, pale of skin with strong features, gentle brown eyes, and light brown hair that they kept tied back. Without exception, they wore silver: pendants shaped like strange creatures, bracelets that curled up muscular forearms, earrings that glinted like third eyes.

The conversations, though loud, were not joyous. Basil was struck by a deep sense of hopelessness in the way they talked, the slope of their shoulders. Following at the woman's elbow, Basil picked his way through the crowded marketplace, keeping his eyes cast down. Finally, they came to a high door set directly in the wall of the main corridor. The woman squared her shoulders, as though bracing herself against what was coming next. As the door swung wide, Basil felt the blood drain from his face. He suddenly realized why the market had felt so stark and barren. There had been no children. Not a single one. Because they were all here.

The sick bay took up the entire mid-deck of a ship. The ceiling seemed oppressively low and it took a moment for Basil's eyes to adjust to the dim light that filtered in through the portholes. The air was oppressively warm, thick with coughing and fevered moaning. Small cots were set up in neat rows that ran the length of the long room. Each contained a small, prone form. Some lay still, while others tossed and turned. Each was desperately pale, and angry clusters of reddish pustules rose from their faces, chests, and arms. Concerned relatives moved among the beds, cooling foreheads and spoon-feeding, ghosts amid the tombstones.

The woman finally stopped at a cot in the near corner. He was probably about seven, with light brown hair and fair skin. He moaned in the midst of fevered dreams. The red rash covered half of his face, and he scratched at it with a flaccid hand, but did not wake. The woman dipped into her bag once more and pulled out a waterskin. She dabbed at the boy's tortured face with a moist cloth. Basil could see in her eyes the highest kind of agony, the helpless misery of those who stand on the shore as the river of death takes their loved ones away.

"Your son?" asked Basil quietly.

"Yes," replied the woman. Her voice wavered. "Caspar. He is dying. So are all of these, all of our children. Can you save them?"

His own discomforts forgotten, Basil's mind clicked into analytical mode. He reached forward, pulling blankets from the boy's chest. The red rash clawed its way across the boy's chest in spidery veins; Basil could almost feel the heat of fever radiating from the skin. Pushing back the thick cuffs of his overcoat, Basil's hands did their work, tapping on the chest, gently palpitating the throat, feeling the heat of the forehead. The boy murmured, but didn't wake.

"No adults have been affected?"

"None. Only the children."

"Are these all of them? Are they anywhere else on the….ship?"

"Colossus, we call it. It's our home. Yes, this is all of them. As soon as the outbreak started, we put them all in one place, but it hasn't seemed to help. They just keep getting sick."

"When did it start?"

"About three weeks ago. Our ships patrol the skies around Colossus for leagues, to keep Outsiders away. The ones who get too close are brought in for salvage. Three weeks ago, a Sovereign dreadnought came within three leagues of here. When they were stripping the vessel, they found a boy, hidden on a cot on one of the lower decks. He was young, younger than my son. He was an Outsider, but he was an innocent. We tried to ease his passing on the ship, and he died two days later. A few days after that, the first of our children became sick."

Basil nodded. He studied the angry, red rash. What could cause such a thing? He let the pages of his textbooks float back up into his mind, page after page slipping through his memory.

"Fifteen have died," said the woman. "We don't know how to stop it."

"We need medicine. What do you have?"

"Not much," replied the woman. "We Marauders are a hardy people, and we only have what we collect from our farms hidden in Panagiottis. We have a few herbs that we use for headache, height sickness…"

"Bring those and some more water. Also, did you loot the ship? The dreadnought?"

"We salvaged what we could, yes."

"Did you bring the medical kit on board? A square chest with metal bindings, with a bronze leaf on the front."

"I can look," replied the woman. She got up to leave. "My name is Gwyneth."

Her footsteps disappeared out the door and down the stairs. Basil looked around the sick bay again. In the dimness, no one was paying any attention to him. He knelt by the boy's bedside, allowing the sounds of misery and despair to wash over him. For a moment, the eyelids of Gwyneth's son fluttered open, but whether they saw him or some fevered phantasm, Basil couldn't tell. As he peered into those pale brown depths, Basil was once more standing on the streets of Kwalz, defenseless as the fires leapt up and claimed the lives of good people. His people. Basil clenched his fist around the cot's frame. This time would be different. This time, there was something he could do.

Gwyneth returned shortly. Basil could tell by the apologetic way in which she handed him the small chest that its contents would not be terribly impressive. Most of the vials and beakers were gone, but a few useful ingredients remained. The small mortar and pestle had been left as well.

"I had to pull it from a barge," said Gwyneth. "Whatever is not useful, we throw away. Burdens cannot be unnecessary on Colossus."

"It will do," said Basil. He began to pull out the vials, memorizing them as he did so.

Under Gwyneth's watchful eye, he went to work. Finally, he managed to produce a small quantity of greenish solution. Gwyneth helped Basil raise the boy's head, and the thin tea trickled down the boy's throat. Initially, he coughed and sputtered, but Basil massaged his neck, allowing the tea to pass.

"This should break the fever, but it won't stop the infection or the nerve damage."

"So it will not cure them?"

Basil took off his glasses and rubbed his eyes. His headache was coming back.

"No. I have never seen this particular disease before, but it bears certain similarities to the saffron fever. If I could get back to my…"

Basil stopped when he saw Gwyneth's expression. She was no longer looking at him, but at someone over his left shoulder. Her face was defiant, but fear lurked in her eyes. Basil turned.

Redleg Melloch seemed to rise all of the way to the ceiling, blotting out the doorway like a storm blots out the sky. His great brown beard obscured the majority of his face like a thundering cloud, and the light brown of his eyes glared with lightning intensity. He raised a mighty hand and struck Basil across the side of the head. He crumpled like a leaf, landing with a clatter on the decking just below the boy's cot. Basil struggled to stay conscious as the room spun haphazardly around him.

Melloch roared something in the harsh Marauder tongue, jabbing a finger at the woman. She returned with a similar retort. They went back and forth, with Gwyneth repeatedly pointing at the boy on the cot. Basil stole another glance at the boy, Caspar, with his fine features and pale almond hair. *I am Redleg Melloch. My son is Caspar Melloch.* Redleg Melloch's son. And Gwyneth's.

Other Marauders in the room were stirring, gathering to where the fight was taking place, standing back from the fury of Redleg Melloch and looking at Basil with wide eyes. When Melloch became aware of the audience, he drew back, chest heaving. He drew the axe from his back, and fixed Basil with a murderous gaze.

"I should have killed you on the spot. I know what your ruse is, spawn of the Liar. It was very clever. You sent a ship here that contained a sickness, a sickness that would not affect the crew. You deliberately sent it in search of us, passing through the skies of Panagiottis until it came close enough to be caught in our nets. Then, when the disease began to strike down our children, you infiltrated Colossus, seeking to 'cure' the illness and set yourself as king over us."

Melloch slammed his axe into the deck, his face a mask of twisted rage.

"Well, I tell you that I will have NONE OF IT! Remember my face well. When we meet on the far side of the mountains of death, I will pursue you until eternity dawns."

Basil could only lie helpless as the Marauder leader took a slow step toward him, and raised the axe above his head in preparation for a killing blow. The blood pumped forcefully in Basil's ears, and he was suddenly aware that it may shortly be spilled all over the deck.

At the moment Basil was sure he was going to die, he felt something break the cold sensation that had chilled his entire body. Small, warm fingers closed around his own, gripping him tightly. Redleg Melloch had stopped. He didn't put the axe down, but the huge man was now looking over Basil's shoulder, at his son. The boy was sleeping peacefully, one hand grasping Basil's.

"If you're going to kill me," said Basil, heart hammering. "I can't stop you. I don't know what Lorus has done to your people, but I am not Lorus. My family has many debts to pay the people of Cor Nova, and if I am successful, yours will be among the first. I can cure your son, and all of these children, if you allow me to live."

"You *do not* understand," said Redleg Melloch. His great chest heaved. "You do not. You were not there when Lorus turned his back on my people, or when Titus forced us from our homes and attacked our strongholds in the mountains. You were not there when our warriors sacrificed themselves at the Bourdigan Pass to cover the escape of our survivors to Colossus. You have not been here as we are, starved and hunted. Now, we're dying. You do not understand."

"You're right," said Basil, unconsciously gripping the sleeping boy's hand tighter. "I don't. I can't. But I can try to make things right. My uncle may have sent this disease to you, but I know how to cure it. The critical component is on board my ship, *Philomena...*"

"Do not speak!" roared Melloch. He turned to some men standing by. "Bring him to the Lorehall."

"Redleg," said Gwyneth. Her hands were like fragile birds landing on Melloch's arms. Her voice was light. "Please. Caspar is dying. He's dying."

With a grunt, Melloch shook her off and stormed out.

CHAPTER TWENTY-FIVE

Cyprian had sailed to many far-off corners of Cor Nova during his years in the air. He had seen many strange and magnificent sights, but none matched the ring-ship of the Marauders in its sheer size and scope. *Philomena's* crew, bunched together on the bow of one of the Marauder ships, could only gape wide-eyed at the impossibly large ramshackle construction of ships and canvas. As the Marauder ship swooped up to the deck of the ring, *Philomena,* crewed by Marauder airmen, was lashed to the rail alongside them.

A few dozen Marauder men were standing along the rail of Colossus, leaning over and jeering at the proceedings in their strange tongue. A large contingent of heavily armed Marauders stormed on deck. They were dressed in furs all the way down to their heavy boots, with silver talismans and bangles tinkling from wrists, heads, and earlobes. One of the Marauders standing on the deck of Colossus thumped a gloved hand against the rail of the huge ring, calling for silence. He was a short, squat man with big shoulders and a large hat with a silver moon medallion on the front. He had bushy eyebrows and spoke each word with a strange bounce.

"You are the shipmaster, old man?" he said in heavily accented Sylvan, pointing at Francis Lightlas.

"Yes."

The spokesman turned to rejoin his fellows and the Marauders began to argue about something, pointing and gesticulating wildly. Finally, they seemed to come to a consensus.

"You are too old," said the Marauder spokesman. "Who is the deckmaster?"

Cyprian saw Lightlas falter, uncertainty in his eyes.

"I'm the deckmaster," said Cyprian, pulling the brass oculus out of his belt as proof of his office.

The Marauders gave him a once-over, then shared an agreeing nod. The heavily armed Marauders dragged the rest of the crew off the ship and down one of the wide, dark hatches into the ring, until only Cyprian and Lightlas were left on deck. Veronica's dark eyes were the last of the crew that Cyprian saw, disappearing into the darkness. Next, they seized Lightlas and put him on the deck of the enormous ring, while Cyprian was left on *Philomena*. Here, they relieved him of his pistol, deckknife, oculus, and anything else that might have been useful. They cleared out the weapons lockers and nailed sturdy planks over the hatches leading belowdecks.

"Now that we've made the preparations," said the spokesman as the other Marauders clustered eagerly around the rail above *Philomena's* deck. "I believe the hostilities can commence. Stranger, state your name."

Cyprian shrugged, jamming his hands into his pockets.

"I'd rather not."

With a grunt, the Marauder drew an extremely large pistol, pulled the hammer back, and pointed it at Cyprian's head. Cyprian felt the sudden clarity of mind that these situations bring.

"Maybe better to cooperate, my boy," said Lightlas, eyeing the loaded gun barrel.

"Cyprian Fields," Cyprian said promptly. "Of Misericordiae."

The Marauder holstered the weapon, and began to speak in a drawling manner, as though he was reciting from memory.

"Cyprian Fields of Misericordiae, in accordance with our Lore, it is unlawful for any Marauder to take the ship of another man outside of warfare. He must instead defeat her master in equal combat. Only then will the ship truly serve him. Your shipmaster is too old to adequately perform this duty, so you will take his place. I am Shaldur, and as I speak your tongue, I am the master of these proceedings."

Cyprian blinked at Shaldur.

"You're going to make me fight for *Philomena?*"

"She will be given a more suitable name when we have thrown your lifeless corpse from her decks, but yes."

A different Marauder whipped over the gunwale onto *Philomena's* empty deck. He was tall and sinewy, and had a long mustache, each dangling tip capped with a piece of ornamental silver. His smile was yellow and menacing. From his leather belt, he drew a thin blade that whizzed through the air like a wasp.

"This is Baztuk," said Shaldur. "He will challenge you on this day for the ownership of your ship."

Baztuk whipped his blade at Cyprian again, barking something menacing in the Marauder tongue. The other Marauders laughed, Shaldur the loudest.

"Baztuk wishes to say that he will make a gift to his woman of your disembodied eyeballs. She has never seen a grey-eyed man before, but the rest of you is not so interesting. Baztuk does not speak the Sylvan, and therefore I will be delivering the ceremonial taunts in his stead. Your shipmaster may deliver the taunts for you if he so desires. I have here your weapon."

He recognized the blade the Marauder tossed down onto the deck as an old, rusty Fleet saber. It was heavy, unwieldy, impractical against such a quick opponent. He would have been better off wielding Burt Spacklebrook by his feet.

"I don't get my choice of weapon?"

"It is better than nothing," shrugged Shaldur. "It is best not to make questions of our generosity."

Cyprian grumbled something impolite, picking up the rusty weapon. Baztuk was advancing slowly up the deck with his blade, his evil smile getting wider with every step. He said something else, and Shaldur translated.

"Baztuk says that he will soon make grisly artwork on the deck with your entrails."

Baztuk lunged. Cyprian barely had time to parry, swerving right and left as Baztuk made two more lunges. The Marauder backed off and barked in the Marauder tongue, a smile curling his lips. Cyprian knew that he was being tested, played with. He took another step back, gaining footing on the bottom step of the command deck. Baztuk smiled again and prepared for another attack.

"Step off a plank, you slimy illiterate scum-guzzling pirate!" roared Lightlas from the deck of Colossus.

The Marauders seemed surprised, almost impressed, by this outburst. For a half-second, Baztuk's concentration was broken, and that was all that Cyprian needed. He launched himself from the step, allowing his momentum to take him straight into the advancing Marauder, blade first. Baztuk barely blocked in time, and the blow sent him staggering across the deck.

"Nice ceremonial taunt, shipmaster!" called Cyprian.

But he had no time to hear Lightlas's gruff thanks, because Baztuk and his blade were rushing upon him again. This time, the crooked smile was gone; the Marauder was not playing anymore. Up and down the deck they fought. Baztuk was perilously fast. It took all of Cyprian's skill to keep the Marauder's razor-sharp blade at bay. He leapt, parried, dodged, and rolled, using every dirty trick he could think of. But the Marauder just kept coming, even as the taunts flew left and right.

"Baztuk wishes to inform you that he will greatly enjoy carving the name of his mother into your ship's bowsprit once he has relieved it of your possession."

"The shipmaster wishes to inform Baztuk that he's a greasy, unscrupulous twit and that if his mother really loved him, she'd use his sword to cut off that ridiculous excuse for a mustache."

As time went on, Baztuk became steadily more dangerous. His blade hissed and flicked back and forth, and Cyprian felt fire erupt in his left arm and across his back as the blade nicked him. His arms and lungs burned, he could feel hot blood seeping down into the sweat-laden shirt beneath his coat. He had to outsmart this Marauder, or all Shaldur's taunts were going to come violently true. And then, out of the corner of his eye, just to the Marauder's left, Cyprian saw one of the mooring cables. For the second time that day, an unlikely plan blossomed in his mind.

Cyprian dodged Baztuk's next thrust and swiped out wildly to the left. The heavy saber swung well wide of the Marauder, but bit deeply into the forward mooring cable that held *Philomena* to Colossus. With a series of pops, the rope untwisted itself and snapped. Baztuk turned his head, distracted by the sound. It was an opportunity not to be missed. Cyprian dealt the Marauder a healthy kick, shoved the saber into his belt, and swung himself up the ratlines, heading for the envelopes. He heard a loud shout in the Marauder tongue from below, Shaldur yelling over the booing of his comrades.

"Baztuk reflects on the cowardice of a man who runs from a fight."

"Oh…er… shut your fool mouth!"

Cyprian ignored both Shaldur and Lightlas. Baztuk could reflect on whatever he wanted, so long as it wasn't Cyprian being dead. Lungs still burning, he pulled himself up onto the surface of the midships envelope. He barely had time to steady himself when the lean, mustached face of Baztuk cleared the opposite side, lithe of step over the envelopes with blade in hand.

"Do not believe that you will fare better up there, boy," called Shaldur from below. The other Marauders and Lightlas had to back up to see them. "The Marauders are at home anywhere on ship. There is nowhere you can run."

The envelope beneath Cyprian's feet was soft and springy. He bounced from foot to foot, ready to meet the attack, but Baztuk seemed equally comfortable. They circled twice, the silvered tips of Baztuk's mustache swinging back and forth. His villainous face split into another evil grin as he followed Cyprian step for step.

Fast as a striking snake, Baztuk sprang forward with his blade and Cyprian felt a sharp sear of pain along the side of his neck. He had dodged just in time to avoid becoming headless. Baztuk attacked again, this time with a stab; Cyprian turned the blade, but not far enough. The silver blade grazed his thigh. Blood began to pool in the base of Cyprian's boot.

There were speckles of blood on the ship's envelope, as though it too had been wounded. Suddenly, Cyprian had another idea. Baztuk lunged again, slashing his blade down on top of Cyprian's. The two hilts collided, blades locked together. Cyprian held tight, looking right into the Marauder's almond eyes.

"Greasy. Unscrupulous. Twit."

With all the strength in his body, Cyprian threw the Marauder back, lifted his blade, and swung it downwards. It bit through the sturdy rope netting and into the canvas of the envelope. With a great whoosh, thick white whorls of aether enveloped Cyprian, roaring their way into the sky. The pressure of the escaping aether forced the tear even wider, and the envelope's top shifted and shrank. Cyprian stumbled, trying to find his footing. With a roar, Baztuk came leaping over the chasm of hemorrhaging aether. But, he overstepped. Cyprian, using his lack of balance, bulled into the Marauder with all the strength he had left.

Cyprian felt his feet leave the canvas, and both he and the Marauder plunged into the center of the envelope.

For a few moments, the whole world was upside down, drowned in whiteness. Cyprian could feel himself sinking through the chunks of sea sponge that helped to keep the aether contained within the envelope. The Marauder was still struggling, reaching for him. Cyprian had the presence of mind to grasp the muscular wrist holding the sword, but Baztuk was so powerful, he knew he couldn't hold him off for long. The white substance burned his mouth and lungs, as though he was trying to breathe empty space.

Finally, he felt the canvas of the underside of the envelope against his back. Somehow he had managed to keep his the saber by his side. He swung it wildly, felt a tear, and then the world jerked. He was falling.

He barely felt it when he hit the deck.

CHAPTER TWENTY-SIX

At first, Veronica could not make up her mind as to whether she should be more amazed or afraid.

The fear, she decided, was fairly commonplace. It stemmed from the dozen well-armed, silver-bedecked Marauder warriors roughly escorting the crew of *Philomena* through the endless wooden passages. The warrior who was occasionally dealing Veronica a zealous poke in the back with a spear was beginning to grate on her nerves. After one jab nearly drew blood, Veronica turned to say something, and nearly stopped in surprise. The face that looked back at her was plenty fierce, with almond-colored eyes and pale skin, but it didn't have a beard. Veronica noted with surprise that this warrior was a woman, her hair plaited and held back by a large, silver band twisted into the shape of an eagle.

Veronica turned around and kept going, brow furrowed. Her father had always said that Marauders were strongly patriarchal. If there were female warriors, they must be running low on men indeed.

On the whole, the crew was quiet, taking in their surroundings with wide eyes. The enormous ring was a labyrinth, layer upon layer of jagged ships and decking stacked upon one another. Her father had told her stories of Marauders, also called the Sky-rovers, the Restless Children of Lightning. According to legend, they'd arrived centuries before from the mythical land of Norum across the Shrouds and been unable to return. In doing so, they had brought the much of the lore of shipbuilding to Cor Nova. They had their own language, their own customs, their own tongue. Throughout the centuries, the Marauders kept largely to themselves, and that made people distrustful.

Once Titus came to power, he hunted the Marauders as enemies of the Dominion, claiming that they plotted sedition against the Imperium with their solitary and suspicious ways. Sensing trouble, most Marauders had fled to a hidden rally point at the misty Bourdigan Pass, in a remote corner of Korkyra. It was there that the Imperium Fleet had found them.

Veronica couldn't help but feel a small thrill. That was where the amazement came in. The Imperium had declared that the Marauders were obliterated in the Battle of the Bourdigan Pass, but obviously this was a lie or maybe even ignorance. There were hundreds of Marauders here, maybe thousands. If the Marauders had managed to evade the Imperium, even here at the edges of society, then perhaps there was hope for Basil as well.

Finally, they emerged into a cavernous empty hull that formed a whole section of a ring. She immediately recognized it from one of her father's books. At one time, this must have been an independent ship, fiercely protected at the center of any Marauder Fleet: the Lorehall. It was strung with tapestries, an ancient history of the dead woven by the fingers of the living.

The Lorehall was full of Marauders, several hundred at least. A few looked on with interest, a spark of cruel delight in their eyes. But most of them were silent and still, almost embarrassed. The men's eyes were pale behind their beards, and the women had a drawn, thin look. Veronica realized that there were no children; she was probably the youngest person in the room.

The icy wind was blowing fiercely from a large open portal at the far end of the hall, bringing with it the sound of someone speaking loudly in the Marauder's harsh tongue. Outlined by the frozen sky at the portal's mouth, a single pale figure stood on unsteady feet. Veronica was elated to see Basil alive, but he looked beaten and dazed. A large purple bruise was forming on the side of his head, and his clothes were ripped down the front of his chest. He seemed on the verge of collapse. A pair of Marauders stood on either side of him, preventing him from falling out of the large portal into the frozen abyss. A few feet in front of him, one of the iron braziers flickered. Apparently, it was important to keep the guards from freezing.

There was an enormous Marauder at the front of the crowd, and it was he who was speaking. As the new captives approached, he fell silent, watching them with hatred in his eyes. He was taller than Benttree, musclebound and fierce. A large silver gauntlet encased one muscular wrist, and a fearsome battleaxe was slung across his back. His beard tumbled down in knots, giving him the look of a primal polar beast.

The Marauder guards prodded them forward, forcing *Philomena's* crew to stand along the frozen lip of the portal on either side of Basil.

At Veronica's back, the howling, icy void beckoned. The wind stung at her neck, and she was forced to think about the reality of being thrown from this portal. Far below, the icy crags passed, silent and forbidding. How long would she fall before striking the ground? Would she feel the impact? Would her mother die alone? Imprisoned at the Abyss?

Her chest tightened, but she curled her fists tightly, forcing herself to think, to take in her surroundings. Benttree was to her immediate right, with Paschal beyond him. Both looked terrified.

Content that his captives were now fully at his mercy, the huge man jabbed an enormous finger at all of them in a sweeping motion, roaring something to the people in the Marauder tongue. The guards approached, spears and swords at the ready. The one on the far end was pushing his swordpoint into Spacklebrook's bony chest. The boy whimpered and moaned, forced to take a step back toward the void. There were mere feet between him and oblivion. Next to him, a burly Marauder with an axe advanced on Oakum. Veronica's guard was giving her a look of particular menace, spear leveled. Behind her, the fire in the iron brazier cracked and flickered, giving her a fiery penumbra. Veronica knew she had to act now, or she wouldn't be acting ever again. She hoped that the guards didn't understand Sylvan. As faintly as she could, she whispered to Benttree.

"Hit...her...when...I...say..."

For a moment, she was worried that he hadn't heard. Then slowly, Benttree nodded, not taking his eyes off his own approaching guards, two monstrous fellows with matching silver noserings. The great Marauder was still railing, even as the heels of Spacklebrook's boots approached the edge of the floor. The redheaded deckhand leaned backwards, eyes wide and stammering, away from the sharpened swordpoint that now menaced his throat.

"Now!" Veronica said, and she ran straight toward the brazier. With a roar that made the planks beneath their feet shudder, Benttree barreled toward the female warrior, driving his shoulder directly into her and slamming her sideways. Veronica bulled straight through the space where she had been, seizing the uncharred end of one of the burning hunks of wood in the brazier. She yanked it free, ignoring the searing pain in her hand and scattering blazing coals all around. The quicker nosering warrior took a sprawling swipe at Veronica, but she danced aside, catching him a blow on the shoulder and neck with the burning log.

There was a loud thump as four Marauders forced Hugh Benttree down. Taking advantage of the confusion, Paschal had managed to land his guard a strong blow to the head, but he was laid flat by another Marauder, who leaned over Paschal, holding a sharp silver knife to his throat.

"Easy there," Paschal muttered, eyes locked on the Marauder. "There's a fine boy…"

"Slash his throat!" cried Redleg Melloch in Sylvan, his face livid with rage.

"You'll do nothing of the kind!" said Veronica, her voice ringing in the Lorehall.

Hundreds of pale faces turned to her, and, nearly as one, blanched. Veronica held her burning log under the nearest fluttering tapestry, allowing the flames to come within inches of the weathered, ancient tassels at the base of the immense work of art. Melloch's face twisted with hatred, and not a little fear.

"Outsider," he said, through gritted teeth. "It would be very foolish of you to do such a thing."

"Let us go," Veronica said, doing her absolute best not to shiver. "And you won't have to discover the depth of my intentions."

CHAPTER TWENTY-SEVEN

Cyprian's senses returned with the wild yelling of Marauders and the sound of cracking and creaking wood.

His eyes snapped open. Above him, the torn remnants of the midships envelope were collapsing like a giant folded leaf. Cyprian threw himself sideways, down the slant of the deck, just avoiding the mass of rigging that crashed down next to him. He could see the form of Baztuk, struggling to escape from the folds.

Baztuk's friends on the deck of Colossus didn't seem too interested in helping their fallen comrade. They had developed another problem. With the loss of one of her envelopes, *Philomena* was sinking, her weight pulling down on the superstructure of the enormous ring. There were pings and snaps as supporting cables and wooden planks began to snap under the pull of the sinking freighter's mooring lines. A network of jagged cracks yawned in the hull beneath the ring's deck.

With frantic cries, Shaldur and company dashed to the ropes that bound *Philomena* to Colossus, attempting to free the ship before their icy refuge sustained more damage. This gave Francis Lightlas the perfect opportunity to hop arthritically over the gunwale.

"Does Baztuk have any comments he'd like to share now, Mr. Shaldur?" he roared with a laugh.

Shaldur didn't reply, but instead drove his blade through the rear mooring cable. In moments, *Philomena* was free. With aether still bleeding in plumes from the lost envelope, she began to sink freely through the icy sky. Cyprian heard the shouts and yells of the Marauders diminish to nothing as *Philomena* descended, shaky and unsteady. Within moments, she was nearly down to the base of Colossus, spars groaning as she swung through the icy wind in an uncontrolled spin.

"We've got to get some more aether in her," said Lightlas, stumping his way toward the wheel. "The valves. Can you get into the ship core?"

Ignoring the pain from his wounds, Cyprian jumped down through the grated hatch into the shipcore, throwing wide the valves sending aether to the two remaining envelopes. Even as the spinning intensified, he felt the descent of the ship first slow, then reverse. Lightlas got on the wheel, muscling through the jolting that ran through the ship's workings. After a few tense moments, the spin began to lessen until it finally stopped.

"That's it!" Cyprian cried, thumping the valve panel with a bleeding hand and kissing a brass fitting. "That's my girl!"

He pulled himself back up on deck and yelled up to Lightlas. They had their ship back; now they needed her crew, and quick. Cyprian could already see the forms of Marauder ships converging on *Philomena*, ready to obliterate her in a hail of gunfire. Cyprian scanned the full circumference of the enormous ring. Where would Marauders keep their prisoners? As if in answer to the question, a high, piercing shriek rang over the sky, and a streak of gold and grey swooped over the deck, whizzing past Cyprian's ear before taking off toward a section of the ring.

"Good to see that bird earning its keep!" cried Lightlas, turning the ship so that her bow aimed to follow Petros's path.

Cyprian squinted into the distance. The kestrel flew towards a section of Colossus formed from the hull of a very large freighter. There were figures poised in the large hatch that opened inward into the ring. He saw the hulking form of Benttree, Burt Spacklebrook looking positively terrified, Nolan Paschal silent and still. Then, with a thrill, Cyprian saw Basil. He looked positively exhausted, but he was there, alive. He counted. They all were. And then, there was Veronica, poised with a torch in her hand, just beneath one of the

Marauders' precious tapestries. Cyprian almost laughed. Those poor Marauders. Sometimes when you go fishing, you catch something with teeth.

"Holding an entire century of Marauder history hostage!" cried Lightlas. "That girl is something different."

With no crew to adjust the sails or the ailerons, all of the work fell to Cyprian. At Lightlas's direction, he shortened and hauled line after line, ignoring the blades of pain that pressed through his arms and legs as he strained every muscle to keep the sails full of wind. Twice, furious gusts nearly tore *Philomena* from their grip, threatening to send her tipping into the frozen void. To make matters worse, a few of the Marauder ships were nearly in firing distance. Lightlas tracked their paths, adjusting *Philomena's* course to avoid them as best he could. With each passing moment, the huge hatch in Colossus grew larger until they were upon it. Lightlas tried to pull *Philomena* directly up to its lip. But, the wind and the weakness of his arms had other plans. Spacklebrook and Paschal had to leap out of the way as *Philomena's* forward bow crashed into the hatch with a shuddering bump.

"Get on board!" said Veronica, not taking her eyes off the monstrous Marauder who was glaring at all of them, powerless to do anything, a muscular tower of pent-up rage.

The airmen complied, rushing aboard as quickly as they could. They took up their positions on deck, searching frantically for weapons, but found none. Burt Spacklebrook nearly had a panic attack when Baztuk flopped, groaning, from the tangled mess of *Philomena's* midships envelope. Paschal and Oakum seized him and pinned him to the mast. Cyprian saw Basil order Benttree to unblock the main deck hatch, which the enormous man did. Then, the ship's cook disappeared into the decks below.

Lightlas handed the helm over to Masterson and walked to the gunwale. An enormous Marauder stood outlined against the opening of Colossus, his large fur cape blowing in the wind. With a great hand, he pointed out to the sky. The Marauder ships were converging, guns brought to bear.

"There is nowhere to run," he called over the rush of the wind.

"No, but you will let them go," said Veronica. She was still standing beneath the tapestry, the torch in her hand. Her face was pale, but resolute. "If you don't, I'll turn this tapestry to ash."

Cyprian's heart beat faster. She was going to sacrifice herself, ransom her own life for *Philomena's* escape. He felt a pang of anguished loss. The men seemed likewise horrified; they looked to Francis Lightlas, his weather-beaten face inscrutable behind his grey beard. Was it better to fight and die than to allow a woman to die in your place?

With a bang, the main hatch clattered open again, and Basil emerged, his spectacles skewed across his face. In one fist, he clutched a large vial containing a cluster of leaves, hurriedly labeled.

"What is that?" Cyprian demanded.

"A critical ingredient. To cure their children."

Basil reared back his arm, prepared to throw the vial over the gap. Cyprian immediately grabbed his wrist. He wrestled the vial from Basil's protesting fingers.

"Hold on a tick. Cure their children you said?"

"Yes," Basil said, snatching ineffectually at Cyprian's hand. "Saffron fever. Cyprian, they will all die if they don't have it. Give me the vial."

"And the staff?" Lightlas asked.

"I don't have it. The big one, Redleg Melloch, knew I was looking for it. He snapped it in two in front of my face and threw it out of the Lorehall door. Cyprian, hang it all!" Basil was still jumping to reach the vial. "They're children. They have no part in this. It's not for us to take revenge."

"Basil," Cyprian said quietly. "I know that I'm not speaking from a position of authority here, but if you think that, you have a lot to learn about kinging."

Lightlas turned to the huge figure standing in the Lorehall portal.

"Mr. Melloch and friends," he called over the gap. "I've just spent the last hour or so enduring your ceremonial taunts, so I'm of a mind to deliver a few of my own. And considering how much of an inconvenience you've been to me today, they would be very colorful indeed. But, I'm a businessman and I'm sure you are all very busy, so I think it would be wise to skip the formalities and come to a reasonable agreement."

Lightlas seized the bottle from Cyprian's fingers, waggling it at the fuming Melloch.

"Mr. Melloch, I take it that you're the chief of this tribe. Basil, the son of Lorus, tells me this is the herb needed to cure your children of their disease. As you can tell, he is very generous. I, however, as a businessman, am not. I require payment."

Redleg Melloch's face twisted in anger. He raised his giant arm. Out of the corner of his eye, Cyprian saw the Marauder ship crews tense over their gun barrels, awaiting the signal to fire. But a woman, tall, slender and fair, appeared from out of the crowd. She placed a staying hand on Melloch's arm.

"What payment do you propose?" she called, her chin held high.

Lightlas produced a winning smile, and Cyprian noticed a few of the Marauders actually seem to relax a bit.

"I require two things. And both I will have, or I will send this little bottle the way all high things eventually go. First, I require my friend Ms. Stromm to be placed gently and whole onto the deck of my ship. She is not to be harmed in any way. Second, I require safe passage from this place to the border of Panagiottis."

Redleg Melloch's chest heaved, the axe-handle on his back moving up and down with the motion. Suddenly, something lit up in Cyprian's mind.

"And a third thing!" Cyprian said, pointing. "We require the axe on your back."

"What are you doing?" Basil hissed. "Who cares about the stupid axe?"

"No!" Melloch said, pushing the woman away. "You will not have it unless you come and take it."

Lightlas raised a finger.

"My deckmaster is very wise. If you are to have the medicine, we will have the axe as well. I will add to it my solemn word that we will not breathe a word of this place to any living soul. The location or nature of Colossus will not leave the deck of *Philomena*, until you are welcomed back into Cor Nova as equals, as brothers."

Melloch gave a sharp, barking laugh.

"No such thing will ever happen while I am alive."

"There is good for those willing to fight for it," said Lightlas. "For those who are willing to fight for a just king. For a Sovereign."

With a nod from Lightlas, Cyprian handed the vial back to Basil, who accepted it gently. For a moment, the sky was quiet save for the whipping of the wind. Every Marauder eye was fixed on Basil, a slim figure in black who held all of their hopes in one gentle hand. Basil looked back, fixing his eyes on Redleg Melloch.

"You set that trap on the skiff," Basil said. "You know who I am, what I'm here for. I can't speak for the inaction of my father, or the action of my uncle. I am not a Marauder. But I am an outcast, as are all of my friends. We are chased and hunted, too. I can't promise riches or gold or fame or plunder. All I can promise that I will try to make things right."

He held the vial up in the air. His words hung with the icy particles in the air, blowing among the tapestries of ancient Marauder history. Melloch shook his great hairy head, his arms crossed in mistrust.

"Do we have an accord?" asked Lightlas. "Swear it on your silver."

Melloch glared at the old shipmaster. His wife whispered urgently into his ear. His face did not soften, but finally, after what seemed like an age, his voice boomed out into the silence.

"I swear upon my silver to give you your girl, safe passage, and my axe. In exchange for the cure."

With a single motion of his brawny arm, he pulled the axe from his back and sent it spinning, end over end, toward *Philomena*. With a thud, it buried itself in the gunwale, blade sparkling in the icy light.

Cyprian nodded. As he stabilized the ship, Basil scrambled over the side of *Philomena*, went up to the huge Redleg Melloch, and deposited the vial in his hands.

"Good fortune to you," he said. "Come on, Veronica."

Veronica followed him, and all were aboard. Benttree tossed the limply struggling Baztuk across the gap to his comrades, Lightlas gave a command, and *Philomena* was off into the white sky.

CHAPTER TWENTY-EIGHT

The shipmaster's trust of the Marauders did not run deep. Lightlas ordered every piece of available sail to be set. Basil's first impulse, weak though he was, was to grab a rope and assist in working the ship's ailerons, but Veronica marched him into the cartorium, where it was fairly warm, and informed him at rapier point that if he emerged and wasn't dying, he would be in serious trouble.

Basil sat down on one of the crates, every joint stiff and protesting. The crew would be constantly looking back into the swirling frozen sky behind, expecting to see the sharp bows of a dozen Marauder vessels running them down, but Basil didn't feel that was too likely. Beside the far-off sounds of ship-life happening on the deck outside, the cartorium was quiet and warm. Basil allowed himself to rest against the bulkhead, his eyes slowly growing heavier.

A slam and a blast of cold air jerked Basil from sleep. Cyprian stood in the doorway, thoroughly caked with snow and ice. Behind him, the sky was dark. Basil picked himself up as Cyprian stomped the ice from his boots and the similarly frozen forms of Shipmaster Lightlas and Veronica followed him. Petros fluttered in behind them as the cartorium door slammed mercifully shut.

"What in all the blessed blue hazes?" said Francis Lightlas, arthritically stripping off his coat and shaking icicles from his beard. "Possessed you to gamble everything on a souvenir?"

Cyprian threw Redleg Melloch's axe on the map table, pulling off his own jacket and dabbing at the shallow cuts on his shoulder and arm.

"It's not a souvenir," he said. He lifted the axe up to the light. The head was large and rough with a cruel bend at the end. Cyprian ran a thumb along the blade.

"Perfectly ordinary axehead," he said, next tracing his fingers up and down the length of the haft. "But the handle...This is not a normal axe handle."

Suddenly, Basil's heart began to beat very fast. He stood up and leaned forward, looking carefully. Cyprian was right. The haft was too thin to be a proper weapon's handle, and perfectly round. Where it was not covered by a tightly braided leather grip, the wood was dark and whorled, the grain swirling into complex patterns up and down its length. As the others watched, silent, Cyprian lifted the axe by its head, and gave the bottom of the haft a solid thump against the decking. The axehead came free from the top of the haft, taking the braided grip with it as it fell down the length of the handle.

What remained on the floor, a perfectly straight rod of ancient wood, unbent by the years, unbroken by famine and toil and struggle, raised over battlefields and festivals, was the Elm Staff, the lone companion of the Sovereign of Cor Nova. The very Arm of Sylvanus itself. Veronica gasped, her eyes wide. Basil reached out, almost trembling as his fingers closed around the haft.

"How did you know?" he asked Cyprian, who was looking radiantly smug.

"A powerful man never throws away a valuable asset. If Melloch destroyed a staff in front of you, it was a fake. He would have kept the real one close. Very close. And, as we've established, this struck me as a somewhat suspicious axe."

A warm feeling flooded Basil's body. They had found two relics. The Amulet was a warm lump in his pocket, and now the Elm Staff was in his hand. A glimmer of real hope shone through the icy fog.

There was a knock at the door. Bartholomew Oakum's face, flushed with anxiety, poked around the doorjamb. He was dirty from head to foot, and sweat glistened on his forehead.

"Shipmaster," he said. "Something you should see. Down in the steerage."

With a groan, Lightlas stood and followed Oakum out, and, after taking one more moment to marvel at the Elm Staff, Cyprian went with them. Elated at their discovery but exhausted from her struggle, Veronica went below to change her clothes. When her footsteps disappeared down the stairwell, Basil was left alone in the cartorium save for Petros, who was snoring lightly amidst the scrolls on the maptable. He turned back to the Elm Staff, setting it carefully on the table in front of him. He laid the Amulet beside it. Two of three. Now only one remained: the Astral Crown. Basil pulled the Rule of Sylvanus from across the table, its brass bindings clinking on the planks.

He opened it to the inside cover, and read from the poem again.

The Sovereign's eye, that sees from height,
Turns on brows of wooden sight.
Third and sixth and third once more.
At Ivory's first, behind the door.

He closed the book. It was a meaningless jumble of words. He turned the Amulet over and over in his hands as he thought. The Amulet led to the Staff. Maybe the Staff would lead to the Crown. Basil turned up the wick of the nearest lantern, and his eyes searched the entire length of the staff, sensitive fingers feeling for any hidden markings. The wood was ancient, and nearly as smooth as marble, but warm. His fingers traced the top of the staff and felt only the same smoothness. Then, they travelled to the bottom. Here, the texture changed.

Basil turned the staff over, letting the lantern light fall directly on the end of the staff. There, etched in three straight, shallow lines, was a perfect triangle. Basil's brow furrowed. What could it mean? It was not a common symbol of the Sovereign. He hadn't seen it anywhere in the Rule.

Then, Basil's eyes fell on the enormous map of Cor Nova beneath his fingers and an idea blossomed. Basil began to shove things off the table. Scrolls, pencils, instruments, and a squawking sea kestrel rained to the planks in a clatter. Disregarding the annoyed flutterings of Cyprian's bird, Basil found a piece of red chalk and a rule, then ran his sharp blue eyes over the map. A blue circle denoted the spot where they had met the O'Larre in the Osmanthus. One corner. A second, farther north, showed the Old Man's Tooth. The second corner.

Basil scrawled calculations on a corner of the map, measuring the distance between the two and figuring angles. Then, with the rule, he drew lines on the map, completing the triangle. Flush with victory, Basil tapped on the spot where the lines intersected, forming the third point of a perfect triangle across Cor Nova.

Folding the enormous map haphazardly, Basil hurried to the main hold. Down in the forward end, there was a large open hatch. Somber voices and shifting lantern light emerged from the opening. Basil stuck his head in, hailing Cyprian and Lightlas. They beckoned him.

"Watch your step, now, Basil," came Oakum's reedy voice from up ahead. "Dark as blazes. Liable to fall and fracture your bits in here."

The steerage was dark and musty and smelled slightly of straw and cats. Holding the map, Basil had to tread carefully along the top of the keel, a huge piece carved from a single Misericordiae cedar. Basil could make out the shapes of Cyprian, Lightlas, and Oakum crouching in the darkness, with only a single lantern between them. He heard Oakum's voice from up ahead, muffled in the gloom. Basil guessed that they were somewhere about amidships, directly below the crew bunkroom and the shipcore.

"I noticed it when I came down a few minutes ago. I had my suspicions after that fancy landing when we were running down the mountain. Got a kind of sick feeling in the pit of my stomach. Came down here to check to see if there was anything amiss. Turns out, there was."

When Basil came up near them, he could see what Oakum was taking about. There, in the middle of the giant keel was an enormous crack, a jagged black gash that ran from one side of the keel into the center at a vicious angle. It was nearly two yards long.

Lightlas leaned heavily against the bulkhead, his head bent, his face pale, the victory of the last few hours flushed away.

"What can we do?" Basil asked.

"What can you do when you have a man who's back is broke?" said Oakum. "We can brace it with something. For now."

Cyprian traced the crack with a calloused hand.

"Once," Lightlas said. "When I was a hand on a treasure trawler out in Corundum Falls, we were paired with a hardy ship, a cedar freighter, like *Philomena*. She was old, a ship that shouldn't have been trusted in the first place. They pulled a tight turn coming out of a storm, and the keel cracked, almost as bad as this one. The shipmaster didn't land her. Tried to get her to port. That night, I was on watch, atop the envelopes. Three hours before dawn, I heard a noise like a twig being snapped, but deeper, louder. By moonlight, I saw the whole hull fold up in half, like a clam shutting. The hull was busted open, and gravity and the envelopes ripped her apart. There was nothing we could do. Not a soul survived."

He turned to Oakum.

"Brace her as best you can. Use whatever we have. It has to be enough to get us somewhere we can get her fixed."

Lightlas turned toward Basil, who was crouched on the keel with a fistful of map.

"Basil, what are you doing? Is that my dominion map?"

For a moment, Basil didn't answer. It was unnerving to see the airmen, usually pillars of confidence bordering on arrogance, so shaken.

"Yes," Basil said finally, unfolding the map as much as he could in the limited space of the keel. "Look at this. There was a triangle on the bottom of the staff. I plotted the spot where we found the Amulet, then where we found the staff. Then, I calculated the angles and found where they intersected to make a perfect triangle. See the third point?"

Cyprian blinked, following the lines with his fingers.

"Misericordiae," he said. "Right in the center. *Ivory's* first. The Ivory City's first. But first what?"

Lightlas, Oakum, and Cyprian looked at each other, both with the look of defeat in their eyes.

"It's a thousand leagues," Lightlas said. "We'll never make it there with the ship in this condition. The keel must be braced before we can do anything else."

Basil felt his hopes deflating. How long would that take? Would Titus have reached the Sarcophagus by then?

"Where can we go?" asked Oakum. "Not back to Kwalz? Or Niev?"

"No," said Cyprian. If the fear in his face had unnerved Basil before, it scared him now. "We'll need to ask for help, the help of a man I hoped I would never see again."

Chapter Twenty-Nine

Cyprian went to bed that night with the screams from Lightlas's doomed treasure trawler echoing in his ears. He lay for a long time, watching the lantern above his bunk sway with the movement of the ship. The wind rattled the windowpanes, and occasionally Petros squawked in his sleep, jerking Cyprian back to wakefulness. Every bump in the night filled his head with the vision of *Philomena* ripping to splinters, the hull crunching in on itself, the envelopes tearing skyward. And throughout this horrific vision, like a gathering storm, leered the mutilated face of Bartimaeus Cain. In a few short hours, they would be at Wailer's Gap.

Finally, Cyprian pulled on his boots and slumped through the ship, heading up to the deck. The air was chilly, but nowhere near as frigid as it had been a few hours before. The clouds, too, had evaporated, leaving behind a starlit night. At the helm, Masterson gave a respectful nod as Cyprian passed. There were no lights in the rolling, barren wilderness beneath. Far on the northern horizon, there was the vague suggestion of the endless flatness of the Great Northern Mar. All was quiet, save for the creaking of wood and the billow of sail. The starlit night opened up wide over *Philomena's* deck, and Cyprian couldn't help but feel a strange peace steal into the midst of his anxiety. He mounted the rope ladder leading up to the tops of the envelopes, pulling himself hand over hand toward the brilliant black and purple of the sky.

Cyprian cleared his throat as he cleared the top of the envelope, ready to tell the lookout that he could head down to the galley for something hot, but there was no airman there. Instead, it was Veronica, sitting at the lookout's small wooden bench with her sketchbook in hand, looking up. The starlight glimmered on the midnight blackness of her hair, and the wind tugged at the hem of her skirt. She straightened with surprise.

"Ah, hello," she said, smoothing her skirt and repositioning her sketchbook on her lap. "Spacklebrook was up here. I told him he could stretch his legs on deck for a little while. I guess I'm not doing a terribly good job, looking out. I wanted to draw, but stars are impossible. You can't capture the blackness… I'm really just looking up."

Cyprian nodded, and sat down beside her.

"Well, that's what you're supposed to do when you're on top lookout. The men on deck can see all around, but their view above is obstructed by the envelopes. You're supposed to look up, see if anyone is coming down from above."

Veronica nodded, a small smile playing on her lips.

"Maybe I'll be an airman yet."

Cyprian folded his arms, leaning back against the bench. It was easier to look up than to look at her, as though the stars emitted a lesser brilliance.

"Not on my ship, you're not," Cyprian said. "You're insubordinate, too strong-willed. You'd be a pain in the neck as a deckhand."

Veronica shook her head, putting the pencil to paper once more. Cyprian watched her for a moment, but she just traced the pencil in idle spirals around the blank page, her head tilted.

"Shipmaster Lightlas told me about the keel. You really think that Bartimaeus Cain is our only option?"

Cyprian's stomach turned over at the mention of his name, but he did his best not to let it show.

"Cain's our only option. It'll take molten iron to fuse the keel properly. Cain is the only one with the means not in a major city and Lightlas thinks that we have enough leverage to get him to help us."

Veronica nodded. She didn't seem convinced. Cyprian didn't blame her.

"Truth be told," he said finally. "I think you already are an airman. When you save a whole crew of airmen from taking the long step, that more or less qualifies you. That was a sticky situation, with the torches and the tapestry. I'd give you a proper airman's belt, but I've had to use my extra one. Seems my old belt was damaged…in an unfortunate accident."

This time, to Cyprian's relief, Veronica laughed.

"Those things happen, unfortunately," she said. "If you're fishing for an apology, you're not going to get one. You were a proper idiot that time and I'd do it again in a heartbeat. But, I'll admit it, Cyprian. You've surprised me. I wouldn't have been able to save the crew on Colossus if you hadn't been there to save all of us."

Veronica went back to her spiral for a moment as her words washed over Cyprian. He suddenly felt very warm.

"You know," she said. "Basil is straightforward. He's a person who knows what he wants, knows what he has to do. He's powerless to present himself as anything other than he is. And for a Sovereign, I think that's a good quality."

Cyprian nodded slowly. He didn't know where she was going with this, but he had the suspicion that he wasn't going to like it.

"I say it's dangerous for a leader," he said. "To have everyone know what you're thinking."

"I know you think that," Veronica said. "Because you make it very hard for anyone to know who you are. I don't know if you're the swashbuckling rogue merchant, the Young Rooster, who will sacrifice anyone or anything it takes to win glory and fame and prestige, or if you're Cyprian, the deckmaster who will do what he knows is right even if a whole fleet brings every weapon in the world to bear against him. I don't think anyone on this ship knows who you really are. But, that doesn't bother me too much. What bothers me is the possibility that *you* don't know."

She turned to look at Cyprian. Her eyes were like twin pools of star-speckled night. Her skin was marble-white and the wind ran invisible fingers over her ebony hair. It was quiet save for the clanging of a lantern against its post down below. Cyprian didn't know what to say. The question struck him as the kind that women are all too prone to ask: pointless to the verge of being unsettling.

What difference did it make to anyone else what he called himself? He was Cyprian Fields, son of Augustus, deckmaster of *Philomena*. What more was there to say?

And yet, captured in those beguiling dark eyes, Cyprian found himself tumbling through his own history. He was a little boy, standing at the knee of his father, a great pillar of leather, brass, and confidence. He remembered the great boom of his laugh, the strength of his brawny arms, his smell of tobacco, sweat, and freshly wound rope. It was on this very ship that he inherited his father's thirst for wide tracts of open sky. Before he could read, he could tie every knot, name every sail, sharpen any knife. And then, he was a hopeless boy in Misericordiae, watching his invincible father die in the Merchant's Rebellion. Years passed, and he was abroad, wandering the world as an orphan, never staying on a ship long. And then, he was in Misericordiae beneath the Old Concourse with Lightlas, looking up at the gently smiling memory from years long past. Then, came a mysterious ship's cook with a strange heritage.

And now, a pair of sparkling dark eyes that demanded him to make sense of it all, to make sense of himself. He knew that anything he might contrive to say would be a lie, and Veronica was not someone to be swayed by lies. So, he didn't say anything at all and she, mercifully, seemed to understand. Together, they looked up into the starlit sky, which now seemed to Cyprian uncomfortably immense and unbelievably beautiful.

"This ship," Veronica asked finally. "I imagine she reminds you a lot of your father."

Cyprian nodded, blinking rather quickly.

"She does."

"That's funny," Veronica said. "You know what she reminds me of? She reminds me of my father, too. And my mother. She reminds me of home."

Veronica didn't say anything after that. Neither did Cyprian. Until the pink rays of dawn crested the horizon, they were content to sit in the immense quiet that only the birds and airmen know. And strangely, thoughts of the damaged keel or Bartimaeus Cain or the Imperium didn't seem so terrifying.

It was the middle of the day when *Philomena* emerged into the lonely valley of Wailer's Gap. The large, ragged encampment outside of the cavern had grown larger and more desperate since Cyprian had last been here. The tents stretched a long ways down the river, and the ground was muddy, churned beneath the feet of thousands of people and animals. Hundreds of lean grubby faces, some sneering, others slack-jawed, turned upward to watch the ship pass over. The crew was immediately apprehensive. Benttree shifted his mass uncomfortably, and Paschal kept spitting over his left shoulder. Spacklebrook channeled his anxiety by talking incessantly.

"Never in all my born days," muttered Bartholomew Oakum, glowering. "Did I think I would be willingly going within any appreciable distance of Bartimaeus Cain."

A few of the other men grumbled their assent, until Cyprian dispersed them to their duties.

"Well, if every man is to come out of here with all of his parts intact, we need to look sharp."

Swallowing his own misgivings and trying not to look at the white scar on the back of his hand, Cyprian oversaw the deck as Lightlas ordered Masterson to steer *Philomena* further into the valley. To everyone's relief, no bandit ship rose to meet them.

"Put her just beyond the cavern's mouth," Lightlas said, pointing to a spot just outside the shadow of the mountain, at the very top of the encampment.

Veronica and Basil stood at his side as *Philomena* descended. The mouth of the cavern opened dark ahead of them, its stalactites like glistening teeth.

"There's a concourse inside," she said.

Lightlas shook his head.

"We need a free route to the open sky. There's no knowing what Cain might try to pull."

As gingerly as he could, Masterson set the ship down where Cyprian indicated, careful to keep the fragile keel from striking the ground. Several of the crew jumped from the gunwales, spooling out long lengths of cable behind them to moor the ship to the rough earth.

"I don't need to tell you to have caution, my boy," said Shipmaster Lightlas, as the crew put out the gangplank. "Cain is a dangerous animal, and must be treated as such. All our hopes rest on you. Best of fortune."

Cyprian nodded.

"I took care of myself once here, I can do it again."

He gave Veronica and Basil an awkward wave as he set off down the gangplank and into the cavern. Once out of the daylight, Cyprian felt the subterranean chill sink into his skin. Several bandit ships were moored on the stone concourse, but they were silent and empty, their empty portholes like vacant eyes as Cyprian passed. The steps of his boots echoed loudly in the cavern. After a few minutes, he managed to find the path that led off into the darkness.

His heartbeat and breath quickened with each step as the square of light behind him grew smaller and smaller. The clamminess of the cave was like damp fingers caressing his neck, and he found himself checking his belt again and again for the reassuring hilts of his pistol and deckknife. He turned right and left, trying to remember his way, half-expecting a leering half-formed face to dart around every corner.

Finally, he made the last turn, and there crouched like a fat, contented spider in the murk, was the enormous golden ship, as though she had welled up out of Cyprian's nightmare. As she had those weeks before, she shone with a red-golden light of lanterns, but there was no tent on her deck. This time, he could clearly see reveling figures dancing back and forth between the gunwales, throwing spastic shadows against the cave wall. The smells of a feast and the whirling of frantic music permeated the dense musk of the cavern.

As Cyprian approached the great bandit ship, Cyprian expected to be rushed by Lizard, Rabbit, and Jackal, but not a soul challenged him as he stepped over the threshold of the large open hatch. He mounted the steps leading inward, his fingers trailing along the woodwork, the carvings so lustrous they almost looked alive, burnished with gold leaf. An oaken staircase inlaid with marble spiraled upward, and Cyprian followed it. As he passed through the decks, he thought he could see strange shapes just beyond the light, fleeing above him and coming up from below, whispering into the dark, urging him onward. He had almost lost count of the turns in the stairs by the time he emerged onto the deck, into the whirling maelstrom of a party.

The music reeled crazily, the crowd a mass of masks and twisting limbs and voices, the air alive with the smell of sweat, wine, and spices. But for all the motion, Cyprian could feel their eyes on him, watching him. Cyprian searched the crowd, looking for Cain. The partygoers continued dancing, pitching, and swaying as though he were not there. Finally, Cyprian cleared his throat, shouting to be heard over the din.

"I would like to speak to Cain."

At first, it seemed that no one had heard. Then, a fire dancer whipped out of the melee.

"Name yourself," she whispered as she flew past his face, whirling a flaming brand on a long chain.

"Cyprian Fields," Cyprian said. "Of Misericordiae."

With a twirl, she melted back into the throng. There was laughter, and a dancing piper streamed past, blasting shrill notes over the crowd. He took the pipe from his mouth, but the music kept coming. With a manic light in his eyes, the piper spoke to Cyprian.

"Old Cain isn't here."

Then, he too was gone.

"He ate an old nutapple and passed away, gone from the life of men," agreed a prancing juggler on stilts.

Cyprian stood his ground as the partygoers danced closer, faster.

"I'm the son of Augustus Fields, heir to the Fields Trading and Supply Company."

More laughter.

"He died," said a nubile dancer, stroking Cyprian's chin before flitting away. "Blown over the Shrouds, probably burned up in the sunset."

"The young Rooster," Cyprian continued, although more weakly. He felt somewhat drowsy, out of sorts, as though his senses were fading in and out.

The partygoers whizzed by in a dizzying whirl.

"Killed by a one-legged man."

"Strung himself from an old oak and ended it all."

"Buried."

"Gone."

"Deceased."

"Bit the dust, as they say."

The courtesans carried on and on, deaf to Cyprian's words. Cyprian breathed in and out. He knew what he had to say: the only words that Bartimaeus Cain wanted to hear.

"I would like to speak to Cain," he said to the reveling crowd.

"Name yourself," leered the fire dancer again.

Cyprian held up his hand, clenched into a fist so that the shape of a blade, scorched white on the back of his hand stood out against the firelight.

"I'm Cyprian Fields. I've done what they all do. I've come back."

Suddenly, they were silent, and Shipmaster Bartimaeus Cain was standing directly next to him, clicking with every breath. The face was the same one that had haunted Cyprian's dreams, deformed, mangled, layered with gold and gems. The eyes contemplated him, almost lovingly.

"Cyprian Augustus Fields," he said, rolling each word as though it were a delicious morsel. "What stories come to me on the wind! You resurrect your father's ship. You take on a mysterious passenger. And, next I hear, you are dashing through the Dominion, outrunning our Imperium's Fleet, tangling with O'Larre and Silverspoon and Marauder. And with each new wild tale, I grew more certain that the generous winds would blow you back to me."

Cain pressed a slender glass of something red and syrupy into Cyprian's hand, raising his own goblet in a toast and drinking deeply.

"You have accomplished much," Cain said, wiping his half-mouth with the back of his hand. "But for what? I would like to hear more. Then again, perhaps you are not the best one to tell it."

He flicked a finger at one of the serving men standing nearby, and someone brought a red silk upholstered couch. There was a thundering in the stairwell. The bandit leader who had apprehended Cyprian emerged, escorting Basil and Veronica. Cyprian noticed with satisfaction that the one escorting Veronica was beginning to develop a black eye.

"Thank you, Admetos," said Cain, settling himself on the couch. "So, Cyprian, you have hidden from me your finest acquisitions. I wonder why you didn't bring them to the party. You didn't think these two would be of some interest to me?"

At Cain's order, Admetos pushed Basil and Veronica forward with the point of his sword. Cain's eyes slithered over Veronica, who glared at him with unmitigated contempt.

"Such a pretty young thing," he said. "And I would wager there is much more to you than that. You are Hector Stromm's girl? A man who knew too much for his own good, if there ever was one. You seem to be following in his footsteps. But, lovely as you are, you are not the real prize. No, not you."

He swept past Veronica, and those dark, intelligent eyes found Basil.

"Oh," he crooned. "You have aroused my interest."

Basil didn't say anything, his fists tightening at his sides.

"You are the famous Basil, the son of Lorus. I will tell you, when I first heard that whisper, I doubted. I doubted strongly. But you look like him. Take that out of your pocket. Don't look at me like some kind of dumb ox. A king acts with decision. Take it out!"

Reluctantly, Basil pulled the Amulet out of his pocket. It twinkled in the firelight, the stone flaring with color as it rotated, casting its light across Cain's hungry face.

"Sylvanus's Riverstone Amulet if I ever saw it. You have been busy, Basil, son of Lorus. But industry, sadly, is not everything. The odds are stacked against you. It is highly unlikely that you will do anything but lose. And die."

"We are in need of help," said Cyprian.

"I know," Cain replied, selecting a succulent fruit from the pile offered to him. In three swift motions of his knife, he flayed the skin from it so that the flesh shone orange in the torchlight. "Otherwise, you wouldn't be here. You'd be off in search of the Astral Crown, wouldn't you? And such an object is not to be found among my treasures. You need something else from me. Desperately. Those are the only kinds of men who find their way to the Shadow Court. The desperate and the lost. Now, pray you tell old Cain what it is you're in need of."

"Our ship has a cracked keel," Cyprian said. "If your shipwrights could brace it with molten iron, we could continue on your way."

Cain's gaze snapped back to Cyprian, but all of the affection was gone. Now, he looked at Cyprian like an annoyance, a wheedling insect. He gnashed his teeth behind the gold mesh, then directed his attention at Basil once more.

"You look just like him. Just like Lorus," said Cain. "And he and I knew each other quite well. He chased me for many a year, across the bounds of this dominion of his. Many times, he very nearly succeeded in taking a piece out of me. Once, he did."

Cain raised a finger to his mangled cheek.

"Yes, Basil Black from Osmara, I know who you are. And I know that there is no way that you can possibly win. Despite your relics and your old dusty book."

Basil didn't quail beneath Cain's gaze.

"We have taken possession of two of the relics."

"Yes?" said Cain with feigned excitement, as though addressing a small child. "And what has that achieved, precisely?"

"There is much we have yet to do," said Basil. "If you help us, I can give you amnesty. I can bring you peace."

Cain burst forth with a laugh that rattled the jewelry on his face.

"Peace! You think I fear the Imperium? Tell me, Basil, do I seem to be…wanting?"

Basil looked around, taking in the rich fabrics, sumptuous wines, and golden finery of the huge ship.

"No," he said.

"Well-observed," said Cain. He gestured to his cheek again, bobbing his head so that the gold glimmered and his teeth were visible. "I hear you are quite the doctor, Basil. But I would never ask you to attempt to heal a wound such as this. Not because I don't believe that you could, but because I would not want you to succeed. Some wounds have purpose."

Cain leaned back on his couch, bare muscles rippling, dark eyes running over them.

"The Imperium keeps people scared, desperate. And desperate men do desperate things. I place myself in a position to benefit from this. With the Fleet running to quell so much unrest, I am left virtually unmolested. I have to repel the odd probe into my borders, pay off the local Fleet officers. The Imperium, without knowing it, is most generous to me. Lorus was never so."

Cyprian cleared his throat.

"Then it seems that we should best be on our way."

Cain held up a long finger, bringing it to his lips. At this moment, a pair of brawny airmen came in, and advanced to Cain's side. They whispered something in his ear, and he dismissed them with a wave of his hand. He never took his eyes off Cyprian, but only spoke once the two were gone.

"Now wait, Cyprian, my boy. Wait. I did not say that I would not help you, nor that I would let you go. My men have inspected your ship. As an act of good faith, they are repairing your keel with molten iron as we speak and I will not prevent you from going on your way when their work is finished. I ask only that you spend the evening here with me. I seldom entertain such company."

Veronica met Cyprian's eyes, distrustful, warning. But what else was there to say? Cyprian forced a smile.

"Of course."

Cain raised his glass of red wine in a toast, drained it to the last drop, and the music and dancing swung back into full delirious force.

With a cheer, the dancers closed in again around him, and Cyprian was lost among them. He could not see Basil or Veronica. Whether it was hours, minutes, or days that passed in that maelstrom of drunken revelry, Cyprian couldn't tell. It was an endless carousel of demonic faces, and Cyprian could not find his way out of the maze. But suddenly, he heard a sound that was familiar; the call of one of his deckhands. The music stopped. The deck snapped back into focus. He could see both Veronica and Basil, a little ways away, both seemingly coming to their senses as well.

"Fields!" cried Oakum, struggling mightily against the muscle-bound bandits that held him fast at the top of the stairwell. "Dreadnoughts! Dreadnoughts over the ridge, a whole battalion of them. We've been double-crossed! We've been-"

There was a crack, and Oakum jerked backwards, blood blossoming in a red flower across his chest. He slumped to the deck, his bandana sliding off his head in the hands of a bandit, his eyes still fixed on Cyprian, glassy and lifeless.

Cyprian whipped around, and there was Bartimaeus Cain, standing over his silken couch with a heavy pistol in his hand, smoke twisting from the barrel. The manic light of victory was in his eye, his face twisted into a grotesque grin. Overcome by fury and grief, Cyprian reached for his belt. His pistol had been taken, but he drew his deckknife. Cain's pistol fired again, there was a crack of metal on metal, and the blade went twirling off into the dark.

"Don't try to fight me, Cyprian," Cain said, his voice booming. "It would be the last thing you ever attempted in the sad little production of your life."

He spread his arms over the howling mass of partygoers.

"My friends! Our Imperium's dogs have answered the call! I am inclined to think it is time we passed on to greener pastures!"

There was a rumble of hooting and stamping and cheering, and the horde broke into activity. Within seconds, the party was collapsing around them, piles of riches and incense and gold were thrown into barrels and cases, troupes of dancers and singers with their instruments whirled around up into the naked masts, pulling with them golden envelopes and sails. Her lamps fore and aft were lit, coated in silk that gave everything in bloody radiance. Her envelopes bellied out and gangplanks were shipped. Suddenly, Veronica was at Cyprian's side, but Cyprian couldn't wrench his eyes away from Cain, who leered over them with the sheen of victory on his mutilated face. Kneeling to the deck, Basil carefully removed Oakum's red bandana and closed the machinist's eyes, then beckoned toward the stairwell.

"Come on!" he called.

"You may stay behind with the masses of brainless nobodies outside," Cain said with a contemptuous flourish to the mouth of the cavern. "There are always more sheep willing to follow. Hide yourselves among them. Perhaps you will escape the Imperium yet. But I think not. Ambry is a tenacious dog."

Veronica and Basil had to drag Cyprian toward the stairwell, but he resisted, pulling and yanking to have at Cain. First McElhaney, now Oakum. Someone had to pay.

"Cain!" roared Cyprian. "You'll regret this. If I live a hundred years..."

"You won't," said Cain, his smile a terrible mask. "And you forget. I don't fear the dead."

Cyprian was still in a murderous haze as Basil and Veronica dragged him down the stairwell, out the front hatch of the great ship. It snapped shut behind them with a thunderous boom. And then, *Queen* was vanishing upward into the ceiling of the cavern, her envelopes scraping past stalactites. There was the snapping of vines and the rumble of falling rock as the enormous ship smashed upward through the cavernous roof, piercing the cavern with fingers of silver moonlight. As Cain's ship disappeared, Cyprian felt his rage begin to dissipate, supplanted by a heavy grief. Basil and Veronica were deathly pale, shaken.

"Come on," Cyprian said. "We have to find the crew."

"And then what?" asked Veronica as they followed him toward the moonlight at the cavern's mouth. They started at a walk, then broke into a run.

"I'll think of something."

But Cyprian was lying. He couldn't think of anything. His head was swimming with the leering grin of Bartimaeus Cain, the crumpling form of Oakum. Finally, they burst into the moonlight. The stone concourse was empty, the bandit ships gone. The hillside was alive with the lights of a hundred cookfires, and the sky beyond was lit with lamps. Dreadnoughts. At least twelve. A whole battalion. They hovered like great predatory beasts, luminous and menacing. Behind them, the yellow nightmare of Cain's ship ascended into the sky, shedding rock dust and vines as it climbed. The dreadnoughts didn't move to intercept it. They kept their guns trained on the hillside.

Below, everything was chaos. The large mass of people who were trailing behind Bartimaeus Cain, hoping that some good fortune would fall to them, could only watch him leave. There were small ships and skiffs attempting to follow, some grinding along the earth, lacking either the sense or the aether to get airborne. Some were fleeing on foot, carrying anything they could. The air was filled with shouts of panicked confusion, the bray of animals, the bitter reek of fear.

"Quick," Cyprian said, and they ran toward where *Philomena* was moored. He tried to make himself think, to devise a way out of the situation, but nothing came to him. His mind was dull, clouded, clogged with the merciless sense of defeat. There was no way he could outwit or outrun that many ships.

"There she is!" said Veronica, panting behind Cyprian.

Philomena rose up, a silhouette against the lights of the dreadnoughts. Her crew was on the ground, Paschal in front with Benttree and the others forming a rough line across her bow. And as they drew closer, Cyprian could see why. There was a mass of people advancing up the hillside, bedraggled, shouting, angry.

"Shipmaster!" Paschal called. He was holding an old musket, shifting from foot to foot, not taking his eyes off the advancing mob. "What do we do? This lot looks like it wants to take a piece out of us!"

"Stand your ground," said Lightlas from the bow, his own weapon trained on the crowd. "Clear out! All of you!"

"Basil!" said Veronica.

"What?"

Basil looked just as bewildered as Cyprian, the lights of the mob and the dreadnoughts flashing in his spectacles. Where was the greater danger? Up or down? Veronica pulled out her rapier, then seized Basil by the collar.

"Say something to them," she said, pointing to the mob. "Get the staff, put on the amulet. Say something, anything!"

Basil's eyes were wide.

"They won't hear me…"

"Get on the bow!"

"I don't…"

Veronica did not look in a mood to be trifled with.

"I hate to tell you this, but sometimes kings take orders. Do it now!"

CHAPTER THIRTY

Ambry watched the golden ship ascend like a demon moon over the hills of Wailer's Gap. The immense ship's lamps were shrouded in crimson silk, giving her a cruel, bloody glow. Ambry could swear that he heard the trilling of music and cackle of high, loud laughter.

"*Queen*," said the signalman standing next to him on the battleship's deck. "I could have sworn that she was just a myth, all the stories they tell about her."

"Well, now you've seen," said Ambry. There were stranger things in Cor Nova, but few more dangerous. He gauged the golden ship's distance, her speed and heading, but knew that there was no hope of running her down. A murderous old skydog like Bartimaeus Cain would never take such a chance. He would have his escape route planned. It didn't matter. For whatever reason, Cain had decided to turn Basil Black in to the Fleet. Why he had done this was anyone's guess, but Ambry considered it useless to contemplate the motives of a maniac. With a noise of derision, he ripped the gold-trimmed parchment that bore Cain's message in half and threw it over the gunwale of the Imperium battleship *Courage of Titus*.

The Grand Admiral scanned the valley floor. The small campfires and torches down below were being snuffed out and trampled. He could see motion on the decks of some of the ships, men fleeing, their envelopes gaining aether as they prepared to flee. Ambry ignored them. Right at the top of the encampment, below the gaping blackness of Wailer's Gap, was a freighter, illuminated faintly by the light of the ascending *Queen*.

Several figures, the crew perhaps, were forming a defensive half-circle around the bow of the grounded ship. A large contingent of Cain's rabble, shouting angry slurs, were making their way toward them. Ambry could see the fire of torches, the glint of blades in the crowd. He pulled out his oculus, looking hard into the figures that stood at the defense of *Philomena*. There was a man with a sleek black beard, another man who was enormous, a willowy red-headed boy who seemed to be concentrating very hard on not running away. He also spotted the golden hair of Cyprian Fields. He didn't look so cocksure any more. Beside him stood a girl in a blue dress, her hair a mass of black. Ambry felt a surge of dislike. Veronica Stromm. There was a score to settle there. But where was Basil? He scanned the oculus back and forth. Nowhere. Abducted by Cain? Killed? Ambry had to at least find a body, or Titus's wrath would know no limits.

Then, he saw motion on the deck of the freighter by the bow. He focused the oculus, and clearly saw the slight, dark form of Basil Black, standing behind the ship's figurehead. The carved figure oddly drew Ambry's attention for a moment. It was a star-crowned young maiden, standing on a globe, her expression one of profound peace, even confidence. With a shake of his head, Ambry turned his attention back to Basil. He was wearing the Riverstone Amulet around his neck, and had the Elm Staff in his hand, but his head was bare. No Astral Crown. He looked as though he was preparing to say something.

"Signal the battlegroup," said Ambry to the signalman, who snapped to attention. "Train all guns on the mob, but keep clear of the freighter. Prepare to fire on my command. Also, every ship is to maintain absolute silence. I will hear whatever it is that this boy is about to say."

With a click of polished bootheels, the signalman began to run colored signal flags up the rigging. There was the sound of rolling shot and tamping rods before the dreadnoughts fell to silence, hovering in the air, watching, waiting.

Only a heartbeat passed before Basil Black was speaking. Fortunately for Ambry, the wind was blowing in their favor, and his voice was just audible over the expanse of sky. Basil Black stood at the bow of *Philomena*, arms outspread.

"My friends," he said. "Listen to me."

"Why?" demanded a voice from the crowd. "It's you and your kind that has brought this upon us!"

There was a roar of approval from the mob, and Basil had to shout to make himself heard.

"I'm Basil Black. Lorus was my father, the Sovereign of Cor Nova. You're here because you wanted someone to follow. You thought a great man like Bartimaeus Cain would bring you peace, safety, power. You thought that he would watch out for you, make you his own. Well, Bartimaeus Cain was never going to do any of those things. And I cannot either."

There was another wave of derision from the crowd.

"Then what the blessed good are you?"

"Shut up! I'd rather hear your screams than your words!"

Basil stood his ground, grip tightening on the figurehead.

"Tonight, we all stand at the mercy of the Imperium, of a madman who does not know what it is to care about anything but himself and his power."

Basil pointed to the dreadnoughts.

"And tonight he has brought that power to bear against us. I don't ask that you follow me. I only ask that you let me and my friends have a chance to make things right!"

"If you are the Sovereign, then you should be able to save us all!" came another voice, somewhere deep in the crowd.

"Yes!" cried another. "Use the High Sylvan, call up the mountains to protect us!"

"Aye, or the storms to sweep them away!"

Basil was silent, and for a moment, it seemed to Ambry that he was trying to pull the power out of himself, to do what only Sovereigns could. But whether he tried or not, nothing special came from Basil Black. The discontent, the underlying rage of the mob, bubbled higher.

"I say we kill him! At least before the Imperium has a chance to kill us!"

"That Amulet will look nice around my neck!"

"Kill the liar!"

And then, the night was filled with lightning and thunder. The ground beneath sections of the mob exploded, sending people and earth cartwheeling into the air. Ambry cursed aloud. Two of the dreadnoughts were firing, their guns pouring hot metal down onto the encampment.

"What the blazes is going on?" he demanded of the signalman, who was hurriedly rearranging the signal flags. "I gave no command!"

"The flags, sir…" replied the signalman, trembling. "I made a mista-"

"Cease firing!" roared the Grand Admiral, smashing a fist against the side of the signalman's head, so hard his mask slammed, ringing, to the deck. "Send the signal!"

The signalman, gasping and frantically searching the flags, tried to rectify his mistake, and Ambry swung the oculus down onto the mountainside. The barrage had not stopped. The ground rippled and boiled under the onslaught, most of them falling short of the freighter.

Then, as though it were fate, one ball came in high. Ambry could almost see it before it hit, a smudge of speeding black against the night, heading directly for the bow of *Philomena*, where Basil stood.

Ambry's mouth slid open in horror. The boy was frozen in time, looking down with shock on the whole scene before him. And then, someone else emerged from the fog, stumbling up the deck as fast as he could run. It was an old-timer with a slightly hunched back, his long legs wind-milling, beard trailing, eyes determined. The face was strangely familiar, as though Ambry had dreamt it once. With one spring of an arthritic leg, the old-timer leapt, locking his arms around Basil Black. And then, the shell hit, directly into the deck, just behind the figurehead. The deck vanished in a spout of flame, shredded wood, smoke. Gone too were Basil Black and the old man.

By the time the oculus fell slack in Ambry's hands, the firing had stopped. Cain's hordes were fleeing the smoking deck of *Philomena*, now twisted and black where Basil Black had once stood. If the remains of the boy could not be found, Titus's fury would be boundless. Ambry wrenched his weapon from its holster and shot the quailing signalman. Another officer stepped into his place, his fists quivering at his sides.

"Your orders…sir."

Ambry swallowed, collected himself.

"Send a dreadnought. Round up any crew who remain and bring them for questioning. Any other rabble, we bring with us to the Abyss."

The officer nodded.

"And the freighter, Grand Admiral?"

Ambry turned and walked away, toward the huge cartorium doors of the battleship, eager to lose himself in the blackness beyond.

"Lance her hull. Then, drop her into the sea."

CHAPTER THIRTY-ONE

The Imperium needed hands to dig his Abyss, and he did not seem to care whose. All over its base, like an army of ants, the women carried buckets. They overflowed with earth, rock, and sand, dredged up from the bowels of the earth, where gaunt men swung pickaxes and rusty shovels in agonized silence, clawing and scratching desperately through the barren earth. Among their number were graceful, sun-browned Stella Marians, sturdily-built lumbermen's wives from Panagiottis, dark-haired Terra Altans with regal brows. Some were dissenters, others had been in the wrong place at the wrong time. Fleet taskmasters paced back and forth across the heaving mass of humanity, sweat running down their necks from beneath their masks. They brandished long, iron pikes, and weren't shy about using them. The air was clogged with constant dust, the far-off sound of clanging iron and grunting men, a smell that might have been blood.

A crack. A shout. Veronica bent to the ground, lifting another yoke of buckets onto her shoulders. The hundred women before her did the same, as did the hundred behind. Following the long bedraggled line of bucket-laden women, Veronica carefully stepped over one of the narrow plank bridges that spanned one of the smaller pits. More than once, Veronica had seen a woman fall here, keeling over from exhaustion and strain. The line never stopped for them.

From above, the Abyss had seemed to Veronica like a circular wound in the flowing, green Fields of Carath, wider across then ten dreadnoughts, end to end. Now, from the below, the sky was no more than a pale disc of light atop the ramshackle rings of rickety scaffolding, gangways, and pulleys. Manlifts bearing untold tons of rock and earth groaned skyward, where a straggling parade of old freighters bore the load out into the desolate mountain range of rubble that rose up from the fields. Half-rotted waterwheels and dripping aqueducts diverted the underground streams that broke through every porous layer of rock. They all ran down to a large, septic pool in the base of the Abyss, where a huge waterwheel turned, churning water choked with refuse and rock dust into a draining whirlpool.

Far away, to the west, Veronica knew the green hills and white marble of the city of Carath rose to the sky, the great domes and vistas of Soliodomus, the ancient house of the Sovereigns, at its crest. Somewhere within those halls, Titus clenched Cor Nova in his fist. But here below, there was no white, no green. There was only the dusty brown of dirt and rock and sand, the visceral red of bleeding hands, the dull grey that was as bright as the sunlight got at the bottom of the Abyss.

She had been in the Abyss for three weeks. Her hands were blistered, her shoulders and ankles and back raw from the rub of the yokes and the blows of Fleet taskmasters. But what pained her most was recognizing that, on *Philomena*, they'd had a chance. A small one, perhaps, but a chance all the same. And people had believed in it. When Veronica had first arrived in the Abyss, some of the others recognized her name. For the first and only time, they raised their eyes from the dust, ignored the constant trudge of buckets and dirt and blood, and in hushed tones they asked about Basil, about *Philomena*. Veronica, not knowing what else to do, told them the truth. Even as the words fell from her mouth, she saw the lights die away in their eyes. They walked away like dead people, their last hope extinguished. Over and over again, she asked herself what she could have done differently. She should have protested the plan to seek help from Bartimaeus Cain. She could have convinced Lightlas and Cyprian to do something, anything, different than what they did. But none of that mattered anymore.

Ignoring her protesting muscles, Veronica heaved her bucket into the enormous pile at the manlift, and went back to the pits for more. She was just one more sad figure in a long line of failures. McElhaney was dead. Oakum was dead. Lightlas was dead. Basil was dead. Those words were a mournful heartbeat, punctuating her every waking hour. The Riverstone Amulet and the Elm Staff were lost, the Astral Crown never found. There was no other heir to Lorus. No hope for a new Sovereign. Not that it mattered. The Imperium's rule could continue forever. All she would ever see of it was this hole in the ground.

To make matters worse, more than once she had caught sight of some of *Philomena's* crew. Paschal and Spacklebrook were assigned to a sandpit somewhere near the eastern side of the Abyss, slogging along with scores of others through endless streams of shifting earth. Masterson was placed with the rock-breakers, wielding a pickaxe until his fingers grew numb and stiff. It had taken her several days before she ran across Benttree, who was forced to wrench massive boulders out of the earth.

Under the eye of the Fleet taskmasters, she couldn't speak to any of them. She just continued to carry her buckets. Sometimes, they shared an intimate nod, a mere acknowledgement that the other was there. Then, back to work. Through the days, Veronica kept an eye out for golden hair, grey eyes, the sound of a sharp tongue. But Cyprian was nowhere to be found. Several times, she had looked skyward, certain that she saw the quick shape of Petros flicking across the sky above. But the kestrel was never there, only the empty grayness. She had not seen Cyprian since he was taken to a separate dreadnought the night at Wailer's Gap, fighting all the way. Veronica tried not to think about him, but he continued to reappear in her fitful dreams, always facing away from her, looking out over *Philomena's* bow.

Veronica seized another full bucket, then began the long trudge back across the base of the Abyss toward the manlift. Another step. Another bucket. Another barrel. Another day. Veronica could keep going, she knew. She, after all, had one tiny pinprick of light to keep her on her feet. She had found her mother.

CHAPTER THIRTY-TWO

Basil's eyes slid open. The diamond stars were suspended above him, twinkling in the midnight black of the sky. For a moment, Basil was everywhere and nowhere, adrift in the nothingness. He was still, quiet, at peace.

He moved his fingers. The grass was cool beneath Basil's head, crisp and soft, like book pages. He could feel it on his hands and the bare skin of his leg, where his pants had been burnt away in patches. The wind was a gentle caress across his face, and he could hear the low cooing of birds and the creak of insects in the dark treetops. There was a sudden fluttering by his hand, and something nipped him sharply on the thumb.

He looked down. There, perched on his palm, was a venerable golden sea kestrel, glaring at him.

"Petros..."

It all came rushing back.

He was in Osmara, running for his life, in Misericordiae, in the Crypt of the Bleeding Elm, in the O'Larre City, in Kwalz, on the heights of Kamallak, reeling in the Shadow Court, and then he was on the bow before an angry crowd. Something dark and fast was flying toward him. Then, Basil felt the lean, wiry grip of Francis Lightlas jerk him sideways. The old shipmaster had opened his mouth and spoken in a language older than the earth. High Sylvan. The words knit themselves together into a silvery nexus. The shell struck, an impossible blast of light and sound, and they were both flying away. Petros must have been caught within Lightlas's protection as well.

Basil jerked himself into a sitting position, eyes wide. The Amulet hung against his chest, the Staff lay in the grass beside him. Where was the crew? Where was *Philomena*? And where was Francis Lightlas? Although every muscle in his body protested, Basil pulled himself to his feet. He was standing on a hill in the mouth of a green moon-lit valley. A burbling stream wound its way through the base, its banks bordered by green meadows and sentinel trees. The crickets chirped, the wind blew. There was not another soul to be seen. With a low cry, Petros flapped off up the hill. At its top, there was an ancient elm tree, bent and twisted with age. At its base, Basil could make out a figure. Hurriedly, he picked up the Elm Staff and scrambled his way up, grabbing at the soft tufts of grass for grip.

Francis Lightlas lay at the foot of the tree, his wizened head propped up on a root, his blue eyes gazing up at the starlight and the waving branches. He looked small, frail, beneath the giant elm. His body seemed shrunken and oddly contorted, as though he had hit the ground hard, perhaps shielding Basil even as they struck. One wizened hand raised up to lightly touch the golden sea kestrel that lighted on his leg.

"I'm afraid, Basil," he said, his voice coming in labored wheezes. "That I have been foolish."

Basil knelt by Lightlas's side and immediately searched for his pulse. It was fast, weak.

"Lie still now," Basil said, reaching to unbutton Lightlas's jacket. "I'm going to help you, shipmaster."

"Shipmaster," coughed the old man, waving him back with a limp hand. "If you knew who I am, you would not be so keen to help. "

Basil sat back, looking hard into that old face, usually so stern and resolute. Now it was clouded by doubt and regret, but less guarded, more sincere. Inexplicably, the faces in Stormalong's fire flashed in his mind, one after the other, a stream of regal strangers rising and falling from the flames. And at the end of them, there was Lorus, a tall, proud young man with the fire licking at the hem of his robes. The fiery visage glowed and flared, and Basil realized that this face was no stranger to him. If that face had been defeated by more evil than any normal man faces in a lifetime, if it had born the weight of fifteen years of failure and exile, it would look very different indeed. Lorus, his father, the last Sovereign of Cor Nova, was not dead. He was right here, hidden in plain sight.

Basil searched for words, but found none. Francis Lightlas's eyes were sad, pale blue in the moonlight. Blue eyes, Basil realized, that very much resembled his own.

"I was going to tell you once you had the crown in your possession. But, as it happens, that is not how it's meant to be."

"But everything the Silverspoon said about... about you..."

"True. All of it. But he did not tell you everything. Basil, my time is running out. You'll have it all from my lips."

Lightlas swallowed, then began to speak in a low voice. Basil had to lean over him to hear.

"When my brother Titus returned from the Boneless Moors in victory fifteen years ago, it was with real joy that I welcomed him back to Soliodomus. But, as time went on, I began to notice strange things. He did not laugh like he used to. He seemed to be suspicions and angry. All the time.

"One dark night, Titus came to me very agitated. It was clear that he wasn't thinking clearly. We had an argument, and a kind of manic rage possessed him. Suddenly, that blackened sword was in his hand, and he was fighting me in High Sylvan, with a strength that I didn't know he possessed. It was wild, unstable, but overwhelmingly powerful. There was little I could do but try to stand my ground. When my strength was gone, the fire rolled all the way up into the Sanctum, and I remember how the stones fell. They closed over my head and I was gone."

Lightlas had to pause for breath. His eyes grew bright, and Basil saw tears gathering in their corners.

"The next I knew, I awoke in a small house in the outer streets of Carath. I had been blown clear of the wreckage, my clothes burned away, my hair singed to nothing, and I looked different. I was aged, bent, as though something in that fight drew my very life away. I was unrecognizable. I was found in the street that night by a shipmaster named Augustus Fields, who was heading back to the concourses.

Not knowing what else to do, he carried me back to his freighter and had his physician look after me."

Basil's eyes widened.

"*Philomena.*"

"Yes. When I finally came to my senses, I had no memory of who I was. When Fields discovered that I knew how to do figures, he hired me as a loadmaster. I spent several years on board his ships, traveling the world. I met Cyprian at that time, a very promising young lad. Bright, strong, extremely talented, like his father. I was not in Misericordiae when the Merchant Rebellion happened. I was in another port, conducting business on Fields' behalf. When I heard, I experienced a rage and a hurt that went deeper than any I had ever experienced. Somehow, deep in the depths of myself, I remembered."

Basil imagined Lightlas standing on a street corner in some far-off city, with the weight of reality crashing down upon him. Somehow, Basil could understand how it felt.

"Why didn't you expose yourself? Rally an army?"

The old man coughed weakly, then shook his head.

"Who would have believed me? I had been dead for almost ten years. I looked nothing like my former self. I couldn't speak High Sylvan. I lost that power, until tonight. I had no way of proving my authenticity, at least not enough to draw major support. And as soon as Titus found out, I would have been hunted and destroyed. There was never any hope for me. I was too old, too weak and worn out.

"So I began to search. In those days, there were many whispers of a plot to reinstate the Sovereign. Finally, after many false trails, I heard of the Bookkeepers, and the closer I got to them, the more I came to believe that you had been born and somehow survived. Your mother was very dear to me, Basil. I am told Colleena passed shortly after my defeat. You remind me much of her."

Basil nodded, numb. He remembered the black Fleet skiff at rest beneath the Old Man's Tooth, her name engraved on a brass plate. The Bookkeepers' tribute to a fallen queen.

"Even as I pursued Bookkeepers, Titus's own search for them accelerated. I managed to reach the last one before he was killed, a former court doctor named Galen Black. He was older than I, dying, unable to outrun my brother any longer. He had known me since I was a boy, and he looked past my appearance, saw me for who I was, the first to do so in ten years. When my body didn't seem likely to be found after the fire, he planted false remains and replaced the true relics with facsimiles. This explained why Titus did not come looking for me. He also masterminded your escape from Soliodomus when you were only just born, placing you with his own brother in Osmara, a metallurgist."

Lightlas's cough was stronger, wetter this time. A fleck of blood appeared at his lips. Basil reached to help, but Lightlas waved him away again.

"I discovered that you had to be transported to Anne Stormalong, that she was the gatekeeper of the Bookkeepers plan, the guardian of the Rule, which would be your guide. When Galen was arrested, the last Bookkeeper was silenced. They had hidden the relics and the Rule, but the mechanism to put you on the path to take them up again had been broken. I alone stood in the gap. They had extracted your location from Galen, and I knew that I had little time. My messenger was only barely able to alert Thon Black that they were coming. Since then, I have tried to keep you safe."

The old man's eyes met Basil's own, and Basil tried to imagine him as he once was, standing proud and tall in the Sanctum of Soliodomus. Lightlas reached out a hand, as though to touch the side of Basil's face.

"Why didn't you tell me?" Basil asked, his voice wavering. "Why couldn't you have just said…"

"I had no answers for the questions you would have asked. I could do you little good as a father. I was of more use as a shipmaster… I'm sorry…"

Lightlas's eyes grew faint again, then sprang open. His breath was shallow, faint.

"I have failed my Dominion twice, Basil. I failed to stop Titus and I failed to give you the ability to face him."

"Lightlas…" Basil said. He didn't know what else to call his father. "You haven't failed. We've come so far. I'm not going to stop…"

"Good!" Lightlas said, suddenly grabbing Basil's vest. "You can't. Once Titus is successful in reaching the bottom of the Abyss, he'll use that twice-cursed sword to open the Sarcophagus within, unleashing the Sidia on the world. He thinks that he can control them, but he can't. They will tear this world apart, just as they tried to in Sylvanus's time. The Sovereign alone stands between Cor Nova and the ruin of the Old World."

"I must have High Sylvan to stop him. I need the Crown."

Lightlas shook his head, his throat quivering. He struggled to speak.

"*The Sovereign's eye that sees from height, perched on brows of wooden sigh. Third and sixth and third once more. At Ivory's first, behind the door. Philomena* was located in Lot 363, beneath the Ivory City's first concourse. The map points to the ship. Ambry will have sunk her, lanced her hull and thrown her into the sea. You must have her back. You must speak to the Marlord."

But, the old man's eyes were flickering, his fingers weak.

"I'm sorry, Basil," he said, his voice barely a whisper. "I've brought you not much but pain and uncertainty. I have not been able to use High Sylvan since my duel with Titus, but now, at the end, I have a little."

He raised a quivering hand to Basil's chest, pressing his thin fingers there. Basil felt a strange warmth, an unravelling, a singing that rose from a low hum deep within himself.

"*Philomena*...." said Lorus. "The Marlord...my...boy..."

The wind sang through the boughs of the ancient elm. The stream flowed and the insects creaked and groaned. Lorus, the last Sovereign of Cor Nova, died in the arms of Basil Black. For a moment, the night seemed to grow darker, as though the Dominion bowed at his passing.

CHAPTER THIRTY-THREE

The light that filtered into the roughly-cut sleeping cavern was feeble, as though starved.

Cyprian could sympathize. He lay on the hard ground, surrounded by the sounds of fitful, exhausted slumber. Some men moaned or talked in their sleep, sometimes crying out, calling for parents or wives or children long lost. The sounds of work and the roar of Fleet overseers in the Abyss beyond penetrated the rock. Day or night, the work knew no end.

Cyprian lay on his back, sleepless, staring vacantly at the single candle that guttered on the cave wall, struggling to remember what a star looked like. He turned over onto his side, so that he could be in the darkness. He didn't want to think about stars. He didn't want to think about anything.

His filthy shirt stuck to the wounds on his chest, still red and raw from the torture that they had inflicted on him in the battleship's stinking brig. Before the first strike, he had told them everything he knew. With Basil dead, there was nothing to defend. He saw the explosion of fire and earth again in his mind, and Basil was gone, surely disintegrated and burned to ash. Him and Francis Lightlas. Better for both of them that they weren't here. Better for everyone.

Somewhere further down, deep in the bowels of the Abyss, the crew was slaving away, their backs bent beneath the iron pikes of taskmasters. Maybe some of them were dead, worked to the brink of death. His next thought was of Veronica, imprisoned with the women, and yet another wave of bitterness rolled through him. He had done this to them. Cyprian clenched his fist so that the knife outline in the back of his hand stood out white. He'd been a fool to believe that Bartimaeus Cain would ever help them. He'd have been better off risking the failure of *Philomena's* keel. If only Lightlas had turned Basil away from the start. What fools they'd all had been to suppose that there was any hope of defeating the Imperium. Now they would all suffer and die in this place. All because of the foolish kind of nobility that gets men killed for no practical reason.

Augustus Fields would not have been captured. He would not have lost Basil, quenching the only hope of an entire Dominion. What kind of airman would his father consider him if he could see him now? No airman at all, a voice inside told him. Nothing but a foolish boy. Cyprian closed his eyes tighter, wishing that the cavern would fall in and crush his misery.

Cyprian paid no attention when the Fleet airman at the mouth of the cavern stiffened, his grip tightening on his weapon as he peered up the passage. He may as well have not been there at all. There was nowhere to run in the Abyss. No one had the strength or the heart to try. In the Abyss, there was no way to go but down. Suddenly, there was a noise like a low whistle and a crack. The airman gasped, then sighed, and Cyprian heard a sound like a heavy sack hitting the ground.

Ignoring sore muscles, Cyprian sat up, and saw the guard crumpled on the ground, his musket on top of him. A hollow, sharpened reed stood out of the side of his neck. There, standing in the tiny trickle of light, was another Fleet soldier. He was shorter than most, and his uniform seemed oddly ill-fitting. He reached up with a dirty, rather graceful hand, and removed his mask. His dark hair fell over his face, and round spectacles glimmered in the pale lantern light. Cyprian's mouth dropped open. Surely, it wasn't true. It wasn't possible. How could it be?

The boy stood stone still. He glanced left and right across the prisoners, lying exhausted and inert. Then he whispered.

"Cyprian?"

Cyprian was sure that he was hallucinating. The boy said it again, somewhat louder.

"Cyprian?"

Cyprian opened his mouth, trying to get words past his cracked lips. How was it possible?

"Basil," he croaked.

Basil rushed to his side. He pulled a waterskin out of his bag, and lifted it to Cyprian's lips.

"Here," he said. "It's bitter, but it will give you some strength."

Cyprian pushed the skin away.

"How?" he rasped. "How did you-"

"Later," said Basil. "We have to go. Drink. Quickly."

Cyprian obeyed. At first, the mixture was thick and cloying on his lips, but then it began to go down easier, and Cyprian drank it in gulps. Within a few moments, his head was clear and he felt a little more strength in his arms. Cyprian tried not think about what kind of apothecary's madness was in the concoction. With Basil's help, he dragged himself to his feet.

"I'm disguised," said Basil, looking slightly smug.

"I saw that," Cyprian said. "Nicely done."

"You'll need to be too. Some of the guards know your face. We were pretty famous by the time we got here. Hold still."

Basil pulled a large bandage out of his bag and wrapped it around Cyprian's head, so that it covered one eye. He dabbed it with blood from a bottle. The result was a convincing bandage. Basil also daubed some dark soot on his chin for good measure.

"Not as bad as it could be," Basil said, inspecting his work. "We're going down before we can go up. We need Veronica."

"I don't know where she is," Cyprian said, adjusting his bandage.

"I do," said Basil. "I bribed one of the airmen. He was a dolt, didn't recognize me. Then I drugged him and took his uniform."

Cyprian felt a real grin plaster itself on his face, the first in weeks. The feeling was sensational.

"My Basil, how you've grown."

Basil smirked back.

"Don't start congratulating me yet. As long as we're in here, we're as good as dead. Petros is alive, by the way. He stayed with me most of the way here, but then he disappeared into the woods. Hunting or something, I imagine."

Cyprian allowed himself a laugh.

"Lazy old feather duster."

They picked their way through the sleeping men and continued downward into the bowels of the Abyss via a spiraling passageway bored into the rock. They passed Fleet men shoving crowds of prisoners, exhausted from work and dehydration, but none stopped to challenge the lone guard and his captive. Even behind the mask, Cyprian saw Basil's eyes wandering into the depths, watching the figures below with intense pity. Several small passages led off to the side, more rough-hewn caverns for sleeping, but Basil did not stop. Finally, when they were near the bottom, they came to one of the larger caverns. Two guards stood at its mouth.

"This is it," Basil said. He reached into his pocket, pulling out a thin, hollow reed and two more of the darts. Cyprian was astonished at how fast he moved. In the space of seconds, both guards were slumped to the ground with hardly a gurgle.

"Blue hazes, Basil," said Cyprian as they pulled the two inside the cavern, out of sight. "That was impressive."

"They'll wake in about an hour," Basil replied. "Won't remember a thing. I practiced on toads for a whole day. Good thing people don't hop as much."

"Good thing," Cyprian agreed quietly, and followed Basil around the corner of the passage.

They seemed to be in the right place. The cavern they entered must have contained two hundred women, lying on the floor. The sounds of fitful sleep arose from most of them as well. Some were awake, and greeted the two boys with wide eyes, unwilling to speak. There were young girls no older than five or six, and silver-haired old ladies. As long as they could carry buckets, Cyprian heard, they were spared.

"Where is Veronica?" Cyprian whispered, scanning the room. He looked for dark hair, anything blue.

"I don't..." said Basil. A few long moments passed. Then he pointed. "There."

Cyprian's heart skipped a beat. There she was, worn, blistered, and thin, but alive, leaning against one of the walls of the cavern. Her eyes were closed, asleep.

Cyprian followed Basil clumsily, tiptoeing through the sleeping women to get to her. Basil kneeled down at her side.

"Veronica," he said.

Her eyes slid open. She blinked, unbelieving.

"Basil…"

Basil smiled.

"Hey."

She threw her arms around him, pulling him close, holding him as though she never wanted to let go. And then, Veronica saw Cyprian. Still hugging Basil, she reached out her hand and took Cyprian's. Her dark eyes looked right into Cyprian, with tears brimming in them. It was like cold, clear water rushing into Cyprian's soul. He decided that he could die right now, and he would feel whole.

By the time Veronica let Cyprian and Basil go, most of the women were awake, sitting up and peering at them, blinking tired eyes. The woman directly next to Veronica stirred. She had long black hair that framed the fair skin of her face, her noble cheekbones and forehead, her thin body covered by a meager blanket. Her eyes were dark and warm, but there was a weakness to her, a fragility, like a little bird.

"Is it them, Veronica?" asked the woman.

"Yes," Veronica said, picking up the woman's hand. She looked at Cyprian. "I found her."

Cyprian shook his head in disbelief. Veronica's mother. How Veronica had managed to find her, Cyprian could not say. Basil seemed to sense Amelia Stromm's weakness. He slid next to her, placing his hand across her forehead, feeling for her pulse. Veronica's mother watched him, inspecting his face.

"You are like he said you would be. You look like Lorus….And like Colleena…" she reached up to touch his face. "Hector always said that you would come. I never believed. Never had enough hope to believe."

"We'll make things right," Basil said, not removing the frail hand that traveled across the side of his head. "We will. But you need to lie still. You have to rest."

"I know," she said with a smile. "And I know that you will do all that you can. We all do."

She took his hand in her own, and slowly, reverently, she kissed it. Out in the cavern, the women were sitting and standing, all looking at Basil, with hollow eyes and slack limbs. They said nothing, just watched, but Cyprian saw something change in them, like a fire kindling behind their eyes. As with all fire, it was fiercely contagious.

It was the kind of fire that men in power will work themselves into a frenzy trying to quench, only to find that it is very adept at springing back from ashes. Hope.

Then, Veronica's mother trembled and fell back against her thin bedding, eyes closed.

"Is she all right?" Veronica asked, grasping her hand.

Basil checked her pulse again, and dribbled some of the contents of the waterskin into her throat. He gently massaged her neck as she swallowed.

"She is very weak. Without treatment, she has a few days."

"What can you do for her?"

"Here, not much more than I already have."

Veronica stood up, her hands fists at her sides.

"You should go," said one of the women nearby, her hands streaked with veins and worn by care. "We will look after her. She will be unhappy if she awakes to find you have not gone to help the Sovereign."

A few others nodded.

Slowly, looking at her as though trying to remember her forever, Veronica kissed her mother on the forehead, and they stole out into the passageway.

The change of shift would not happen for another few hours, so the passageway was still mostly deserted. Nevertheless, Cyprian kept his head down, careful to meet no one's eyes as they climbed. Veronica did the same. Basil marched along behind them, doing his best to play the dutiful soldier.

"How far to the nearest lift?" Cyprian whispered.

"Just a little ways," answered Basil. "Up around the next bend."

Cyprian's heartbeat quickened. They were close. So close. He imagined seeing the sky again, flying over the treetops, skimming the stars. Then, he felt Basil stiffen. A man in an immaculate red uniform was coming around the corner, his footfalls precise measured steps. He came abreast of them, and for a moment, Cyprian was sure he would pass. Then, his head turned. A blade flashed in the passageway. The hard, gray eyes of Grand Admiral

Khyber Ambry swept over them. He glanced at the stripes stitched on Basil's sleeves.

"Corporal," he said, his voice soft. "Perhaps you could tell me what you are doing."

Basil was silent for a moment, and Cyprian could feel his arm shaking as he scrambled for a response.

"Escorting these prisoners, Grand Admiral."

Ambry nodded slowly, and inclined his head toward Veronica, who was silent and still.

"You'll forgive me if I find that suspect, Corporal. I was just on my way to visit this particular one and she was under no circumstances to be moved from the holding cell."

"My mistake, Grand Admiral," said Basil. "My orders must have been..."

Ambry didn't seem to be listening. He drew his pistol from his belt and pointed it at Cyprian's face, using the barrel to drag down the bandage that covered his eye. Cyprian stayed stock still. In Ambry's eyes, there was no triumph, no twitch of emotion, only the solemn weight of duty.

"Good day, Mr. Fields," said the Grand Admiral. "It seems that you're a much better sneak in the air than on the ground. Apparently the initial rounds of interrogation was not sufficient to make you understand that fact."

In his peripheral vision, Cyprian saw Veronica's hand twitch. He willed himself not to look at her. Cyprian gave Ambry a smirk.

"You're watching the wrong captive, Grand Admiral."

Veronica was a blur. With a single jab, she knocked the pistol aside, and Cyprian and Basil bulled into the Grand Admiral as one, slamming him against the wall of the cavern. It took every ounce of Cyprian's flagging strength to keep the Admiral restrained. His muscles were like knotted cords beneath his uniform. The struggle knocked Basil's mask aside, sending it clattering to the cavern floor. Ambry's eyes grew wide, and he was suddenly pale and still, staring at Basil as though he were a ghost. Cyprian took the opportunity to slam his unresisting hand against the cavern wall and take his pistol.

"Admiral Ambry," said Basil, still breathing hard. "I don't have to be your enemy."

"No..." Ambry grunted. "I watched you die. One of my own ships... An impostor..."

277

"You above all people should know how tenacious life can be. Particularly when one has a reason to live. Look at my face. You served my father before Titus. You know what he looked like. Tell me I'm not his son."

Ambry's gray gaze only hardened.

"Your father was a danger, unworthy of the Throne. You are foolish to doubt my loyalty to the Imperium."

Basil was looking deeply into the admiral's eyes. It was the same expression he used when searching for a piece of shrapnel in a wound, powerful, shrewd, uncompromising. And suddenly, the young boy and the Grand Admiral seemed to change places. Basil appeared to grow larger, the admiral to shrink.

"I don't question your honor," said Basil. "Only your capacity for evil. Once you were young like me. Once you looked up at the dreadnoughts in the sky, at the men in black and gold, who flew the Sovereign's colors and did his justice from Shrouds to Seas. You wanted to be one of them, to be a protector, a guardian, a watchful sentinel. You craved an adventurous life, an honorable death. And what are you now? A murderer in red, a mercenary beneath a tyrant's flag. You were once more, Ambry. You can be more again."

A flicker of doubt passed across the Admiral's face. His mouth opened, then closed, his brow furrowed. Then, there was a clatter from below. A group of Fleet soldiers emerged into the passageway, chatting idly. As soon as they saw the Grand Admiral pinned against the wall, their hands immediately went to weapons as well. The spell was broken. The Grand Admiral lunged with near-superhuman strength, sending them stumbling.

"Run!" Cyprian yelled, and the three took off up the hallway.

Bells sounded up through the Abyss. With the airmen at their heels, they dashed around two more bends in the passageway. They no longer cared who saw. They bulled right through plodding prisoners and Fleet airmen alike.

"Look!" Basil said, pointing to a contraption that was mounted in the passage ahead. "A lift!"

They clattered aboard.

"Going up?" Cyprian said, eyeing the lift assembly.

"Do it!" yelled Basil.

Cyprian dealt the mechanism a kick. With a force that forced all three of them to its planks, the platform rattled skyward. Bullets started whizzing around them, as airmen began to fire on the racing platform. Cyprian ducked as chunks and splinters of wood came flying off where the balls struck. His momentary elation quickly evaporated. They had nothing to fight with, nowhere to go. They neared the top of the lift's range, and the next ledge approached quickly. Over the lip, Cyprian could see gun barrels and red uniforms. There was nothing waiting for them there but a hail of bullets.

"Going back down?" asked Basil, seeing the same thing.

"You got it," Cyprian replied, and slammed the lift's lever into reverse.

With a jerk that left them momentarily weightless, the platform stopped in mid-air, then plunged back downwards. The rocky, weeping walls of the Abyss went whizzing past, and Cyprian had to cling tightly to Basil and Veronica to prevent them from being whipped away. Beneath them, the floor of the Abyss was rushing up. The gear next to Cyprian was spinning so fast that the smell of burning wood and hot iron filled his nostrils. If they didn't stop soon, they would dash against the floor of the Abyss.

"Basil!" he yelled over rushing wind. "Your coat!"

Basil looked at Cyprian like he'd gone mad, but yanked off the red coat. Cyprian snatched it.

"Hold on!" he said, and thrust the coat into the whirling gear of the lift.

With a juddering series of snapping noises, the gear tore through the thick wool, jamming the gear mechanism with its fibers. Cyprian was nearly thrown from the bucking platform before he managed to seize one of its cables.

Finally, there was an almighty snapping sound, and the platform broke away, spinning freely into void. With cries of alarm, Veronica and Basil collided directly with Cyprian, and they shot outwards in a tangle of limbs.

Wump.

Cyprian opened his eyes, surprised to find himself alive. Basil's foot was somewhere near his head, and Veronica was lying across his chest, apparently dazed. They were sprawled, half submerged, on a large pile of sand. About five feet above his nose, the shattered remains of the lift swung back and forth against the backdrop of the dusky circle of sky. For a moment, Cyprian lay stunned, until the sound of Basil spitting out large amounts of sand, the stamp of boots above, and the crack of a musket resounded in his ears. Then, he was up again, dragging Basil and Veronica, tumbling head over heels down the pile of sand. Before them lay the base of the Abyss, pitted with the labor of a thousand hands at pickaxes and shovels, a treacherous labyrinth of walkways and rock-piles among the digging crews. The souls in the pits rose from their work, watching wide-eyed as the three dashed by.

"Where are we going?" asked Veronica.

"I don't know!" Cyprian said, turning down a random walkway, dodging among the boulders. Another hail of gunfire peppered the ground behind them. The soldiers were getting closer. A number of the taskmasters, whips brought to bear, were making their way toward them. Cyprian dealt the closest one a hearty punch to the jaw as they sprinted past. He couldn't help but smile.

Basil pointed ahead, his hand bobbing up and down with each panicked step.

"The waterwheel!"

Cyprian had no plan, so he didn't see the point in arguing. As one, the three jumped a trench and ran down the causeway leading to the enormous waterwheel and drainage pool. As they drew closer, Cyprian could see the dark water swirling with refuse, thick with mud. It all coalesced into a colossal whirlpool that drained down into some underground hole.

They stopped when they reached the edge of the pool, gasping for breath. Soldiers were approaching from every side. They had put aside their guns for the moment. Swords gleamed. There was nowhere for their prey to run. The taskmasters dashed towards them as well. One of them was looking particularly murderous, rubbing a bruised jaw.

"What's the plan, Basil?" Cyprian asked. "Talk fast."

"Cyprian, Veronica," said Basil. He looked Cyprian hard in the eyes. "Do you trust me?"

Veronica nodded. Cyprian felt something twist in the bottom of his stomach.

"I'm going to hate this, aren't I?"

"Yes."

Cyprian looked at the swirling, murky water. It made a greedy sucking sound as it disappeared under.

"We're going to jump, aren't we?"

"Yes."

Cyprian thought back to his escape from Bartimaeus Cain, the rushing black water, the way his lungs had burned, screamed for air. At least then, he'd known where the river would lead.

"Do you have any idea where it lets out?"

"With any luck," said Basil. "The sea. Hold on tight to me."

Veronica seized Basil's right arm. Cyprian took a final, longing look at the oncoming battalion of red uniforms and gleaming steel.

"Maybe I'll take my chances-"

Veronica seized his arm.

"Don't be an idiot."

And then, they leapt. In one whirling moment, Cyprian was up to his neck in the fetid water, and grabbed onto Basil. Then, he felt a tug around his ankles, an irresistible pull that yanked him around once. And then, they were sucked down into the blackness.

Chapter Thirty-Four

Basil fought to stay conscious as they were sucked through the rushing, swirling dark. Beside him, Cyprian and Veronica held on with all their strength, trying not to slip loose from his grip. For one horrendous moment, he felt Cyprian's rough hand depart his own. Only a wild fling of Basil's arm brought him back in contact, and they were away again, yanked by the might of the roaring river.

Summoning his failing senses, Basil reached into himself, into the small, warm glow that Lorus had left. The High Sylvan sprang like a living thing from his lips, guiding them past jagged rocks and unseen screens of debris. Suddenly he could hear the words that the river spoke, a deep bass thrumming that echoed through earth and rock. It sang its path, and Basil murmured along with it.

Once, twice, they emerged into pockets of air, managing to suck in a breath before being dashed along again. Around one bend, something large and scaly stirred in the deep, watching them with two golden eyes, contemplating how they might taste. Basil uttered another syllable, and the river pulled them away before the creature had the chance to spring. As the moments passed, Basil could feel his strength weakening, the High Sylvan words growing feeble and faint. He lost track of the river's song. He was going blind, and they would be lost, swept along forever.

A punch in the gut, a feeling of flight, and suddenly, Basil's face was half-buried in sand. He was breathing cool, salty air.

The grit bit against his cheek, scratching his spectacles. With a groan, he sat up. His sodden shirt was like lead on his shoulders and his head was still whirling, but he was alive. He was sprawled in a small, sandy cove, surrounded entirely by thick groves of palms and white sands, at the base of a large cliff. A few yards above, a large outlet spewed the murky water of the Abyss into the pool. The moon shone in the starlit sky above. Beyond the mouth of the cove, Basil could see the rhythmic waves of the ocean.

A little further up the cove, Cyprian had hauled himself onto the sand, where he flopped like an ungainly fish, his face as green as the sea.

"Nature not agree with you, Cyprian?" Veronica asked. She was already on her feet, wading through the pool, the thrill of escape lighting her eyes.

"Not this particular kind of nature," said Cyprian, rolling over onto his back. "Ay, gerrofme!

The sandcrab that had decided to nip his finger went sailing off and plopped into the surf.

"Sandy little twit," muttered Cyprian, drawing himself upright.

They found the beach to be deserted, and the sky was clear on all sides. After searching a little ways down the coast, they found a spot where the palm trees gave good cover. Here Basil told them the tale of his adventure and tended to their wounds as best he could. The lacerations on Cyprian's chest were red and raw, some of them beginning to show signs of infection.

"How did you survive?" Veronica asked.

"It was Francis Lightlas," said Basil, squeezing palm oil onto Cyprian's shoulder. "He jumped in front of me, said something in High Sylvan that protected us both."

"High Sylvan?" Veronica said. "That means…"

Cyprian and Veronica were silent for a minute, looking at him. The surf pounded in the distance.

"He was Lorus," said Basil.

Veronica's eyes grew wide. Cyprian swore loudly.

"Not possible," he said. "I've known him since I was a kid. He was one of my father's men. Lorus was tall, handsome, everything a king should be. Old Lightlas was a cantankerous old man."

"I know," said Basil, carefully placing a makeshift palm bandage. "He survived the duel with Titus…"

And Basil told the whole story. Cyprian and Veronica listened carefully, interrupting only occasionally to ask questions. When Basil had finished, they sat back in silence for a moment, listening to the buzzing of the cicadas in the trees.

"Blue hazes…" Cyprian said. "Makes you wonder who around here's NOT royalty."

"And High Sylvan?" Veronica said. "I heard it, through the water, when we were getting pulled along. How did that come about without the three relics? Did you find the Astral Crown?"

Basil shook his head.

"He gave me the High Sylvan. Lightlas did. Somehow. Before he died, he said he hadn't had it since his duel with Titus. Somehow it was blocked until he saved me on *Philomena* back at Wailer's Gap. It was just like how I used it in Osmara once. Before he died, he managed to pass what little he had rediscovered to me. It's incomplete, like I know some of it but not all. And it's finite. It runs out when I use it. I don't know exactly how to explain it."

Veronica nodded.

"And did he say anything about the crown?"

"Only that it could be found on *Philomena*."

Cyprian dug his fingers into the sand in front of him.

"Doesn't do us a lick of good. Ambry had her sunk. In the ocean. Fifty leagues up the coast, at least. Even if we could get back to the site, and she was in shallow water, I don't know how we'd get into her."

Basil stood up. He looked out over the ocean, the moonlight sliding across the rolling waves.

"I might know a way."

He walked down the beach. The Mar seemed to call to him, each lap of the waves against the shore a beckoning finger, curling toward him. Basil waded into the water, feeling the sand pull away at his bare feet. *The Marlord*, his father had said. And where to find a lord but in his domain? In a moment, Basil was waist-deep in the waves. Cyprian and Veronica watched from the shore, outlined in the moonlight.

"Do you mind letting us know what it is that you're doing?" Cyprian asked over the crash and rumble of waves. "We just got done nearly drowning ourselves, don't tell me you're going to finish the job."

Veronica slid her hand down Cyprian's arm.

"Cyprian, just wait."

Basil reached down deep within, feeling the stirring, the last warmth that Lorus had left behind. Then, he opened his mouth, and he spoke High Sylvan in rhythm with the waves that pulsed against his chest. He felt a swirling in the water, tugging first at the hems of his pants, then growing upwards. He looked down. A rotating bubble had formed in the seawater. Smooth as glass, the seawater retreated from his legs and waist, as though he was inside an invisible glass capsule. Basil took another step. The water followed the curve of an invisible shell around him. He took another step. The waterline reached his shoulders, then his neck, then his head. Finally, the waters closed above him, and the crash of waves disappeared. There was only a sound like a deep rhythmic swirling, as though he was at the center of some immense living beast.

Ahead, the moonlight penetrated the surface, shafts of silver piercing the unending green and blue. Occasionally, a dash of scales or the flick of a muscular tail passed through these pillars of radiance. Basil whispered into the still air, and the bubble glided forward into the moonlit sea, sinking as it went. Beneath him, shelves of coral slid by, alive with schools of flitting luminescent fish, sea creatures of every imaginable shape and size, and waving plants. He imagined, here and there, the crippled spars of airships fallen over the Mar, of gold and treasures long forgotten. After a moment, the floor of the ocean dropped away to blackness, and Basil was suspended in an endless dark void of crystalline blue.

A cloud of stars blossomed in the blackness, round pearls of light pulsing pink and orange and gold. The long tails of the jellyfish trailed into the blackness, creating delicate contrails of radiance all around him. For a long moment, Basil stood suspended, taking in a beauty that few had ever seen. Then, the lights began to go out. One by one, they fell away, and Basil was left in the deepest dark he had ever known. His one companion was the deep groaning of the sea, which seemed to grow louder with each passing moment. Then, out of the blackness, Basil saw a deeper blackness moving. It was long and rippled past like a shroud in the gloom. Then, there were more shapes, a churning forest. It was as though something was beyond, waiting, watching. Basil cleared his throat.

"I'm looking," he said. "For the Marlord."

At his words, the sea blossomed with light once more, and Basil gasped. This time, the sea looked back.

Basil was a mere fleck floating before the monstrous eye, a enormous pool of blackness bordered by an iridescent green iris and veinous purple skin. The creature's mottled flesh was a map of scars and markings, encrusted with barnacles. An immense tangled web of tentacles, bristling with flexing suckers, encircled Basil. Schools of blind fish and sinuous eels flitted in and out them. A swirl of lanternfish, stripes of bright light running down their flanks, rotated around Basil, illuminating the void.

A voice sounded in Basil's mind. A voice that spoke in High Sylvan, encrusted with age.

You are a traveler in a place you do not belong.

"I'm…" Basil paused as he searched for the words. "Looking for something."

All are looking for something.

Basil did not have a reply. No book could have prepared him for the immensity and age of this creature. The Marlord regarded him, its massive eye unblinking.

What is it that you look for, Son of Sylvanus? Those who live in the deep know many secrets.

"I am looking for Sylvanus's crown. People calling themselves the Bookkeepers have guided me to you."

And what did they have in mind that I should do? The fate of many rests upon you. I knew all of your forefathers, even if they did not all know me. It is their duty to protect those above. It is mine to protect those below. If the greed of men were not so prone to flow down the rivers and into the Great Mar, I would have no interest in helping you. Again, this Crown is not mine to give, it is yours to find.

"Please, if you're as wise as you say, there must be something you can do for me. I believe the Crown is in my ship, which was lost to the sea."

The Marlord was silent, the black eye staring. The great tentacles uncoiled toward the bubble, close enough for Basil to reach out and touch. He didn't dare.

What the sea takes she is loathe to return. Perhaps the Crown does not reside in your ship at all. What is this piece of man-work to you, that I should bring her from where she rests?

Cyprian cleared his throat, recalling the words of Anne Stormalong.

"Humans become attached to things, to beginnings. *Philomena* is one such beginning."

The Marlord did not reply. For a moment, they hung suspended in the blackness of the sea. Then, an abysmally low sound echoed in the deep, a groaning like the plates of the earth grinding against one another. Basil tore his gaze from the Marlord's eye and looked down. Out of the darkness, a long, regular form was emerging. *Philomena* rose from the seabed trailing contrails of sand and ripped sailcloth, her hull entangled in flexing tentacles, her figurehead unbowed by the black desolation of the sea. The ship finally stopped when her main deck touched the soles of Basil's feet, his bubble a pearl in the midst of floating sailcloth and rope. The Marlord's eye regarded him.

Good luck to you, Basil Black. Remember that men ask many questions. Often, the answers to these questions is the same.

"I don't know what that means."

All finds its place at the proper time.

Basil felt a twinge, and noticed that the surface of the bubble was rippling. Suddenly, spurts of black, icy water were striking Basil from all sides. He tried to speak High Sylvan to push it back, but the warmth that Lorus had put in his chest was gone. The blackness of the sea threatened to crush him. Still he heard the voice rumbling through the deep.

Borrowed power fades. Your time runs short.

And suddenly, *Philomena* was rising up out of the water, carrying Basil along with her. The force of the rushing, salty water forced Basil to the deck. Finally, with a plume of spray, the ship broke through the surface of the sea. Waves crashed against the side of the airship, and her envelopes hung limp. Enormous purple tentacles cradled the hull, pushing her into the shore. As the hull ground against the sand of the beach, *Philomena* tipped leftward, sending Basil sliding into the gunwale near the bow. When he finally pulled himself to his feet, he heard the slap of boots on sand coming down the beach.

"*Philomena!* Basil, what did you do? What in the blue hazes did you blessed do?" cried Cyprian as he and Veronica came without shouting distance. Then, his eyes caught the huge, purplish tentacles that were retreating back into the watery depths. He stood with mouth agape. "What…. did you do?"

Still coughing up seawater, Basil slid over the gunwale into the surf.

"I saw…" he said, his knees suddenly weak. "I saw the Marlord. I saw it…"

"What did it say?" Veronica asked, her face alive with wonder. "What was it like?"

"I don't really know…" Basil said. It was all a blur. "But it gave me back the ship! Although it wasn't really any help on finding the crown."

"So, you haven't found it."

The voice seemed to come from nowhere. For the second time that day, Cyprian swore loudly, grabbing a piece of driftwood, prepared for a fight. But it wasn't Titus or Ambry or some other lackey of the Imperium standing on the beach. It was a woman, wild and silver beneath the moon. Her buckskin was torn in places and a large gash in her forehead trickled blood down her cheek. She was very apparently annoyed, and while Basil didn't find this frightening exactly, those piercing silver eyes made him decidedly uncomfortable.

"Do I mean to understand," Stormalong said. "That you do not have the crown?"

"You know," said Cyprian, dropping the driftwood. "It is not usually prudent to sneak up on nervous people in the dark."

"Enough of you and your inanities, boy!" snapped Stormalong. "If I want to hear foolishness spoken, I'll ask for it. I want the answer from the one on whom the burden rests."

Her silver eyes bored holes into Basil. He shifted in the sand with an uncomfortable squelching sound.

"No," he said. "We have the staff, and the amulet, but not the crown."

Stormalong's eyes hardened even more.

"Your mission was to collect the relics of Sylvanus, not be captured by every group of people you had the misfortune to inconvenience on the bumbling way you went about it."

"Well, come on now…" Cyprian said.

"Did I release you from silence?" demanded Stormalong. She counted on her fingers. "The O'Larre. The Marauders. Bartimaeus

Cain. And finally, the Imperium himself. And from what I have seen, you have just finished conversing with the Marlord. You're lucky that he didn't feed you to any of his fish-folk."

"Yes," Basil said. "Francis Lightlas gave me High Sylvan. But he wasn't Francis Lightlas. He was my father."

Stormalong didn't bat a silver eye.

"You knew?" Basil asked.

"You say 'was'," Stormalong said. "He is dead then? Lorus is dead?"

"Yes. Why didn't you tell me?"

Stormalong's expression softened slightly.

"For the same reason that he did not tell you. What would he have done? He knew that his time to rule was over. He knew that the best chance for freedom in Cor Nova was to reinstate his heir as Sovereign."

They were silent for a moment.

"Lorus wasn't defeated," said Veronica. "At least, he isn't until we are."

Stormalong looked at Veronica, then nodded, a small smile just visible at the edge of her lips.

"Ably spoken. But we may fare no better than he. Come away from this wreck. Prying eyes will see it before anything else. Back to the treeline."

They stumbled back up the beach to where the ferns and palm trees took root, settling in the little cove.

"There are bad tidings," said Stormalong. "The abominable pit of Titus nears completion."

"We saw," said Cyprian, stretching his arm to show the scars. "We helped."

"You and many other reluctant hearts. The work nears completion. The Sarcophagus lies just beneath the surface. Titus flies there at this very moment with an entire Fleet battalion. When he arrives, he will open the Sarcophagus, and attempt to control them."

"The Sidia," said Basil.

"Yes," replied Stormalong. "Men were not made for power, particularly not the kind that has been bred in the Sidia. It pollutes the souls of men. Look at the effect of a single Sidiom on Titus, the one imprisoned in the sword. The power it lends to him is fantastic, but it has driven him near to madness. He will be unable to contain the Sidia for long, if at all. When he breaks, the scourge of the Old World will be released once more. And there will be no Sylvanus to save it this time."

"How much time do we have?" asked Veronica.

"My messengers tell me tomorrow, before the sunset."

"So, none," said Veronica, looking to the wreck of *Philomena*, rocked by the waves on the shore. "At least the Marlord gave us back the crown."

"All my thanks to Mr. Tentacles," said Cyprian. "But even if we were able to find the Crown, there's no way we could reach the Abyss in time. With no ship…"

Stormalong's brow furrowed. She pointed to the hulk on the coast.

"I believe that is a ship, is it not?"

"It was a ship," said Cyprian. "Although she's more like driftwood now. She has a broken keel, for starters."

Stormalong stood up and strode down the beach toward *Philomena*. Shrugging at one another, the three stood up and followed her. She was silent, her arms straight at her side, thinking intensely.

"So, we have no weapon," said Basil, as they walked out onto the beach. "But what about you? You have High Sylvan…"

"Nothing to the degree of Titus," said Stormalong. "Or the Sovereign. Mine is a pale shadow of that ability. As different from the light of the moon to the light of the sun. I would fare no better than Lorus would have."

Philomena rocked gently with each salty blast of the ocean, the green seawater spilling into and out of her ports as the waves broke against her. Stormalong waded over to the large break in the hull about midships, ripping aside a splintered plank. Cyprian winced.

"Anne, could you please-"

Stormalong continued unheeding, until Cyprian finally shook his head and lent her a hand. In a few moments, the moonlight fell on the exposed keel of *Philomena*, awash with seawater. The immense trunk of cedar had shorn completely through, in two long jagged pieces almost exactly amidships. Cyprian was suddenly very quiet. This was a near-incurable wound for a ship *Philomena's* age.

Stormalong bent carefully over the keel. She reached into her bag, and putting something here and there on the broken sides of the keel. Basil leaned closer to look. They were small, wrinkled seeds. Stormalong stood up, and sighed. The salty air seemed to blow more quickly through the keel, the waves to beat more rhythmically. And she spoke High Sylvan, soft as moonlight. At first, the seeds were still. Then, they rocked back and forth. And erupted.

Like tiny fingers, white roots burst forth and sank into the wood. Twisted green sprouts spiraled upwards, shoots thickening and leaves spreading with every passing second. Veronica and Cyprian sloshed back to avoid the reaching arms of the vine, but Basil stood transfixed as the shoots exploded into tiny white flowers shaped like stars.

"Look," whispered Veronica. "Look at the break."

It was closing. The vine and the roots thickened, tightening around the long split in the keel so that the black sliver shrank with every passing second. The keel juddered against the sand as the broken pieces realigned. And then, all was still. Stormalong dealt the keel a hefty kick. The thump reverberated through the whole ship, but the keel was solid as a rock.

"Blue hazes," Cyprian said, running his hand over the vines. "We have a ship."

"And, I would suspect, garrulous son of Augustus," replied Stormalong. "That you have a plan as well. You're the kind who comes up with them. Let's hear it."

Cyprian rubbed an affectionate hand against the old freighter. A familiar light was glinting in his eye.

"I don't think you're going to like it."

Basil looked up. The moon was overhead, the night already half gone.

"At this point," he said. "I don't think we have the luxury of being able to like it."

CHAPTER THIRTY-FIVE

The wind moaned low and forlorn through the night. Fitful clouds came and went over the lonely moon, causing the tombstone mountains of rubble to fade in and out of blackness. Worn, broken-down freighters drifted among them like ghosts, trailing torn sailcloth like burial rags, their prisoner crews listless with exhaustion beneath the whips of Fleet officers. They traced endless loops, carrying the guts of the earth up from the Abyss, dumping them and returning for more.

Not a single one of the ghostly slave ships seemed to notice as one more broken, forlorn ship slipped into the rubble mountains. It was a mid-size Misericordiae freighter, riddled with battle scars, her charred, broken spars near the bow hastily covered with canvas. Her second envelope was shredded to tatters, and the other two were slowly leaking aether in wispy trails to the sky. A close observer would have noted that a large portion of her was encrusted with algae and barnacles. But the men on board the other rubble ships didn't seem to know or care. Perhaps the fear of the whips of their Fleet overseers kept their eyes down to their work. Perhaps they had just lost the will to look up.

Whatever the reason, Cyprian decided, he was blessed thankful. It had been a pain to guide *Philomena* low over the coast and up through the valleys back into the Fields of Carath. At every moment,

Cyprian had to prevent the ship's hastily mended keel from clipping the earth and keep her silhouette well below the horizon, invisible to any watchers above. If not for the clouds over the moon, Cyprian doubted they would have had a chance.

Cyprian slid his hand over the worn wood of the ship's wheel, giving it a rough pat. He had to give it to the old girl, even after three weeks in the grip of the ocean, it had only taken a few hours of frantic rigging to get her flying. But, as he'd discovered, there was a yawning chasm between flying and flying well. The brine had clogged and corroded her aether pipes, making her vents difficult to control, and the ravages of the sea had caused a lot of her rigging and cables to weaken and unravel. Several had snapped inside the housings and pulleys that threaded the shipcore. In addition, several of her control surfaces were nearly completely useless, tattered to mere shreds. He reached for one of her pitch levers, and was rewarded with a spray of rancid seawater to the face. Muttering furiously, he did his best to wipe salty water from his eyes.

Cyprian was inwardly cursing whatever miserable mollusk had gnawed off the main knob of the aetherolabe when Veronica emerged from below, looking gloomy. Her dark eyes swept the horizon, pausing warily on the ghostly rock freighter that was drifting ahead of them, dumping its load of gravel on the nearest ever-growing pile of debris.

"Don't worry," Cyprian said in a low voice, guiding the sodden *Philomena* through another silent turn in the maze of rubble. "None of them have so much as glanced at us since we've pulled in. So long as we keep our distance, they shouldn't notice anything amiss."

Veronica nodded, her dark eyes still searching the night, as though trying to pull back the layers of darkness. Cyprian had the feeling that her mind was elsewhere, maybe still mentally searching the ship with Basil, maybe somewhere in the depths of the Abyss, kneeling by the weak form of her mother.

"I've been watching the sky in the east," Cyprian continued. "But I haven't seen any ships from Soliodomus yet. Either they're biding their time or they're already here. Have you found anything?"

Veronica's eyes widened; she was looking at something off the bow.

"Careful!" she said in her loudest whisper, jabbing at a finger at the mountain of rubble that was now looming alarmingly close to the rightward gunwale.

Cyprian jerked the wheel around leftward, dragging one of pitch levers back. There was a low thud in the shipcore, signaling that the cable servicing it had broken. Cyprian rolled the wheel back and seized a handful more levers, barely managing to get the ship back under control and out of danger, at least mostly. They both winced as the hull clipped the pile of crushed rock with a juddering groan. Finally, there was silence. No alarm was raised, and Cyprian and Veronica were left looking at each other in the dark. Cyprian swallowed.

"So. How's the search coming along?"

"Nothing yet," Veronica said, a small smile at Cyprian's embarrassment emerging on her face. "I just came up to see how you were faring. I think I have a reasonably good idea of that now. Do you need help?"

"Veronica, I'm a remarkably good airman…"

"Do you want me to steer?"

"No," Cyprian said, kicking the helm, which shuddered. "I don't want you to blessed steer. This is like flying my grandmother's busted old wardrobe. The cables are rotted through, the pitch controls are a mess, and some insufferable cephalopod has chewed the knobs off my aetherolabe. What in blue hazes are you smiling at? I have a hard time seeing what's so blessed funny. We're at the very maw of death itself, you know."

Veronica shook her head, still smiling.

"I'm going to go help Basil. As I said, no trace of the crown yet. We've been through everything aft of the galley, most of the holds, and Basil's in the steerage now."

"Wonderful. Excellent. I'll just try to hold off certain death and so on. By all means, go on giggling and helping my ship's cook find his tiara."

Veronica was still grinning as Cyprian coaxed *Philomena* into a low bank around the next mountain of rubble. A pale, orange light broke across the bow. Innumerable torches and oil fires lit the mouth of the Abyss, casting orange radiance to the fevered sky. Even now, the lifts and wheels were turning, churning the guts of the earth upward to be discarded on the Fields. Veronica's laughter was instantly extinguished. Her grip on the helm tightened.

"We're getting too close," she said.

For once, Cyprian didn't have a smart remark. The sight of the pit gave him a horrible, twisting sensation in his stomach. He nodded, turning the wheel, but his eyes stayed locked on the furious activity that surrounded the Abyss. Clustered like vermin around a rotting carcass, dreadnoughts pulled against their mooring cables at the top of the enormous pit. Veronica brushed her hair over her ear, her face awash with orange light.

"Stormalong was right. A whole battalion. At least… twenty, thirty. But I don't see a flagship."

A flood of figures in red descended from the ships, marching down the ramps and lifts in rows and columns.

"They're deploying," Cyprian said. "Either they're fortifying it for Titus, or they're planning something else… Why would they need that many soldiers?"

Both jumped at the sound of a hatch banging. Basil emerged from the companionway below. He looked even more rumpled than usual. His vest was faded and tattered, now shiny with the salty ooze that coagulated in the steerage. The baleful lights from the Abyss flashed across his spectacles as *Philomena* turned and passed again into the depths of the rubble mountains.

"Still nothing?" Veronica asked.

Basil shook his head.

"No. I just dredged through the whole steerage. Nothing except for another belligerent octopus and at least three species of crab. There's not a sign of the crown anywhere. We went through every locker in the galley, down through the holds, tore apart every bunk. We even looked through Lightlas's cabin."

Cyprian went through the ship again in his mind, trying to conjure up any place that he could think of.

"You're sure it was *Philomena*?"

Veronica nodded.

"That's what Lightl- er, Lorus said. *Third and sixth and third once more at Ivory's first… Philomena's* berth beneath the Ivory City's first concourse was number 363. It has to be here. Somewhere."

"*Perched on brows of wooden sight…*" Basil murmured.

"You checked the figurehead?" Cyprian asked. "She has wooden eyes, wooden sight."

"Twenty times, at least," Veronica said, cradling her head in her hands. Her eyes were rimmed with red. It had been a long time since any of them slept. "The crown that's on her head is all wood. I don't see what else we can do besides saw her in half."

"Which wouldn't work," Basil said. "I think it unlikely there's anything inside her. She's a solid piece of cedar. And she's as old as the rest of the ship, maybe even older. Still nothing from Soliodomus?"

As one, they looked out over the dark plain toward Soliodomus and the city of Carath. There was nothing moving in that blackness. At least, not yet. Cyprian shook his head.

"Old Titus hasn't stuck out one rotten toenail. Although, it looks like Stormalong was right. The Fleet is deploying at the Abyss, gearing up for something big. Whatever is down there, it seems like they'll be going after it. And soon."

Basil wandered to the gunwale, looking out into the endless mountains of rubble, now slicing the moonlight night into slivers of darkness. The wind whipping through them was a low, mournful moan, picking at his coat and hair.

"We know perfectly well what's down there," Basil said to the night. "If Titus gets to the Sarcophagus, there'll be no hope for any of us. The Sidia nearly destroyed Cor Nova once. Once Titus releases them, there's nothing to stop them from finishing what they began. And without the Crown, there's no way to stop Titus."

The wind's keening seemed to rise slightly.

"Don't forget Stormalong," said Veronica. "She'll come with the reinforcements."

"Right," Cyprian grumbled. "An army of pinecones and sparrows. And somehow she's going to go all the way to other end of the dominion and back?"

Veronica punched him in the arm, flicking her eyes at Basil. "I have a feeling," she said. "That Anne Stormalong is the kind of woman who knows more than one way to get around."

Basil did not seem encouraged. He plunked himself down on the final step from the command deck.

"It's not here," he said. "We've looked through everything. We must be missing something."

Veronica sat down next to him. She looked ashen.

"We have to think," she said, resting her head against the worn cedar beams. *"Brows of wooden sight…"*

And they lapsed into silence, each to their own thoughts, *Philomena* rocking in the restless wind. Cyprian sat next to Veronica to rest his legs. He did his best to think of think of anywhere a crown might be hiding on *Philomena*, but his mind was growing cloudy. His thoughts wandered.

When Cyprian's eyes opened, the dawn was rising red. He jumped to his feet, inadvertently startling Veronica, whose head had been resting on his shoulder. Basil was standing on the rear gunwale, looking out over the mountains of rubble. In the aggressive shafts of dawn light, ships were approaching from the white city far off in the east. They were large, red, flying in close formation. Basil's shoulders bent, as though beneath a great weight.

"You could have woken us, Basil," Cyprian said.

Basil didn't move. His voice was low.

"He's coming."

Cyprian brought his oculus to bear, tightening the focus on the formation. It was a host of dreadnoughts, cut down lean and bristling with weaponry, encircling a large battleship, its great bow a hammer splitting through the sky. A group of interceptors flew on the fringes, their decks alive with watchful eyes and quick guns, scanning for any danger. Every ship flew great crimson banners with the Imperium's seal, furling out behind them in the sky. Cyprian centered the oculus on the battleship, a formidable behemoth of cedar and oak, polished metal and colored glass.

"It's him all right," Cyprian said, passing the oculus to Veronica. "Earlier than we thought."

Basil nodded.

"Eager."

Veronica collapsed the oculus with a decisive click.

"What are we going to do?"

"The only thing we can do," Cyprian said. "Wait. Alone, we're on a suicide mission. The interceptors would shred *Philomena* before we had even half their altitude. Stormalong's reinforcements had better be good, because they're all we've got."

"No," Basil said. The warships were drawing ever closer to the Abyss, predatory shadows against the red dawn sky. "We have to get to Titus. I'll have to…improvise."

Basil began pacing up and down the deck, his face a mask of concentrated determination. Cyprian did his best to keep a level tone of voice.

"Basil, now is not the time for some kind of hare-brained scheme…"

"Now that's new!" Basil said, not breaking his stride. "How come it's always a good idea when you come up with it, and a hare-brained scheme when it comes from anyone else?"

"Basil has a point…" Veronica said.

Cyprian rubbed his forehead.

"Look, I know I've been on the business end of a fair number of dubious doings, but none of them included a quarter of the Imperium Fleet and the actual fate of the blessed dominion. I mean… Cut me a little rope…"

Veronica gave Cyprian a significant glance, all pursed lips and arched eyebrows. It was the one that advised him to stop talking.

"Fine," Cyprian said. "Sorry. Basil, what's your idea?"

"We have no choice," Basil said after completing several circuits of the deck. "I have the staff and the amulet. That has to count for something…"

Now it was Cyprian's turn to catch Veronica's eye. Basil could do nothing against the power of Titus, and the amulet and staff alone would be no help. Still, it was hard to disagree with so little time left. And besides, Basil's mind seemed to be made up.

"I'll do what I can," he said. "All we have to do is distract him until Stormalong returns with reinforcements. How close can we get?"

Cyprian didn't voice again his lack of confidence in Stormalong's reinforcements. The delegation of Fleet ships was nearly at the mouth of the Abyss, the interceptors falling back in towards the bow of the great battleship, tightening their defensive perimeter around the formation.

"To the battleship?" Cyprian said finally. "We won't get anywhere near her. Getting into the Abyss would be easier. I don't think anyone is watching the concourses. If they're expecting trouble, it will come from the sky, not from a half-wrecked rubble ship."

Basil gave a grim nod. Wordlessly, almost not believing what he was doing, Cyprian got on the helm and gave Basil and Veronica direction. He brought *Philomena* up as high as he dared. Then, he pointed her bow into the line of ships approaching the rock-strewn concourse of the Abyss. The three of them worked silently, doing their best to pay attention to ropes and sails, all the while watching the battalion of Fleet ships descend toward the Abyss. The warships stopped, venting aether to the sky, directly over the enormous pit, fiery dragons prepared to plunge down on their prey. Dozens of interceptors patrolled the perimeter, but they paid the rubble ships no mind.

A half-dozen other weathered hulks were at a standstill on the loading concourse, their spiritless crews looking up at the hovering battleship with empty eyes. With only a slight grinding against the rough oaken planks, Cyprian managed to bring *Philomena* in beside them. He nearly leapt out of his skin when a cannon blast and a fanfare of trumpets split the air. A huge hatch in the hull of the battleship was splitting open like an upturned scarlet flower. Out of its depths, a gondola, trimmed in red with golden banners, emerged descended into the Abyss on twin spools of golden chain. A single figure, tall and angular, stood on the gondola. Titus was immaculately attired in a trim Fleet uniform, with a black sword at his hip. Immediately, the soldiers poised on every tier of the Abyss exploded into furious applause and cheering.

Cyprian felt an acid anger start bubbling in his gut. This is how the world honors a man who ordered this cavernous monstrosity, who buried freedom beneath an avalanche of burning books, who celebrated the death of his father as a national triumph. Up and down the line of battered ships, the prisoner crews watched the Imperium descend, their eyes devoid of any emotion. It was too much work to care.

"The Imperium makes his entrance," Cyprian said, as Titus waved a lean hand, his expression one of cultured benevolence. "To thunderous applause."

Veronica's voice was twisted with bitterness.

"It's how it always goes," she said.

Basil alone was moving. He reached up to the boom winch that hung over the deck, releasing the winch platform.

"Basil," Veronica said. "You can't."

"I'm going down," he said, swinging the arm of the winch out over the ship's side. Just a few feet beyond, the Abyss yawned wide. The platform swayed in the fetid gusts of wind that rolled up from below.

"Basil," said Cyprian as Basil swung aboard. He carried nothing but the Elm Staff, the Riverstone Amulet around his neck. He almost looked incomplete without his medical box. "This is suicide. You don't have High Sylvan... You don't even have a gun. There has to be something..."

Basil pointed to the lone figure descending in the gondola, a fuse that was about to reach the powder.

"There is no more time, Cyprian," said Basil. "Two of three relics will have to be enough. Now, release the winch. It'll have to be quick."

"I'm coming with you," said Veronica resolutely. She only hesitated a moment before joining Basil on the creaking platform. "My mother is down there and I'm not letting you go alone."

"Well," Cyprian said, checking the pair of rusty pistols he'd scavenged from the ship's holds. "You're sure as hazes not going without me. I'm the only one of us who can fight half well..."

Basil shook his head.

"Cyprian. Someone has to run the winch."

Cyprian's mouth shut. He knew that Basil was right. There had to be a strong hand up at the top to man the mechanism. For a moment, a thousand options ran through Cyprian's mind. He thought about conscripting one of the slack-jawed prisoners. He thought about trying to rig the complicated system. But none of them were viable.

Reluctantly, Cyprian laid his hand on the winch lever. Veronica's dark eyes penetrated him, and he thought he could gaze into them forever. Perhaps, this would be the last time he ever saw those eyes. Suddenly, he realized that the two people he was about to drop into the most dangerous place in Cor Nova were his two truest friends in the world. There were many things that he felt that he should say, but none seemed to fit in his mouth correctly.

"I'm coming down after you," he said finally, swallowing to keep the thickness out of his voice. "One way or another. Don't start any of the fun without me."

Basil smiled.

"Never."

Cyprian nodded. He pulled the lever. With a steady creak, the spool turned, sending Basil and Veronica down the side of the Abyss. Carefully, Cyprian adjusted the levers, doing his best to keep the platform steady. He looked up and down the rim of the Abyss. No one was paying attention to the line descending from *Philomena*. It was just one more in the endless contraptions clinging to the walls. Occasionally, he chanced a glance over *Philomena's* gunwale. The platform had nearly disappeared among the endless scaffolds and lifts of the Abyss. Once, he thought he saw Veronica looking back up at him. The spool ran and ran. Then, there was a bump, and the rope went slack. The platform had reached the bottom, or as near to it as it could go.

Meanwhile, Titus's gondola had reached the floor of the Abyss as well. The taskmasters were driving captives back, clearing the pocked ground for the Imperium. He was a speck of red down below, but he seemed to draw every eye as he stepped from the gondola, as powerful as gravity. Cyprian rushed to the gunwale, aiming his oculus down into the Abyss. Titus was speaking, but Cyprian was too far away to hear the words.

He drew his blade, and the hair on the back of Cyprian's neck stood up. The temperature dropped and the air grew darker. With blade poised high, Titus spoke High Sylvan. It was reedy and twisted, a pale and terrifying shadow of the speech of Stormalong or Basil. Nevertheless, the heavens heard and answered. With a blinding crack, a bolt of lightning crashed down from the sky above into the upraised blade. Cyprian watched horrified as Titus moved the blade downward and swept it around, tracing a huge circle around himself. The lightning from the sword jetted outward, striking and tearing chunks of rock and earth to the side. The whole Abyss shone with demonic light as the lightning bolts arced, smashing rock and turning sand into glass wherever they struck. The gunpowder smell of burning rock rolled upward with the dust and the fetid air of the Abyss.

Cyprian's heart hammered in his chest. If Titus had that much power, there was no way that any amulet or staff alone would be of any use to Basil. He needed the Astral Crown, and the power of the Sovereigns, or he would be turned into so much grayish paste beneath Titus's bootheel. Somewhere, down in that murderous hole, Basil was utterly alone. He had no weapon, no ship, no allies beyond a temperamental girl with a rapier. If any help was coming from outside, it was too late. And there was nothing that Cyprian could do about it.

In that moment, he was the little boy on the weather tower again, watching *Philomena* plunge in and out of the clouds of smoke, watching his father's life be extinguished before his eyes. He was powerless. And then, Cyprian's mind seized strangely on another figure in that memory. He saw, clearly, the figurehead of *Philomena*, her eyes. Her smile. The world beneath her feet. And suddenly, the words inscribed on the cover of the Rule of Sylvanus sprang to his mind. *The Sovereign's eye that sees from height, perched on brows of wooden sight…*

With effort, Cyprian tore his gaze from the Imperium. He dashed up the deck to the figurehead. There had always been something about her, something in the way she confidently smiled out over the wide world. She knew a secret. She had known it for a long time. Cyprian ran his hands over the figurehead's wooden head again. It was wooden all the way through. Likewise her face, her hands, her feet. Just as Basil had said, her body was a single intricately carved piece of Misericordiae cedar.

Finally, with the Imperium's lightning still rattling in his ears, Cyprian looked deep into her wooden eyes. His breath caught. There, in the cedar depths of her eye, a pattern was visible. Anyone but a born airman would have taken it for a mere curiosity of the wood, a sunburst formed by the grain. But Cyprian saw the shape clearly, crafted expertly in miniature at the center of the eye. It was round, with spokes radiating outward. A ship's wheel.

With a whoop, Cyprian swung out and kissed the figurehead on her cedar cheek. He tore up the deck, slashing loose the tie-downs on the spars and sails. They snapped to the fore, ripped and tangled as they were. The prisoners on the other ships took notice, but Cyprian didn't care. He put his hands on the wheel, which, he knew, was more than a wheel. He slammed back the last pitch lever, sending the last of *Philomena's* aether into her remaining two envelopes.

"One more rise, old girl," he said.

The old freighter bled aether from torn canvas, her keel groaning, reluctant to take to the sky.

"Come on," he said, turning the valves wider, grinding his teeth. "Come on. For McElhaney, for Oakum, for old Lightlas or whoever he was. For Dad."

And slowly, with great effort, *Philomena* rose just enough to clear the concourse. Cyprian pushed the pitch levers, propelling *Philomena* forward into the open space of the Abyss. In the absence of wind and buffeting, the merchant ship slid through the air. Cyprian heard a shout from the Imperium vessels above, but he just increased the airship's speed, throwing wide the vents. *Philomena* bled a trail of aether all the way down.

CHAPTER THIRTY-SIX

No one was watching Basil and Veronica as they descended toward the floor of the Abyss. The show unfolding below drew every eye. As the gondola glided downward on its chains from the battleship above, the Fleet taskmasters cleared an enormous circle, driving the prisoners back with their pikes and lengths of chain. With the faint clicking of telescoping legs on the bottom of the gondola, the magnificent carriage rested perfectly level on the base of the Abyss. The glass-paned door slid open, and the Imperium Titus emerged.

Basil had never seen Titus before, but he was immediately struck by the strange resemblance between him and Lorus. Although Titus was now tinged with gray, they had the same strong features and sharp blue eyes. Basil's eyes. His heart thumped loudly in his chest. Titus was a grand sight in his ceremonial uniform, and he walked with measured step down the gangplank, giving small waves and nods to the blank slaves and cheering Fleet men at every level of the Abyss. The gondola rose up into the air behind him. Finally, Titus stood alone amid the rocks like an explorer stands on top of a mountain, victorious.

Veronica was standing next to him, one hand nervously drumming the hilt of her rapier. She was watching for possible obstructions that would get in the way of the platform's descent, occasionally pushing it one way or another off the rocky wall.

"Veronica," Basil said. "When we get to the bottom, I don't know what's going to happen."

Veronica nodded.

"I know that."

"I don't even know what I'm going to do."

"I know that too. Look, Basil, whatever happens I'm going to be there beside you, watching your back. I've lived my entire life risking my neck. Now, the time has come to risk it all. I'm ready."

Basil suddenly felt a warmth. He would not be totally alone in this.

"Just promise me," he said, "If anything happens to me, get to your mother and get her out of here, along with anyone else you can find."

"I will, Basil."

Finally, Titus raised a hand for silence.

"My friends…" he intoned. His voice was deep and melodious, echoing off the walls like thunder. "My friends! Loyal citizens of your Imperium! Faithful followers of the true leader of Cor Nova! My greetings to you on this day of days, this hour of hours!"

The resounding applause from the soldiers was enough to drown the solid thump of the platform coming to rest on mound of broken rock at the base of the Abyss, cloaked on either side by tall piles of earth. Basil and Veronica clambered over the broken rocks to the floor of the mighty pit. Up ahead, there was the crowd of prisoners, gathered all around the wide empty circle in which the Imperium stood.

"Look at what we have accomplished!" he continued. "The mettle of man against the tyranny of nature! The work of muscle and steel against dumb earth and stone! And all of this so that we men might discover our true power, that our Dominion may accept her true destiny."

Basil and Veronica crept forward through the crowd, closer to the Imperium with every step.

"For many, many years, my forefathers held this land captive. Groaning beneath the weight of asinine tradition, irrelevant history, and ancient platitudes, the Sovereigns kept the children of Cor Nova plodding through the years. They denied men the power that they would need to move on, to move forward, to assume the destiny that we have chosen for ourselves. But no more!"

Finally, Basil emerged into the first row of prisoners. Across the expanse, he could see the tall form of Titus, a lone stony pillar in the mutilated earth. The Imperium spread his arms wide, chest outthrust. He reached to his side and unsheathed the black saber. It slid free of its sheath with a single, ringing note that filled up the void of the Abyss for a long moment. Basil's hair stood on end. A wave of deep unease spread across the crowds. The temperature dropped. The sky darkened. Titus's eyes were lit with a far-away power, the blade in his hand almost alive.

"There was power in the Old World, and my brother and his kin raised you to hate and to fear it. You were raised to see it only as a weapon, but weapons are tools, dear friends. And tools can be used to build greatness."

The sky around swirled and darkened. Titus swung the blade high, and High Sylvan sprang from his lips, the syllables crashing into one another. The grey clouds split with light, like quartz running through granite, and a column of lightning roared down from the heavens, crashing into the blade. With an almighty roar, Titus brought the saber down like a hammer against the scarred and torn earth of the Abyss. In plumes of molten rock and hot dust, the ground rolled and rocked, sending boulders spinning end over end. The air was filled acrid smoke. All that was left in the center of the Abyss was an enormous wide circle of bare, green stone, with Titus alone at its center, not a single hair on his head out of place. The black-hilted blade steamed in his hand.

In a moment, Basil knew that he was looking at the Sarcophagus. It was immense, at least as wide across as four ships bow to stern. The dark green stone was furrowed, rounded in places. Basil had seen that before, when melted rock went through the forges of the metallurgists. It was as though the rock had been liquefied and then drawn like a curtain over whatever lay beneath. Basil knew it was no metallurgist, but Sylvanus himself, who had spoken this impenetrable rock into place eight hundred years before.

Titus was taking a moment to appreciate the beauty of the Sarcophagus himself, but it seemed that the sword had other plans. It hummed with energy, and tracking in the Imperium's hand, raising and extending Titus's arm, its blade wavering over the thousands of faces that peered down at it, until it rested directly between Basil's eyes. The sharp, blue gaze of Titus, Imperium of

Cor Nova, fell on him. Titus's angular, once-handsome face contorted briefly into a look of confusion and hatred, his lip curled, his eyes widened in disbelief. Basil was supposed to be dead, and here he was, alive.

For the first time, the prisoners realized his presence as well. Those near Basil backed away, leaving him exposed, with only Veronica at his back, her rapier drawn, her expression defiant. The murmurs spread through the crowds, and the desperate hopelessness of the Abyss seemed to flicker. There was the sound of far-off shouting and shoving as units of Fleet airmen pushed their way through the crowds toward him. Finally, Titus's face flexed into a rueful grin, as though Basil was merely a small child out of bed.

"And look who has come to celebrate this day of days," he said. "But the elusive Basil Black. My, my, but don't you look a sight. Come a bit closer, dear boy."

The utterance of Basil's name caused more stirring in the crowds, but Titus didn't seem to notice. With cool derision, the Imperium's lips moved once more. Basil felt a feeling of constriction, as though his chest was being squeezed in a giant fist. Titus flicked the blade upward, and Basil was flying through the air, turning over once before smashing to the cold, green stone at the edge of the Sarcophagus. The Elm Staff clattered away from him as he landed hard, the air driven from his lungs. The Sarcophagus was icy against his cheek.

"Good day, nephew. It seems that you come bearing gifts. I dare say your travels have yielded many such prizes. Let us have a look."

With a harsh pair of syllables, Titus swiped the saber once. With a clatter, the Elm Staff leaped from the stone floor and swooped to Titus's feet as though blown by the wind. The Amulet, too, leaped towards the Imperium, dragging Basil along on by the neck on its chain for several yards before the strap broke, and the Amulet too sailed towards Titus. Titus caught the round necklace neatly in his free hand. He hefted it, giving it a cursory glance.

"Pretty trinkets," mused the Imperium. "The Riverstone Amulet. The Elm Staff. But no Astral Crown. Alas, Basil, you have fallen short. The magic number is always three."

Basil struggled to his feet, massaging his neck where the chain had bit savagely into his throat. His vision was swimming, the taste of blood filling his mouth. Through the haze of pain and confusion, he was aware of thousands of faces, watching him. But ahead of all of them was the tall, leering form of Titus, a pillar of power and control, now holding Basil's only meager resources. Basil felt the last of his resolve flow out of him. He had lost this fight. He had been losing it ever since the day the messenger came to Osmara.

"I've heard many wild tales about you, young Basil. The wildest is that you have come to see me finished, to do away with me and put yourself on the Just Throne. I would very much like to dismiss such stories for the skydog's tales that they are. Come on now. It is no time to be shy. Have you come to dethrone your Imperium or not? We have many witnesses eager for your answer."

Titus swung a hand out toward the throngs of people standing at every level of the Abyss. It was easy to see them as nothing more than a mob, a collection of faceless prisoners. All the same ragged limbs and labored breathing, all stained the monochrome dirt color. But now, Basil looked at their faces. Down to a man, they were watching him, reading his every move, anticipating the words that would come from his lips. Each one, he realized, was as much an individual as he. Each one now had a hope to cling to. It was not within Basil's rights to take away that hope, however slim, however fragile. Basil squared his shoulders, and looked at his uncle.

"I have."

A stir went through the crowd. A few of the soldiers laughed. Titus's lips tightened.

"That is quite painful to me, Basil. It is always good to maintain the ties of family. You could be a part of our great project. Not the stuff of leadership, but you would make quite the clerk."

Basil reached into the satchel at his waist. He pulled out the Rule of Sylvanus. It was heavy, warm in his hand, the brass mending plates on the cover smooth against his fingers.

"Have you read this?"

"Speak up, boy."

"I said, have you read this?"

Titus laughed again.

"I'm a vital man, nephew, but my eyes aren't a hawks'. I don't know what book you are holding, but it looks as though it has seen better days."

"It was your blade that did the cutting."

"Hmm. Quite Lorus's son you are then, if you carry his old copy of the Rule around with you."

"Have you read it?"

"I have no use for Lorus's dusty book. As you may be aware, it was of no use to him either. Nor to any of our forefathers. Nor to any person here. It is not right for modern man to bend his back beneath such meaningless platitudes."

Basil opened the Rule. He held it high.

"I've read it. One day, one of these books will rest in every home in the dominion again."

Titus's grip tightened on his saber. His patience was running out. Basil knew he would have to talk quickly.

"Our family has ruled Cor Nova for four hundred years. We have had wise Sovereigns. We have had foolish ones. Many were something of both. But if you had read the rule, Titus, you would know something about what separates the wise and the foolish."

Basil began to walk, slowly, toward Titus.

"Wise Sovereigns use the power that they are given, only ever asking how it can be used to serve. Foolish Sovereigns take power that does not belong to them, only ever asking how it can serve them. You and I, Titus, both know what is inside this Sarcophagus. We both know that in the Sidia, there is enough power to destroy a world. But only you are foolish enough to think that you could possibly control it."

Titus's lip curled in derision.

"Ah, yes, Basil what a fool am I. Clearly, you've steeped yourself in the wisdom of the Sovereigns. But you'll have to excuse me if I doubt the ability of eight hundred years of dead kings to know what is best. Let me ask you, Basil. The Sovereigns have wielded the powers of the earth, the Tongue that made the World, the nigh-limitless weapons of nature. And what were the Sovereigns kings of? A sleepy and dusty world, a world of farmers and airmen and blacksmiths. The Sovereigns were content to sit and watch the world wile away its time, one generation after the next."

With a spiteful swing of his arm, Titus threw the amulet and staff. They clattered to the green stone a few yards from where Basil stood, the Amulet's strap wrapped around the Elm Staff.

"But I," Titus spat. "I am no Sovereign. I am the Imperium. When I combine High Sylvan with the power of the Old World, I will have power sufficient to build towers to the sky, expand the borders of Cor Nova beyond the Shrouds, lead our people into greatness never before imagined. We will be new Cor Novans!"

Titus's voice sounded colossal in the Abyss. He thrust a viciously pointed finger out at all the prisoners.

"Does anyone side with this king?" he thundered. "If I am an impostor, then by all means, come forward and stand by his side. Kneel before this boy and he will pledge you his protection. If any man or woman of you would be the subject of the Sovereign, speak now!"

The thousands of faces were silent, looking down at Basil with wide eyes.

"Do you hear that, Basil? It's the sound of men. They are no more than animals, needing direction and the whip."

"No," Basil said. "It's the sound of fear. You should recognize it. I believe it's the only language that you know how to speak anymore. Sidia cannot be intimidated. They won't obey you."

With a hiss of hatred, Titus raised his blade to the darkened heavens. The steel crackled with electricity, the sparks dancing in frenzied sparks. Basil could sense the malevolence of the blade, the dark, coiled something that screamed within, eager to unleash its rage on the world. In the bizarre lightning glow, Basil couldn't hear Titus's words, but he saw the words form on his lips.

"Oh Basil," he said. "They already do."

The lightning condensed, the sword slid downward and bucked once. An arc of pure white heat raced straight for him.

Basil suddenly felt very far away, as though he was no longer standing in his beaten, unraveling shoes. He was aware of a collective gasp, a groaning rush. From the corner of his eye, he saw a freighter plummeting through the Abyss, broken spars and masts rattling with sails flapping behind.

Alongside it, a lanky blur flew free, swinging on a rope attached to a plunging mast. Cyprian's coat and golden hair billowed out behind him, his jaw set, storm-grey eyes glinting. In his free hand hung a large circular object. Then, the whole world blazed white. Basil was unsure of whether he was feeling life leave his body, or if the normal flow of time had passed him by. He was certain that everything was over, that he had let them down, that thousands of people were seeing the last Sovereign of Cor Nova die at the hands of his uncle. He had failed them, failed every last one.

Then, Basil's vision cleared. He was lying on the ground, and he could barely breathe. He opened his eyes and saw the dark, swirling circle of the sky above the Abyss. Fine splinters of cedar were raining down around him, some of them charred and black. He looked down. A large, thick plank of scorched cedar was lying on his chest. Scarcely believing he was alive, he pushed it off. In the center of the Sarcophagus, Titus still stood, the sword now by his side. But between the two of them, a wreck of cedar spars, charred cable, and burning canvas was in the final stages of collapse. Great plumes of aether were venting from the ship's wrecked envelopes, her bulkheads splintering beneath the weight of her decks. At one end of the wreck, a figurehead of a fair, confident maiden broke forward and thudded to the ground. The lightning blast from the saber had connected right at the center of *Philomena's* keel, blasting her to smithereens about midships.

Titus stood frozen, his expression strangely cool and vacant, as though the merchant ship was a mere raindrop from the sky, as though a dead pigeon had fallen from on high. Then, the Imperium disappeared, blocked out by the figure of a man now standing in front of Basil, still bent in the crouch he'd landed in, the hem of his jacket smoking from residual lightning strike. Basil felt a calloused hand in his own, and he was yanked to his feet.

"I forget what number rescue we're on," Cyprian said as he thrust the Elm Staff and the Amulet into Basil's hands. "But we're really going to need to discuss my fee."

Basil's mind was whirling. Numbly, he put the Amulet around his neck.

"Cyprian, what are you doing?"

"What I've been tasked to do," he said, bending to pick up the circular object at his feet. It was *Philomena's* battered ship's wheel. "In the business, we call it earning your wages. Which, as I said, will need to be re-evaluated."

Cyprian lifted the wheel high, and smashed it to the dark stone floor of the Sarcophagus. With a crack, the carefully milled segments of the wheel broke cleanly around its joints, but something remained behind, a ring of starlight embedded in the wood. Extracting it carefully, Cyprian lifted the Astral Crown carefully between his fingers. Droplets of light slid around the crown's rim. Basil shook his head.

"How did you know?"

Cyprian gestured toward *Philomena's* broken figurehead, confidently smiling face now turned upward toward the sky.

"Pattern embedded in the figurehead's eye. *Brows of wooden sight.* Old *Philomena* knew better than we did. Now, I believe it's considered bad form to put this on yourself."

And before Basil knew it, Cyprian had placed the Crown on his head. Basil's heart beat against the Amulet that hung around his neck. The Elm Staff was warm in his hand. The Crown encircled his head, as light as a breeze and as strong as a helmet. Instantly, Basil felt something stir within himself, a warmth that reared its luminous head against the dark. It was the feeling that rose up within him when he helped the life surge back into something dying. For the first time in a long time, Basil knew exactly what to do. He straightened his glasses.

"So," Cyprian said, bouncing slightly on his heels and casting an anxious glance toward the Imperium. "Are you the leader of the free world now? What's cooking?"

"He will attack the people," said Basil.

"What?"

"We are going to fight," said Basil, nodding toward the Imperium. "When I don't yield to him, Titus will try to make me yield by attacking the people. He knows they're my weakness. Get them out. As many as you can."

"Ah," Cyprian said, his eyes glancing around at the enormous masses of gaping prisoners that filled the Abyss. "Well, there are a lot of them…"

"And Cyprian?"

"Yes?"

Basil reached out and clasped Cyprian's hand.

"You've been a friend to me. For everything you've done, I can never thank you enough."

Cyprian nodded.

"As your acting shipmaster, good business practice obligates me to lie and say that this was a great experience. As your friend, honesty obligates me to tell you I am never doing this for you ever again."

Basil smiled as Cyprian gave him a final punch on the arm and took off, away from the Sarcophagus. Basil went in the opposite direction, past the great wreck of *Philomena*, toward Titus. The ship lay like a broken butterfly, the skeleton of a living thing, and Basil felt a momentary pang of sadness. She had been their fortress, their home. And now, having carried them all this way, she was gone. One more wrong to be righted.

There was a flicker of uncertainty in Titus's blue eyes as he watched Basil advance, his gaze lingering on the crown on Basil's head. Still, Basil kept coming, walking faster. The Imperium leveled the saber. The blade bucked with lightning once more, the brilliant white bolt streaking straight for Basil's head.

But Basil felt no fear. He felt his mind light up like the lamps in the Crypt of the Bleeding Elm, clear and bright. As quickly as thought, words welled up within him, words that were powerful, words that were spoken when the world was made, words that summoned the being from the void and existence from nothingness. He thought of the deep, protecting green of the sea. The High Sylvan came to his lips, the words exploding into life around them as he spoke them.

Out of the air, glistening droplets of salty water formed, pulsing and growing as they danced around him. In moments, a rotating shield of water enveloped him. The lightning crashed into it, blazing diamond veins in the rotating orb of emerald. With a roaring hiss, the water burst into steam. Basil remained in the midst of it, sopping wet but unburnt. There was an immediate outburst from the crowd, a great swelling. The soldiers began to yell and curse, trying to keep the people under control. Titus, in the midst of impending chaos, kept his composure, but Basil could sense the façade falling, the madness creeping upward as whatever dwelled within the sword stretched its black tendrils toward the Imperium's mind.

"So now you wield Sylvanus's power? And you think that you can use this as a weapon to destroy me? This won't go well for you, Basil. But, it is the way it should be, with the power of the old extinguished against the power of the new."

Titus raised the sword skyward and spoke High Sylvan. But the words were ugly and dark, as though they were being spoken backwards, as though time itself was coming unravelled. The great disc of sky above turned dark and brooding, the air cold and clammy, the wind quick and bitter. It screamed over the rim of the Abyss, an ancient shrieking song that no men were ever meant to hear. And in the depths beneath Basil's feet, something shifted with a low rumble, as though a key were turning in a lock. Spidering cracks appeared in the green stone, lines of blackness that spread ever further outward. One crack ran directly between Basil's legs, and he could see it growing wider with each passing moment. Titus stood with sword still poised, his eyes alight with their own crackling lightning as he watched the Sarcophagus's slow blossoming. Sylvanus's work was being undone.

"Perhaps you have the trappings of the Sovereign," said Titus, face twisted into a triumphant leer. "But you are no Sylvanus, boy. You are no match for what comes next, if you live to see them."

Then, Titus uttered a single syllable in High Sylvan, and the black saber erupted into towering orange flame. He lashed out, the column of fire snapping whip-like through the air. Basil leapt back, the flames licking at his vest. Once more, he called up the green, towering column of seawater, but this time, he urged it forward, a wave that crashed toward Titus, lapping into the widening gaps in the Sarcophagus as it went. Titus slashed outward, blasting Basil with searing steam, and the entire Sarcophagus was covered in a dense fog.

For a second, there was only silence, a dense unending grayness, but then the sword screeched again. Lightning slashed streams of searing brilliance in the fog. With a word of High Sylvan, Basil wrenched columns of stone and sand from the earth. The lightning crashed into these, and steaming droplets of molten glass rained down around him. Basil stood alone in the fog for one breath. Then a second.

Titus lunged out of the gray, saber gleaming with vicious purple radiance. Basil uttered two syllables of High Sylvan, and a shockwave of keening wind blasted Titus sideways off his feet. Titus found his balance and recovered, thundering in High Sylvan. An army of boulders rose into the air around him. With a thrust of Titus's sword, they cannoned toward Basil. Basil ducked and rolled, blocking the rain of boulders with blasts of storm, waves of water, and his own bolt of lightning. Basil fended off a boulder strike with his own volley of rock, but was too slow to see the one coming from behind. The force of the blow lifted him off his feet and knocked him savagely to the ground. He saw stars, and every breath inflamed his chest with pain.

His head lay right beside one of the cracks. They were widening with every passing second, the earth groaning as though in pain. The whole earth shook, as if its very foundations were shuddering. And then, Titus was on him. The Imperium's gloved hand clamped mercilessly over Basil's face so that he could neither breathe nor speak. The haunted saber pressed into his throat. He could feel a bead of hot blood trickle down his neck. There was a flash, and Basil suddenly saw the face of Lorus, when he was young and fair and powerful, lying against the floor of the Sanctum of Soliodomus beneath this very blade, begging for his life.

"There are no good men," the Imperium said. "There are no evil men. There are only men who understand the reality of life, who look forward to the future. And before you die, you should hear what the future sounds like."

With merciless strength, Titus plunged Basil's head into the blackness of the widening chasm. It swallowed all of the light around him. Basil could hear a terrible, mournful scrambling deep inside, a malevolent presence that waited, overflowing with hatred and power. Somewhere in the dark, a thousand horrible things circled. Titus pulled him back upward. Basil was able to draw half a desperate breath before Titus clamped down over him again, his malevolent stare haloed by the storm.

"Do you hear them? That is the power that will bring Cor Nova to her destiny."

And he thrust Basil downward again. This time, the presence beneath surged around him. He saw Thon Black, his death prolonged by the torture of Fleet interrogators, the leering face of Bartimaeus Cain, *Philomena* on fire. He saw a thousand faces, watching him, hopeful, until the moment of his death. He watched the hope die in their eyes, the dark scream its victory over the desolation. Who was he to stand against the powers of evil?

Titus yanked again, and once more Basil was in the light, in the Imperium's manic grip. But this time, there was something else in the stormy background, something that looped and spiraled between the Fleet ships on flickering wings. It wheeled directly over Basil and Titus, looking down at Basil with a single golden eye. It was a sparrow. A single lost sparrow.

Suddenly, it was not alone. Over the gunfire, the sound of wings rippled through the air. Hundreds of sparrows were circling above the top of the Abyss, cutting a spiral of wings in the gray circle of light. With a chorus of echoing roars, black shapes leapt outward from the rim, outlined in the gray sky, and came rushing downward toward the Fleet vessels. With a crash, the witchbears slammed into the decks, enormous ivory claws burying themselves into the wood, the spikes and stripes of red fur along their backs flared in rage. Another beast leaped from the edge, larger than the others. On its back, raising a wild cry, was a woman in buckskin with luminous silver hair. Anne Stormalong.

And behind her, outlined in the sky, there came a host of ships, tilting down in to join in the fight. At the front were Marauders, their warships silvered and swift, with warbells clamoring in their rigging. Immediately beside them, ships with hulls carved from single trunks of enormous Osmanthus trees descended. On each deck, masses of bark-armored O'Larre swung their thin vine slings, entangling the rigging of the Fleet dreadnoughts. And behind these came a mass of ships of every imaginable shape, size, and color. There were ancient militia carracks with rusty guns and wizened deckhands, merchant schooners from the north, hardy freighters from Misericordiae and the lands beyond. There were caravels, skiffs, clippers, and galleons. They flew the colors of a hundred trade unions, all seven provinces, towns and cities, even a few bandit clans. Each deck swarmed with airmen, commanded by officers of every shape and size.

Basil could scarcely believe what he was seeing. They had come. They had come because they believed. Titus's face was twisting into a rictus of hatred, anger, and desperation.

"Why?" he spat.

"If you understood that," Basil said. "We wouldn't be here."

But the manic light of victory had not left Titus's eye. All around them, the blackness was bulging out of the rifts in the Sarcophagus. Something crept out of the blackness, a limb that morphed and changed even as Basil looked at it. First a claw, then a talon, then a hoof. Then, an enormous amorphous head, bristling with tentacles and spines blasted from its ancient prison, screeching into the first light it had tasted in centuries. The scream coalesced into a lance of pale, throbbing dark that sliced a Marauder ship clean in two. Screams resounded through the Abyss as the ship's pieces rained down, her crew still clinging to the remainder. And with a roar like an avalanche of broken rock, more limbs burst from the wounds in the earth, devouring ship after ship, Imperium dreadnought and rebel alike.

Taking advantage of the distraction, Basil sucked in all the breath that he could, and shouted in High Sylvan. A series of silver threads, twisted and unraveling sprang into the air in front of him, knit themselves together and blossomed outward. It was a barrier, the same kind that Lorus, his father, had conjured to protect him from the cannon blast in the camps of Bartimaeus Cain. It rose over the base of the Abyss, closing away the sky and the light, trapping the Sidia beneath. They screeched and screamed, spasming limbs assuming thousands of forms as they sought to escape.

"Fool!" cried Titus, tightening his grip on Basil anew. "You're only delaying the inevitable."

"Then you don't have anything to worry about," Basil said. And, with both hands, he seized Titus by the lapels of his uniform and rolled sideways, sending them both tumbling sideways into the screaming dark.

CHAPTER THIRTY-SEVEN

The Abyss was a sea of mayhem. Ships of every shape and size pitched above and within the pit, guns roaring death and orange flames. The O'Larre fought like tigers, slinging themselves from the decks of their ships, whipping through rigging as easily as if they were the boughs of the Living Sea. A Marauder vessel went streaking past, unleashing a fearsome hail of burning shot directly into a Fleet dreadnought, which exploded into flame and ground against the wall of the Abyss. Ancient militia vessels and merchant ships turned their guns to the interceptors that swung past, fire blossoming from their decks. Missed hits smashed the walls of the Abyss to rubble and destroyed lifts, scaffolds, and cranes.

"Find cover!" Veronica yelled into the mass of panicking prisoners, but she was pushed aside by the mob. They tumbled over each other as shards of pulverized rock and burning wooden fragments rained down from the battling ships above. Even soldiers and taskmasters were scattering, every bit as confused as the prisoners.

Veronica had seen the lights and sounds of High Sylvan as two figures did battle far below. One red, one black. Also there in the pit, the remains of *Philomena* smoldered. She had held her breath, her chest a pounding vacuum, until she'd seen Cyprian swing free of the wreck of his ship. Veronica shook her head in grinning exasperation. Somehow, he had found the Astral Crown. That boy.

Veronica turned her attention back to the mass of prisoners. She was seized by the impulse to search for her mother, but she forced herself to think reasonably. There would be no finding one sick woman in this sea of confusion. The prisoners were running without direction, stumbling and falling, some in danger of being crushed beneath the feet of those fleeing. Veronica tried desperately to organize them, but she could not shout loud enough over the hellfire noise of the Abyss.

She nearly gave up when she caught sight of an enormous man wading through the chaos toward her. His wide back bore a hundred wounds and scars, the marks of beatings untold. But, beneath the dirt and blood, he still had the face of a Misericordiae farmboy.

"Benttree!"

"We have to get you out of here," he rumbled.

"Not a chance," she said. "I'm staying. Can I use your height?"

Benttree took a knee, offering Veronica an enormous hand. In two sprightly leaps, she was up on his knee, then on his enormous back, standing tall on his rock-steady shoulders.

"Listen!" she cried.

A few of the faces looked up at her, eyes wide.

"You're Veronica Stromm!" yelled someone. "You're with Basil!"

"That's right, and if you want to live, you'll listen. We can't stay here! We need to get under cover, and then back to the surface. Lifts, causeways, whatever we can find! At the top, there's a concourse with rubble ships, most of them manned by prisoners like you. They can be commandeered. There must be airmen among you."

There were nods in the crowd. A few tattooed hands went up. A few of them even wore the tattered remains of airmen's belts.

"Let the women up first-"

There was a rumble that fairly shook the Abyss from top to bottom. For a single moment, every head turned, pistols, swords, and bare fists poised silent in the air. There was something horrible and forbidding about the blackness that lay beneath the cracks of the Sarcophagus. Something ancient and hungry dwelt beneath that rock, and it was eager to be free.

"Go!" Veronica said. "Now!"

In a solid mass, the prisoners fled, shoving guards and clambering up the huge causeways. All through the Abyss, others began to follow. Prisoners shouted direction to one another, pointing upward, and a mass migration began. Veronica turned her attention back to the fighting. Above their heads, ships filled the sky of the Abyss, grinding one another against the rocks, releasing thunderous clouds of fire and iron at each other, dueling with blades and fists as rigging and envelopes entangled in close quarters. Down at the base of the Abyss, where several dreadnoughts had deployed legions of Fleet airmen. The red-uniformed troops formed a huge, ragged ring around the rim of the Sarcophagus, brandishing steel and wheeling light cannons into position. It took Veronica only moments to see why.

On the bare rubble at the base of the Abyss, a wave of rebels was rushing the Sarcophagus, intent on reaching the Imperium. Marauders and O'Larre, having leapt free from burning ships, were strengthening their numbers. At their sides stood rickety old militia men wearing moth-eaten black Fleet uniforms, hard-bitten merchants and highwaymen with nothing to lose, and students with illegal printings of the Rule of Sylvanus jammed in their pockets. There were prisoners there as well, holding picks and shovels and lengths of chain.

And then, someone called the charge. Veronica clearly discerned two figures at the head of the offensive. The first was the huge, loping form of Redleg Melloch, his beard wild and tangled, a massive battle-axe swinging from his mighty fists. And to his left, a running silver form as light as Melloch was heavy, Anne Stormalong reached out her hand. The swarm of sparrows spun and wheeled ahead of her, converging on the crews of the light cannons. With a crash of steel and the boom of powder, the two sides met in furious battle.

At the center of the ring of fighting, a huge expanse of open pits remained, and a pair of figures dueled at the center, one red, one black. Between them, the wreckage of *Philomena* lay, now charred and smoldering. The ground was riddled with cracks. The roaring of ethereal fire, the smashing of ocean water, the crack of lightning, the rumble of falling rock had rent the earth, now billowing with evil steam.

"Benttree," she said, sliding down from the big man's shoulders. "I'm going down there."

Benttree nodded, moving to follow her.

"Never seen anyone quite so dead set on saving the world as you."

She turned around. There was Nolan Paschal, dirty and perilously thin. Behind him stood a reedy, redheaded teenager and a small, serious man with an enormous mustache.

"If you're going, we're coming with," replied Paschal, elbowing Spacklebrook in the chest when he squeaked in objection. "Can't let a lady take on such dangerous goings as this by herself. You see that trick the deckmaster pulled?"

"If you can call that a trick," Veronica said. They all turned toward the Sarcophagus, the shattered remains of *Philomena* a sad mess of cedar and canvas on the green stone. Paschal whistled through his teeth.

"Didn't reckon we'd see that old girl again."

They plowed their way through the crowds of prisoners escaping upward, Benttree splitting the enormous crowd with his width. Veronica and the others followed in his wake. A few soldiers appeared here and there in the tunnel, but they were quickly bowled over by the fleeing prisoners. More than one, faces stricken with terror by the battle outside, joined them, stripping themselves of their uniforms as they merged into the throng.

"Thanks kindly," said Paschal as he relieved one such deserter of his pistol and saber. He handed the blade to Masterson.

They were nearly at the level of the Sarcophagus when Veronica saw a new wave of prisoners coming up from the sleeping caverns. Between them, they carried prone forms on makeshift stretchers of axe handles and spare canvas. On one of the hastily made stretcher poles, a hand rested, as pale and delicate as a bird. Veronica's heart pounded. She dipped out from behind Benttree, pushing and shoving her way toward the stretchers. Finally, she was beside her mother, keeping pace as the two haggard women bearing the stretcher trudged upward. Amelia Stromm was even paler and thinner than when Veronica had left, only a day before. Her eyes were half open. When she saw Veronica, a very faint smile played at the corners of her lips.

"Mother," Veronica said. "I'm sorry I had to leave you."

Veronica's mother squeezed her hand. It was distressingly light. "You must help that boy. He needs you."

"Basil. Yes, mother…"

"And the other. The rough one. He needs you more."

Veronica was speechless for a moment.

A shriek broke through the Abyss. From one of the enormous black cracks that was fracturing the base of the Abyss, something hideous emerged from the deep, flailing tentacles and talons as it came. It unleashed a hideous bolt of darkness that rent the pale light of the Abyss, shredding a ship into two pieces. Veronica felt her heart lurch in her chest. Both Cyprian and Basil were down there. If the Sidia were coming through, then Basil wasn't doing well. If Basil wasn't doing well, then Cyprian would be pulling some harebrained move to try to save him. Veronica's mother was speaking again, her eyelids growing heavier by the moment as the stretcher swayed.

"When the Sovereign fell, your father used to doubt whether he was doing the right thing in being a Bookkeeper. Sometimes, late at night, he would agonize for hours over whether he was putting us in danger for no reason, risking his family against an Imperium that would never be defeated. In those moments, he would sit by your bedside, and watch you sleep.

"And then, he would go back to work, his doubts at rest. He never told me why, but I think I know. Even from the time when you were that little, you were so full of fire, so intelligent, so loving. You couldn't stand for anyone, man or beast, to be mistreated, and you wouldn't rest until you saw a wrong righted. I think you gave Hector hope because he understood that as long as there were people like you in Cor Nova, the Imperium would never be safe."

Tears were welling up in Veronica's eyes, a wild cacophony of emotions stirring in her heart. What a wonderful and terrible thing it was to be loved like this.

"He was right… Hector was right…" Amelia Stromm said, her consciousness failing. "Go, Veronica. I will be well. They need you…those boys…"

Her mother's hot, limp hand fell away from Veronica's own as her stretcher bore her up and away, towards freedom. Veronica murmured her thanks to the stretcher-bearers, who said something about it being no burden.

Then, the shots rang out again in Veronica's ears, the sounds of furious battle, raging with even more fury than when it had started. Veronica wiped her eyes with the back of her hand, then reached up and pulled a pin from her gathered hair. It tumbled down over her back, a cascade of shining ebony. Then, she drew the pearl-handled rapier free from her belt, and looked for the remains of *Philomena's* crew. They stood stock-still on the far side of the passageway, wide-eyed. Burt Spacklebrook looked particularly struck.

"Blow. Me. Down."

But Veronica was wasting no time.

"Come on!"

They tore down the passageway, the dwindling flow of prisoners coming up parting as they hurtled down, Veronica in the lead with the others trailing her. All the way, Veronica kept her eyes trained on the rebels throwing themselves against the line of Imperium airmen around the Sarcophagus. They were ferocious, but the Fleet had the benefit of organization and numbers, and they were pressing their advantage. Interceptors swung out of the fray above, banking hard and blasting their cannons down into the rebels. Beyond the fighting, the whole earth was screaming as the green stone split, gaps widening into frightening blackness. There were flashes of deeper darkness within, like a snarling dog throwing itself at a half-open door. The figures at the center of the Abyss were almost entirely concealed by a black mist that seemed to huddle over them. Occasionally, flashes of silver, blue, and yellow reared against the blackness, outlining figures before plunging back into darkness.

"It's hopeless," Veronica shouted as another round of cannonfire pounded the rebels. "They'll never break through if they fight separately..."

"Look!" Spacklebrook called, pointing as they finally grew close to the fighters. "There! That's Fields, sure as anything!"

Veronica squinted into the smoke, above the roar and ruin, and saw a tall shape with shoulder-length sandy hair, his coat slashed in several places. He dealt an oncoming airman a mighty punch to the stomach before bringing a shovel down with an almighty clang on his helmet. At his right, a witchbear of all things snapped and lunged, bowling over two more airmen coming from the right. Veronica and the three airmen ran out over the scarred battleground.

"Cyprian!" Veronica yelled over the din as she leaped into the fray, the rapier glimmering in her hand. "Cyprian! Get over here!"

And suddenly, Cyprian was there. He was covered head to toe in dirt and soot, blood trickling from a nasty cut on his scalp. He smelled like burnt gunpowder and his chest heaved with exertion. Together, they took shelter in the lee of a huge boulder.

"Good of you to show up!" he shouted over the din. "You know, these witchbears aren't so bad when they're on the same side as you. Have you done something to your hair?"

"The Sarcophagus!" Veronica said. "The Sidia are going to come through, and this crowd won't stand a chance. We need to fall back!"

Cyprian and the airman looked at each other.

"We'd have to leave Basil!"

"There will be no one to fight for Basil if those things are loose! It took Sylvanus himself to get them imprisoned here. There's no amount of swords or guns or ships that can keep them contained! Only High Sylvan will be able to put them back!"

And then, there was a deafening series of cracks like rolls of thunder, and a mass of enormous black figures rose from the base of the Abyss, lashing out from their prison, morphing into tentacles, spines, and claws. They smashed another three ships, and several of the fearsome limbs smashed to the ground, leaving destruction in their wake as they blindly searched for victims among those on the ground. The fury in the air was now tinged with panic, as ships turned their guns temporarily away from one another and towards the horror.

And then, a voice rose, Basil's voice. The High Sylvan was warm and natural, like the far-off rumble of approaching rain on a day choked with dry heat. It rolled around the Abyss, and the air over the black mist began to take shape. Silver threads as soft and gentle as moonlight began to form, weaving themselves into a fabric that stretched over them, binding the Sidia and pulling them inward. For a moment, the fighters stood in awe.

"It's a barrier," said Veronica. "Trapping the Sidia beneath it."

They were frozen, the airmen who braved a thousand storms, who looked down on the world, the kings of the sky. They stood silent and open-mouthed, looking up at the monstrosity. Cyprian's gaze hardened. The enormous silver dome, the dark shapes unfurling and raging within it, reflected in the greyness of his eyes.

"So Basil's trapped with Titus and the Sidia. They can't get out, but that doesn't mean we can't go in."

Veronica looked at him in that moment. She found herself recalling the first time she had ever seen him, stomping into her cabin on *Philomena* on that first day. She remembered the surge of dislike and mistrust that she had felt then; he'd seemed so untrustworthy and immature. Then, the rest of their adventures played back in her head, all the times he had saved her, and she had saved him. All the tenderness that existed beneath his rough exterior, how he was a boy trying to fill a man's boots. For all of his foolhardiness and sarcasm, there was courage and honor in him as well. And now, they were plotting to enter into the most dangerous place in Cor Nova, to fight an evil that nearly tore the world apart centuries ago. She could not think of anyone she would rather have at her side.

And the other. The rough one. He needs you more.

She grasped the side of Cyprian's head, ignoring the grit, dirt, and blood, and kissed him once on the cheek. There was a light thud as his shovel fell to the ground. When she pulled away, Cyprian looked slightly dazed and (Veronica thought) very, very young. But his slack jaw quickly found its way back to his customary smirk, and the bright spark of his grey eyes reignited.

"Well," he said quietly. "If that's how you feel about it."

"It is," she replied.

There was a moment of stunned silence.

"Blow. Me. Down."

"Shut up, Spacklebrook," said Paschal, checking the breech of his pistol.

Cyprian looked again at Veronica, and then at the amorphous blob of pulsating blackness in front of them as though it were another feat of airmanship to be conquered. To make matters worse, the fighting had reignited with a vengeance, and a small battle lay between them and it. But Cyprian didn't seem worried.

"For Basil, then."

They took off running once more, jumping crevices and crags to close the gap between them and the fray. Above them, the sounds of warring warships sounded, and fragments of wood, iron, and flame rained down. Even as they plunged themselves into the fighting, Veronica saw that pushing through would be impossible. The red line of Fleet airmen was impenetrable, and the fire of light cannons kept them pinned down. Not even the witchbears were able to close the gap.

"Interceptor!" called Masterson, from behind.

A lean red warship was closing in from the fray above, banking sharply so that her guns were trained on them. Veronica looked for cover from the coming barrage, but there was none. A thunder of cannon fire rang out, but all that fell on them was a hail of burning splinters. A second Fleet interceptor, expertly tracing the air around the first, had blown its enemies' keel out. The first interceptor crashed into the side of the Abyss in flames. Veronica watched in awe as the new interceptor came about, bringing her opposite guns to bear against a section of the Fleet line, and fired, blasting a gap in the Imperium's defense. The rebels were stunned.

"Blue hazes..." Cyprian mumbled.

Then, the main hold doors of the interceptor sprang open, and a dozen figures swung out, sliding earthward on lines. But, these were not the Imperium's men. They wore uniforms in majestic midnight black bordered with gold. On their chests was the crest of the Sovereign Dominion of Cor Nova. Cyprian had no memory of the Fleet before Titus had reformed it, but he'd heard about the heroes in black who did the Sovereign's bidding about the skies of Cor Nova. They were the knights of the air, the Long End of the Elm Staff, the Sons of Midmorning. The men of the Seven Armadas of the Sovereign Fleet. It was like going back in time.

One of them was taller than the rest, his hair a dark gray streaked with white, his eyes hard and silent. He unclipped himself from his line, drawing sword and pistol. Behind him, his men did the same.

"Admiral Ambry," said Veronica, unable to hide her surprise.

"Good day," said the former Grand Admiral, his eyes on the already-reforming line of Imperium soldiers ahead.

"What are you doing?" she asked.

"Once," he said. "I was too much of a coward to stand against the power of Titus. As I've told you before, Ms. Stromm, we all must make a choice. Years ago, I chose wrongly. It is too late for me to save Lorus, but I can save his son. I may have lived a coward, but as long as there is breath in my body, I will not die one."

He turned and Veronica could see his face. There was pain there, the heavy residue of a thousand terrible deeds. But behind it, Veronica could see a resolve that bore the pain upward, into the light.

"I trust you intend to go through the barrier. My men and I will go before you and clear the way. We will only be able to protect you for a short time, so you must follow closely. Do not stop. And tell the Sovereign..."

The Admiral paused for a moment, searching for the words.

"...tell the Sovereign that I am sorry."

And Ambry ordered the charge. The battleground of the Abyss streaked by as they ran for the barrier, the men of the Sovereign Fleet turning to protect them from the onslaught of red soldiers that converged from all sides, enveloped in cannonfire and the clash of steel. Ambry was at their head, his saber flashing, his pistol firing. And then, the forces of the Imperium and the Sovereign were behind them. Veronica, Cyprian, and *Philomena's* airmen around were clear. The flexing barrier of silver and black towered up ahead of them.

They didn't stop. They didn't slow down. They passed through.

Chapter Thirty-Eight

The darkness boiled and raged around Basil. His fist was still clenched around Titus's collar, and even as they fell, the Imperium was lunging for him, a powerful hand seeking Basil's face and neck. The saber sang a horrible song as it sliced back and forth through the dark. And then, with a blow that drove all the air from Basil's lungs, they slammed to a cold, stone floor. Titus's grip failed and he tumbled off into the darkness.

Basil's fought to remain conscious. The air of the place was stale and fetid. The spiderweb of cracks admitted pale slivers of light that balked and failed against the crushing pressure of the blackness. The floor that he lay on was the same dark green as above. But this rock had known the wrath of something terrible. Over and over again, the rake of talons and the gnash of desperate teeth had ripped jagged wounds across its surface. Basil's pulse quickened, and he was suddenly aware of the Sidia. The malicious, hateful blackness encircled him.

Basil picked up the Elm Staff, holding it close. Deep in those depths, something seethed, unraveling coil upon coil of sinuous murder, clacking talons scraping against exposed bone. There were thousands of them. They had halted in their rising, sensing the long-forgotten warmth of things living. A few yards from Basil, Titus's voice sounded in the dark, his figure outlined in the feeble light, blade unnaturally agleam.

"My soldiers," he said, eyes filled with triumph. "You have been here for a long time. Waiting for this day."

The Sidia were still, poised. Titus brought the blade to bear. It gleamed in the blackness, a sliver of silver light, like the half-open eye of something murderous. The Sidia followed its passage, like tame animals. Titus laughed, delighted that the Sidia bent to his will.

"You doubted, Basil," he said with a leer. "The power that Sylvanus squandered I will use to make the world over again."

Titus brought the blade down toward Basil.

"And you have the honor of being the first to fall."

He gave a command in High Sylvan, and with a chorus of screeches, the Sidia rushed toward Basil. As quick as thought, the High Sylvan sprung to Basil's lips. Once more, the rotating shield of ocean water rose up around him, but the Sidia crashed through, salty droplets hissing against spectral skin. Onward they came, horrible members coiling and stretching out toward Basil. Something locked around his lower leg, spines digging into his flesh. Basil spoke again, and gouts of orange fire exploded out into the darkness. The Sidia flailed backwards, but kept coming. Tentacles and talons descended, wrapping themselves around Basil's neck and head, icy cold. Their sound was suddenly loud in his head: screaming. Whether it was from pain or rage or both, Basil could not tell, but their anguish was limitless. These had once been living souls, broken and turned into nameless horrors. They were hollow husks of evil. He felt no pity for them, only pity for what they had once been.

Then, Basil was conscious of a new scream, long and high. He managed to turn his head, and saw the figure of Titus, writhing in the grip of a dozen phantom limbs. His face was aghast in confusion and pain as the tendrils of black wrenched the saber from his hands. It floated in the grip of the Sidia, fibrous spectral muscles tensing against the steel. With a shrieking ping of metal, the blade snapped, exploding into infinitesimal shards of steel. A blackness exploded outward, rejoining its fellows, which surged all the more violently in on both Basil and Titus.

In the screaming dark that raged over him and through him, Basil saw Thon Black disappearing into the darkness in Osmara, the bound figures on the fire in Kwalz, Nolan Paschal dying on

Philomena's deck, an ocean of beaten humanity laboring to their death in the Abyss. There was no end to the murder and the pride and the stupidity, all because of Titus's insatiable craving for power. Basil had failed to stop him, and now all of Cor Nova would be devoured. Basil seethed and raged, and whether he was screaming his own scream, or the Sidia were feeding on him and growing louder he could not tell.

Despite the darkness, something compelled Basil to open his eyes and look at Titus again. The Sidia were ensnaring him just as they had Basil. And, even as Basil watched, his struggling became feeble and Titus grew old, bent, withered; the vigor that had enlivened his body disappeared into the sucking, venomous ether. The natural blue of his eyes shone with fear. Basil recognized his own eyes, his father's eyes.

Suddenly, Basil felt his hatred ebb. He felt something quieter well up within himself. It was the same feeling he felt in Osmara when someone brought him something wounded and struggling in a wooden box, the same feeling he felt when the sick Marauder boy grasped his hand on Colossus, the same feeling he felt when he was on board *Philomena.* It was the certain knowledge that all good things are connected, and that men only become evil once they have severed themselves from what is good. It is the way of evil to sever, the way of good to heal.

Basil felt the weight of the Astral Crown on his head, the smoothness of the Riverstone Amulet pushed against his chest, the strength of the Elm Staff that he still clung to despite the wrenching of the Sidia. He was Basil, the ship's cook, the healer, the Sovereign, the son of a brave man who called himself Francis Lightlas, and he realized with stunning clarity the only thing that he could possibly do. The Sidia were now squeezing him down, crushing him with terrifying strength. With all the breath he had left, Basil called up one last syllable of High Sylvan. A final gout of orange flame stabbed the enveloping dark, and the Sidia flinched, their grasp loosened for just a moment. One hand sprang free. With it, Basil reached out, and seized Titus by the arm.

Suddenly, all was light.

Howling, the Sidia recoiled, exploding backwards and away from Basil and Titus. All around them, shadowy figures burst into brilliant being. They were tall and short, male and female. Each one held the

Elm Staff, wore the Crown and the Amulet. And now that he had read the Rule of Sylvanus, Basil knew their names. He recognized Analisa and Proteus, Casimir and Kyril, Chrysanthe and Celeste, the twins Linus and Elos. Sovereigns all. And somewhere behind them, a luminous multitude, more numerous than the sands on the seashore or the raindrops in a storm. Cor Novans who had gone before.

First among them, but somehow equal, was a tall man in long, ancient robes, his wrinkled brow furrowed and sunburnt, his face that of a shepherd who had lived under the stars. Sylvanus was not looking directly at him, but seemed to be looking onward, as though towards the dawn. At his side, a tall Sovereign with dark, flowing hair and clear blue eyes stood. Francis Lightlas, Lorus. He too, was looking onward, his expression one of serene calm that Basil had never seen in life.

As though in agony, the Sidia boiled with rage all around them, an undulating maelstrom of gnashing teeth. Their horrible, rending scream had risen to a cataclysmic pitch, raging against the luminous multitude that now filled the emptiness of the Sarcophagus with brilliance. But now, Basil wasn't listening.

When he raised the Elm Staff, its luminous replicas did the same. And when Basil spoke High Sylvan, he was not alone. The voices of the Sovereigns past combined in a brilliant symphony, every tongue forming the words in perfect unison, as though reading from the same book, drawing from the same source. All around the great multitude, a crown of luminous golden fire blossomed, pushing outward into the blackness, radiating brighter with each majestic syllable.

Turn back, you cruelty of ancient men. Turn back as the shadow from daybreak. Turn back as the silence from song.

For you stand against the words that formed the stars in their cradles, the planets in their cycles, the oceans in their deepness, the skies in their wideness.

The words that called the mountains skyward, that bid the rivers flow, that forged hearts to beat within men, that birthed the wide world in all of its many wonders.

Turn back.

The crown of gold flame was a dazzling sun of radiance.

Turn back.

331

Arcs of golden flame thrust outward into the Sidia. They shrieked and recoiled, but Basil could barely hear them. The song of the ancients beat onward.

Turn back.

The tendrils of golden flame wrapped themselves around writhing black bodies, entangling them in nets of radiance. The screams grew louder and longer as the Sidia were forced back down into the depths in an ever-tightening vortex, tongues and talons and teeth scraping against their ancient prison.

But Basil felt his strength beginning to wane, and with it, the ancient Sovereigns began to grow dim. He looked upward. The fractures in the Sarcophagus were still visible, pale earthly radiance shining through. The only way Cor Nova would be safe would be to do as Sylvanus had done. Basil pulled the barely conscious Titus close to himself and tightened his grip on the Elm Staff. With a word of High Sylvan, the dark green stone beneath his feet kicked upwards, launching them both high into the dark void. The waning golden radiance of the trapped Sidia fell rapidly away. The ancient Sovereigns had faded to mere shadows. The pale light of the fracture drew close.

Basil stretched out his free hand, still holding the staff, reaching for the light of freedom, the lip of the breach in the Sarcophagus. With all the strength left in his arm, Basil swung the Elm Staff upward, so that the far tip reached for the gap. But it was not close enough. It was less than a yard to freedom, but Basil had no more strength. With the last wisp of his power, he whispered into the dark, and bid the stone to close, to trap the Sidia beneath forever. At least Cor Nova would be safe. Basil and Titus hung for a moment, weightless, and then gravity reclaimed them for its own. The Sidia, sensing a second chance at their prey, shook off their golden tethers. From above and below, the light faded, and Basil and Titus fell back into the void.

Chapter Thirty-Nine

Cyprian and Veronica passed through the barrier effortlessly. One moment, Cyprian felt a gentle, pulsating warmth, and then they were through. The screaming struck Cyprian like a lance, forcing him to his knees. The sheer might of anguish and rage contained within the barrier overwhelmed him, threatening to crush him beneath its weight. The others, too, were on their knees, trying to block out the horrible unending scream. Even Veronica was terribly pale, her mouth parted in silent horror, her eyes overflowing with tears.

The barrier had cast the lid of the Sarcophagus in a weird twilight, the ships beyond mere shadows, the sounds of their cannons muffled. The green stone beneath their feet was split open into great fissures of sucking blackness, and up from these great wounds clawed legions of black, formless horrors. The Sidia shrieked and roiled within the barrier, dashing themselves against the boundary in a seething rage. Then, as though sensing the presence of the living, some of the creatures turned toward them, phantom eyes alight and spectral nostrils flaring.

Hopelessness welled up inside Cyprian, stealing his will. But, a little ways from them on the Sarcophagus, an angular mass of wood and canvas lay crushed against the rock. It meant something. Cyprian blinked hard, trying to screen out the scream that dominated his whole brain, trying to remember. And then, the light

333

shifted, and his eyes fell on the broken figurehead that lay tumbled on the ground. A maiden with a crown of stars, with the world under her feet, her smile calm and confident, watching over them. Just as she had watched over Francis Lightlas, Cor Nova's forgotten Sovereign. Just as she had watched over Augustus Fields.

Almost as one, the Sidia shrieked even more horribly and tore towards them, changing form rapidly, each form more horrible than the last, terrible limbs drumming against the rock of their tomb, tattered wings beating against the air. Cyprian's grip tightened around his pistol, storm-grey eyes glaring into the soulless eyes of the Sidia, now staring them down with a potent malice. The maiden had seen Augustus Fields through the battle of his life. Now, she would do the same with Cyprian.

When Cyprian stood up, it was though gravity was a thousand times stronger, yanking him down towards the earth, his mind rebelling with every inch. But with each passing moment, the scream faded. He felt stronger. He seized Veronica by the hand, her grip icy and shaking, and then she was on her feet too. The airmen, likewise, began to rise, helping one another and stumbling as they did. Benttree, the first on his feet, seized Spacklebrook by the collar. Paschal and Masterson steadied one another. For a moment, the scream fading in his ears, Cyprian looked at them all, and wondered how he had ever doubted them. These men had stayed with him all the way from a dirty ship's cradle on the Old Concourse to the very pit of destruction itself. These flawed, broken, wonderful men. They had done it for him. They had done it for Veronica. They had it done for Basil. They had done it for a better world. And now, he was going to let some nightmare of the Old World consume them all?

"To blue hazes with that," Cyprian said, his gaze falling back to the oncoming wave and the broken remains of *Philomena*. They were getting out. All of them. And he had just the idea.

Cyprian pointed toward the wreck of *Philomena* and the Sidia beyond. He grinned. Veronica and the crew watched him, unbelieving.

"Last one to the ship takes watch!"

He took off running. And, wonder of wonders, the crew followed, though still wincing against the scream.

"We trust you, here, shipmaster…" said Paschal, panting beside him. "But I hope that there is some kind of plan."

Cyprian nodded.

"Of course, Paschal. Titus was able to destroy or at least trap one Sidia with a sword-"

"And High Sylvan," Veronica reminded him.

"Let's focus on our haves rather than our have-nots, shall we, Veronica? In any case, our pistols are too small to get us any headway against them. But I know where to get some guns that have a little more punch."

"*Philomena's* falconets!" said Paschal, eyes growing wide. "Reckon we'll be able to get to the powder? The whole mid-deck is collapsed."

Cyprian pointed toward the bow, now just a few yards away.

"There was a reserve in one of the forward holds in sealed casks. When I crashed her, that whole section of the hull ripped open. Should be completely exposed. We can light and fire in no time."

"It'll have to be fast," Spacklebrook yelled up from behind, his voice high with fear. The Sidia were roaring towards them now, their screams growing ever louder.

"It will be," Cyprian said, reseating his pistol. "Spacklebrook, you and Benttree get on deck and reposition those guns. The rest of us will retrieve the ammunition. As long as we can get volleying before they breach the gunwale, we should be able to hold them back long enough to figure out how to get Basil out."

They leapt on board the remains of *Philomena*, her deck now a landscape of broken spars. Forward, Cyprian could see casks of powder falling out of the hull just where he said they would be. In an impressive show of brute strength, Benttree repositioned the guns into firing position against the oncoming wave of black. The crew moved with blurring speed, loading all of the cannons on *Philomena's* leftward side with powder and shot. The Sidia were so close the ground rumbled.

"Ready, Fields!" called Paschal from his gun, where Masterson stood ready with a firing rod. He was barely audible over the inhuman shrieking.

Despite the wave of terrifying black, Cyprian grinned. He was feeling himself.

"Fire!"

Philomena's broken decks rumbled and the blaze of cannonfire flashed against the underside of Basil's barrier. The Sidia broke against the concussive wave of gunfire, cast back and reeling. The crew rushed to reload, and repelled a second thrust with another blast. But the Sidia were learning. A few flanked the ship, smashing over the gunwales, talons and snapping snouts swiping at the crew. Veronica set to with her rapier, parrying the thrust of a cruel, curved beak, defending the gun crews as best she could, but the tide of invading creatures only grew stronger.

One of the creatures was able to get through their defenses, smashing into Paschal and bowling the red-hot cannon he and Masterson were firing over *Philomena's* side. Paschal was smashed across the chest by a huge claw before Benttree tackled the rapidly changing limb. They managed two more volleys, but the sea of Sidia was too much. They poured toward the wrecked ship in a fresh assault.

Cyprian was rolling a new cask of powder into position when he was struck by another idea.

"Benttree!" he called, kicking the barrel toward him. "Toss!"

With one flex of his massive arms, Benttree hefted the barrel and threw it end over end out into the darkness. Cyprian trained his pistol on the cask until it was nearly swallowed by the murk, and fired. A huge blossom of orange fire exploded outward, casting the Sidia back. For a moment, Cyprian was able to see the inky blackness of the large, central crack in the middle of the Sarcophagus.

"He must be there!" Veronica called over the din, her rapier ringing as she sliced through something that shrieked. "Under the surface! We have to get to him!"

But Cyprian didn't see how. They were surrounded, their guns silenced, the Sidia seemingly poised over them, savoring their terror. And then, Cyprian heard a new sound cleaving through the terrifying wail. It was as though it came from somewhere far away and yet from within, a glorious sound. The cracks of the Sarcophagus blazed with light, as though the sun itself was contained beneath. Pillars of golden flame erupted from the fractures, winding blazing tendrils around the ever-shifting talons and trunks of writhing Sidia. They spasmed and shrieked as they were dragged downward through the cracks. The airmen gaped, every bead of sweat on their foreheads reflecting droplets of golden light.

"High Sylvan," Veronica said. "He's doing something."

"Drawing all those beasts down in there with him," Cyprian said. "Like a blessed hero. Hopefully he sics a couple of them on Titus."

"The barrier," said Masterson, pointing upward.

They looked up. The barrier was disappearing. Like melting snow, silver fibers unraveled themselves into nothingness. Above them, the fighting had stopped. Ships drifted in mid-air, red-hot gun barrels leaving trails of smoke through the sky. Fleet and rebel alike, the fighters on the ground were still, their weapons still poised in their hands. All watched the luminescence escaping the cracks of the Abyss with a silence fueled by anticipation and exhaustion. The golden light pulsed once, twice, casting beams of radiance all the way up from the base of the Abyss to the gathering twilight sky. And then, it began to falter, dwindling and fading, leaving only grayness in its wake. The air grew tense, the peace thin.

"What's happening?" asked Paschal from where he lay, nursing a broken arm and a few cracked ribs.

"I… can't tell," Veronica said, squinting.

Cyprian whipped out his brass oculus, its lens now cracked. He trained it on the fissure. The light was gone now, and the green rock was moving, the fissure closing. Cyprian's heart sank. Basil was going to be trapped beneath. He looked up to the rigging. The winch boom was snapped in several places, but the spool was still intact and slung with rope. He seized the end, running out the winch behind him as he hurdled the gunwale and dashed over the Sarcophagus toward the fracture. Once or twice, the spool jammed, nearly sending Cyprian sprawling, but Veronica and Masterson worked the mechanism, freeing the kinks as Cyprian ran. In moments, Cyprian was at the edge of the fissure. The golden radiance was only a pale glow at the bottom, but he spied a shape below him the darkness. He couldn't tell how far away. Cyprian whipped the rope once around himself, and leapt. For a long moment, he was a javelin falling through the nothingness, and the strange screaming of the Sidia below grew louder.

Then, from the corner of his eye, Cyprian saw something move, whipping in the blast of stale air. Almost on instinct, he lunged, one strong hand closing around a staff of straight elm wood. He was yanked forward, his whole body lurching as the rope's slack ran out and the weight on the Elm Staff pulled at the same time, slamming Cyprian to a stop. Beneath him, in the blackness, he could see the dark form of Basil Black, his head hanging, arm quivering with the effort of hanging on to the staff. And gripped against his body, slipping with every passing moment, the suggestion of a lean form in a red uniform, head lolling against Basil's shoulder. Despite the pain, Cyprian huffed in disgust. Basil. Did he have to help everybody?

The gold radiance below was paling to nothing, the fissures above them closing with every second. Once more, things stirred in the deep. Tentacles and claws raked against one another. There were things down there that Cyprian had shot once or twice. No doubt they would remember him.

"Up!" he roared, yanking back and forth on the rope. "Now, Veronica!"

And suddenly, they were rising. Then, there was fresh air, and hands pulling him upward, seizing Basil and Titus as well. He was free, with Veronica's arms around him, but all eyes were on Basil. The young ship's cook was lying on his back, eyes only half open, looking up at the clearing sky. The Riverstone Amulet glimmered faintly on his chest, the Astral Crown was a ring of pale light across his forehead, and the Elm Staff lay in the dust beside him. The base of the Abyss rumbled once as the ever-diminishing cracks of the Sarcophagus sealed themselves shut.

All was still. There was no sound save the agonized breaths of Titus. The former Imperium's body lay curled, shrunken and perilously weak.

The airmen gathered around, Benttree almost apologizing for his immensity, Paschal with his arm in a makeshift sailcloth sling, Spacklebrook looking willowy ands pale as usual, and Masterson with half his mustache burned off by a cannon blast. Behind them, an immense throng of people craned their necks to see the fallen Sovereign. The airmen of hundreds of ships looked down, the battle forgotten as they watched the wheel of history turn. Once more, on the Fields of Carath, a Sovereign had arisen, and saved them all. Behind the ships, in the ring of sky above the Abyss, the moon broke through the gray clouds, flanked by thousands of stars.

Basil was deathly pale, but his blue eyes were now open, taking in a peaceful sky. He coughed, his voice little more than a croak.

"I think we won."

Epilogue

The ornately carved white marble of the Way of Kings sparkled brilliantly in the afternoon sunlight. To the east and west, the Fields of Carath spread in endless flowing waves of green grass. Cyprian swept through the sunshine and the wind, long strides taking him past hundreds of restored statues of Sovereigns that lined the Way of Kings.

Cyprian wore a long shipmaster's coat in deep maroon. Tucked into his weathered airmen's belt was a shining dual-lensed oculus of Terra Altan make, a finely crafted mahogany-gripped heavy pistol, and a custom deckknife with a crowing rooster inlaid in the hilt. For all the finery, his hands were chapped and calloused, worn hard from the work of running an airship. Or several, as the case would have it. Petros sat on his shoulder, what was left of his golden plumage glimmering in the sun, occasionally nipping at Cyprian's ear.

Cyprian only paused for a moment to admire the final statue. The Sovereign Lorus was depicted in all the glory of his youth, his beard kempt and noble, his face unlined. But Cyprian recognized him. In his hand, he held a model of a three-masted freighter, the humble tool he had used to save the world. The colors of the Round Plaza shone up at Cyprian as he approached the Nicholas Gate. A pair of Fleet airman in majestic black embroidered with gold snapped to attention as he approached. One bearing the rank of a corporal saluted.

"Shipmaster Fields," he said.

"I'll admit to that," said Cyprian, reaching into his coat pocket for a folded piece of paper, embossed with the Sovereign seal. "I've received a summons from the Sovereign's Rector of Restorative Efforts. I'm here to turn myself in."

"Yes. The customs official sent a kestrel to inform the Rector when your ship entered Carath. Here she is."

"She…"

The Nicholas Gate creaked and there, standing on the white marble, was Veronica Stromm. Cyprian had never considered what a few months of not living on a ship or running for her life could do for a woman's beauty. Apparently, a lot. Veronica was wearing a smart blue dress, the sleeves of her white blouse rolled up. Her hair, done up in a complex swirl on the back of her head, was the perfect sheen of ebony. Her cheeks were flushed, her eyes gleaming.

"Of course," Cyprian said, making an outrageous bow. "The Sovereign Basil's Rector of Restorative Efforts. Well, Veronica, you didn't have to send out a Sovereign edict just because you missed me."

"I haven't missed you," she said, grinning in spite of herself.

She broke into laughter when Cyprian made a face of defeated rejection, then embraced him warmly.

"Thank you, Corporal," she said. She smiled at Cyprian and made a gesture to the enormous bronze door, standing ajar. "After you."

They entered into a marble atrium, finished floor to ceiling in a stunning marble of pale gold.

"It was Basil's idea to call for you, not mine," Veronica said as the Nicholas Gate swung shut behind them. "Your letters have been just about all the Cyprian Fields that I can stand. If I have to read another self-indulgent blow-by-blow of your most recent merchant's deal gone wrong, I'm going to start sending those kestrels right back to the nearest fancy Fields ship I can find."

"It's not bragging if it's true," said Cyprian with a smirk.

She shook her head.

"You're impossible. But really, Cyprian, it's been good to see your trade union do so well. You deserve it, after everything that happened."

"Yes, I definitely do."

Veronica punched him on the arm, laughing.

"Cyprian Fields, get back on your stupid, pretentious ship! We'll get someone else…"

"Excuse me," Cyprian said. "I'll try to be a little more modest. But it doesn't seem like I'm the only one who's doing well. Someone I know is the new Rector of Restorative Efforts. And, far and wide, I've heard many good things about our man Basil."

"Yes," Veronica replied with a sigh. "Things are stabilizing. The last of the trials for the crimes committed under the Imperium are coming to a close. The resettlement of the Marauders and those displaced by the Abyss is ongoing. The bandit situation is not getting any better, however. That's part of why you're here."

"Ah, I was hoping you'd get to that."

"Yes. We've found something."

"Found something. Color me intrigued."

Veronica turned to the door leading into the Sanctum and pushed it open.

"Come look at this."

The Sanctum of Soliodomus was awash with colored light. Forests, oceans, and plains spiraled up the enormous columns that held the cavernous roof aloft. The ceilings glittered with a vast mosaic of the skies, the sun and moon aglow amid a wash of constellations. Tapestries in majestic blues and greens spilled down the towering walls, depicting scenes from antiquity. Its beauty was breathtaking, but almost as amazing was the activity that was taking place within.

Across the immense marble floor of the Sanctum, what looked like a small city had sprung up. Amid the columns, long aisles of crates, bags, chests, and lockers rose. Each was filled with books, manuscripts, and prints, some of them overflowing into smaller containers or built up to teetering stacks. Through the labyrinthine ways, a small army of uniformed orderlies was at work, stacking, moving, tagging and reorganizing.

"It wasn't just the Rule of Sylvanus the Bookkeepers were protecting," Veronica said. "It was everything else as well. Ancient

works of literature, wisdom, history, architecture, poetry. All the
knowledge and wisdom of centuries. They hid it in caches all over
Cor Nova, but much of it was right here, stored in underground
vaults beneath Soliodomus. Right under the Imperium's nose. It was
hurriedly done, though. There's a mountain's worth of material
here, and it has to be organized, catalogued, and compiled. My
mother is even helping with some of the sorting. Much of it will be
sent into the Sovereign's own libraries, to be copied and sent out to
the rest of the Dominion. It's a colossal amount of work."

"And that's why Basil has you."

"Yes."

They walked down the length of the Sanctum, side-by-side. Here
and there, Veronica indicated choice works or amazing finds in the
mountains of history. Her voice was alive with passion, and Cyprian
understood that, for her, bringing these books back into the hands of
Cor Novans was a way of healing the damage wrought by over a
decade of brutality.

Cyprian couldn't help but think about the day in the Abyss,
before their charge through the barrier. He remembered the feeling
of her lips on his cheek, the look that had passed between them in
that shining moment. What Veronica truly felt for him, Cyprian
didn't know. But he was certain that he thought about her every day.
As much as he loved the freedom of the sky, he often found himself
standing on the deck of his ship looking out over the far reaches of
the Dominion, missing her.

Finally, they reached the front of the Sanctum, where the Just
Throne rose on a dais, speckled with a dazzling rainbow from the
enormous stained glass windows. The Elm Staff lay flat across the
arms of the great stone chair, the Crown resting on a plinth atop the
chair's head.

"So," Cyprian said. "This is all very interesting. But I still don't
see why I'm needed."

Veronica nodded.

"For that, we need to see a certain former ship's cook."

She guided him down wide passageway that led off the Great
Hall, down several quieter hallways, until they came to a tall oaken
doorway. The guard saluted as Veronica opened the door, admitting
a flow of golden light into the corridor.

Basil's library was immense, smelling of paper and sage. The skeletons of a hundred strange things were suspended through the domed ceilings. The polished mahogany surfaces were littered with scales, bones, spines, and feathers. Tiered stacks of cabinets with small, labeled drawers took up a whole wall. A large crystal tank against one wall contained a school of glimmering purple fish. In the midst of all of it, behind a large oaken desk stacked high with papers, books, and samples, sat a boy in smart black vest with the Riverstone Amulet glimmering on the right breast pocket. He was concentrating on writing something, his spectacles flashing in the light that came through the window.

"Well, I'll give you one thing, Basil," said Cyprian, looking around. "It's definitely you."

Basil Black looked up and grinned, putting his pin in the inkwell. He stood up and embraced Cyprian.

"Thanks for coming. Hey there, Petros."

The old bird squawked, leaped onto a bookcase, and started pecking suspiciously at a fossil.

"It seems you're settling very easily into this Sovereign life."

Basil nodded.

"It has its good times and bad. Certainly no end to the work that needs to be done. A lot of people were displaced by the Imperium, people lost, knowledge extinguished. Putting lives back together is not an easy business. We've had to reinstate new provincials along with their cabinets, as well as overhaul the Fleet. I feel that the task would have been much easier if Admiral Ambry had survived the charge at the Abyss. Keeping all the wheels turning means I don't have a lot of time for my other pursuits. I do get to look at them, though."

He made a rueful gesture to the library. For the first time, Cyprian noticed a pathetic figure seated in a padded chair over in the corner, where a low fire burned in the grate. His skeletal hands were folded across his blanketed lap, and his once-powerful blue eyes gazed emptily into space. The once-Imperium Titus was a shriveled hull of himself. Basil followed Cyprian's gaze.

"I'm sure you won't mind if my uncle keeps us company."

Basil sent his steward for some refreshments, and Cyprian soon forgot about Titus. For a long time, they sat in Basil's library, catching up on what had passed within the last few months.

"Now," said Cyprian finally. "This is all very nice. But you called me here for something…"

Basil nodded. He withdrew a key from a chain around his neck and unlocked a heavy bookcase directly behind his desk. Cyprian could see a variety of old-looking volumes within. Basil selected a large, brown folio.

"This was found in one the book vaults underneath Soliodomus."

Basil flipped the front of the folio open, releasing the faint smell of dried mildew and old paper. The pages were covered with scrawling text in black and red, along with hastily drawn images.

"This looks like an old plunderer's map," said Cyprian, tracing a finger along the spidery lines. "You want to go on a treasure hunt?"

"Yes, but not just any treasure hunt," said Basil. "If you remember, the reason that Titus acquired his power in the first place was from an encounter with a wounded Sidia. That leaves many questions. Most importantly, how did such an ancient and powerful creature find its way back into Cor Nova? I believe the answer goes back to an old friend…"

With a nod from Basil, Veronica flipped a page. There, in garish red, was depicted a huge golden ship, its decks festooned in lanterns and covered in festively dancing figures. The golden-veiled face of Bartimaeus Cain flickered in Cyprian's mind. His hand tightened on the desk, the white outline of the knife standing out.

"As Sovereign," said Basil. "One occasionally encounters tasks of a sensitive nature. Sometimes, the Fleet can be a useful tool to deal with them. But in other cases, there are circumstances where a more…personal touch is needed."

Cyprian looked down at the map, trying to quell the excitement that was growing inside him.

"I have a trading company to run."

"I know."

"There are assets to monitor."

"I know."

"Employees to manage."

"I know."

"So what do you know that I don't?"

Basil leaned over his desk, pushing the dusty folio toward Cyprian. He was smiling, his eyes glinting behind crystal spectacles.

"I know that secretaries and orderlies and stewards can be put in place to manage those kinds of things. I also know that some people have a need for wide open spaces and danger and the unknown. And if I recall correctly, the deal only gets sweeter when there's a score to settle."

For a moment, silence reigned in the majestic library of Basil, the Sovereign of Cor Nova.

"Mr. Black," Cyprian said, grinning and extending a hand. "I've taught you well."

A Glossary of Useful Terms

Compiled for this text by V. Stromm, Rector of Restorative Efforts
With the (unsolicited) assistance of C. Fields, Vice Rector of Categorical Nonsense, as revenge for destroying his favorite belt

Aether - A naturally occurring white gas that boils out of fissures in the earth near volcanic sites; its extreme lightness makes it an essential component of aetheronautics - *Not suitable for breathing, unless you're a Marauder with a bad mustache.*

Aetherolabe - An instrument found on board airfaring vessels comprised of a large spinning ceramic or metallic sphere balanced on a layer of aether; can be used to track heading, pitch, roll, and (in some cases) velocity

Aetheronautics - The science and study of the travel through the atmosphere

Aileron - A small, specialized sail mounted to the hull or rigging of an airship; typically controlled by pitch levers from the helm; used to maneuver

Airman - A worker on board an airfaring vessel; more properly referred to as an "aetheronaut" *although any airman who uses this word is a half-baked bean for certain...*

Airship – Common parlance for an airfaring vessel; powered by wind, gravity, and the buoyancy of aether captured in large envelopes; may come in a wide variety of shapes, sizes, and operational purposes; often referred to in slang as "crates" or "ladies" *My favorite term for airship is -insufferable old tub-*

Bandit - A criminal who subsists on stealing and killing in the shipping corridors; may consist of individual ships and crews, but are often organized into clans; examples include the Mazurkas of Stella Maris and the Bowman-McCoys of

Korkyra *And all* **FLEE** *at the name of Cyprian A. Fields*

Bookkeeper - A member of a resistance group dedicated to restoring the Sovereign to the Just Throne by reuniting the Sovereign heir with the three relics of Sylvanus; it is believed that this group was quite small, consisting of no more than ten individuals - *Should we get membership cards?*

Cartorium - A large room found beneath the command deck of an airship that contains maps and navigational equipment; it also functions as a meeting room for officers; the command and navigational center of an airship

Command Deck - A raised deck at the stern of an airship that overlooks the main deck and contains the helm; typically where the shipmaster or deckmaster observes activity on board

Concourse - A large structure built to moor and supply airships; may be stone or wooden in construction

Deckhand - A worker on an airfaring vessel

Deckmaster - Second-in-command of an airfaring vessel; Usually oversees the crew; *Handsome and don't you know it*

Dreadnought - A medium-size warship and main workhorse of the Sovereign/Imperium Fleet

Envelope - A large, lacquered canvas bag specifically designed to contain aether; usually filled with sea sponges to help retain aether in case of rupture *Which seems to happen a lot, distressingly*

Falconet - A light cannon; typically found on merchant vessels

Fleet - The common name for the military armadas maintained by the Sovereign, and later the Imperium; Seven Armadas comprise the Fleet, one for each province

Freighter -A medium to large airfaring vessel specifically designed to transport cargo *You're not the only one who can draw around here,*

Veronica Stromm

Gunwale - The wooden rail that extends around the main deck of an airship

High Sylvan -A language supposedly first utilized by Sylvanus; the speaker has the ability to command nature; very little is known about this phenomenon and it appears much more complicated than originally thought

Imperium - The title assumed by Titus, the brother of the Sovereign Lorus, following his rise to power; under the influence of a Sidiom, Titus's reign as Imperium was marked by an utter disdain for the tradition of the Sovereigns and an obsession with power - *Why even put him in here? Who wants to deal with that?*

Interceptor - A small warship of the Sovereign/Imperium Fleet; well-known for their speed and maneuverability, they are often used for scouting and strike missions

Keel - The large, single piece of wood that forms the lower frame of an airship hull; usually made out of cedar or oak; its integrity reinforces the entire ship

Loadmaster - A ship's officer responsible for the loading and welfare of cargo; is often also responsible for the tabulating yields and calculating profits

Machinist - A ship's officer responsible for maintaining an airfaring vessel

Marauder - An airfaring race apparently indigenous to the land beyond the southern mountain range known as the Shrouds; during the reign of the Sovereign Obelius, a small refugee armada was apparently blown over the Greater Shrouds; these were the ancestors of the modern Marauder community in Cor Nova; they are extremely capable silversmiths and shipwrights, but their secrecy and isolation has made them the subject of much suspicion among Cor Novans

Marlord - An ancient, intelligent guardian of the Great Northern Mar; little is known of its origins or whereabouts, but Cor Nova's Sovereigns have interacted with it on various occasions *Ah yes, Mr. Tentacles*

Moonwise - In aetheronautics, the motion of an airship when turning left

Mordonoc - A feathered reptilian creature that plagues the shipping corridors of Cor Nova; violent and unpredictable, mordonocs fly in packs and can bring down a large freighter; through extreme measures, they can be trained to obey human masters

O'Larre - A tree-dwelling race living in the Osmanthus Forest; their origins and customs are mysterious *Well, if you lived in a tree and ate bugs all day, you might be a little enigmatic yourself*

Oculus - A hand-held spyglass used by ship's officers; a silver oculus typically denotes a shipmaster, while a brass oculus denotes a deckmaster; other metals may be used by lower-ranking officers

Old World - The common term for the socio-political state of affairs preceding the rise of the Sovereign Sylvanus; it is believed that humans at that time exercised extremely powerful abilities similar to what is now called High Sylvan, but allowed these to fall into corruption; the resulting wars (sometimes called The Scourge) eventually brought humans to the mercy of the weapons they had created to destroy one another

Osmanthus - A large region of tropical forest located in eastern Misericordiae; also known as the Living Sea

Province - The seven geo-political divisions of the Sovereign Dominion of Cor Nova; each one began as a separate city/state from the fall of the Old World; following that event, all of the nations united under the Sovereign Sylvanus; the provinces maintain much autonomy *Go MISERICORDIAE*

Provincial - A leader of one of the provinces; each provincial has a different title and a varying level of power and responsibility according to the laws of the province

Rule of Sylvanus - A text written by the first Sovereign Sylvanus to guide the actions of his successors; it is traditional for each Sovereign to add a chapter to the text before passing the Amulet, Staff, and Crown onward

Shipcore - The mechanical center of an airfaring vessel; contains gears and pulleys for rerouting cables and valves to control envelope buoyancy

Shipmaster- The commander of an airfaring vessel. On ship, their word is law. Any disobedience toward a shipmaster's will is considered mutiny.

Sovereign - An ancestral leader of the Sovereign Dominion of Cor Nova - *I tried to draw Basil but I can never get his stupid, intelligent nose right.*

Sidia - An army of undying, powerful soldiers developed by humans as a weapon at the end of the Old World; overcoming their human masters, they nearly caused catastrophic destruction of life before being stopped by Sylvanus, who imprisoned them in a Sarcophagus beneath the Fields of Carath

Silverspoon - An information-peddling brotherhood that is at least several centuries old; each Silverspoon is intensely secretive and vastly knowledgeable, although it is unclear exactly how individual Silverspoons know so much when they are separated by such large distances; they were persecuted in large numbers during the reign of Titus; also known as "Rumormen"

Sunwise – In aetheronautics, the motion of an airship when

turning right

Venegast - A species of giant ground-dwelling mollusk found in the Osmanthus; capable of producing hallucinogenic toxins that stun and disorient prey *Veronica, really, what is with all this flowery language? Can we not just say -horrible underground murderslug- and have done with?*

ACKNOWLEDGEMENTS

The first edition of *Philomena* ended with acknowledgements to those who have encouraged my development as a person and an author. For all they have done and continue to do in my life, thank you again to David and Nancy Guiney, Deacon Dave Galvin, Dennis Barron, Fr. Fred Byrne, and George and Jeanne Rishell.

Thank you to Rebecca Corbell, Grace Drnach, Angie Cummings, and Sofia Cummings, who loaned this project their sound judgment and good humor. I have also benefited from the enthusiasm and contributions of the Cummings family, the Calis family, the Galvin family, the Buede family, Jason Miles, Zach Morse, and Matt Przybysz.

Finally, this book would not exist in its present form without Peter Mongeau, who saw a stronger story lurking within the original edition. It would seem that he, along with Cyprian Fields, Basil Black, Veronica Stromm and all who took part in this project, understands the beauty of taking something earthbound and making it fly.

32295240R00231